Return items to **any** Swindon library by closing
time on or before the date stamped. Only books
and Audio Books can be renewed - phone your
library or visit our website.
www.swindon.gov.uk/libraries *EVE*

EVEN SWINDON
LIBRARY
TEL: 486113

6/6

23. JUN 1

23. JUN 1

*WITHDRAWN
From Swindon
Borough Libraries*

eve Ton
9/6/16
DUE 05/10/17.

L4

Copying recordings is illegal. All recorded items
are hired entirely at hirer's own risk

D0552667

IN THE BOSS'S CASTLE

BY
JESSICA GILMORE

First Published in Great Britain 2016
By Mills & Boon, an imprint of HarperCollins*Publishers*
1 London Bridge Street, London, SE1 9GF

© 2016 Jessica Gilmore

ISBN: 978-0-263-91984-4

23-0516

Our policy is to use papers that are natural, renewable and recyclable products and made from wood grown in sustainable forests. The logging and manufacturing processes conform to the legal environmental regulations of the country of origin.

Printed and bound in Spain
by CPI, Barcelona

A former au pair, bookseller, marketing manager and seafront trader, **Jessica Gilmore** now works for an environmental charity in York. Married with one daughter, one fluffy dog and two dog-loathing cats, she spends her time avoiding housework and can usually be found with her nose in a book. Jessica writes emotional romance with a hint of humor, a splash of sunshine and a great deal of delicious food—and equally delicious heroes.

For Audrey, Rob, Josh, Michaela and Lily.
With much love always x

PROLOGUE

Hi, Hope,
Truthfully I was a little shocked when they asked
me to job swap with you for six months. I thought
I was way too far down the food chain, especially
since I changed careers and found myself back at
the bottom of the ladder again. But I've never left
the US—so my bags are packed, I actually have a
passport and I'm on my way to London before they
change their minds!

I guess you want to know a little about the
stranger coming to take over your life? There's no
big scandals you'll be glad to know, so no need to
warn the neighbours or hide the family silver. I'm
Maddison and I've been working for DL Media for
just over three years, I started out in the PR and
events team before Brenda, my boss (soon to be
yours) poached me for Editorial. It's a step down
in some ways—back to making coffees and book-
ing taxis and a lot less managing my own time,
but somehow she convinced me that it'll be worth
it. It's nice to be wanted for my brains and not my
contact list, at least that's what I tell myself when I
pick up her dry cleaning. Because, in between the

taxis and the coffee pick-ups, she is teaching me a lot—you're lucky to be working with her.

She's very focused, doesn't see the point of any life outside work and is absolutely obsessed with glass ceilings and reaching full potential, blah-blah-blah. It's not that I don't want all that, I'm as ambitious as they come in some ways, but I do want more. I want it all. I want to meet the right guy and settle down, picket fence, big dog, rugrats and all. Don't tell Brenda that!

I thought I'd found the right guy. Bart. AKA Bartholomew J Van De Grierson III. But turns out he's not The One or rather I'm not The One for him. At least not right now. He wants a break. Thinks we should 'explore other options'. So this opportunity has come at the right time for me. I'm exploring other options on the other side of the Atlantic and putting my career first for a change. Maybe working with Brenda has influenced me more than I knew!

I do hope he misses me at least a little, though...

So—New York! It's the greatest city on earth, I promise. My biggest advice? Pack light! The good news is you'll be living in the Upper East Side and it is fabulous! The bad news? No one expects to swing a cat in a New York studio, but mine...? You couldn't swing a mouse. But, hey, location is everything, right? And when you sit on the fire escape with your morning coffee and watch the sun rise over Manhattan you won't want to be anywhere else.

Welcome to New York. City of reinvention, city of dreams...
Maddison.

* * *

Hi, Maddison...

Welcome to London and London's greatest borough. I've compiled a 'Welcome' file which tells you absolutely everything you need to know, in alphabetical order, from where the boiler is—and the number of a good plumber—to the best place to buy coffee locally. There's a guide to buses and Oyster cards (no Tube here in Stokey) under T for Transport, and a comprehensive section on work (W for Work) to help you find your feet right away.

I hope you feel at home here. Stoke Newington is pretty sought-after now, but when my parents moved here it was still a scruffy, community-minded part of the East End—and even with all the swanky bars and yoga studios I miss the place I grew up in. Not so community-minded when you are more likely to bump into nannies and cleaners than neighbours, and everyone is obsessed with extending and rainforest wetrooms. But it's still home and I can't imagine living anywhere else. Except maybe New York, of course...

I am so excited about moving to New York for a whole six months. I've always wanted to travel but never had the opportunity. Faith, my younger sister, is on a gap year and seeing the world, lucky thing—but living in a new city and progressing my career? That's an amazing opportunity.

I've also been at DL Media for around three years. Before that I was working at a local solicitors' firm which fitted in with Faith's school hours. But as soon as she was old enough for me to commute to work I came to DL, at first as a general

PA, before getting the opportunity to work with Kit Buchanan as an editorial assistant.

Brenda sounds like just what I need—a real mentor. Kit, your boss-to-be, is... Well, he's brilliant. Everyone agrees with that. It's just I'm not sure he ever sees me. Sometimes I feel like I'm just a piece of efficient office furniture.

In fact it's been a really long time since anyone has seen me as anyone worth knowing. It gets a little lonely, to be honest, especially now that Faith is making it very clear that now she's grown up she doesn't need me to fuss over her.

Maybe she's right. Maybe it's time to put me first.

Starting with New York!

Enjoy London.

Love, Hope x

CHAPTER ONE

MADDISON CARTER OPENED the opaque glass door, leaned against the door frame and held up her perfectly manicured hand, a piece of paper dangling from her fingertips. 'Messages,' she announced.

Kit Buchanan pushed his chair away from his desk and blinked at her. His expression might seem sleepy and unconcerned to the casual observer but after just four weeks Maddison knew better. 'You could email them to me,' he suggested, a teasing gleam in his blue eyes. This conversation was getting as predictable as the sunrise. So she used paper and a pen and preferred her lists on thick white paper, not on an electronic device? It didn't make her a Luddite, it made her efficient.

'And have you ignore them? I think not.'

Kit sighed. The soft *here she goes again* sigh he used about this time every day. 'But, Maddison, maybe I like ignoring messages.' His eyes laughed up at her but she refused to smile back, even a little. She wasn't colluding with him.

'Then get an answering service. Or a machine or just answer your cell phone every once in a while and then I…' she brandished the list '…I wouldn't have to tell your girlfriends that you're in a meeting twenty times a day.'

His eyebrows rose. 'Twenty times? How very keen.'

Okay, she might have exaggerated slightly but just one conversation with the terribly polite and terribly condescending Camilla was enough and three definitely enough to drive the most precise person to hyperbole. Maddison ignored the interruption and, in a deliberately slow voice, began to read from the paper. 'Right, your mother called and said please call her back, today, and confirm you are going to the wedding, it's a three-line whip and if you don't RSVP soon she will do it for you. Your sister called and said, and I quote, "Tell him if I have to go to this damn wedding on my own I will make him suffer in ways he can't even imagine and don't think I won't do it…"'

Maddison paused as she reread the words. She liked the sound of Kit's sister, Bridget, with her soft, lilting voice and steely words.

'And Camilla called three times, can you please answer your cell, how can she expect to get ready for a wedding in just a couple of weeks if you won't even confirm that you're taking her, you inconsiderate bas…' She looked up and allowed herself one brief smile. 'I didn't catch the rest of that sentence.'

'The hell you didn't,' he said softly. The smile still curved his mouth and he was still leaning back in the vast, black leather chair but the glint had disappeared from his eyes. 'Everyone seems *very* keen to make sure I attend this wedding.'

'If you would just RSVP they'd stop calling.' Maddison didn't care whether he went to the darn wedding or not. She just wanted to stop fielding calls about it.

'I will, as soon as I've decided.'

'Decided?'

'Whether I'm going or not.'

Maddison heaved a theatrical sigh. 'Great. Can I beg

you to do just one thing? Put Camilla out of her misery.' Sure, the woman spoke to Maddison as if she were some sort of servant, and sure, she sounded like a snooty character in a Hugh Grant movie, all clipped vowels and lots of long *r*'s, but she was getting a little more desperate with every call. Maddison would never allow herself to beg for a man's attention but she knew all too well what it felt like to see the spark die even as she did her best to keep it going. Knew what it felt like to see the emails and texts diminish, hear the call go straight to voicemail.

Kit stared at her, his eyes narrowed. 'I didn't know that advising on my personal life was in your job description.'

Maddison took a deep breath, willing herself to stay calm. 'Nor did I and yet here I am, taking calls from your girlfriend eight hours a day.'

'Ex-girlfriend.'

'She…what?'

His eyes caught hers, the blue turned steely. 'Ex-girlfriend. She just wants to come to the wedding. Thinks if I take her to meet the parents then things might start again between us. So you see, I'm not a total git.'

Whatever *that* might be. Maddison stared down at the list, her righteous indignation draining away. 'Okay. I apologize—although in my defence it seems that Camilla doesn't understand the *ex* part of your relationship. Maybe she needs reminding. And you *really* should call your mother.'

He didn't respond for a long moment and Maddison kept her eyes on the list, knowing she had gone too far. She was normally so good at keeping her cool but Kit Buchanan was just so…so *provoking*.

She started at his unexpected laugh. 'There are times when you remind me of my school matron. I will, I promise. How are things looking for tonight?'

The abrupt turn of subject was a relief. She had spent far too long today on Kit Buchanan's social life; work was a much safer subject. Maddison looked at her list again, composing herself as she did so. 'The caterers are already there and setting up, so are the bar staff. The warehouse confirmed that they have sent two hundred books across ready for the signing. I got late acceptances from five people, their names have been added to the entrance list and the door staff are primed; three people sent in late apologies, I replied on your behalf and arranged for books and goody bags to be sent to their offices. Oh, and I popped into the venue last night after work and took a last look around. Everything is in order.'

'Very efficient, as always, thank you, Maddison.' The words were perfect but the amusement in his tone took the edge off his praise and despite herself she could feel her cheeks flush. Kit always seemed to be laughing at her and it was…unsettling. She wanted respect, not this knowing humour. But so far, no matter what she did, respect seemed to be eluding her. And, dammit, it rankled. She was usually so much better at impressing the right people in the right ways.

She certainly wasn't used to feeling discombobulated several times a day.

She eyed her boss. He was still lounging back in his chair, an unrepentant gleam in his eye as he waited for her response. Hoping that she would lose her cool, no doubt. Well, she wasn't going to give him the satisfaction but, oh, her fingers curled; it was tempting.

It didn't help that Kit was young—ish. Handsome if you liked brown tousled hair that needed a good cut, dark stubble and blue eyes, if you found scruffy chic, like some hipster cross between a college professor and an outdoorsman, attractive. Maddison didn't. She liked her men clean-cut, clean-shaven and well turned out.

But, even if he wore head-to-toe *couture*, Kit Buchanan still wouldn't be her type. *Bart* was her type: tall, athletic, with a good job in banking, a trust fund and a bloodline that ran back to Edith Wharton's innocent age and beyond. Not to mention the brownstone. Breaking up with the brownstone was almost harder than saying goodbye to the man. She'd invested eighteen months in that relationship, spent eighteen months moulding herself into the perfect consort. All for nothing. She was back at square one.

Although, he *had* said a break. Maddison clung on to those words, hope soothing the worry and doubt clawing her insides. Everyone knew that taking a break wasn't the same thing as breaking up. And if Bart saw that she was having an amazing time in London without him then surely he would realize he had made a very big mistake? Maybe this distance, this time apart was a good thing, the push he needed to take things to the next level.

She just needed to start *having* the amazing time. So far Maddison's London experiences had been confined to work, takeaways and working her way through Hope McKenzie's formidable box-set collection. Watching *Sex and the City* instead of living it. Surely she at least deserved to be *flirting* in the city?

Kit's voice brought her back to her present surroundings—thousands of miles away from her unexpected failure. 'Anything else on that list of yours or is it all neatly ticked and crossed out?'

Okay. This was it. She'd spent the last four weeks regrouping, licking her wounds, grateful for the opportunity to recover and plan far away from the all-too-knowing eyes of her New York social group. She'd been so *sure* of Bart, shown her hand too early and lost spectacularly. But it was time to reassert herself, professionally at least. Then maybe she would get her confidence—and her man—back. Maddison willed herself to sound composed, her voice not to tremble. 'I think you should rewrite your speech for tonight.'

Kit went very still, like a predator watching his prey. 'Oh? Why?'

'It's very clinical.' She kept her eyes focused on him even as her knees trembled and every instinct screamed at her to stop talking and to back out of the door before she got her ass fired. 'You've spent the whole four weeks I've been here absolutely absorbed in your work. You barely noticed that Hope had gone. You've been in before me every morning, not stopped for lunch unless you had a meeting and who knows what time you leave? But the speech? It has no passion in it at all.'

Kit didn't take his eyes off her, his face utterly expressionless. 'Have you read it? The book?'

Had she what? 'I…of course.'

'Could you do a better job?'

She flinched at the cold words, then tossed her head up and glared at him. 'Could I write an introductory speech that sounds like I value the author, think the book is worth reading and convince the room that they need to read it too? Yes. Yes, I could.'

'Great.' He pulled his chair back to his desk and refocused his eyes on his screen. 'You have an hour. Let's see what you come up with.'

'Great speech.'

Kit suppressed a sigh as yet another guest complimented him. It *had* been a great speech and he'd delivered it well, a nice mingling of humour and sincerity. Only he hadn't written it. Embellished it, ad-libbed a little but he hadn't written it. Maddison had been annoyingly right: his own effort had lacked passion.

Kit knew all too well why that was. Three years ago he'd lost any passion, any zest for life, any hope—and now it seemed as though he'd lost the ability to fake it as well.

Which was ridiculous. He was the king of faking it—at work, with the ever so elegant Camilla and her potential replacements, with his friends. The only place he couldn't convincingly pretend that he was the same old Kit was with his family. Especially not with his family and with the wedding looming on the horizon like a constant reminder of all that he had lost. He needed to sort that out and fast. He knew he had to RSVP. He knew he had to attend. He just couldn't bring himself to commit to it because once he did it would become real. Thank goodness for his new project. At least that helped him forget, for a little while at least.

Forgetting was a luxury.

He caught sight of Maddison, gliding through the crowds as untouchably serene as ever. Kit's eyes narrowed as she stopped to murmur something in a waitress's ear, sending the girl scurrying off with her tray. As usual Maddison had it all under control. Just look at the way she glided around the office in her monochrome uniform of black trousers and perfectly ironed white blouse like some sort of robot: efficient, calm and, until today, he could have sworn completely free of any emotion.

It was a shame. No one whose green eyes tilted upwards with such feline wickedness, no one with hair like the first hint of a shepherd's sunset, no one with a wide, sweet mouth should be so *bland*.

But she hadn't been so bland earlier today. Instead she

had been bursting with opinions and, much as she had tried to stay calm, not let him see the exasperation in those thickly lashed eyes, she had let her mask slip a little.

And then she had written that speech. In an hour. Yes, she definitely had hidden depths. Not, Kit reminded himself, that he was planning to explore them. He was just intrigued, that was all. Turned out Maddison Carter was a bit of an enigma and he did so like to figure out a puzzle.

Kit excused himself from the group of guests, brushing another compliment about his speech aside with a smile and a handshake as he slowly weaved his way through the throng, checking to make sure everyone was entertained, that the buzz was sufficient to ensure the launch would be a success. The venue was inspired, an old art deco cinema perfectly complementing the novel's historical Jazz Age setting. The seats had been removed to create a party space and a jazz band set up on the old stage entertained the crowd with a series of jaunty tunes. Neon cocktails circulated on etched silver trays as light shone down from spotlights overhead, emphasizing the huge, jewel-coloured rectangular windows; at the far end of the room the gratified author sat at a vintage desk, signing books and holding court. The right people were here having the right sort of time. Kit had done all he could—the book would stand or fall on its own merits now.

He paused as Maddison passed by again, that damn list still tucked in one hand, a couple of empty glasses clasped in the other. He leaned against the wall for a moment, enjoying watching her dispose of the glasses, ensure three guests had fresh drinks, introduce two lost-looking souls to each other, all the while directing the wait staff and ensuring the queue for signed books progressed. A one-woman event machine.

How did she do it? She looked utterly calm, still in her favourite monochrome uniform although she had changed her usual well-tailored trousers for a short skirt, which swished most pleasingly around what were, Kit had to admit, a fine pair of legs, and there was no way the silky, clingy white blouse, which dipped to a low vee just this side of respectable, was the same as the crisp shirt she had worn in the office. Her hair was no longer looped in a loose knot but allowed to curl loosely around her shoulders. She looked softer, more approachable—even though she was brandishing the dreaded list.

She was doing a great job organizing this party. He really should go and tell her so while he remembered.

By the time Kit had manoeuvred his way over to Maddison's corner of the room she was deep in conversation with an earnest-looking man. Kit rocked back on his heels and studied her. Good gracious, was that a smile on her face? In fact, that dip of her head and the long demure look from under her eyebrows was positively flirtatious. Kit neatly collected two cocktails from a passing tray and watched as the earnest man slipped her a card. Did he know him? He knew almost every person there. Kit ran through his memory banks—yes, a reviewer for one of the broadsheets. Not a bad conquest, especially if she could talk him into positive reviews.

'Flirting on the job?' he said quietly into her ear as the earnest man walked away, and had the satisfaction of seeing her jump and the colour rush to her cheeks, emphasizing the curve in her heart-shaped face.

'No. I was just…'

'Relax, Maddison, I was teasing. It's past eight o'clock. I think you're on your own time now. This lot will melt away as soon as they realize that these are no longer being served.' He handed her the pink cocktail before tasting his own blue confection and grimaced as the sweet yet medicinal taste hit his tongue. 'Or maybe not. Is this supposed to taste like cough syrup? Anyway, cheers. Great job on the party.'

'Thank you.' It was as if a light had been switched on in her green eyes, turning them from pretty glass to a darker, more dangerous emerald. 'Hope started it all. I just followed her instructions.'

'The party favours were your idea, and the band, I believe.'

Her eyes lit up even more. 'I didn't know you'd noticed. It just seemed perfect, nineteen twenties and a murder mystery.' The guests' goody bags contained chocolate murder weapons straight out of a golden-age crime novel: hatpins and candlesticks, pearl-handled revolvers and a jar-shaped chocolate labelled Cyanide. The cute chocolates had caused quite a stir and several guests were trying to make sure they went home with a full set. Turned out even this jaded crowd could be excited by something novel and fun.

'Excuse me.'

Kit looked around, an enquiring eyebrow raised, only for the young man hovering behind him to ignore him entirely while he thrust a card in Maddison's direction. 'It was lovely to meet you earlier. Do give me a call. I would love to show you around London. Oh, and happy birthday.'

'Thank you.' She accepted the card with a half-smile, sliding it neatly into her bag. Kit tried to sneak a look as the card disappeared into the depths. How many other cards did she have in there? And what had the young man said?

'It's your birthday?'

Maddison nodded. 'Today.'

'I didn't realize.' Kit felt strangely wrong-footed. How hadn't he known? He'd always remembered Hope's birthday although, come to think of it, that was because she made sure it was in his work calendar and lost no opportunity to remind him that flowers were always acceptable, chocolates even more so and vouchers for the local spa most acceptable of all. 'I'm so sorry you had to work. I hope you have exciting plans for the rest of your evening and weekend?'

Maddison paused, her eyes lowered. 'Sure.' But her tone lacked conviction.

'Like?' Kit cursed himself as he pushed. She'd said she had plans so he should take her word at face value and leave her in peace. He didn't need to know the details; she was a grown woman.

A grown woman in a new city where she knew hardly anyone.

Maddison took a visible deep breath before looking directly at him, a smile pasted on to her face. 'A film and a takeaway. I'm going to explore the city a little more tomorrow. Low-key, you know? I don't know many people here yet.'

'You're staying in alone, on your birthday?'

'I have a cocktail.' She waved the glass of pink liquid at him. 'It's okay.'

He'd heard the lady. She said she was okay—and, judging by the cards she was collecting, the room was full of men who would gladly help her celebrate any way she wished to.

Only she was new to the country... Kit had thought his conscience had died three years ago but some ghost of it was struggling back to life. 'What about the other girls at work? None of them free?'

'It's a little awkward, you know? Technically I'm at the

same level as all the other assistants but they all sit in the same office and I'm on the executive floor so we don't see each other day-to-day.' She hesitated. 'I think Hope didn't really socialize so there's this assumption I'm the same.' She shrugged. 'It's fine. I just haven't prioritized making friends since I got here. There's plenty of time.' She attempted another full smile; this one nearly reached her eyes. 'I'm actually quite good at it when I try.'

His conscience gave another gasp. He should have thought to check that she was settling in, but she had been so efficient from day one. *Besides*, the annoying ghost of conscience past whispered, *if you had noticed, what would you have done about it*? But she *had* put a lot of work in tonight and it *was* her birthday... Even Kit couldn't be so callous as to abandon her to a lonely night of pizza and a romcom. 'I can't possibly let you go home alone to watch a film on your birthday, especially after all the hard work you put in today. The least I can do is buy you a drink.' He looked at his blue drink and shuddered. 'A real drink. What do you say?'

CHAPTER TWO

SHE SHOULD HAVE said no.

The last thing Maddison needed was a pity date. Even worse, a pity date with her *boss*. But Kit had caught her at a vulnerable moment. Nice as it was to be flirted with by not just one, or two, but several men at the party, all of whom had their own teeth, hair and impressive-sounding job titles, she couldn't help but remember this time last year and the adorable little inn in Connecticut Bart had whisked her off to. Three months ago she was reasonably confident that this birthday he'd propose—not break up with her two months before.

Which meant she wouldn't be married at twenty-seven and a mother by twenty-eight. Her whole, carefully planned timetable redundant. Somehow she was going to have to start again. Only she had no idea how or who or where…

Happy birthday to me. Maddison sighed, the age-long loneliness forcing its way out of the box she had buried it in, creeping back around her heart, her soul. It wasn't that she minded the lack of cards and presents. She'd got used to that a long time ago. But she couldn't help feeling that at twenty-six her birthday should matter to someone. Especially to her. Instead she'd been in denial all day. She wasn't sure why she'd mentioned it to the young sales guy, maybe some pathetic need to have some kind of acknowledgement, no matter how small.

That's enough. She wasn't a wallower, she was a fighter and she never, ever looked back. Maddison pushed herself off the plush velvet sofa and paced the length of the room. If she did have to wait in Kit Buchanan's house while he changed then she might as well take advantage and find out as much as she could about him. From the little she had gathered he was a constant source of speculation at work, but although the gossips were full of theories they had very few solid facts. A few juicy titbits could give her a way in with the social groups at work. She couldn't just bury herself and her sore pride away for the whole six months like some Roman exile marooned on a cold and damp island.

After all, the weather in London was much nicer than she had expected.

At least it was just her pride that hurt. She'd never be foolish enough to give away her heart without some kind of security.

Stop thinking about it, Maddison scolded herself, looking up at the high ceiling as if in supplication. She had five months left in London; she needed to start living again so she could return to New York full of European polish and fizzing with adventure. If that didn't bring Bart back on his knees, diamond ring in one hand, nothing would. After all, didn't they say absence made the heart grow fonder? Think how fond he could grow if word got back to him of just how good a time she was having in London…

A piece of elaborate-looking plaster work caught her eye. Original, she'd bet, just like the tiles on the hallway floor and the ceiling roses holding the anachronistically modern lights. The huge semi-detached house overlook-

ing a lushly green square was the last place she'd expected Kit to live; she would have laid money on some
kind of trendy apartment, all glass and chrome, not the
white-painted Georgian house. It was even more impressive than Bart's brownstone.

She hadn't seen much in the way of personal touches
so far. A tiled hallway with no clutter at all, just a hat
stand, a mirror and an antique sideboard with a small
bowl for his keys. There was nothing left lying around
in the living room either except a newspaper on the coffee table, neatly folded at the nearly completed crossword, and just one small photo on the impressive marble
mantle—a black-and-white picture of two teenage boys,
grinning identical smiles, hanging over the rail on a boat.
She had no trouble identifying the younger one as Kit,
although there was something about the smile that struck
her as different from the smile she knew. Maybe it was
how wide, how unadulterated, how wholehearted it was,
so different from the cynically amused expression she
saw every day.

The sound of footsteps on the stairs sent her scuttling
back to her seat, where she grabbed the newspaper and
scanned it, carefully giving the impression she had been
comfortably occupied for the last ten minutes.

'Sorry to keep you. I spilled some of that green stuff
on my shirt and didn't fancy going out smelling like the
ghost of absinthe past.' Kit walked into the room and
raised an eyebrow. Maddison had kicked off her shoes
and was curled up in a corner of the sofa, the newspaper
on her knee, looking as studiously un-detective-like as
possible. 'Comfy?'

'Hmm? No, I was fine. Just finishing off your crossword. I think it's Medusa.'

'I beg your pardon?'

'Six down. *Petrifying snakes.* Medusa.'

'Here, give me that.' He took the paper off her and stared at the clue. 'Of course. I should have thought…' He looked back up and over at her, his eyes impossibly blue as they took her in.

'Do you like puzzles, Maddison?'

'I'm sorry?' It took all her resolution to stay still under such scrutiny. It was as if he were looking at her for the first time, as if he were weighing her up.

'Puzzles, quizzes? Do you like them?'

'Well, sure. Doesn't everyone?' He didn't reply, just stared at her in that disconcertingly intense way. 'I mean, when I was a kid I wanted to be Nancy Drew.' When she hadn't dreamed of being Rory Gilmore, that was. She swung her legs to the floor. 'I believe you mentioned a drink.'

He didn't move for a long second, his eyes still focused on her, and then smiled, the familiar amused expression sliding back on to his face like a mask. 'Of course. It's not far. I hope you don't mind the walk.'

Maddison hadn't known what to expect on a night out with Kit Buchanan: a glitzy wine bar or maybe some kind of private members' bar, all leather seats and braying, privileged laughter. She definitely hadn't expected the comfortable pub Kit guided her into. The walls were hung with prints by local artists, the tables solid square wood surrounded by leather sofas and chairs. It was nearly full but it didn't feel crowded or loud; it felt homely, like a pub from a book. The man behind the bar nodded at Kit and gave Maddison a speculative look as Kit guided her to a nook by the unlit fire before heading off to order their drinks.

'I got a sharing platter as well,' he said as he set the bottle of Prosecco on the table and placed a glass in front of her. 'I don't know about you but I'm starving. I never get a chance to eat at those work parties. It's hard to schmooze with a half-eaten filo prawn in my mouth.'

'When I started out in events sometimes canapés were all I did eat,' Maddison confessed, watching as he filled her glass up. 'New York is pricey for a girl out of college and free food is free food. Some days I would long for a good old-fashioned sub or a real-sized burger rather than an assortment of finger food! Turns out a girl can have too much caviar.'

'Happy birthday.' Kit handed her a glass before taking the seat opposite her, raising his glass to her. 'You worked in events?'

She nodded. 'After I graduated I joined a friend's PR and events company.' It had been the perfect job, working in the heart of Manhattan with the heart of society—until her friend had decided she preferred attending parties to planning them, being in the headlines rather than creating them. 'After that I landed a junior management role at DL Media and then Brenda poached me. I've only worked in editorial for the last six months,' she added. She still wasn't sure how Brenda had persuaded her to leave the safe world of PR for the unknown waters of editorial. It was the first unplanned move Maddison had made in a decade. It still terrified her, both the spontaneity and the starting again.

'Six months? I did wonder why you were still at an assistant level when you are obviously so capable.' The words were casually said but Maddison sat up a little straighter, pride swelling her chest.

She looked around the room, not wanting Kit to see just how the offhand praise had affected her. 'It's nice here. Is this where you bring all the girls?'

'You're the first.'

She turned and looked at him, laughter ready on her lips but there was no answering smile. He was serious. 'Consider me honoured. Why not? It's pretty convenient.'

Kit shrugged. 'I don't like to bring anyone home. It gives them ideas. One moment a cosy dinner, the next a sleepover and before you know it they're rearranging the furniture and suggesting a drawer. Besides, Camilla and her ilk only like to go to places where they can see and be seen. This place isn't anywhere near trendy enough for them.'

It sounded pretty lonely. Maddison knew all about that. 'So if you don't want to share your home or local with these girls, why date them?'

His eyes darkened for a stormy moment. 'Because I am in absolutely no danger of falling in love with any of them.'

He had said too much. This was supposed to be a casual 'thank you and by the way happy birthday' drink, not a full-on confessional. He didn't need or deserve absolution. Maddison stared at him, her eyes wide and mouth half-open as if he were some kind of crossword clue she could solve, and for once he couldn't think of the right kind of quip to turn her attention aside. He breathed a sigh of relief as the waitress came over, their Mediterranean platter balanced high on one hand, and broke the mounting tension.

'If I'd known you had overdosed on canapés I'd have ordered something more substantial,' he said, gesturing at the bowls of olives and sundried tomatoes, hummus and aioli. 'The bread's reasonably sized though.'

'No, this is good, thanks.' But she sounded thoughtful and her eyes were still fixed disturbingly on him. Kit searched for a change of subject.

'Have you heard from Hope?' That was safe enough.

Maddison speared a falafel and placed it delicately onto her plate, every movement precise, just as she was in the office. 'A couple of emails. I think she's settled in.' She smiled then, a completely unguarded, full-on smile, and Kit's chest twisted at the openness of it. 'She intimidates me a little. I thought I was organized, but Hope? She beats me every time. Did you know she left me a printed-out file, all alphabetized, with instructions on what to do if the boiler breaks and when the trash goes out? Half of it is about what I need to do if her sister, Faith, comes home early from her travels or phones or something. I mean, the girl's nineteen. Cut her some slack!' But although the words were mocking there was a wistfulness in Maddison's face that belied them.

She took a deep breath and her features recomposed until she was back to her usual calm and efficient self. 'Anyway, some of her neighbours have dropped round and been welcoming, which is very kind but they're older and have kids. They're nice but a night spent in talking about the cost of childcare isn't exactly something I can contribute to.'

Kit grimaced. 'No, I can empathize with that. It seems that every time I go out now someone is talking about nannies or the importance of organic baby food.' Each time it was a reminder that his friendship group was moving on without him, the teasing about his bachelor status beginning to grate.

She raised her eyes to his. 'Don't you want kids? One day?'

He laughed shortly. 'Why does it all come back to kids and marriage? I thought society had evolved beyond that. Why not just enjoy some company for a while and then move on?'

Maddison was frozen, her fork in her hand. 'That's really what you think? Poor Camilla.'

Kit frowned. 'She knew the score. I don't pretend to be anything different, to want anything different, Maddison. If she wants to change the rules without checking to see if I'm still playing along then that's not my problem.'

'People change. No one goes into a relationship expecting it to stay static. Relationships evolve. They grow or they end. It's the way it has to be.'

'I don't agree. It's perfectly possible for two people to enjoy themselves with no expectations of anything more. Look, Camilla said she was happy enough with a casual thing but it didn't take long before she started pushing for more. If she'd been more honest with herself, with me, at the beginning, then she wouldn't have got hurt.'

'Wow. You've actually made me feel a little sorry for her.' The colour was high on her cheeks and he opened his mouth to do what? Defend himself? No, to put her straight, but anything he might have said was drowned out as the pub's PA system crackled into life with an announcement of that night's quiz.

Maddison straightened and looked around, her eyes bright like a child promised a treat. 'Oh, I haven't done a quiz since college. Do you want to…? I mean, we've barely started on the wine and there's all that bread to eat.'

Interesting. Kit sat back and looked at her; she was practically fizzing with anticipation. His mind flashed back to the completed crossword, to the way she had meticulously sorted every single problem that had come his way for the last four weeks. *I wanted to be Nancy Drew*, she had said.

Could he trust her? It wasn't just that he didn't want any of his commercial rivals getting any hint of what he was up to; he didn't want it known internally either. He didn't want project-management groups and focus studies and sales input. That would come, but not yet. Not while he was enjoying the thrill of the new.

'Maddison,' he said slowly. 'How would you like to be my guinea pig?'

'Your *what*?' She couldn't have looked more outraged if he'd asked her if she wanted to eat a guinea pig.

'Guinea pig. Testing out my new product.'

Her eyes narrowed. 'How very marketing friendly of you. I was under the impression that we produced books.'

'Oh, we do. I do.' He considered her for a moment longer. She didn't really know anyone to tell and didn't strike him as the gossiping type anyway. He should trust her. He hadn't come this far without taking some risks.

Kit had started his publishing career while still at Cambridge, republishing forgotten golden-age crime books for a nostalgic audience. Two years later he'd diversified into digital genre publishing before selling his company to DL Media for a tidy sum and an executive position. The sale had paid for his house and furnished him with a nice disposable income and a nest egg, but lately he'd been wondering if he'd sold his soul, not just his company.

He had had no idea just how different things would be. The sole guy in charge of a small but growing company was a million miles away from a cog in a huge international corporation—even an executive cog. And although the perks and salary were nice—more than nice—he missed the adrenaline rush of ownership. This project was making his blood pump in almost the same way as building up his imprint had. While he was working on it he almost forgot everything else that had changed in the last few years.

Maddison's eyes were fixed on his face. 'So what is this product?'

Kit watched her every reaction. 'Okay, so we produce entertainment and information. I am planning to marry the two together.'

Maddison frowned. 'And you want me to bless the happy couple?'

'I want you to road-test them.' He took a deep breath. He was going in. 'I'm planning a series of new interactive guidebooks.'

'Okay…' Scepticism was written all over her face. 'That's interesting but does anyone even use guidebooks any more?'

Kit had been expecting that. 'Guidebooks available in every format from eBook to app to good old-fashioned paper copies.'

'I still don't see…'

He took pity on her. 'The difference is that they don't tell you what to see, they give you clues. Each guidebook is a treasure hunt.'

She leaned forward, a spark of interest lighting up her face, transforming her from merely pretty to glowingly beautiful. Not that Kit was interested in her looks. It was her brains he was after; he was certainly not focusing on how her eyes lit up when she was engaged or the way her blouse dipped a little lower as she shifted forward. 'A treasure hunt? As in X marks the spot?'

He tore his eyes away from her mouth. *Focus, Buchanan.* 'In a way. Tourists can pick from one of five or so themed routes—historical, romantic, wild, fictional or a mixture of all the themes and follow a series of clues to their mystery destination, taking in places of interest on the way. Each theme will have routes of varying length ranging from an afternoon to three days, allowing people to adapt the treasure hunt to their length of stay, although I very much hope even cynical Londoners will want to have a go.'

'Yes.' She nodded slowly, her still-half-full plate pushed to one side as she took in every word. 'I see, each hunt would have a unique theme depending on the place like, I don't know, say a revolution theme in Boston? It wouldn't just be tourists, though, would it? I mean, something like this would work for team building, bachelor and bachelorette parties, family days out...' Satisfaction punched through him. She'd got it. 'And what's the prize—or is taking part enough?'

'Hopefully the satisfaction of a job well done, but successful treasure hunters will also be able to pick up some discounts for local restaurants and attractions. I'm looking into building some partnerships. To launch it, however, I am planning real treasure—or a prize at least.'

Maddison leaned back and picked up her wine glass. 'And you want me to what? Source the prize for you?'

Kit shook his head. 'No, I want you to test the first few routes. The plan is to launch next year, simultaneously in five cities around the world. Each launch will open up on the same day and teams will compete against each other. But for now, in order to present a full proposal to marketing, we've been concentrating on drawing up the London routes—and I want to know how hard it is, especially to non-Brits, if the timings work and, crucially, if it's fun.'

'So, this will be part of my job?'

Kit picked up his own glass; he was about to ask a lot from her. 'We're still very much in concept stage at the moment. This would be in your own time at weekends. But...' he smiled directly at her, turning up the charm '...you said yourself you needed to get out and about...'

'I didn't say that at all. For all you know I am completely happy with takeaways and box sets. Maybe that's the whole reason I took this job,' she protested.

He watched her carefully, looking for an advantage. 'But you're spending your weekends alone. I know the routes but not the clues so I want to see how it works in practice. I was going to go around on my own but here you are, new to London. A non-Brit. It's perfect. You can follow the clues and I'll accompany you and see how it works.'

'I...'

'I don't expect you to do it for nothing,' he broke in before she talked herself out of it or pointed out that spending every weekend with her boss was not her idea of fun. 'Each route we complete has a prize. An experience of your choice, fully paid. Gigs, concerts, theme parks, restaurants—you name it.'

'Anything I want?'

'Anything.' Now where had that come from? He would be spending all week and most of the next few weekends with her, did he really want to add in leisure time as well? But before he could backtrack Maddison held out her hand.

'In that case you have a deal,' she said.

In for a penny... He took her soft, cool hand in his. 'Deal. I'm looking forward to getting to know you better.'

Why had he said that? That wasn't part of the deal. So she was proving to be a bit of an enigma, a girl who liked a challenge? They were reasons to stay away, not get closer. But this was purely business and business Kit could handle. It was all he had left, after all.

CHAPTER THREE

ALTHOUGH CLISSOLD PARK couldn't hold a candle to her own beloved Central Park, the small London park had a quirky charm all its own. There might not be a fairy-tale castle or boats for hire on the little duck-covered lakes, but it was always buzzing with people and a circuit made for a pretty run.

Maddison increased her pace, smiling as she overtook a man pushing a baby in a jogger. Not so much difference between Clissold and Central Parks after all—and yes, right on cue, there it was: a t'ai chi ch'uan class. City parks were city parks no matter their location and size.

The biggest difference was that dogs roamed unleashed and free through the London park; in Central Park they would be allowed to walk untethered only in the doggy-exercise areas. Maddison nervously eyed a large, barrel-chested brown dog hurtling towards her, the sweat springing onto her palms nothing to do with the exercise. Could it smell her fear? She wavered, torn between increasing her pace and stopping to back away from it when it jumped, running directly...past her to retrieve a ball, slobber flying from its huge jowls. Maddison's heart hammered and she gulped in some much-needed air. She hated dogs; they were unpredictable. She'd found that out the hard way—and had the scar on her thigh to prove it.

At least her mom had dumped that particular boyfriend after his dog had attacked Maddison, but whether it was the dog bite that had precipitated the move or some other misdemeanour Maddison had never known.

Maddison increased the pace again, the pain in her chest and the ache in her thighs a welcome distraction from thoughts of the past—and the immediate future. In one hour Kit Buchanan would be knocking on her door and she would be spending the whole day with him. Whatever had possessed her to agree?

On the other hand she didn't have anything better to do. And despite her reservations she had had fun last night. For the first time in a long time she had been able to relax, to be herself. She only needed to impress Kit professionally; what he made of her socially wasn't at all important.

It was a long time since she hadn't had to worry about that.

Maddison turned out of the park and began to run along the pavement, dodging the myriad small tables cluttering up the narrow pavements outside the many cafes and coffee shops that made up the main street, until she reached the small road where she was staying. Her stomach twisted as she opened the front door and stepped over the threshold, the heaviness in her chest nothing to do with the exercise.

Try as she might to ignore it, staying in Hope's old family home was opening up old wounds, allowing the loneliness to seep through. It wasn't the actual living alone—apart from the semesters sleeping in her college dorm Maddison had lived by herself since she was sixteen. No, she thought that this unshakeable melancholy was because Hope's home was, well, a home. A much-loved family home with the family photos clustered on the dresser downstairs, the battered kitchen table, the scuff marks in the hallway where a generation of shoes had been kicked off to prove it.

And sure, Maddison wouldn't have picked the violet-covered wallpaper and matching purple curtains and bed-spread in her room, just as she would have stripped the whole downstairs back for a fresh white and wood open-plan finish, but she appreciated why Hope had preserved the house just the way it must have been when her parents died. There was love in every in-need-of-a-refresh corner.

Losing her parents so young must have been hard but at least Hope had grown up with them, in a house full of light and happiness.

Maddison's childhood bedroom had no natural light and pretty near little happiness. The thin bunks and thin-ner walls, the sound of the TV blaring in if she was lucky, silence if she wasn't. If she was alone. It was only tem-porary, her mother reassured her, just somewhere to stay until their luck changed.

Only it never did. That was when Maddison stopped believing in luck. That was when she knew it was down to her, only her.

Maddison found herself, as she often did, looking at the photos displayed on the hallway sideboard. Both girls were slim with dark hair and dark eyes but whereas Hope looked perpetually worried and careworn, Faith spar-kled with vitality. Reading between the lines of Hope's comprehensive file, Maddison got the impression that the older sister was the adult in this house, the younger protected and indulged. But Faith was nineteen! At that age Maddison had been on her own for three years and was putting herself through college, the luxury of a year spent travelling as remote as her chances of discovering a secret trust fund.

Maddison picked up her favourite photo. It was taken when their parents were still alive; the whole family were grouped on a beach at sunset, dressed in smart summery clothes. Faith must have been around six, a small, merry-faced imp with laughing eyes and a naughty smile, holding hands with her mother. Hope, a teenager all in black, was standing in front of her father, casual in his arms. She was probably at the age where she was so secure in her parents' love and affection she took it for granted, embarrassed by any public show. It used to make Maddison mad to see how casually her schoolmates treated their parents, how dismissive they could be of their love.

One day Maddison wanted a photo like this. She and her own reliable, affectionate husband and their secure, happy children. A family of her own. It wasn't too much to ask, was it? She'd thought she was so close with Bart and now here she was. As far away as ever. The heaviness in her chest increased until she wanted to sink to her knees under the burden.

Stop it, she told herself fiercely. Kit would be here soon and she still had to shower and change. Besides, what good had feeling sorry for herself ever done? Planning worked. Timetables worked. Things didn't just happen because you wished for them or were good. You had to make your own destiny.

It didn't take Maddison long to get ready or to post a few pictures of her evening's adventures onto her various social-media accounts, captioning them 'Birthday in London'—and if they were carefully edited to give the impression that she was a guest at the party, not working, and that there was a whole group at the pub, well, wasn't social media all about perception?

Her phone flashed with notifications and Maddison quickly scrolled through them. It was funny to see life carrying on in New York as if she hadn't left: the same parties, the same hook-ups and break-ups. She chewed her lip as she scrolled through another Friday night of cocktails, exclusive clubs and VIP bars. At least her bank balance was healthier during her London exile. Keeping up with the Trustafarians without a trust fund was a constant balancing act. One she was never in full control of. Thank goodness she had landed a rent-controlled apartment.

Still, she had to speculate to accumulate and if Maddison wanted the security of an Upper East Side scion with the houses, bank balance and guaranteed happy life to match, then she needed to make some sacrifices. And she didn't just want that security, she needed it. She knew too well what the alternatives were and she had no intention of ever being that cold, that hungry, that despised ever again.

The sound of the doorbell snapped her back to reality. She stood, breathing in, trying to squash the old fears, the old feelings of inadequacy, the knowledge that she would never be good enough, back into the little box she hid them in. She should have learned from Pandora; some things were better left locked away.

The doorbell sounded again before she made it downstairs and she wrenched the front door open to find Kit leaning against the door frame, looking disturbingly casual in faded jeans and a faded red T-shirt. Morning. Recovered from your victory yet?'

Maddison felt the heat steal over her cheeks. Maybe it hadn't been the most dignified thing in the world to fling her arms up in the air and whoop when she and Kit were declared pub-quiz champions but it *had* been her birthday. And they had won pretty darn convincingly. 'Are you kidding? I want a certificate framed for my wall so I can show it to my grandkids in forty years' time.'

She grabbed her bag and stepped out, pulling the door shut behind her.

Kit waited while she double-and then triple-locked the door as per Hope's comprehensive instructions. 'Right. As I mentioned yesterday we need to keep things as simple as possible. The idea is to give people a fun and unique way of seeing London, not to bamboozle them completely. Plus our target market is going to be tourists, the vast majority of whom aren't English, so we need to make this culturally accessible to everyone whether it's a girl from New York...' he smiled at Maddison '...or a family from China or a couple from France.'

'More of a scavenger hunt than a treasure hunt?'

'A mix of the two. Every destination is accessible by Tube or bus to make it easier, at least to start with, and we're putting the nearest stop with each clue with directions from that stop. On the app and on the online version you won't get the next clue until you put in an answer for the current quest but that would be impossible on paper. The discounts you get will be linked to how many correct answers you have in the end.'

'And what's to stop people going online and cheating?'

'Eventually? Nothing. But hopefully the fun of the quest will stop them wanting to find shortcuts. And the discounts will be the kind you get with most standard tourist passes so nice to have but not worth cheating for.'

'Have you thought about randomizing it? You know, every fifth hundred correct—or completed—quest gets something extra? Just to add that bit more spice into it.'

'No.' He stared at her. 'But that's a great idea. I'll plan that in. Good thinking, Maddison.'

'Just doing my job.' But that same swell of pride flared up again. 'So, what's the plan? Where are we starting off? Literary? History?'

Kit held up a map and grinned. 'Neither. How do you feel about seeing the wild side of London?'

'When you said wild...' Maddison stood still on the path and stared '...I thought you meant the zoo!'

'Nope.' Kit shook his head solemnly but his eyes were shining with suppressed laughter. He seemed more relaxed, more boyish out and about. It was almost relaxing. But last night's words beat a warning tattoo through her head. There was a darkness at the heart of him and she needed to make sure she wasn't blinded by the veneer.

Not that she was attracted to Kit. Obviously not. A handsome face and a keen brain might be enough to turn some girls' heads but she was made of stronger stuff. No being led astray by blue eyes and snug-fitting jeans for Maddison, no allowing the odd spark of attraction to flare into anything hotter. Think first, feel after, that was her motto.

Speaking of which, she was here to think. Maddison looked around. She was used to city parks—Central Park was her gym, garden, playground and sanctuary—but the sheer number of green spaces on the map Kit held loosely in one hand had taken her aback. London was surprisingly awash in nature reserves, parks, heaths, woods and cemeteries. Yes, cemeteries. Like the one lying before her, for instance. Winding paths, crumbling mausoleums and trees, branches entwining over the paths as they bent to meet each other like lovers refusing to be separated even by death. Maddison put one hand onto the wrought-iron gate and raised a speculative eyebrow. 'Seriously? You're sending people to graveyards? For fun?'

'This is one of London's most famous spots,' Kit said as he led the way through the gates and into the ancient resting place. Maddison hesitated for a moment before following him in. It was like entering another world. She had to admit it was surprisingly peaceful in a gloomy, gothic kind of way. Birds sang in the trees overhead and the early-summer sun did its valiant best to peep through the branches and cast some light onto the grey stone fashioned into simple headstones, huge mausoleums and twisted, crumbling statues. 'There's a fabulous Victorian cemetery near you in Stoke Newington too but there's no Tube link so I didn't include it in the tour.'

'You can save it for the future, a grave tour of London.'

'I could.' She couldn't tell whether he was ignoring her sarcasm or taking her seriously. 'There are seven great Victorian cemeteries, all fantastic in different ways. But I love disused ones best, watching nature reclaim them, real dust-to-dust, ashes-to-ashes stuff.'

'Don't tell me.' She stopped still and put her hands on her hips. 'You wore all black as a teenager and had a picture of Jim Morrison on your wall? Wrote bitter poetry about how nobody understood you and went vegetarian for six months.'

'Naturally. Doesn't every wannabe creative? You forgot learning two chords on a guitar and refusing to smile. Does that sum up your teen years too?'

It certainly hadn't. She hadn't had the luxury. People didn't like their waitresses, babysitters, baristas and cleaners to be anything but perky and wholesome. Especially when their hired help had a background like Maddison's. She'd had to be squeaky clean in every single way. The quintessential all-American girl, happy to help no matter how demanding her customer, demeaning the job and low the pay.

'Not my bag,' she said airily. 'I like colour, light and optimism.'

Kit grinned and began to pick his way along the path.

On either side mausoleums, gravestones and crumbling statues, some decorated with fading flowers, formed a curious honour guard. 'What was your bag? Let me guess: cheerleader?'

Maddison tossed her hair back. 'Possibly.'

'Mall rat?'

'I would say Mall Queen,' she corrected him.

'Daddy's credit card, a cute convertible and Homecoming Queen?'

'Were you spying on me?' she countered. Actually it had been a rusty bike she had saved up for herself and then repaired. Not a thing of beauty but she had been grateful at the time.

He fell into step beside her, an easy lope to his stride. Her brightly patterned skirt, her neat little cashmere cardigan and elegant brogues were too bright, too alive for this hushed, grey and green world and yet Kit fitted right in, despite his casual jeans. He belonged. 'So where did you spend your cheerleading years?'

'You wouldn't have heard of it. It's just a typical New England small town.' Maddison was always careful not to get too drawn into details; that was how a girl got caught out. She didn't want anyone to know the sordid truth. She much preferred the fiction. The life she wished she had led. So she kept the generalities the same and the details vague. 'How about you? Have you always lived in London?'

He looked surprised at her question. 'No, I'm from Kilcanon. It's by the sea, on the coast south of Glasgow on a peninsula between the mainland and the islands. Scotland,' he clarified as she frowned.

'You're Scottish?' How had she not known that?

'You can't tell?'

'You don't sound Scottish, you sound British!'

He laughed. 'We don't all sound like Groundskeeper Willie, well, not all the time.'

'Do you miss it?' She only had the haziest idea about Scotland, mostly bare-chested men in kilts and romantic countryside. It sounded pretty good; maybe she should pay it a visit.

'Every day,' he said so softly she almost couldn't hear the words. 'But this is where I live now.'

'I love living in New York but I wouldn't want to raise my children there.'

'Children?' He raised his eyebrows. 'How many are you planning?'

'Four,' she said promptly. 'Two girls, two boys.'

His mouth quirked into a half-smile. 'Naturally. Do they have names?'

'Anne, Gilbert, Diana and Matthew. This week anyway. It depends on what I've been reading.' Actually it was always those names. They gave her hope. After all, didn't Anne Shirley start off with nothing and yet end up surrounded by laughter and love?

'Let's hope you're not on a sci-fi kick when you're actually pregnant then, or your kids could end up with some interesting names. Why so many?'

'Sorry?'

'Four children. That's a lot of kids to transport around. You'll need a big car, a big house—a huge washing machine.'

'I'm an only child,' she said quietly. That, for once, wasn't a prevarication, not a stretch of the truth. And she had vowed that when she got her family, when she had kids, then everything would be different. They would be wanted, loved, praised, supported—and they would have each other. There would be no lonely nights shivering under a thin comforter and wishing that there were just one person to share it with her. One person who understood. 'It gets kind of lonely. I want my children to have the most perfect childhood ever.'

The childhood she was meant to have had. The one she had been robbed of when her mother refused to name her father. All she had said was that he was a summer visitor. One of the golden tribe who breezed into town in expensive cars with boats and designer shades and lavish tips. Maddison could have been one of them, but instead she had been the trailer-trash daughter of an alcoholic mother. No gold, just tarnish so thick hardly anyone saw through it to the girl within. Even when she had got out, the tarnish had still clung—until she left the Cape altogether and reinvented herself.

Kit looked directly at her as she spoke, as if he could see through to the heart of her. But he couldn't; no one could. She had made sure of that. And yet her pulse sped up under his gaze, hammering so loudly she could almost hear the beat reverberate through the cemetery. She cast about for a change of subject.

'How about you? Do you have any brothers and sisters besides Bridget?'

Kit wandered over to a statue of a lichen-covered dog waiting patiently for eternity. Maddison shivered a little, relieved of the warmth of his gaze, pulling her cardigan a little tighter around her. 'There were three of us.'

Were?

Her unspoken question hung in the air. 'My sister's a lot younger, she's still at university, but my brother…he died. Three years ago.'

'I'm sorry,' she said softly. 'You must miss him.'

He turned, his smile not reaching his eyes. 'Every day. Okay, where are we headed?'

Maddison swallowed. It was a clear change of subject.

He was not going to discuss his loss with her. There was no reason why he should; they barely knew each other. And yet there had been a connection last night, and now as they wandered through the gravestones. Maybe she'd imagined it. After all, didn't she know how powerful imagination was? How important.

She held up the piece of paper and read out the first clue once again. '"Take the Northern line to Archway. Walk up Highgate Hill and through Waterlow Park to the final resting place of the city. Unite at the grave where you have nothing to lose but your chains. The last words on the fourth line are…?"' She paused and looked up at Kit. 'Unite at the grave? What does that mean? We have to split up?'

'See, this is where in the actual trail you'll read the information about Highgate Cemetery in the guidebook and hopefully work the clue out from there. Here.' He passed her his phone. 'Read that.'

She took it carefully and squinted down at the screen, angling it away from the sun so that she could make out the words. '"Famous people buried here include Douglas Adams, George Eliot and Christina Rossetti, although many people bypass even these luminaries and head straight to the grave of Karl Marx…" Oh! Of course.' She read through the rest of the list. 'Lizzie Siddal's buried here too? I'd love to see her grave. I did a paper on the Pre-Raphaelites at college.'

'Take your time. The whole point of this is that it's fun and a way to explore London, not to tear around like some kind of city-wide scavenger hunt.'

'True, but I'm testing it, not doing it for real,' she pointed out. 'I can come back. I might even explore the one in Stoke Newington. Maybe you've converted me to gothic tourism.'

'That's the aim. I'll get you on to a Ripper tour yet. Look, there's a tour guide. Why don't you ask him the way?'

'Only if you take my photo when we get there.' Maddison examined the picture of the grave in fascination. 'I've seen a lot of hipster beards since I got to London but Karl Marx has them all beat. I want to capture that for posterity.' It wasn't quite the type of picture she had intended to fill her social-media sites with but hey. Let Bart see she had hidden depths.

And more importantly that she was out, about and having fun.

Only, Maddison reflected as she walked towards the guide to ask for directions, it wasn't all for show. She probably wouldn't have chosen to spend her weekend in this way but she *was* having fun. And even more oddly, until the last minute she hadn't thought about Bart once all morning.

She'd been banking on absence making the heart grow fonder but in her case it seemed that out of sight really was out of mind. Well, good. Maddison Carter didn't hang around weeping about any guy, no matter how perfect he was. And the more she made that clear, the more likely he would be banging on her door the second she got back to New York, begging for a second chance.

That was the plan, wasn't it? But the image didn't have its usual uplifting effect and for the first time Maddison couldn't help wondering that if she had to go to such extraordinary efforts to persuade Bart that she was the girl for him then maybe, just maybe, he wasn't the guy for her.

And if he wasn't, then she had no idea what to do next.

CHAPTER FOUR

'WHAT HAVE YOU got planned for me today?' Maddison looked up at the threatening-looking sky and wrinkled her nose. 'And what did you do with the sunshine?'

'I forgot to order it.' Kit gestured towards the end of the street. 'Shall we?'

'Okay, but there better be more transport today because, I am warning you, my feet are planning on going on strike after two miles.'

He wasn't surprised by her declaration. They had covered a huge amount of distance the day before, walking to Hampstead Heath from Highgate where, after deciphering the clue, Maddison had found out the opening times of the famous all-season open-air pool. From there they had travelled to first Regent's and then Hyde Park before searching for Peter Pan's statue in Kensington Gardens. Less a leisurely treasure hunt, more a route march through London's parks.

And Maddison hadn't complained once.

She had turned all his preconceptions on their head this weekend. She had surprised him, shamed him a little, with the speech she had produced, with her sharp criticism of his own effort. Charmed him with her unabashed competitiveness in the pub quiz; and yesterday she had unflaggingly followed the clues, suggesting improvements and possible new additions. Not once had she moaned about sore feet or tried to steer him into a shop. He tried to imagine Camilla under similar circumstances and suppressed a smile. Unless her treasure hunt took her down Bond Street she was likely to give up at the first clue.

What was he doing with women like Camilla? He'd thought he was choosing wisely, safely, but maybe he would be better off on his own. It was what he deserved, after all. Although sometimes his dating habits seemed like some eternal punishment, his own personal Hades.

Maddison stopped. 'The bus stop is just here. I was a bit horrified when I realized I was going to have to bus in to work but actually I love that I spend every day on a real red double-decker. It's like an adventure. I never quite know where it might take me.'

Kit's mouth curled into a reluctant smile, his bitter thoughts banished by her enthusiasm. Turned out Maddison Carter had quite the imagination. 'Doesn't it stop at the bus stop outside work?'

'Well, yeah, that's where I choose to get off. But sometimes I wonder if it might turn an unexpected corner and poof. There I am, in Victorian London, or Tudor London. Even in New York I don't feel that. Oh, we have some wonderful old houses back home but they're babies compared to some of the buildings I see here.'

'We'll have to do the history tour next. That will blow your mind.' The bus pulled in at that moment and they got on, tapping their cards on the machine by the driver before ascending the narrow, twisting staircase to the top deck. Yesterday was the first time Kit had been on a bus in a really long time, and personally he was struggling to see any hint of adventure travelling in the slow, crowded vehicle, but to test the routes properly he needed to travel the way his intended market would. However long it took.

He would taxi home though; that wouldn't be cheating.

The bus lurched forward as he slid into a narrow seat beside Maddison. She was wearing the same brightly patterned skirt as yesterday teamed with another neat cashmere cardigan, this one in a bright blue that emphasized the red tones in her hair. She looked like a bird of paradise, far too elegant for the top deck of a bus—or a hike through a park. She had turned away to stare out the window, no doubt daydreaming of time-travelling adventures as the bus progressed slowly down a narrow street, stopping every few hundred yards to allow passengers on and off.

It was a good thing they had all day.

Kit shifted in his seat, trying to arrange his legs comfortably. 'Did you have a nice evening? A date with one of your conquests from the party?' Whatever she had done it had to have been better than his evening, an engagement party for an old friend. Camilla had been there, all quivering emotion and hurt eyes, his attempt to speak rationally to her thwarted by tears. It was funny, he thought grimly, how he had stuck to his word and yet somehow ended up the villain of the piece. At least she finally seemed to have accepted that they were over, had been over for some weeks and, no, he wasn't going to change his mind.

'A date?' Maddison turned and stared at him. 'I only met those men on Friday. It would be a bit early for me to accept a date off any of them even if they did ask me.'

Kit grinned at the indignation in her voice. 'Oh, I'm sorry. Do you need references and to meet the parents first?'

She didn't smile back, her face serious. 'No, but you

never accept an invitation to a same-weekend date. Especially not for a first date.'

'You don't? How very unspontaneous.'

'Of course not.' She was sounding confused now. 'A girl needs to make sure any potential guy understands that she's a busy person, that she won't just drop everything for them.'

Kit frowned. 'But what if you don't have plans? What if you're turning down a night out for a box set and a takeaway?'

'It doesn't matter. If he doesn't respect you enough to try and book you in advance then he never will. You'll be relegated to a last-minute hook-up and once you're there you never move on.' Maddison turned to him, her eyes alight with curiosity. 'Isn't it like this in London?'

'I don't think so. Not that I've ever noticed. I say, "Want to grab a drink?" They say yes. Simple.' Simple at first, anyway.

'Or no. Surely sometimes they say no.'

Kit paused. 'Maybe.' But the truth was they usually said yes.

'Wow.' Maddison looked around as if answers were to be found somewhere on the bus. 'There's more than just an ocean between us, huh? Guess I'll never get a date in London. Or I'll end up civilizing your whole dating scene. Grateful women will build statues to me.'

The women Kit knew played enough mind games without adding some more to their repertoires. 'Remind me never to talk to a woman of dating age in New York again; I shudder to think of all the rules I must have inadvertently broken.' Although it must make life a little clearer, all these rules. It never failed to catch him unawares how quickly it could escalate—a coffee here, a drink there and suddenly there were expectations.

He suppressed a grin at Maddison's appalled face and couldn't resist shocking her a little more. 'If you want to meet someone in London then you need to be a lot less rigid. Over here we meet someone, usually in the pub, fancy them, don't know what to say to them, drink too much, kiss them, send some mildly flirty texts and panic that they'll be misconstrued and repeat until you're officially a couple.'

Maddison stared at him suspiciously. 'That's romantic.'

'You've seen *Four Weddings and a Funeral*, right? Think about it. If Andie MacDowell had understood the British Way of Dating she would never have married the other man, she would have just made sure she turned up at Hugh Grant's local pub a couple of times and that would be that.'

'Four Weddings, Three Nights Out and a Funeral?'

'That's it. Now you're ready to go. If you're looking, that is—or is there someone with the perfect dating etiquette waiting for you back in New York?'

'We're on a break.' The words were airily said but, glancing at her, Kit was surprised to see a melancholy tint to her expression. Sadness mixed with something that looked a lot like fear.

'Because you came here?'

'Not really.' She shook her head, a small embarrassed laugh escaping her. 'I can't believe I'm telling you this.'

'I don't mind.'

Maddison paused, as if she were weighing up whether to carry on. 'Rule number two of dating,' she said eventually. 'Don't talk about your other relationships. Always seem mysterious and desirable at all times. Remember, rejected goods are never as attractive. Rules are rules, even when you're talking to your boss!'

'Your way sounds like a lot of hard work.' Kit stole a glance at her. Her face was pale, all the vibrant colour bleached out of it. He had been subjected to tears, tempers and sulks by his exes, often all three at once, and remained totally unmoved, but Maddison's stillness tugged at him. He wanted to see the warmth return to her expression; after all, he knew all about pain and regret, what a burden it was, how it infected everything. 'Look, if you want to talk about it forget I'm your boss. I've got a sister, remember? Sometimes I think she uses me as her very own Dear Diary.'

Maddison slid a long look up at him and Kit tried to look as confide-worthy as possible. It wasn't curiosity, not exactly. He just got the impression that she didn't let things out very often. Didn't allow her vulnerabilities to show. 'Rule number three, never assume you're exclusive, not until it's been formalized.' She sighed. 'I didn't assume but I let myself believe it was imminent. That he was in it for the long-term.'

'And you were? In it for the long-term?'

She nodded. 'When I first met him, right then, before we even spoke, before we had coffee or went for a walk or kissed. When I first met him I looked at him and I knew. Knew that I could grow old with him.'

Kit blinked. 'Like love at first sight?' He couldn't keep the scepticism out of his voice.

'No.' She shook her head, strawberry-blonde tendrils shaking with the motion. 'Not love. But compatibility, you know? That would grow into love? Two old people rocking on their porch at the end of a long day.'

'You got all that before hello?'

'The way he was standing, his hair, the cut of his suit. It said he was...' She paused, looking up at the bus roof as if for inspiration. 'He just looked like the way I always imagined my future to look. Does that make any sense at all? Have you never thought that way? That you could grow old with someone?'

Kit hesitated. 'Once,' he admitted reluctantly. 'But not straight away.' But the words didn't quite ring true. The reality was that right from the start he had been so dazzled by the image Eleanor portrayed that he had failed to look beneath the carefully applied gloss to the woman underneath.

'What happened?'

Kit tried to smile, as if it were nothing, but he knew all too well that it looked like a grimace. 'She married my brother.'

Maddison opened her mouth then shut it again. He understood that. What was there to say, after all? Kit pulled his phone out of his pocket and busied himself looking at emails. The subject was closed—it should never have been open at all.

Half an hour and a Tube train later they alighted at Notting Hill. He had been careful not to catch her eye, to start another conversation, knowing one more careless confession would shatter everything he worked so hard to contain. But they were here now and the game was back on. And so must he be. He switched on his usual smile, the one that was barely skin-deep.

'Ready?' Kit handed Maddison the first clue and, with one sweeping, comprehensive look at him, she took it. His message had been received and understood.

'"Turn left out of the station until you reach Holland Walk. What is Henry's man doing outside the place where East meets West and the Dutch play?"' she read aloud. 'How international. Are we still doing wild London?'

'Just for today.' After this he was planning south to the Chelsea Physic Garden and then east to Greenwich

Park. Next weekend he was hoping that they could do the historical tour and literary the week after that—and then he would have enough data to put together a full proposal and Maddison could have her weekends back again.

As could he. The usual long, lonely weekends unless he buried himself with work or left London for two days of something outdoors, strenuous and a little dangerous.

Maddison repeated the clue to herself as they walked up the tree-lined splendour of Holland Park Avenue, past the white-painted, ornately decorated houses of this most exclusive of areas, breathing in a deep satisfied sigh as they turned into the park. 'I do love the countryside.'

Kit grinned. 'This isn't countryside, city girl. Two minutes that way and you're back in the heart of the city.' He stared unseeingly at the nearest tree. 'Back home there's nothing *but* trees and grass, water and mountains. The nearest supermarket's an hour's drive away on single-track roads, nothing remotely urban for miles around.'

'Sounds remote.'

'Yes.' He closed his eyes and pictured Kilcanon on a perfect day, the evening drawing in over the water, the vibrant greens fading to grey. Like Odysseus sitting on Circe's island, he felt a sudden piercing longing for his home. But unlike Odysseus there would be no happy homecoming at the end of his journey. His exile was self-imposed, necessary—and permanent. 'It's like no place on earth. But this is my home now, there's no going back. Not for me.'

And just like that he closed down, just as he had on the bus, and Maddison had no idea how to reach him— or even whether she should try. After all, they weren't friends, were they? They worked together, that was all.

But she didn't like to see anyone in pain and the darkness had returned, his eyes more navy than blue, his lips compressed as if he were holding all the emotions in the world tightly within.

'Because of your ex? And your brother?' The conversation from the graveyard yesterday returned to her and she stopped still, shock reverberating through her as she put the clues together. 'Wait, she married your brother, who died?' She regretted the words the second they snapped out of her mouth; there must have been a more sensitive way to have put it.

'Yes.'

'I'm sorry. For both.'

'Thank you.' They began to wander along the path, following the signs to the Japanese garden, Maddison mentally ticking off part of the clue as she went.

'It can't have been easy for you.' And that, she thought with a grimace, was the understatement of the century.

His mouth twisted. 'I accepted long ago that the Eleanor I thought I was in love with doesn't exist. I just wish I had really been able to forgive Euan while I still could. I said I had, of course, but I never did. Not because she chose him over me. But because *he* chose *her* over me.' His mouth snapped shut and he marched along the path as if, like the White Rabbit, they were late.

Maddison walked slowly behind, giving Kit the space he needed. She didn't know a lot about families but she understood betrayal, knew that the worst wounds were inflicted by those who should put you first. No wonder he wasted his time with women who were safe, women he would never allow in too deep.

But his wounds were festering. When had he said his brother had died? Three years ago? And he still hadn't dealt. If she didn't push now, maybe he never would.

But there were dangers in confidences. That was how bonds were formed, friendships forged. She should know; she'd honed her listening skills a long time ago—the right questions, a sympathetic face. She knew the drill. Used it to navigate her way into the right groups, the right cliques, the right life.

But this time she could use her skills for good. To help. Darn altruism. She didn't have the time or space for it.

She stood, teetering on her decision. Flip the conversation back to clues and parks and grisly tours or probe deeper. She knew which was sensible...

Kit was standing by the entrance to the Japanese garden, a scruffy silhouette, hands in pockets. Maddison picked up her pace and closed the distance between them, mind made up. Light, frivolous words prepared. Only: 'Were you close?' fell from her lips instead.

He turned his head to look at her, his eyes distant, granite-like in their bleakness. Maddison stepped back, the shock almost physical. Gone was the annoying, teasing boss, gone her focused if entertaining weekend companion, in his place a hard-faced stranger reeking of grief.

'Once.'

'Until Eleanor?'

'Until Eleanor.' He walked into the garden, Maddison following, taking a moment to admire the deep oranges and reds in the expertly arranged planting perfectly setting off the delicate waterfalls and sculptures. She joined Kit on the wide stone bridge and stood by him, looking at the koi as they swam in the pond.

'She was everything I didn't know I wanted.'

Maddison's heart twisted at the words. Wasn't that what she aimed to be? Hadn't she tried to learn Bart? To be everything he didn't know he wanted? But her intentions were more honourable; if he wanted her, offered her

the security she craved, she would look after his heart
as if it were her own, do her very best to give him hers.
Not break him into pieces.

'We were close, Euan and I. There's barely a year and
a half between us and he was the oldest—he never let
me forget that. But he had asthma and it held him back
sometimes and I, I didn't let him forget that.'

He paused, still staring into the pond as if the koi
carp could give him the answers she couldn't. But like
her they just listened.

'I was in my last year at Cambridge when I brought
Eleanor home. I'd never brought a girl back before. I
couldn't wait for my family to meet her. But he couldn't
help himself, couldn't help making even her into a competition and this time he won. How was I supposed to
forgive him for that?'

Without thinking Maddison reached across the carefully maintained space between them and laid a hand
on Kit's arm. It was firm, as she'd known it would be,
warm. She wanted to leave her hand there, flesh on flesh,
to allow her fingers to slip down the muscled forearm, to
link around his wrist. Her heart began to hammer, every
millimetre of her uncomfortably aware of his proximity,
of the feel of him under her suddenly unsteady hand.

She had never experienced a visceral reaction like this
over a mere touch before.

She had never had a reaction like this before. Period.

Slowly, as if her hand were an unarmed grenade and
not a part of her own body, Maddison lowered her hand
back to her side. Kit was continuing as if nothing had
happened, as if he hadn't even felt the pressure of her
hand, let alone the almost explosive chemical reaction
when skin touched skin.

Which was good, right? No, it was great. No awkwardness, no apologies. She'd just done what any normal person would do at a moment like this. Offered some comfort. Awkward comfort, sure. But all completely appropriate and above board.

'In that moment I was exiled from my home. Came home for holidays and Christmases, pretended I was fine, that there was no problem on my side. But I couldn't stay for long, not while they lived in Kilcanon. It's got worse since he died. I feel it more than ever. Going back gets harder every time. His absence seems larger every time.'

Maddison took a deep breath, steadying her voice as best she could. 'Did she love him?' She badly wanted the answer to be yes. After all, she'd been ready to love Bart, hadn't she? Ready to give him her body and soul in return for the security he guaranteed. She wasn't one of those gold-digging fakes ready to barter themselves away for a lifestyle. She was just cautious, that was all. Not ready to commit her heart too soon. Not till she knew it was safe.

'I'd like to think so, I really do. At least, I hope he believed she did. I hope he died thinking she adored him just as he adored her. Of course, her forthcoming nuptials to an older, richer and more influential man might point the other way but, hey, what do I know about grief?'

'A fair bit from the sound of it,' she said softly and he grimaced.

'It's been three years. It's time I moved on and accepted my responsibilities to the family. That's what my parents think. Not that *they've* really moved on. I'm not sure they'll ever accept the fact that Euan has gone and I am all that's left. Poor seconds.'

'I'm sure they don't think that.'

He laughed, a short bitter sound. 'You've spoken to my mother. You must have worked out what a disappointment I am.'

'I know she wants to hear from you, that messages through me aren't enough.' What would it be like to have a mother who cared? Who tried and tried to get through to you even when you were too grief-stricken and hurt to respond. 'Wait, Eleanor's wedding. Is that the wedding I keep getting calls about?'

'The very same. She's marrying a neighbour of ours and my parents are very insistent that we all go along and bless her new marriage. It's the right thing to do. And they're right, and yet I just can't bring myself to accept the damn invite. It's like if I do, that's it. Euan has gone and it was all for nothing.'

CHAPTER FIVE

IT HAD BEEN a long day and by the time Maddison had noted down the maker of the clock situated just outside the Royal Observatory in Greenwich Park she was beat. She flopped onto a bench with an exaggerated sigh. 'That's half of London off my sightseeing list.'

'See, virtue is its own reward.' Kit had his trademark amused smile back in place as if the heartfelt conversation in Holland Park had never taken place. Maddison couldn't help thinking that it was for the best. She'd mentioned her hopes for Bart, he'd opened up about his brother. They were even. No more depth required. And next weekend she would be armed with an entire list of small talk and safe topics to make sure they went no further.

'Actually...' she smiled sweetly at him '...reward is its own reward. Event of my choosing, remember?' Even as she said the words she wondered if she was playing with fire, spending more time alone with Kit Buchanan. But an event was different; if she chose wisely they wouldn't have to communicate at all. And it all made good copy for her social-media sites. She had a ton of pictures to add over the week: the Japanese garden at Holland Park, another gorgeous garden in the equally gorgeous Chelsea and the slightly disappointing visit to Vauxhall. It was a perfectly adequate park but she had secretly been hoping that the old pleasure gardens were still intact with winding, tree-lined paths full of lurking rakes, and a ballroom brimming with waltzing, masked partygoers. Now that would have got a lot of 'likes'. A few pictures of her dallying with breeches-clad rakes and surely Bart would have been over on the next plane.

Although given the choice she'd have been tempted to stick with the rakes... Maddison pushed the disloyal thought aside. Her plans with Bart were—had been—about forever. She wouldn't throw that away for a rake, no matter how tight his breeches.

Nor for a pair of blue eyes and an easy smile. Not that the owner was offering.

'Of course. Your prize. What's tempting you? Dinner at Nobu, drinks at the Garrick, Shakespeare at The Globe?' Kit leaned against the railings and looked out at the view and, despite herself, Maddison couldn't stop her gaze skimming over his denim-clad rear. The worn jeans fitted him just right; even breeches couldn't improve that posterior. 'Or some sort of concert? Your wish is my command.'

'Seriously, anything?'

'That was the deal. Why?' He turned, his eyes creased, a wicked gleam warning her that she wasn't going to be impressed with his next suggestion. She folded her arms and glared at him. It had as much effect as bombarding him with kittens. 'Do you fancy something more risqué? I'm unshockable, you know, quite happy to take you to a burlesque club or into Soho for something a little edgier if that's what you fancy.'

Maddison had an irrepressible urge to play along, just to see how far he'd go. 'Burlesque is very two years ago. Once you've spent a year learning how to unfold yourself from a giant martini glass in little more than a feather boa it quite takes the mystique away. It was great exercise, though, really worked the abs and the glutes—especially hanging upside down on a rope.'

'I'd pay good money to see that,' he said softly and Maddison barely repressed a shiver as the gleam in his eye intensified, darkened. Maybe she didn't want to find out how far he would go. Maybe she was the one who was happy staying right here.

'I'm out of practice.'

'Isn't that a shame?'

Okay, it was definitely time to change the subject. 'Opera. I'd really like to go to the opera, in Covent Garden.'

The gleam was wiped away as if it had never been. 'Opera?'

'You did say anything,' Maddison pointed out sweetly, enjoying the look of horror on his face.

'True. I am a man of my word. But are you sure? Huge ladies in nighties collapsing and dying over twenty minutes of yowling? Because I'm sure there's a complete extended *Lord of the Rings* trilogy showing somewhere. You, me, twelve hours of orcs?'

'You have a very outdated view of opera. Not the twenty-minute-dying thing,' she added truthfully. 'That's pretty standard, but the casting and staging is equal to the singing now. But if you really hate the idea I'll go by myself.'

'No, no, I promised. Any preference?'

The temptation to demand a full repertoire of Wagner almost overwhelmed her but she resisted. 'You choose, whatever's on. The experience will be enough.'

He shook his head. 'Opera,' he muttered. 'Okay, caterwauling and extensive death scenes it is, but you have one more task before you fully earn it. I want to walk under the Thames, see if it's worth including in a tour, and as we're so close you can come with me. Tell me if it should be on every tourist's wish list.'

'Walk under the Thames?' Maddison stared up at him. 'I hate to break it to you but I left my scuba-diving stuff at home.'

'Luckily for you there's a staircase and a fully tiled tunnel. No masks or tanks required. I believe it's perfectly safe. About one hundred and twenty years old though so there may be a few cracks...'

Maddison's pulse had already sped up at the words *walk* and *under* but *cracks* sent it hammering into overdrive. 'Why walk when there are perfectly good bridges and cable cars?'

'History. It was put in to help dock workers get to work on time from the other side of the river. I'm joking, Maddison, it's perfectly safe, not a crack to be seen. The damage from World War II was repaired, well around then I think. It's a great addition to the history tour but I just want to see how long it takes and look for things I can use for a clue. If you really hate the idea then...'

'No. It's fine.' It wasn't but no way was she playing the weak, pathetic female. 'I just think you exceeded the walking quota for today and now here you are adding a whole river's worth of extra steps. I'm just calculating how much it's worth. Interval drinks at the opera for a start.'

It wasn't that she was claustrophobic, not at all. She was fine in her tiny studio, wasn't she? And sure, she didn't like flying, but nobody really liked being cheek by jowl with a bunch of strangers in a tin can in the sky. It was just she didn't like feeling that she had no escape. It was too much like the tiny, airless room in the trailer, the door shut and not being allowed to come out, not even to use the toilet or to get a drink. It was being help-less that got to her. And walking under a river seemed a pretty darn vulnerable thing to do.

'Drinks as well? That might make the actual opera part a little more palatable.' He extended a hand. 'Come along, Miss Carter, we can't be lounging around here all day. We have waters to conquer.'

Why had she agreed when it was obvious how much she didn't want to go into the tunnel? Daniel had probably been much more eager to go into the lions' den—but, unlike Daniel, Maddison had no need to martyr herself. Kit had suggested more than once that she could wait for him by the domed entrance but she brushed his sugges-tion aside with a curt, 'I'm fine, honestly.'

Which was the least honest thing he had heard this week. Fine didn't usually mean pale, big-eyed and mute.

The entrance to the tunnel was by the Cutty Sark, the permanently moored Victorian clipper, and Kit made a note to try and work the boat into the history quiz—with the Royal Observatory so close it would give treasure hunters a good reason to come this far east. But he didn't stop as he steered Maddison past the tourists queuing up for a tour; if she was going to insist on doing something that so obviously freaked her out, then they should get it over with as soon as possible.

They bypassed the glass door lifts at the tunnel en-trance, choosing to access the tunnel through the spiral staircase instead, and began the descent still in silence. There must have been one hundred or so steps and Kit breathed a sigh of relief when they reached the bottom, Maddison still safely by his side.

'Okay, keep your eyes out for clues,' he said as cheer-fully as he could, as if a mute, white-faced Maddison were a completely normal companion. 'Interpretation, some carving or plaque we could use. I was wondering about the number of steps but lost count halfway down.'

'So did I.'

'She speaks! So, what do you think?'

Maddison swivelled, taking in the tunnel. It was, Kit had to admit, less than spectacular, the floor a grubby gravel path, the circular walls curving low overhead, completely covered with white rectangular tiles. A line of lights ran ahead, murkily lighting the way. If he was planning to write a crime novel, then this would make a perfect location. If it weren't for the CCTV and other pedestrians, that was. He stepped aside as a family came by, the children yelling excitedly as their voices echoed off the walls.

'It's a little like being in the Tube. If I didn't know I wouldn't have guessed we were under the river.'

'Those Victorians missed a trick. They should have put in glass walls so we could gaze in delight on the murky depths of the Thames, looking out for shopping trolleys and the occasional body.'

'Charming. I so wish they had.'

'Ready? I'm going to warn you now that we're not getting out the other end; there's not a huge amount to see there and I want to take a closer look at the Cutty Sark.'

'There and back again? That's going to cost ices *and* drinks at the opera.' But her voice wasn't so stilted and her posture more natural. Whatever Maddison had been afraid of obviously hadn't materialized—and she was right: it was very much like walking through a connection tunnel at a Tube station. A long connection tunnel. One the width of the Thames, in fact.

And the Thames was wider than he'd realized. 'Seen anything?' They had walked maybe around five hundred yards and he had yet to see a single identifying item that would make the tunnel suitable as a treasure-hunt destination.

'Not a thing. Maybe there will be something at the other end we can direct them to.' She sounded completely normal now, if a little weary.

The lights flickered and she froze, her eyes wide. Not so normal after all, just putting on a good front. Maybe they would have to exit at the far end after all. Kit wasn't sure he wanted to bring her back through the tunnel if she was going to be so jumpy.

'Maybe, otherwise...' But before he could finish his suggestion the lights flickered again and then a third time, before with no further ceremony simply blinking out. Kit blinked and blinked again, the darkness so very complete he didn't know where the tips of his fingers were, which way he was facing.

'What the...?' he swore softly. 'Maddison, where are you? Are you okay?' She didn't reply but he could hear her breathing, fast, shallow, panicked breaths getting hoarser and hoarser as her breathing sped up.

'Maddison.' He put out a hand, feeling for her, conscious of a mild panic, a little like playing blind man's bluff, that moment when you reach out into the unknown, patting the air gingerly, hoping to touch hair or a sleeve. But there were no answering giggles, just increasingly hoarse breaths. He felt again but his hands brushed nothing more substantial than air. Damn.

'Maddison, it's okay. I'm going to get my phone. It has a light on it. Okay? Just slow down, lass.' The affectionate word slipped from his tongue before he was aware. A word that belonged at home, to a past life, a past time. 'Breathe. Breathe.' He kept speaking in a low, measured voice while he fumbled for his phone, breathing a sigh of relief when he located it. It took him three expletive-ridden tries to press his fingerprint onto the lock screen but eventually the phone was on and he could press the torch icon. Immediately a beam of light sprung out from the back, casting a pale glow over the wall in front of him. He moved it to the side and finally located Maddison.

She was utterly rigid, her eyes wide in shock, the blood completely drained from her face as if she were looking into Hades. Kit reached out and took a hand, wincing at the iciness of her flesh. All thoughts of boundaries and assistants and company policies when it came to line managers and their staff disappeared as he shrugged off his jacket, wrapping it around her and pulling her in tight so that he could rub her arms, her back, her hands, trying desperately to transfer some warmth from him to her. She was shaking now, her teeth chattering, but her breathing slowed as he held her. She still didn't utter a single word.

It could only have been a minute at the most but it felt like an eternity. The silence as absolute as the dark, punctuated only by her panicked breath and his murmured comfort. It was almost a shock when the lights came on with no ceremony, just with a dull flicker. Maddison started, stared at the light—and then burst into tears. Convulsive, silent sobs that racked her body as if they would tear her apart.

'Hey, hey, it's okay.' Kit continued to rub her back, his hands moving in slow, comforting circles, but now the lights were back on, now she was responding to his comfort, albeit in a damp, sobbing way. It was hard for him not to notice just how perfectly his hand fit the contours of her back. How her hair was lightly fragranced, a subtle floral scent that made him think of spring. Of how perfectly she fitted into him, her head under his chin and her breasts—oh, dear God, her breasts—nestled enticingly against his chest.

No, not enticingly. She was in pain and shock. What kind of monster found that enticing?

Her waist was supple and her legs gloriously long. The kind of legs a man wanted wrapped round him…

Kit swallowed, his hands stilling as he tried to push the unwanted, forbidden thoughts away. She was in love with someone else, remember? She wanted a porch swing with that someone, which wasn't a sign of commitment he was familiar with, it must be some American thing, but it sounded serious. And even if she weren't…

She was bright and quick and ridiculously attractive, not to mention the perfect breasts and the long legs and the hair. Girls like Maddison deserved to be put up on pedestals and worshipped. Even if she were free she wasn't for him. He didn't deserve her, would never deserve a woman like her. He deserved shallow and superficial and downright annoying at best. Really he would be better off on his own. He deserved a lifetime of loneliness.

After a few minutes during which Kit studiously counted the tiles over her shoulders, anything to take his mind off just how closely they were pressed together, Maddison's breathing slowed down to the odd gulp, her sobs transmuted to small shudders, her tears finally stemmed. 'I'm so sorry.' She stepped back and he was instantly cold, instantly empty. He wanted to drag her back against him, allow his hands to explore every inch of her body in a way that had nothing to do with comfort, everything to do with lust. Kit's eyes dropped to the lush tilt of her mouth, swollen from tears, and wanted to crush it under his until her sobs were a distant memory.

He took a step back of his own. 'That's okay. Come on, let's get out of here.'

'I...I...I'm not good in the dark.'

'You don't have to explain anything.' His voice was gruff as he forced the words out. 'Are you okay to walk? I think we both need a stiff drink.'

Maddison cradled the brandy Kit had insisted on buying for her. 'I am really...'

'Sorry,' he supplied. 'I know. But you don't need to be. There is absolutely nothing to apologize for.'

'A twenty-six-year-old woman so afraid of the dark she has a meltdown? That's beyond an apology.' She buried her head in her hands. 'I am completely pathetic. Do you know I sleep with a night light? Like a little kid?'

She had slept with a night light since she was eight, since the night she had woken to hear a noise snuffling outside her trailer. There were coyotes on the Cape but her mind had immediately jumped to bears—or something worse. Maddison had blinked against the total darkness, heart hammering, mind buzzing with a fear completely alien to her eight-year-old mind.

'Mommy.' But her voice was hoarse with fear, the word barely more than a whisper. 'Mommy?'

At some level she'd known, known even if she could call out it would be no use, that her mother had gone out once she was asleep, that she often went out when Maddison was asleep, known that she was all alone in an old trailer in the middle of the woods. That anyone or anything could come and break into the trailer and nobody was there to save her.

Maddison looked up at Kit, her hands gripping the brandy, and took in a deep, shuddering breath, trying to get the panic back under control, where it belonged. 'You know what I love about living in New York? It's never dark. The light shines in through my window all night long.'

Kit reached over and laid his hand over hers, a warm, comforting clasp. She wanted to lace her fingers through his and hold on tight, let him anchor her to the daylight and the sunshine and the busy city street, pull her out of the darkness of the past.

But only she could do that. She needed security, she needed a family of her own to make up for her long, lonely childhood. She wanted the kind of money that meant walls were always thick, lights were always on and that she never, ever had to spend a night on her own.

'We all have our Achilles' heel,' he said, his fingers a comfortable caress on hers. 'No one has to be strong all the time, Maddison.'

She shook her head. He really didn't get it. 'I do,' she told him as she eased her hand out from under his, ignoring the chill on her now-empty hand in the space where he had touched her, the need for his warmth. 'I do. Weakness makes you vulnerable. Strength, security, that's what counts, Kit.'

He was looking at her as if he wanted to see into the heart of her but her barriers were well crafted and she wasn't letting him in. 'What happened, Maddison?'

She picked up the brandy and took a hefty swig, coughing a little as the strong liquor hit the back of her throat. 'Nothing happened, Kit. It's just life is like this treasure hunt of yours. There are winners and there are losers and you should know by now, I really like to win.'

CHAPTER SIX

'IS THIS WHAT you were hoping for? Because we can always duck out and do something else. Something that doesn't take quite so long.' Kit stared down at the programme, dismay written all over his face. 'Three acts? *Three.*'

'It's less than three hours in total,' Maddison looked around at the glittering sea of people and suppressed an excited shiver. 'And it could be a lot worse. Just think, it could have been Wagner.'

Kit shuddered dramatically. 'I'm definitely not putting this in the guidebook.'

His voice was a little loud and several heads turned disapprovingly. She elbowed him meaningfully. 'It's culture, you have to include it. You can't assume everyone is going to be a philistine just because you are. Besides, you must have known what to expect. This can't be your first opera.'

'Oh, it can. It will also be my last,' he said darkly. 'I didn't realize your cooperation would have quite so high a price. And I'm not just talking about the tickets—or these gin and tonics.'

Maddison repressed a smile. He might be acting all grumpy, but Kit had gone well above and beyond their agreement. 'Thank you.' She squeezed his arm. 'I didn't expect a gala night. This is really incredible.' She managed to stop the next words tumbling out before her sophisticated girl-about-town image was well and truly blown, but she couldn't keep her eyes from shining her gratitude. *No one has ever done anything like this for me before...*

Maddison looked around for the umpteenth time, trying to keep her excitement locked down deep inside. *Play it cool, Maddison Carter, you belong here.* And tonight she really did. Kit hadn't just brought her to the Royal Opera House, he'd gone all out and hired a box at a first-night gala performance of *Madame Butterfly*.

The cause was fashionable, the tickets sought after and London's great and good were out in force, the women's jewels competing with the huge, dazzling chandeliers, the men in exquisitely cut tuxedos. It was like stepping back in time to Edwardian England—and she, Maddison Carter, was right in the middle of it. A real Buccaneer. She might not own any heirloom jewels, but the man on her arm was one of the most striking in the room and she had intercepted more than one envious glance in their direction.

And everything was fine. She'd been worried on Monday that he would be careful with her, that her breakdown would change his attitude. It had been a relief when he had been his usual, slightly annoying self. In fact it was as if the weekend, the confidences, had never happened. Which was as it should be, because there had been moments when she had felt far too close to him, far too at ease.

Far too attracted.

Maddison sipped her drink, the sharp notes of the gin and tonic a relief. Where had that thought come from? Tunnels aside, she was having a good time with her extracurricular work, but treasure hunts and a heart to heart weren't going to get her the happy-ever-after, all-American dream, were they? She needed to remember her goals: a good marriage, a family of her own, security—emotionally and financially.

She took another sip. Tomorrow. She'd remember it tomorrow. It would be rude not to give her total concentration to the night ahead.

'Do you actually like opera?' Kit murmured in her ear, his breath warm, intimate, on her bare shoulder.

She turned to face him, pushing the disquieting thoughts away. 'I love it.' He arched a disbelieving eyebrow and she laughed. 'Honestly. I grew up with it. How could I not?'

For the first time, discomfort twisted in her as she stretched the truth. She *had* grown up with opera, but not in the way she was implying.

Every summer, Maddison would pick out the men she hoped were her long-lost father and watch them, waiting for recognition to spark in their eyes. Only it never did. They didn't even notice her. The year she turned ten she'd spent the summer hanging out on the beach all day, pretending as usual that she belonged to one of the laughing, happy families enjoying their vacation by the sea. Pretend that any moment they would look up, see her and call her, pull her sand-covered body in close, wrap her in a towel, hand her an ice-cold drink while alternating between kisses and scolding her for straying so far away.

It was so much better than the reality—an empty trailer and cold leftovers. If she was lucky.

Her favourite families owned or rented houses right on the beach. As evening fell and the beach emptied she would sit in the dunes and watch them. And that was when she had first noticed him, the tall, broad man who lifted his daughter up with one hand, who spent hours constructing the perfect sandcastle, who sang opera as he grilled dinner for his family on the beach-house patio.

She watched him every summer until the year she turned fourteen and realized that daydreams were never going to change anything.

But she couldn't shed the knowledge that if she'd lived with him, with somebody like him, with her real father, then maybe she would have had the childhood she wanted, the one she invented for herself as soon as she left Bayside: a childhood filled with singing arias, with ballet matinees and Saturday trips to the museum. The moment she hit New York she tried to re-create that childhood and fill in the gaps in her knowledge, spending her wages on cheap matinee seats up in the gods, museum tours, absorbing a childhood's worth of culture.

And it had brought her here, to the most glamorous place she had ever been in her entire life.

Her little black-and-white dress might be on the demure side but it held its own, every perfect seam screaming its quality. She smoothed out the heavy material with a quiet prayer of gratitude to the woman who had hired Maddison as a maid, giving her a room when Maddison left home at sixteen. Thanks to Mrs Stanmeyer, Maddison had had the space and time to study her last two years at school—and her benefactress's influence had secured Maddison a scholarship and bursary at a private liberal arts college in New Hampshire. In its ivy-covered buildings she'd both got her degree and reinvented herself.

And she never forgot Mrs Stanmeyer's advice: Maddison only bought the very best of everything. It meant her wardrobe was limited but it was timelessly classy and made to last. It allowed her to fit in anywhere.

The past faded away as the music swelled and surrounded her. Every note exquisite, every aria a dream.

She squeezed her eyes shut and let the music take over, offering wordless thanks to the man in the beach house. He wasn't Maddison's real father, she knew that now—truthfully she'd known it then—but he'd given her a gift nonetheless. She might have had to train herself to appreciate this music, but her training wheels were long since discarded and she was all-in. Every atom of her.

Finally the last lingering note died away and the audience was frozen in that delicious moment between performance and applause. Still tingling, Maddison turned to Kit. Had he hated it? Was he bored? She really hoped he got it.

That he understood a part of her.

His eyes were open and alert, which was a definite bonus; Bart liked to see and be seen doing culturally highbrow activities, but Maddison suspected if he could have got away with earplugs he would have—as it was she wasn't convinced he didn't snooze the best part of any performance away. Kit, however, was leaning forward, his arm on the balustrade and his eyes fixed onto the stage below.

She couldn't wait any longer. 'So? Did you hate it? You hated it. If you're bored we should go. Honestly…'

Kit reached out and covered her gesturing hand with his, sparks igniting up and down her arm as his fingers clasped hers. 'I wasn't bored. I…I don't know if I'm enjoying it exactly. I mean, offer me a trade for a sticky, beer-covered floor, some drums and guitars and a mosh pit and I'd take it, but I have to admit I'm…' he paused, raking a hand through his hair '…moved.'

'That's a start.' The glow inside was gladness. She'd introduced him to something new, something life enhancing. It had nothing to do with the hand still holding hers, nothing at all. 'Would you come again?'

There was no pause this time. 'Yes. Yes, I would.' Surprise lit up his face as he spoke. 'Wow, that was unexpected. I didn't know I was going to say that.' His fingers tightened, a cool clasp blazing a heated trail straight up her arm. 'Thank you.'

Maddison tried not to look at their entwined hands, not to behave as if this was in any way odd. 'For what?'

'For making me try something new.' The words were simply said but his gaze held a barely concealed smoulder, one that ignited every nerve right down to her bare toes.

'You're very welcome.' She tried to sound non-committal but couldn't stop the soft smile curving her lips, couldn't stop her eyelashes fluttering down in an unexpectedly shy gesture. What was going on? This wasn't how she operated. She hadn't tried to learn him by heart, hadn't tried to mould herself into what she thought he wanted. She was being herself, as much as she ever could be, thinking of nothing but work and yet unexpectedly finding herself having fun.

It had been a long time since fun had figured in her plans.

By some unspoken mutual accord their hands unclasped as Kit ushered her from the box to collect their interval drinks.

The corridors were buzzing with people, the bar even more so. Luckily there was no queuing; instead, here in the rarefied environs of the dress circle on a gala night, trays of champagne and canapés were circling amongst the chattering crowds. Kit neatly snagged two glasses off a passing waitress and passed one to Maddison, raising his own glass to her as he did so.

'To trying new things.' His eyes gleamed a bright blue in the glittering lights, a devilish glint flickering in the depths. Maddison's mind whirled with confusion, with an unexpected, unwanted desire to press a little closer. For those eyes to look at her with even more heat, more devilry. Her dizziness increased as his eyes held hers, the rest of the room falling away.

This was it, a dim, distant part of her analysed as she stood there, staring up at him. This was what attracted Camilla and her ilk to him, even though he warned them away, warned them that he wasn't in it for the medium-term, let alone forever. But when he focused, really focused, he could make a girl feel as if she were the only person worth knowing in the room. The only person *in* the room.

And yet she was pretty sure he didn't do it on purpose; this was no practised trick, no calculated seductive move.

That was what made it so dangerous, made him so very dangerous.

Even she, mistress of her own heart and destiny, might get swept away. For a very little while.

Or not… She was too seasoned a player to fold her hand at the first eye contact and warm, intimate glance. Maddison took a deep breath, stepping back, out of the seductive circle of his spell. 'To new things,' she agreed. 'It's the ballet next.'

Kit smiled appreciatively. 'Oh, no, it's my turn to choose next and I quite fancy seeing the demure and always put-together Maddison Carter in a mosh pit. Up for it?'

A what? Maddison opened her mouth to deliver what was definitely going to be a stinging retort as soon as she could think of one, when a languid hand draped itself on Kit's shoulder, a statuesque middle-aged brunette spinning him around as she pressed a kiss onto his suddenly rigid cheek. Only a muscle beating in his jawline showed any emotion.

Maddison shivered, suddenly chilled. Had they turned the air conditioning up? Hard to imagine how very warm she'd been just a few seconds before.

'Kit, dearest. I thought it was you but Charles said I must be mistaken. Kit at the opera! And yet here you are…'

Kit was still supremely still, only that pulsing muscle and the flash of anger in his eyes betraying any sign of life. 'Not mistaken, Laura. Hello, Charles.' He nodded over Laura's shoulder at the tall, balding man behind her.

'Gracious, Kit, last place I would have expected to see you. Not your usual style of thing.'

'No,' he agreed, his voice smooth. 'It's not. It is, however, very much Maddison's style and so here you find me.' He smoothly stepped out of Laura's possessive clasp and took Maddison's arm, ushering her forward, his hand holding her tight as if he feared she might run—or that he might. 'Laura, Charles, this is Maddison Carter. Maddison, this is Charles and Laura Forsyth.' He paused then before continuing, his voice still as urbanely smooth as the richest cream. 'Eleanor's parents.'

'Lovely to meet you.' Her words were as mechanical as her smile, Maddison's mind sprinting ahead as she watched Laura Forsyth's unsubtle summing up. Maddison held her chin up, as unconcerned as if she hadn't noticed the slow appraisal; she had nothing to hide, clothes-wise at least. Her outfit might be demure but the quality was unmistakable.

'American? How long are you over for? So nice of Kit to take you around.'

Maddison's eyes narrowed at the thinly hidden derisive note in the older woman's voice. Did Laura Forsyth think she could be put down so easily? It had been a long time since Maddison had allowed herself to be dismissed in a couple of sentences.

She would wipe that smile right off Mrs Forsyth's suspiciously wrinkle-free face.

Maddison plastered a bright smile on to her own naturally wrinkle-free thank you very much face and moved even closer to Kit, slipping under his arm, her own snaking round his waist as she turned to him. 'Isn't it? Kit's being very hospitable.' Maddison laid an extra-slow drawl onto the last two words, filling them with an unmistakable innuendo, and felt him quiver but whether it was with humour or anger she had no idea.

What the heck was she doing? Had she taken leave of her senses? She picked *now* to lose her temper, to behave spontaneously? It was going to look great on her résumé when Kit fired her. Reason for dismissal? Inappropriate temptress at the opera.

The older woman's eyes narrowed. 'He always was good-hearted, weren't you, Kit? Eleanor always said you put yourself out for others. We will be seeing you next week, won't we? It would mean a lot to Eleanor. After all, you're still family. I *had* hoped that, well, never mind that now. But for Euan's sake, Kit, you should come to her wedding.' Her eyes flickered towards Maddison. 'You are welcome to bring a guest, of course.'

'That's very kind of you, Laura. I am very busy and we weren't sure we could spare the time, were we, Maddison? But it would be a shame not to show you Scotland while you're here. So, thank you, Laura. We'd love to accept. Please do pass my apologies on to Eleanor for taking so long to respond.'

We? Hang on a second. Maddison worked to keep her smile in place. He was calling Laura Forsyth's bluff, surely. He didn't actually expect Maddison to attend a wedding in Scotland. With him. With his whole family. His ex-girlfriend and dead brother's widow's wedding. Did he?

There weren't enough opera tickets in the world.

The smile faltered on Laura Forsyth's face. 'How lovely. Eleanor will be delighted. We'd better get on. Charles has clients here. I'll see you—both—next weekend.' She kissed Kit again before disappearing into the crowd.

Maddison freed herself and rounded on Kit. He looked completely unruffled.

She folded her arms and glared at him. 'What did you just do?'

'Accepted the wedding invitation.' How could he look so calm and so darn amused? Did he think this was funny? 'After all, you've been reminding me to for weeks. I thought you'd be pleased.'

Thought she'd be *what*? 'I don't care whether you go or not, I just wanted you to decide either way and for the many, many phone calls to stop. I wanted you to make a decision for you. Not for me! Why did you do that? Now she'll think that I… That we…'

'She thought that the second you cosied into me. It wouldn't have been gentlemanly of me to push you away and explain that, sorry, you were my over-familiar assistant, and once she had included you in the invitation it seemed rude to accept for just me.'

Okay, she *had* been the one pressing in close in a proprietary fashion. 'I shouldn't have…' how had he put it? '…cosied into you like that. It was silly. It was just the way she looked at me. I got mad.' This was why she kept her temper, her feelings, under close control—usually, at least. Look what trouble acting impulsively could do.

'Apology accepted.' Maddison nearly choked at his smooth words. 'And now you've accepted responsibility for the whole situation you can see it's too late to backtrack now.' His mouth curved wickedly and she didn't know whether she wanted to wipe the smile off his face—or kiss it off.

Wipe, definitely wipe.

'Too late? I could have had plans. I might have plans.' Kit shot her a knowing look and Maddison scowled. 'Okay, I don't have plans but she doesn't know that. Just tell her I mixed up my dates. Or I'm ill. Or I had to leave the country.'

'Or you could just come with me.'

Maddison stilled. 'Why?'

Kit shrugged. 'Why not? Scotland is beautiful, especially at this time of year, and you really should see more of the UK than just London.'

'Your family will be there.'

'That's okay, they don't bite. You'll be doing me a favour, actually. I think I mentioned that I don't go back often. It can be a little intense. Your presence will relax things a little.'

'You want me to come along to act as a buffer between you and your parents?'

'I said no such thing. You speak to my mother more than I do. She'll be delighted to meet you at last.'

Meet the parents. Not at all awkward. 'Isn't there someone else you'd rather take? An actual real date?'

Kit stilled. 'I don't introduce my dates to my parents.'

'Not ever?' Obviously she never had but there were mitigating circumstances in her case. Kit's mother sounded both sober and present, qualities Maddison's mother had failed to possess.

'Not since Euan died. No, not because I'm too heartbroken.' Her face must have expressed her thoughts and Maddison flushed with embarrassment. 'No. Introducing dates to parents raises hopes in bosoms on both sides and that's something I'd rather not do.'

His words on her birthday came back to her. 'You really don't want to fall in love again one day?'

'No.' His voice was uncompromising. 'I don't believe in love. It's just getting carried away by infatuation and circumstance.'

His views weren't so far away from Maddison's own but it was uncomfortable hearing them so baldly stated.

'Look, Maddison, it's a good opportunity for you to spend some time outside London. Besides, we can work on the way up. I'm quite happy to dictate and drive.'

'You're really selling it to me. A weekend of weddings and work.'

'If you really hate the idea, then of course you don't have to come. But I do know it will be much more fun if you're there.'

Fun? With her? Warmth stole through her at the casual words. Words of acceptance and liking. 'Okay.' Wow, she was easily bought, wasn't she? But Kit was right. She should get out of London and see more while she was here. It had taken her twenty-six years to get to Europe; what if it was another twenty-six before she returned?

And he thought she was fun...not competent or organized or reliable. Fun.

'Great. I hope you brought some warm clothes. Scotland can be nippy even in early summer and I get the impression the atmosphere at Eleanor's wedding will be positively frosty.'

CHAPTER SEVEN

'ARE WE THERE YET?' Kit looked over as Maddison stretched and yawned, noting that she looked more cat-like than ever as she did so. Her hair was a little mussed up from sleeping in the car, her face make-up free. She looked younger, freer. His stomach tightened. If only they were on their way to somewhere where *he* could feel free. Instead every mile closer to the border the air closed in just a little bit more. Duty, responsibility, expectation all waiting to descend on him like an unwanted coronation mantle.

He turned the radio down a little. 'Not even close, I'm afraid. It would help if this section of the motorway wasn't all roadworks—it feels like we're permanently stuck at fifty miles per hour.' It might have made more sense to fly or to get the train but Kit needed to know that he had an escape plan ready and active at all times—and that meant his own transport.

'I don't understand. We've been on the road for hours. England just can't be that big. It's meant to be all little and quaint.' Maddison stared out of the window at the never-ending fields—and the never-ending drizzle—as if she were searching for thatched roofs and maypoles. She'd be searching for some time. The view from the M6 was many things but quaint wasn't one of them.

Besides, there was something she needed to be put right on. '*England* is nearly four hundred miles long and we're driving about three quarters of the length of it, but, as you need to remember before you are thrown out of the country for disrespect, we're not going to be in England, we're going to Scotland. A whole different country.' Despite himself, despite everything, Kit could hear the pride in his voice, feel the slight swell in his chest. Eleanor used to tease him that the further north they got the broader his accent got. Of course, now she rolled her *r*'s as if her home counties upbringing and Oxbridge education belonged to someone else, more Scottish than Edinburgh rock.

'A whole different country,' Maddison repeated. 'Like Canada?'

'But without border patrols and with the same currency.'

'Got it.' She slid him a sidelong glance. 'Are you okay?'

'Fine, why?'

'It can't be easy, watching your ex get married.'

If only she knew the half of it. 'I've had plenty of practice. This is her second wedding and she's still in her twenties. I fully expect to watch Eleanor get married several more times before she's through.'

'It's just…' she hesitated '…Eleanor's mother seemed concerned, as if she thinks you're still in love with the bride.'

'She hopes I'm still in love with the bride,' Kit said drily. 'I bet right now she's instructing the vicar to leave a good long pause after the true impediment part so that I can stand up and claim Eleanor for my own.'

'Leaving me weeping in the aisles?' There was an appreciative gurgle in Maddison's voice as she outlined the scenario. 'If only I had a hat, one with a little veil. Oh! And gloves.'

'There's no need to sound like you want it to happen.'

'I'm just saying if it were to happen I'd want to be appropriately dressed. What's the groom like?'

'Loaded, huge estate in Argyll, another one much further up in the Highlands—rich folk pay a fortune for the hunting and fishing. Plus various concerns in the city, a town house in Edinburgh. He's a catch…'

'I can tell there's an *if* or a *but* coming up.'

To hell with it, he needed to be honest with someone. '*If* you like your life partner to be the other side of forty-five, red-faced, balding and a pontificating know-it-all.'

'He sounds gorgeous.' She hesitated. 'So why?'

'Hmm?'

'I kind of got the impression that Eleanor's parents were all about the money and the image. Aren't they glad she's marrying someone who can keep her in style? An estate sounds pretty grand.'

'The Forsyths all about the money? Whatever gave you that idea?'

'So don't take this the wrong way, you're a nice guy when you want to be and easy enough on the eye, but why does socially ambitious mama want her darling daughter to run off with you? Especially as she already jilted you once?'

'She didn't jilt me. We were never engaged.' Thank goodness.

'You know what I mean. It doesn't make any sense. Unless she's thinking about her grandkids and the gene pool. No male-pattern baldness in your family.' She looked at his hair as if assessing the thickness.

Kit suppressed a sigh; this persistence was useful in his assistant, completely necessary if she was road-testing a treasure hunt. It was a little less comfortable when she was probing into his past. His hands gripped the steering wheel tight, his eyes fixed on the grey lines of the motorway as he eased his way past a lorry. 'As the youngest son I *wasn't* much of a catch. I was a student with his own eccentric business. I didn't plan on going into the City or doing any of the respectable money-making jobs a suitable partner for the Forsyths' beautiful only daughter would do.'

'A girl's gotta eat.' There was something oddly constrained in her voice despite the light words.

'She does. The right food at the right tables in the right households.' Kit hesitated. He liked that as far as Maddison was concerned he was her boss, nothing less, nothing more. But she was going to find out exactly what the future held for him in approximately four hours' time anyway and he would rather she heard it from him. Warts, title and all. Kit took a long drink of water, handing the bottle back to Maddison and focusing on the road ahead as he chose his words carefully. 'Euan was the eldest son and that made him a much better prospect than me. The Buchanans aren't as rich, not nearly as rich, as Angus Campbell, the lucky groom. But our name is older, we have a title, an ancient one, not an honorary one, and the castle has been in our family for generations. For new money like the Forsyths, that's worth more than a second estate. Now Euan's gone...'

He could hear Maddison's breath quicken. What was it with the predatory urge that overtook formerly sane women at the mention of a title and a castle? Kit didn't want to turn and look at her, to see if her eyes were gleaming covetously.

She shifted. 'You're no longer the second son. What does that mean?'

'Mean? It means that I'm the heir. To the title, the estate and the family name.' He laughed but there was no humour in the sound, just the bitter twist of fate. 'Turns out Eleanor bet on the wrong brother all those years ago and she's been kicking herself about it ever since we buried Euan.' Kit was trying to sound matter-of-fact but there was a rawness he couldn't cover. It was a long, long time since Eleanor had had the ability to hurt him. It turned out Kit was completely capable of destroying his own life— and the lives of everyone around him—without her help.

But she'd duped Euan and he would never forgive her for that.

'You don't know that,' Maddison argued. 'She might have really fallen in love with your brother. Hard on you, sure, but just because he was the eldest, just because he was going to inherit stuff, it doesn't mean she used you.'

He swallowed, his mouth dry despite the water he'd just consumed. 'Ah, but you see she told me. A month after we buried Euan. A month after she stood weeping by his grave and shooting me sympathetic glances as I had to come to terms with the knowledge that my brother had died...' The guilt that never really left him pressed down, heavier than ever. Such a stupid death. Such an unnecessary death. And he was to blame... 'She came to me and said she'd made a terrible mistake all those years ago. That she had never stopped loving me. That she knew it was too soon but maybe one day...'

Maddison was staring at him open-mouthed. 'She said all that?'

'Of course, I had just sold that quirky little start-up for a few million quid and a nice, well-paid and respectable job. Add the title and the castle to that and suddenly her old lover was looking all shiny and new. She still had her sights on being the Lady of Kilcanon.'

'I'll bet. What did you say?'

'I said not on her life. And then I got very, very drunk.' His hands tightened on the wheel. All those years of bitterness, the loss of his brother, all because of some *princess* who thought she was entitled to have it all—and damn anyone who got in her way.

But in the end he couldn't blame Eleanor for Euan's death. No. The only person to blame was Kit. And he could never, ever atone. God knew he had tried.

Maddison watched the scenery flash by but if someone quizzed her about what she had seen she would have definitely flunked the test. It was starting to add up: Kit's lack of interest in anything but the most perfunctory of relationships, his reluctance to go back to Scotland. He must have loved Eleanor very much once. Until she betrayed him.

Betrayal was such a strong word. After all, what had Eleanor done, exactly? Married strategically? Could Maddison blame her for that? After all, wasn't that her goal?

But she wasn't prepared to trample over sibling relationships and break hearts to do it. Her case was totally different. Wasn't it?

But the moral high ground didn't feel all that high.

'This must all come as a shock to you.'

She started. 'Sorry? The castle? Yeah, that's unexpected. Is there a moat and dungeons? A talking candlestick? A butler?'

'No to all the above and no, I didn't mean the castle. I meant the unhappily ever after. You believe in love at first sight, don't you?'

She almost laughed. As if. Nothing could be further from the truth; she wasn't even sure she believed in love.

Lust, sure, although she tried to ignore it. It could take a girl horribly off track. Affection, definitely. Compatibility. They were the foundations of a good, solid relationship. Shared goals another. But true love? That was for fairy tales. If Maddison had sat in her trailer waiting to be rescued she'd still be sitting there now. 'What makes you say that?'

'Mr Grow Old on a Porch Swing. What happened when you first saw him? Cupid's arrow straight to your heart?'

'Not exactly.' The mocking tone in his voice hit her harder than any arrow could.

'So what was it? What attracted you to him? How did you know he was the one if you weren't instantly smitten?'

Maddison thought back to the party where she and Bart had first met. It had been thrown by one of her college friends who had just bought, with family money, a fabulous loft apartment on the Upper East Side. Bart had been lounging against one of the carefully distressed brick walls, deep in conversation with a couple of friends. He had just looked so *solid*: tall, broad, blonde, clean-cut with that indefinable privileged air that Maddison worked so hard to cultivate but feared she never could. He wasn't handsome, not exactly, but he was nice to look at—and she could instantly see a future with him. A safe future. She had had no idea who he was at the time—her ambitions were high but not *that* high. But she could tell by his clothes, his stance, his air that he had the background she looked for, the future she needed. He had obviously felt her staring because he had broken off the conversation to look over at her—and then he had smiled and she had been lost in a world of infinite possibilities. A world where she was safe. For a time at least.

'I…' She stopped, unable to go on, and twisted her fingers in her lap, trying to find the right words. But what words were right? She didn't want to lie to him—she who lied to everyone—but there was no truth palatable enough to be served up.

Kit winced. 'I'm sorry, Maddison, it's not been that long, has it? I'm forgetting that not everyone weeps crocodile tears. For what it's worth, anyone who needs a break from you is an absolute idiot. He's not going to meet anyone better.'

No? He might meet someone genuine, someone who wanted Bart for his conversation and body, for his passions and interests, not for their vision of a perfect future. Could she really have done it? Married someone for convenience? Oh, she hadn't used that word before, had she? But that was what it came down to. She had deceived Bart—and she had deceived herself. 'He should. He deserves to. He's a really nice guy. Maybe he was right to call a halt to things.'

'Oh?' He raised an enquiring eyebrow.

Maddison hadn't told anyone the truth for so long there were times she wasn't sure exactly what the truth *was* any more. Not the teachers at school when they had asked about her mom, not her friends, not herself. Especially not herself. And Kit would judge her, he more than most. Maybe that was what she deserved.

Before she could weigh up the consequences of carrying on she spoke, the words almost tumbling out in the rush to unburden herself at long last. 'Bart's full name is Bartholomew J Van De Grierson III.'

But of course that meant nothing to him. 'Poor guy. I thought Christopher Alexander Campbell Buchanan was bad enough.'

She ignored him. 'His family have lived in New York

going back to colonial times. They're as close as we have
to aristocracy, or to royalty. Bart works in the family
business, and by business I mean global, multimillion,
fingers in pies you've never heard of and plenty that you
will have. He owns this incredible brownstone and the
family have an estate in the Hamptons, right by the sea.
It's as big as a small village.'

'Right. You found out all the important things, then?'

She had—and they had terrified her and seduced her
in equal measure. She'd been in well over her head but
how could she turn her back on the possibility of a future
so glittering it obliterated her more modest dreams? She
stared at her hands. 'Have you ever been hungry, Kit?
Have you ever woken up to find out that the electricity
was turned off and there's no hot water for a shower?
Have you ever had to work out which clothes were the
least dirty and turn up for school in them?'

He shot her a quick look but she wouldn't, couldn't
meet his eye. 'I wasn't prom queen and I didn't have a
credit card on Daddy's account. I didn't *have* a daddy.
And my mom wasn't around much.' She took a deep
breath. 'I want a family of my own, Kit. I want security. I want to know that I'm not just a pay cheque away
from eviction, that there is always, always money in the
bank. I want kids.'

'Four of them. I remember.'

She swallowed. How had he remembered that? 'Four
children who will have the safest, happiest, most perfect childhood ever. And I know that people say money
doesn't buy happiness—but I bet you anything those people have never gone to bed hungry. Or been really, really cold. So cold they can't sleep and their bones ache.'

'No, they probably haven't. So Bart wanted four kids
too? He was happy to be your secure happy ever after?'

She laughed. 'People like Bart don't marry people like me, Kit. You must know that. Money calls to money. Sure, he might date a girl like me, walk on the wrong side of the tracks for a little bit, but he wouldn't bring her home to meet the parents, wouldn't take her away with his friends. Wouldn't marry her. I grew up in a small town by the ocean and I saw it all the time—the wealthy summer visitors only mixed with people like them. And I knew that if I wanted to be one of them then I had to transform.' She couldn't stop now she'd started, the words spilling out. It was cathartic; this must be what confession was like, handing over your sins for someone else to absolve or punish.

'Transform?'

'Into one of them. Normal, a little spoiled, entitled. I got to college and created a whole new identity—a prom-queen, cheerleading, hayride, ice-carnival princess identity. Not too detailed, not too fancy, not privileged enough to raise alarm bells but privileged enough for the right groups to let me in. The college I went to was full of prep-school graduates with the right kind of background. It was almost too easy in the end to infiltrate them. By the time I graduated and moved to New York I knew the right kind of people with the right kind of connections to take me to the Upper East Side and from there...'

'You hooked him.'

'I couldn't believe it,' she half whispered. 'I wanted someone from a solid, wealthy background but Bart was beyond my wildest dreams. I worked really hard to turn myself into the right kind of wife for him—made sure I found out about the things he liked, got on with his friends, stuck to the rules. I wasn't clingy or needy or argumentative or sulky. I dressed the way he liked, wore my hair the way he liked, cooked the right food, hiked or swam or played tennis, whatever he was in the mood for. I read the right books…' She gulped in air, shocked by the bitter tint to her voice. 'But in the end I still wasn't good enough. He walked away anyway. It serves me right for aiming too high.' Brought down like Icarus, her punishment for flying too close to the sun.

Kit didn't answer for a long moment and Maddison couldn't look at him to see his reaction. Disgust, probably, maybe dislike. Hatred. After all, she was everything he abhorred. Fake, money-grabbing, conniving…

'Maybe you didn't know him as well as you thought.'

That wasn't what she'd expected him to say. 'What do you mean?'

'Have you been pretending the last few weeks? With me?'

'No, I mean, you're my boss, not…'

'Not a suitable future husband?'

She nodded, mortified heat flooding her. 'I mean, you have a good job and all, and I didn't know about the castle.' Maddison winced. Honesty was probably not the best policy here; she wasn't helping herself sound any better. 'It wouldn't have made any difference anyway. I want the life I missed out on, you know, the prom-queen and hayride life, summers at the shore and clambakes, Fourth of July parties and huge family Thanksgivings life. It's all I've ever wanted. Much as I could come to love London, that life doesn't exist here.'

'All I'm saying is that maybe Bart fell in love with the girl I've come to know. She's witty and clever and annoyingly organized, if a bit too partial to long operas. Maybe he wanted that Maddison, not the Stepford wife you turned yourself into. Just a thought.'

His words sank in slowly, each one dropping perilously close to her heart. 'I thought you'd hate me.'

Kit's face was completely impassive, a muscle beating in his cheek a lone sign her confession affected him at all. 'We've all done things in the past we need to atone for. I'm the last person to judge anyone. But if I were you I'd stop trying so hard. Just be yourself. Do you really think money will bring you happiness?'

Maddison winced. It sounded so cold put like that. 'I know security will…'

'Then make your own. You're a clever woman with a great career ahead of her. I'd advise you to concentrate on that. Marriage to the wealthiest man in the world can't bring you security, Maddison. Just look at Eleanor. She thought she had it made and it all disappeared, leaving her to start again. Bachelor Number Two may be wealthier but he's a bitterer pill to swallow.'

Make her own security? She'd spent so long focusing on just one possible path it hadn't even occurred to her that there could be more than one way to her goal. Maybe she could buy her own apartment in the city, have her own summer house at the shore. Maybe if she relaxed then she'd meet someone who wanted a family as much as she did, who didn't need luring into commitment.

Maybe there was a happy ever after waiting out there for her after all. She stole a glance at Kit, his face still completely unreadable. One thing she knew for sure was that her future didn't include messy brown hair, blue eyes and a lilting accent. Kit Buchanan's idea of long-term was next-day dinner reservations. And that was fine. The ache in her chest wasn't some inexplicable sense of loss. Not at all. She might be considering moving the goalposts but she hadn't changed as much as that. Had she?

CHAPTER EIGHT

'IS THIS IT? Are we in Kilcanon?' Maddison craned her head. 'I can't see a castle. When you said castle did you mean small cottage because, I have to tell you, they're not the same thing where I come from.'

'No, this is Loch Lomond. I need to stretch my legs. Fancy a walk?'

'A walk?'

'It's when people move at a slow pace putting one foot in front of the other in order to get across ground.'

'I know what a walk is. I just…I mean…I wasn't sure whether you wanted company.'

'I could leave you in the car but that seems a little inhospitable.'

But he knew what she meant. She was trying to sound him out, to see if he still wanted her company after her revelations just a couple of hours earlier. Maddison had lapsed into silence after her sudden and startling confession, leaving Kit to sort through a myriad conflicting thoughts and feelings: sorrow, sympathy, disgust. Admiration.

She hadn't said much about her childhood but he could fill in the bleak gaps; her need to be in control at all times, her fear of the dark, it all made sense. As did her overwhelming desire for security.

Her targeting of a rich man to be that security was a little harder to stomach, a little too close to home, and his first instinct had been to drive her to the airport at Glasgow and send her back to London on the next plane. The last thing he needed to do was take another gold-digger back to meet the family.

But she was no Eleanor and he was a lot older and a lot wiser. At least Maddison was honest about who she was and what she wanted. And could he blame her for trying to re-create the mythologized childhood of her dreams?

No. He didn't blame her or dislike her or even pity her. Truth be told he kind of admired her. Life had thrown every disadvantage at her and she had risen above it, made something of herself. So she had made some mistakes along the way? It was better than hiding away, bitter and resentful, or being too afraid to try.

Like you? He pushed the thought away. He wasn't bitter or afraid, he was undeserving. Undeserving of happiness or of love.

Maddison, on the other hand, deserved a lifetime of both.

She joined him at the path, a light Puffa slung on over her jumper and jeans. 'This is a real loch? Is there a monster in it?'

'Several. Don't walk too close to the edge or they might pull you in, kelpies and boobries and…'

'Stop. You know what I mean. A *real* monster.'

'You need to be a lot further north for Nessie, I'm afraid. But if you're lucky you might see a selkie when we get to Kilcanon—watch the seals closely, they're usually the larger ones.'

'I'll do that.' She hesitated. 'Kit, about earlier?'

'It's fine. I'm glad you told me but you don't owe me

any explanation, Maddison. We're colleagues, that's all.'
But the words sounded hollow even to his own ears.

'Good. I've never…I mean, I don't talk about myself
very often. Thank you. For listening and not hating me.'

'I could never hate you.' In a different time, if he were
a different man, he might be in danger of exactly the opposite. But his heart was frozen somewhere back in time
and he had no intention of allowing it to be melted, not
even by this fiery American survivor.

It was a bright, warmish day and Maddison was soon
far too hot in the thick jacket she had layered over her
sweater. 'You told me it would be cold and raining.'

'It could well be when we get to Kilcanon. It's a mi-
croclimate. All of Scotland is.'

'Is it as pretty as here?' She stopped and turned, admiring once again the blue waters lapping gently against
the loch shore and the hills rising steeply on every side,
greens and purples and shadowy greys. She had thought
that they would head down to the loch but instead Kit
had chosen a path that led away, a steep path winding
up into the hills. Turned out even regular running didn't
prepare you for hill-climbing. Maddison could already
feel a pull on her calves and her lungs were beginning
to make themselves felt.

'Pretty? There's nothing pretty about Kilcanon. It's
magnificent… Here, watch out. This is a bit slippy.' Kit
extended a hand and pulled Maddison up the slick, steep
rock. His grip was firm and she had a sudden urge to lean
on him, to allow him to guide her up the narrow, slip-
pery path, but she quelled it firmly, brushing past him
instead to take the lead.

'Come on, Buchanan,' she called over her shoulder
as she set off at a pace, shocked at how her lungs burnt

as she pulled herself up. She had really got out of condition recently; this would do her good. Besides, giving her body a good workout might cure it of some treacherous urges—such as wanting to stare into Kit's eyes, keep hold of his hands or lean into that solid strength.

Oh, no, she was getting sappy. Maddison increased her pace, enjoying the ache in her calf muscles, the fiercer pull in her thighs, the heave in her chest. The distance she was putting between him and her.

'It's not a race, Carter. Slow down and smell the roses—or at least enjoy the view.'

'Slowing down is for losers. You'd be eaten alive in Manhattan,' she threw back as she concentrated on one foot in front of the other, using her hands and upper body to pull her up a particularly vertiginous twist in the path. All she was aware of was the steep rise of the way ahead, the rocks that needed to be navigated, the small treacherous pebbles that could cause a foot to slip, the slicks of mud and the...

'No! Darn it!'

And the deceptively deep puddles. This one calf deep and full of thick mud, cold as it sucked at her foot and leg.

'Ugh. I'm trapped in a swamp! Kit! Stop laughing...'

He came up beside her, slow and easy, folding his arms and eyes dancing with amusement as he took her in. 'Pride comes before a fall.'

'I haven't fallen.' Maddison tried to summon some shred of dignity, hard as it was to do when one foot was caught fast in a miniswamp, the other scrabbling for a firm foothold. Any minute now she was going to tumble and she'd be damned if she was going to fall in front of this man. Any man.

'Yet,' Kit pointed out helpfully.

'You could help me.'

'I could.' The laughter underpinned his words and she glared at him.

'Do you want me to beg?'

'Well...' He leaned in close and her breath hitched. His face was barely centimetres from hers, his shoulder close enough to grab, to hold on to, to bury herself in and let herself be saved.

She didn't need saving, did she? Just a helping hand.

'You could say *please*.'

Their eyes caught, held. His were alive with laughter, a teasing warmth curving his mouth, but behind the amusement was something hotter, something deeper, something straining to break through. And Maddison knew, with utter certainty, that all she needed to do was ask.

She hadn't asked for anything since she was six.

She glared, watching his amusement increase until a reluctant smile curved her lips. 'Please.'

'There, that wasn't so hard, was it?' Kit grasped her hand and pulled. Maddison steadied herself against him, allowing him to take her weight as she heaved her foot free. It took a couple of tugs until, with a nasty squelch, the mud gave up and she stumbled forward, letting out a small yelp of alarm as she toppled, trying to get her balance.

'Easy, Maddison, I got you.'

He had. His arms were around her, steadying her, holding her up, and she allowed herself to be held, to be steadied. Just for a second. What harm could it do? What harm one moment of resting on someone else? One moment of needing someone else? Just a moment and then she would pull back, make some quip and carry on, ignoring the discomfort of her cold, damp boot and the sodden jeans because that was what Maddison Carter did, right? She carried on.

'Thanks.' Her breath was short and she inhaled, taking in the soap-fresh, wool scent of him, allowing her hands to remain on his waist as she pulled back, searching for the right kind of cheery smile that would put this moment behind them, behind her.

It was a lot to ask from a smile. And as she looked into his eyes any urge to laugh the moment off fell away as surely as the path plunged down towards the water, the sounds around drowned out by the blood rushing around her body, pulsing in her ears. All the amusement had drained out of his face, out of those blue eyes, now impossibly molten like sapphire forged in some great furnace. Instead she looked into the sharp planes of his face and saw want. She saw need. She saw desire.

For her.

'Kit?'

He didn't speak, his breathing ragged, his grip tightening on her shoulders. She should walk away; she needed to walk away because this, this wasn't planned. She had never let desire override her common sense before, and yet here she stood, making no move to reassert herself, passive in his grip.

The blood pounded faster, her stomach falling away, an almost unbearable ache pulsing in her breasts, beating insistently deep down in her very core. Maddison had always controlled every step of every seduction, when, how far, what, but now she had no power, no choice at all. Her body was taking over, need flaring up, overtaking sense, overtaking thought, overtaking everything.

She swayed towards him and his eyes flashed as they fixed on her mouth, hunger burning in their blue depths. Hunger for her.

For her. All of her.

Not just her body. She had laid herself bare before

him, let him in to see all the nasty little corners she hid from everyone—and still he hungered. Maddison swayed closer still. His gaze was intoxicating and she could drink it in forever, bathe in the heat, helpless before his acceptance.

Kit released his grip on her shoulders, his hands moving slowly down her arms, each centimetre of her flesh blazing into life where his hands touched before burning with thwarted desire as his hands moved away. She was desperately trying to gulp in air, her chest tight with need.

Walk away, a small, sane part of her urged. *Walk away*.

But she had spent ten years being sane, ten years putting sense first, desire second. Didn't she deserve just a little time out? She was going to re-evaluate her plan anyway; she needed to explore all options, didn't she?

That was all this was. Exploring options. Because Kit didn't do love either. He was safe.

Maddison jumped as he reached out to cup her face, one finger tracing the curve of her mouth, a muscle beating insistently in his cheek. It took everything she had to hold his gaze, to stand there while his fingers explored the curve of her jaw, one tantalizing digit running slowly over her mouth, blazing a trail of fiery need. It was hard to breathe, hard to think, hard to stand still, hard not to step forward and grab him and make him fulfil that lazy promise. Her knees weakened as she watched the lines of his mouth, his eyes soften as they focused on her.

She looked up at him and allowed her mask to slip, just for a while. Allowed the desire and want and hope and need to shine through and as their eyes met she saw any resistance fall away.

She thought he would pull her close, go straight in for the kiss, but instead Kit moved back a little, one hand moving from her waist to the small of her back, leaving a trail of electric tingles as it oh-so slowly brushed over her body. Before today Maddison would have said that it would be impossible for anyone to feel anything under the thickness of her jacket but, like the princess lying on her tower of mattresses, every movement marked her. Claimed her.

'This crosses a line.' The words were so unexpected that Maddison didn't compute them at first. 'I should step away.' But he didn't.

'I think we already crossed that line.' Confidences, opening up emotionally, secret glances of shared amusement—to Maddison they were all far more intimate than mere sex. She suspected the same rang true for Kit. If there was a line to be crossed then they had walked blithely over it that day in the graveyard. Maybe even before then, when he had invited her out for a birthday drink. Maybe they had been heading here since then.

He closed his eyes briefly. 'Maybe you're right.' Then, only then did he step closer. Maddison hadn't appreciated quite how tall he was, how broad he was, how much coiled strength was hidden behind the quietly amused exterior until she was enfolded by him, in him. She had never allowed herself to feel fragile, delicate before, but the look in his eyes, the light, almost reverential touch, made her feel as if she were made of glass, infinitely precious. She shivered, heat and need running through her.

She slid her hands up his arms, allowing herself the time to appreciate the hard muscle under the thick material, until her hands met at the nape of his neck.

She stepped in, just that one bit closer so that leg was pressed against leg, her stomach against his taut abdomen, her breasts crushed against his chest. Desire rippled through her as the heat from his body penetrated her; she could barely raise her eyes to look at him, suddenly and unexpectedly shy. She was laying it all out there for him. What if she wasn't enough?

But the look in his eyes when she finally raised hers to meet his said it all and, emboldened, she pressed close and lifted her mouth to his. Softly at first, hesitant, and then as the kiss deepened she lost all reticence, holding him tighter, pulling him closer, revelling in the all-male taste of him, smell of him, feel of him. His hands hadn't moved, still just holding her close, burning where they touched her until she was almost writhing with the need for them to move, to have every inch lit up with that same sweet, intoxicating flame.

Maddison wound her hands through the soft hair at the nape of his neck, pulling him even closer, but it wasn't enough. The barriers of clothing, of skin too much. Impatient she slid her hands back down his torso, thrilling at the play of muscles under her hands, needing flesh on flesh.

'Maddison.' He broke away and she was instantly cold, even as he captured her hands in his, his thumbs caressing her palms. 'Slow down, lass. We shouldn't…'

'I…I…' She stumbled back, cheeks hot even as the rest of her shivered with an icy chill. 'You're right, we shouldn't…'

'Stay here,' he finished. 'We're a little exposed here on the public footpath.'

'Oh.' She smiled at him a little foolishly, blinking as she twisted in his embrace, aware for the first time in several long minutes of their surroundings. 'Yes.'

'We could get a hotel room, here. If you wanted, that is. We'd still be back in time for the wedding. Only if you want to, though…'

Maddison put a finger on his mouth. 'I want to.'

'Good.' His voice was hoarse, ragged with need. 'I was very much hoping you would say that.'

The early-evening sun slanted in through the window, turning the red-gold of Maddison's hair flame-coloured. Kit pulled a strand of it through his fingers, the silky texture as smooth as her skin. He liked her hair like this, dishevelled, down, free, just as he liked her like this: soft, warm and drowsy.

What on earth had happened? One moment he was stomping up a steep hill, almost blind to the beauty all around him, taking little notice of the fresh air filling his lungs, trying not to mull over their conversation in the car, and the next moment... It hadn't just been the feel of her, soft and pliant in his arms as he'd pulled her free, it hadn't been the way she had looked, so different from her usual neat and tidy self in her jeans and jacket, hair falling out of its elegant twist, face rosy with the exercise. It had been more. Maybe they had been headed here all along.

Maybe it was the feelings she had roused in him in the car. Anger—not at her, *for* her. The abandoned child, the lonely girl, the jilted lover. She deserved more. But not just anger. She made him feel compassion, a need to possess her, protect her.

His mouth curled. As if he could protect anybody. And yet he wanted to, wanted to pull out a sword and challenge all comers, shield her from hurt.

'What are you thinking?' Maddison rolled over, the sheet pulled high, shielding her lithe body from his gaze. It was the body of someone with fierce amounts of control—slim, toned and smooth. It had been lots of fun helping her lose that control. Twice.

'That I hadn't expected to find myself here when we

left London this morning.' That was an honest reply even if it wasn't all he was thinking.

She looked around and Kit followed her gaze, taking in, for the first time, the pink flowery walls, the heavy velvet curtains fringed with tassels, the huge variety of cushions and the shiny pine wardrobe. She smiled at him. 'No, I can imagine not. It's probably a little pink for your tastes.'

'We could have waited and found somewhere a little more boutiquey.' He didn't want to say romantic. This, whatever it was, wasn't about romance.

'No.' She slid a hand over his chest, a smug smile tilting the corners of her mouth as he inhaled sharply. 'This is perfect. Besides, I didn't want to wait.'

'No? Me neither.'

'Do you think the landlady bought it? The impromptu walking-weekend story?'

Kit allowed himself to twist another strand of that sunlit hair around a finger. 'Sure she did. I'm sure she's completely used to couples hammering at her door, throwing cash at her and disappearing upstairs.' The modest B & B had been the first place they had passed with a vacancies sign. It might not boast Egyptian cotton sheets, designer paint or expensive antiques, but it was clean and, most importantly, available. Neither of them had been prepared to wait for something more luxurious.

'I had a valid reason. I was covered with mud. I needed a bathroom.'

Kit whipped the sheet off, ignoring Maddison's squeals as she made a grab for it, and took a long, appraising look down at her legs. 'You still are.' He reluctantly let the sheet drop back down in response to her indignant tug and sank back down beside her. He could have feasted his eyes on her forever. 'You need a good wash. Want me to help?'

She pulled herself up on her forearm and looked down at him. 'Maybe. How good are you with a sponge?'

'Immensely talented,' he assured her and watched her eyes glaze over. 'Want to find out just how good I am?'

'Soon,' she promised him, slumping down onto him, her body hot against his skin. Kit shifted so that he was curled around her, his arm holding her tight, the heavy weight of her breast just under his hand. It had been so long since he had just lain with a woman, caught in that languorous twilight time between sex and the real world. The promise of pleasure still hanging, musky in the air, and yet sated enough to let the promise stand. For now. Maybe. He allowed his finger to circle around the tip of her breast, a light caress, a small possession as he burrowed his face into the sweet spot at the nape of her neck, tasting her skin one more time.

'Mmm…' Her sigh was all the encouragement he needed and he deepened the caress, his other hand sliding along her hip, across the flat plane of her belly, as he nibbled his way along her shoulder. 'Do we have to go to this wedding? Can't we stay here forever?'

Kit found the delicate spot at the top of her shoulder and tasted it, his tongue dipping into the hollow, following the line down towards the top of her other breast. Maddison shifted, allowing him access to her body, submissive under his gentle onslaught.

'I would much rather stay here.' He was taking his time, enjoying the quickening of her breath, her hands fisted in his hair. 'I am suddenly very fond of pink curtains.' But as he kissed his way down her body, sampling her slick, salty, satin skin, revelling in the knowledge that he was responsible for each moan, each cry, each movement, he knew that it was just a pipe dream. Duty called him home. But tonight? Tonight was all about pleasure and Kit intended to make the most of every single second.

CHAPTER NINE

THE MORNING AFTER the night before. It wasn't usually a problem. After all, he always made his position completely clear before anything compromising began—no commitment, no emotional attachment, no expectations. Just two people hanging out, enjoying the moment. And if, in the end, the other person wanted more, well, his conscience was clear. He wasn't the one changing his mind.

But there had been no laying out of the rules this time. No clarity. Just an overwhelming need overriding sense, overriding thought. He could have taken her there and then on the hillside, mud and hikers forgotten. At least he'd had enough sense to call a temporary halt.

But not enough sense to halt it altogether.

Kit gripped the steering wheel until his knuckles whitened. Need meant weakness. Need meant attachment. He didn't do either. He only dated women he was in no danger of falling for. That was the rule.

Maddison Carter broke every rule.

But it wasn't as if she were after anything more serious either. Maddison had her heart set on her perfect marriage to the perfect guy who would give her the perfect family. And he was far from perfect.

Surely she knew that this, whatever it was, was just

an interlude. She wouldn't want it to be anything more any more than he did.

Which in many ways made her the perfect woman.

Although following up a night of mind-blowing passion with a trip to the family home wasn't the best idea in the world. Even the most clear-headed of women would be forgiven for finding the signals confusing.

Maybe not just the women.

Kit turned his attention to the road ahead. Most people headed north from Loch Lomond, past Fort William, up into the deeper Highlands, but to get to Kilcanon Kit took an early turn away from the loch, dropping back down on to the long peninsula that would take them down, past the sea lochs to the coast. The road twisted and turned, climbing up into thickly forested heights where eagles soared before dropping back down to the loch side. Glasgow, just an hour and a half away, felt as remote as London or New York; a bustling city had nothing in common with this wild and natural beauty.

And Kilcanon was possibly the wildest and most beautiful part of all. The Buchanans' ancestral lands were at the very tip of the peninsula where land met sea. The road ahead was achingly familiar; here it was, the first glimpse of home. Every time it hit him anew, a sharp punch to his heart.

'There it is, Castle Kilcanon.' They were the first words either of them had spoken in the last hour and he slowed the car down so Maddison could look out at the sweep of water below, at the round grey castle dominating the landscape like a sentinel.

'That's your home?' She sat up straighter and peered down at the dark, rotund keep. 'Where's the flags on the turrets and the knights galloping over the drawbridge?'

'We don't keep the knights on a full retainer.' The

village spread out across the bay, the harbour home to several small boats bobbing on the sea, the castle on the other side of the bay. The weather had lifted a little and even though the grey of the sea met the grey of the sky on the horizon, the two blending into one, he could still see the craggy, green islands, some impossibly close, others mist-shielded ghosts.

'There's a lookout point. Can we stop?'

Kit didn't reply but he pulled over and sat there for a moment while she got out of the car and walked over to the railings, leaning over them while she took in the spectacular view. Once he'd have been hurrying her, eager to cover the last fifteen minutes' travel as the road wound down and round to the village, but not any more. Now he was glad of the opportunity to delay their arrival by even a few minutes.

In London he could push the memories away with work and play until all they could do was beat at his dreams, but as soon as he set foot in Kilcanon they would surround him, whispering ghosts reminding him that he was to blame. His eternal shame. His eternal punishment.

Maddison's hair was whipping around in the breeze, the red-gold a vibrant contrast to the greens and blues surrounding her. He got out of the car and walked to the rail, leaning next to her. 'It's beautiful, isn't it?'

'Like nowhere else.'

'I'm sorry for yesterday.'

She slid a green-eyed glance over at him, the corners of her mouth curving into a playful smile, which caught him and held him. 'Why? I'm not.'

'It shouldn't have happened. I'm your boss and you were at a low point. I took advantage of you.'

'No, you cheered me right up. Made me feel desirable and wanted when I couldn't even look at myself without disgust.' She turned to face him, laying one slender hand over his. 'Look, Kit, it's all right. I'm not Camilla. I don't expect you to suddenly fall to one knee after one night together, no matter how amazing that night was. I know that's not what you are looking for and I...' She hesitated, lacing her fingers through his, her hand warm against the ice of his. 'I don't know what I want, not any more. It was all so clear-cut a few weeks ago. Even a few days ago.'

'Four children and a rich husband?'

She leaned into him with a playful shove. 'Yes. Well, marriage, a family, security. That is really important, although maybe I need to re-evaluate how I get there. But whatever happens I think I need to start living a little, not plan so much. So you are off the hook, nobody took advantage of anybody. It doesn't have to happen again, although,' she added, her fingers caressing his, 'I'm not saying that I'd mind if it did.'

'Remind me of that later,' he said softly and felt her quiver beside him.

He stared out at the sea—still today, tranquil. 'We used to take boats out over to the island, race them. Sails only, no motors allowed. Go fishing off the pier, kayak across the harbour. Everything was a competition, everything. Even love.'

'You miss him.' It wasn't a question.

'You have no idea how much. I don't feel it so much in London. He never visited me there—the city air was bad for his asthma—but here, by the sea, he was fine. Every time I come back it hits me again, that he's not here. And this evening I have to watch his wife marry someone else, as if Euan never existed.'

'It was three years ago, Kit. She's allowed to move on.'

'Maybe you're right.' He freed his hand from hers and

moved to stand behind her, his arms around her waist holding on tight, allowing her to anchor him to the here and now. 'One of us should move on. We can't both hold an eternal vigil.'

'You are allowed to as well. It's what he would have wanted.'

If only she knew. He didn't think he would ever break free of the chains binding him to his guilt and grief—and even if he could, would he want to? Did he deserve to? Euan was dead and he was alive and nothing would ever change that.

'Come on.' He dropped a light kiss on her hair, breathing in the floral scent, glad that she was here in all her vibrancy and warmth, chasing away the shadows that dogged his every step. 'We have a family to meet and a wedding to attend. Ready?'

'Absolutely. Parents are my speciality. Lead the way.'

Kit took in a deep breath. There was no retreating now. But at least, this time, he wouldn't be alone.

Maddison wasn't quite as confident as the car swept up the long, gravelled drive to the castle. The gravel was grey like the thick stone blocks of the turrets. Grey like the sky above them, the sea behind them, and despite all her good intentions she shivered. 'Is that where you slept?' She tilted her head to look at the top of the keep, the windows narrow slits in the stone. It must be dark in there, dank. Her spine tingled as she imagined a small child, a mop of dark hair and huge blue eyes, sitting forlornly in a round, cheerless room.

'Oh, no, I was down in the dungeons. Kids are always better off behind bars. That's the family motto.' Kit was gripping the steering wheel a little tightly but his tone was teasing and the wink he gave her knowing.

'Of course you were, on a pallet of straw, a bucket in the corner.'

To Maddison's surprise the drive didn't end in front of the imposing entrance, but swept around the castle, finishing in a semicircle in front of an eye-wateringly large house situated on a slanting hill two hundred yards behind the castle. The house was built from the same grey stone as the keep but it seemed softer somehow, maybe because of the wisteria clambering over the front and upwards to the roof, maybe because of the elegant, tall towers flanking both sides, or maybe it was the three tiers of tall windows promising a light, airy interior, the stone in between them decorated with delicate ornamental stonework. Either way, despite its size, it made a more believable—and more comfortable—home than the ancient, thick-walled castle.

Kit braked the car and pointed up to the top floor. 'The nursery floor was up there. Euan, Bridget and I all had rooms up there, along with the playroom.'

She barely took in his words, her mouth open in utter shock. 'It's…it's huge!' Somehow the grand old house was more imposing than any castle could be. Twisting around in her seat, Maddison could see how the ground had been cleverly landscaped so that the keep hid the house from prying eyes and yet the house itself had an uninterrupted view, over smooth green lawns, right down to the sea. Behind the house lawns rose in wide, flower-covered terraces up into the hillside, hints of arbours, patios and summer houses hidden just out of view. She turned back to Kit and eyed him accusingly. 'I can't believe you let me think that you still lived in there.'

He grinned. 'It's a common misconception but the keep's been empty for years. By all accounts it was always cold and uncomfortable and our eighteenth-century ancestors were too nesh to keep shivering in there. With the Jacobite rebellion over they didn't need such thick walls and so they built the big house, as it's still known. Only the old castle gets the courtesy of being Castle Kilcanon, the ancestral home of the Clan Buchanan.' He deepened his voice as he said the last words, sounding more like a documentary maker than a son returning home.

'The big house?' Maddison had never quite got the British art of understatement. The house in front of her made the estates of her college friends seem small—and tacky—even though she had visited homes covering many more acres. She instinctively knew there would be no cinema rooms or bowling alleys here, no infinity pools or gyms. This was real class, real old money. She had no idea how to fake this kind of lifestyle. How to fit in.

For the first time in many years doubt clouded her mind. She shivered again as a raven landed on top of the keep, a foreboding omen.

'Kit!' Maddison had no more time to panic as the huge front door was flung open and a pretty girl in her early twenties ran down the imposing front steps. She was casually dressed in an old sweater and jeans, her dark red hair scooped back and not a hint of make-up on the creamy face, liberally strewn with becoming freckles. Maddison pulled her cashmere jumper down, smoothing it with shaking hands, doubting her outfit. Was it too put together? Artificial?

'Kit! You're home! I can't believe you left it till now. Mum has been spitting feathers. She was convinced you'd let her down and find an excuse not to come. Not that I blame you. If it wasn't a three-line whip I would be far away from here. It sounds utterly dreary.'

'Hey, Bridge.' Kit was out of the car before the girl got to them and reached down, scooping her up and swinging her round. Maddison's chest squeezed. She would give anything to have someone greet her with such uninhibited joy. 'I have plenty of time. The wedding doesn't start until five.'

'I know.' The younger girl pulled a face. 'Evening candlelit ceremony and black tie. So tacky. I blame Angus.'

'I doubt Angus had much of a say,' Kit said drily.

Maddison got out of the car, her legs stiff and awkward as she walked around to meet them, her throat dry and chest tight. She had thought she didn't care what Kit's family made of her, but she wanted this warm-faced girl who so obviously adored Kit to like her. To think her worthy.

Worthy of what? she reminded herself. *One night does not make a future. And you don't want that, remember?*

But it was hard to remember just what she did want as Kit put a steadying arm around her and led her forward. 'Maddison, this is my little sister, Bridget. Bridge, this is Maddison.'

'It's nice to meet you at last.' Bridget held out her hand. 'We've spoken on the phone so often I feel that I know you already but it's much nicer face-to-face. We'll have to have a real gossip straight away and you can tell me all about what a tyrant Kit is and fill me in on all his secrets.' She threw a speaking glance at her brother. 'There's tea and scones waiting in the drawing room. And no, you can't escape. Behave.'

'We should have dawdled more on the way.' Kit squeezed Maddison's shoulder. 'Ready? Some trials involve dragons and daring rescues, others golden apples and races. My mother conducts trial by small talk. It's deadly, it's terrifying but it's possible to survive.'

Bridget elbowed him. 'Don't scare her, idiot. It's not that bad,' she added to Maddison. 'At least the scones are good.'

When Maddison visited her college friends' homes, finding a valid reason to be free from her fictional family over Christmas or Thanksgiving, she rarely saw their parents. She'd arrive at some spacious, interior-decorated-to-within-an-inch-of-its-life mansion, be whisked off to an en-suite room bigger than any apartment she'd ever lived in and then spend the next few days in the kind of pampered bubble the set she chose to run with considered normal. Food was pulled without consideration from cavernous fridges, or prepared by smiling, silent maids. Parents rushed in with platitudes and compliments before rushing back out again to the club, to work, to a party or a personal-training session. Maddison knew how to smile, compliment prettily and make the right kind of impression to be invited back.

But scones and a small-talk-stroke-interrogation in a house older than an entire state was another thing entirely. She leaned a little more heavily against Kit as they approached the front door. The big house might lack a moat but stepping over the threshold felt as final as watching the drawbridge close up behind her.

Bridget led them into a huge hallway dominated by closed, heavy wooden doors interspersed with portraits of stern-looking men in kilts surveying the landscape and even sterner-looking ladies in a variety of intricate hairstyles. Nearly every portrait featured some kind of massive dog and a gloomy-looking sea. A wide staircase started halfway down the hall, sweeping imperiously up towards the next floor with a dramatic curve, the carved wooden bannister shining like a freshly foraged chestnut. She swallowed as her eyes passed over tarnished gilt mirrors and ancient-looking vases.

'This is all very formal.' Kit squeezed Maddison's shoulder. 'Bridge must be trying to make an impression on you. Usually we come in through the back.'

'I didn't think Maddison would want to pick her way through thirty pairs of mismatched wellies, twenty broken fishing rods, enough waterproofs to clothe an army and the dogs' toys,' Bridget said. She flashed a shy smile at Maddison. 'But Kit's right, the front door is usually just for guests. It takes far too long to open it, for one thing, and there's nowhere to dump your coat, for another.'

Maddison couldn't imagine wanting to dump her coat. The air was as chilly as a top New York law firm's offices, only this wasn't status-boosting air conditioning, it was all too natural. 'It's lovely,' she said. 'Very...' She looked up at the nearest portrait for inspiration. The sitter was scowling, his grey, pigtailed wig low on his brow, his sword angled menacingly. 'Very old.'

'The bannister is good for sliding on,' Kit said. 'And when the parents went out we used to practise curling on these tiles. There's no heating at all in the hallway so in winter they get pretty icy.'

Maddison had no clue what he was talking about so she just smiled. But she knew one thing for sure. She couldn't get carried away here, couldn't change her game plan, couldn't hope that whatever had sparked into life yesterday was real. She would never belong in a place like this; there were limits to even her self-deception. So she might as well relax and enjoy it for what it was. A fun interlude before she went home to New York and decided what she was going to do with the rest of her life.

The problem was that her original prize wasn't looking quite as golden as it used to. It wasn't that she didn't want security; she did. She still needed it just as she needed air and water. She still wanted children who teased each other the way Kit and Bridget were, children who were raised with the kind of love that Kit seemed to take for granted and with the same opportunities. She just wanted a little bit more.

She wanted the full package. Security, love and respect. And by raising the stakes she might have just doomed her entire quest to failure.

CHAPTER TEN

THERE WAS SOMETHING incredibly seductive about watching a woman getting dressed for a big occasion. The concentration on her face as she twisted her hair up just so, the way she slid the small point of an earring into her lobe, the purse of her mouth as she painted it an even deeper red.

The way she rolled on her underwear, a subtle mixture of practicality and romance, a little like its wearer. The black silky bra designed to show off her shoulders in the thinly strapped dress, the wispy knickers Kit had to drag his eyes away from because they really, really didn't have time. Yet.

Maddison was wearing the same dress she had worn to the opera, a simple knee-length black dress with a white strip around her waist, echoed by a wider band at the bottom of the dress. The invitation had specified Black Tie and Kit knew that the other female guests would be going all out. Maddison, with her knot of red-gold hair and the pearls in her ears, would probably be the simplest-dressed woman in the room—and the most beautiful, he realized with a twist of his stomach.

His mother had put them in one of the suites, two bedrooms and a shared bathroom, a sign she was unsure of their romantic status. Kit shared her uncertainty—common sense told him to walk away quickly while it was still possible to extricate himself with grace, but his body told him something very different.

Right now his body was winning.

Which had the advantage of both distracting him from the forthcoming wedding and lessening the pain of Euan's absence. So he would let his body win—for now.

'You're looking thoughtful.' Maddison moved towards him, her gait slower, sexier in her high heels, and laid a reassuring hand on his shoulder. 'Let me get that for you.' And with practised ease she adjusted his bow tie. 'Very dapper. Are you worrying about tonight?'

'Not really. I was just admiring how you managed my mother earlier. It was like watching two fencers spar.' His mother's patented brand of tea and interrogation usually either froze her opponents into stunned silence or cracked them open until they had spilled every secret. Not many managed to parry and block with the same deft touch Maddison had shown.

'I had quite a lot of fun. She's a formidable opponent. I had no idea what to call her, though—Mrs Buchanan? The housekeeper says My Lady but I'm not sure I could say that and keep a straight face. I'd feel like a house-maid in Downton.'

'I'm sorry, I should have warned you how absurdly formal it can be here. My father is the Viscount of Kilcanon and my mother is Lady of Kilcanon but in speech you say Lord and Lady Buchanan. Locally, though, they are mostly known as the Laird and Lady. I know,' he said apologetically as her forehead creased in puzzlement. 'It's all a little feudal.'

'Aren't Laird and Lord the same thing?'

'No, not really. Angus, the lucky groom...' Kit cast a look at the clock on the wall, relieved to see they still had an hour before they had to leave '…he's the local laird in Kameskill because he's the biggest landowner, but it's an honorary title. If he sold the estate the title would pass with it. If we sold this estate then Dad still stays a viscount.'

'So wait, do you have a cool title? Do I get to call you Sir?'

Kit sighed. He hated this part. 'Both Bridge and I are Honourables, but neither of us use it,' he admitted. 'And now Euan's gone I'm Master of Kilcanon.'

'Master? How very dominant of you.'

He matched her grin. 'Remind me to show you later…'

'Chicken…' she said softly and his blood began to pound at the challenge.

'Unfortunately we have been summoned to a pre-wedding drink with my family, but wait until we return and I'll show you who is master.'

'I can hardly wait…' She sashayed before him but stepped aside as she reached the door so that Kit could go first.

He touched her shoulder. 'Worried about the dogs? I can get Morag to lock them away.' One of the family pets had wandered into the drawing room when they were having tea and Maddison had paled significantly and made no move towards it, retreating a little when it had stalked nearer her.

'No.' But she didn't sound at all convincing. 'Honestly, I'm fine. It's just they are really *big*.'

'Another thing I should have warned you about. I forget not everyone has grown up with dogs the size of small ponies.'

'Small ponies? Are you kidding? I think they would outrank a medium pony and maybe even a large one.' She was smiling but there was a look of trepidation in her eyes and he decided he'd better keep the dogs away from her. They were very sweet tempered but fifty kilograms of dog could be intimidating to even the most ardent of dog lovers. 'Still,' she said, with that same game smile on her face, 'I guess a smaller dog would get lost in a house this size.'

'There's still a corgi or two somewhere in the west wing and a dachshund stuck in the tower,' he agreed straight-faced and was rewarded with a moment of puzzlement before she glared at him and stalked out of the room.

As was customary, drinks were in the library and, sure enough, when Kit ushered Maddison into the book-lined room two of the family's prized deerhounds were flaked out on a tattered old red rug in front of the fire. One of them raised a lazy head in their direction and Maddison tensed, her arm rigid under his hand, before the dog flopped back down, too tired from its day to properly investigate the newcomer.

Maddison swallowed. 'I feel even more Downton than ever,' she said, and Kit tried to see the familiar room through her eyes: the oak panels, the huge leaded windows, which needed a ladder to reach the top shelves, the leather chesterfield and the old walnut bureau where his father conducted his business just as his grandfather had before him and so on back into the mists of time.

'It's all too dusty to be truly Downton,' Kit whispered. 'No butler either, just Morag, and she never bobs a curtsey and is always gone by six.'

'Kit.' His attention was called away by his father's curt tones. Lord Buchanan was standing by the fireplace, a glass of single malt in one hand. Looking at him was like looking into a portrait in the attic, Kit in thirty years' time. Not that Kit often looked straight at his father. How could he when he was responsible for so much loss? For the lines creasing his father's forehead and the shadows in his mother's eyes?

He ushered Maddison forward. She, he noted, was still keeping a wary eye on the dogs. 'Dad, good to see you. This is Maddison Carter, my very able assistant, who very kindly agreed to accompany me this weekend. Maddison, my father.'

His father nodded briefly at Maddison but didn't speak and Kit was grateful when Bridget pulled her over to the sofa she was sitting on, thrusting a glass of champagne into his hand as she did so. Conversations with his father were rarely comfortable and he'd rather not have a witness.

This was the problem with bringing anyone home. They saw too much.

Lord Buchanan stiffened as he glanced at the champagne Kit was holding, swirling his own whisky as if in challenge. 'It's good to see you still know the way home, son.'

It was going to be like that, was it? He wasn't going to rise, he wasn't... 'Luckily there's always satnav.' Okay, he was going to rise a little.

His father didn't respond to the jibe. 'Whatever it takes.'

Kit looked over at Maddison. She seemed comfortable enough sitting between Bridget and his mother. As he'd expected his mother was dressed traditionally in a long blue dress, a sash of the family tartan over her shoulder fastened with a sapphire brooch. Bridget was less traditional and tartan free, but still in a floor-length dress in a sparkly material. Maddison didn't seem bothered though;

she had that same self-possessed look on her face that she usually wore in the office.

Maddison looked up and caught his eye and for one all-too-brief moment they were the only people in the room. Kit's heart hitched, missing a beat. What would it be like under different circumstances, bringing a girl like Maddison home to meet the family?

His father followed his gaze over and looked at Maddison speculatively before transferring his gaze to his son. His lip curled. 'What are you wearing? A kilt not good enough for you any more?'

Kit tore his eyes away from Maddison and looked down at his neatly tailored tuxedo, shrugging. The last time he'd worn his kilt had been at Euan's funeral; he'd managed to avoid any formal occasion in Scotland since then, wearing a black tuxedo when necessary in London.

'I wore the kilt to Eleanor's last wedding.' He saw his mother look up at that and remorse stabbed him at his bitter words. 'I just couldn't,' he added in a more conciliatory tone.

But it wasn't enough. His father shook his head. 'You get more Londonified by the day. You're needed here. It's time you shouldered your responsibilities and...'

And so it started, just as it did every time he spoke to his father. Every conversation they had had since the funeral. The same words, the same tone, the same message. He was needed here. He was responsible for this mess and he damn well better clean it up.

Didn't he know it? And that was why he couldn't be the son his father wanted. How could he come here and just take Euan's place as if he deserved it? Step into his dead brother's shoes?

'I have shouldered them. I can just as easily watch you ignore every suggestion I make from London.'

His father fixed him with a glare from eyes so familiar it was like looking in a mirror. 'You'll be responsible for this place one day and God knows I'll make sure you know how to run it.'

Admit it, you wish I had died instead. Kit took a deep breath, swallowing the bitter words back. 'Did you look at diversifying the cloth making and selling directly to the public like I suggested? How about setting up our own distillery? Doing up the holiday cottages?' His father remained silent and Kit threw his hands in the air. 'I did business plans for all those projects, found the right people. If you're not interested…'

His father interrupted, red in the face. 'You just want to change things. You have no interest in the traditions of the place.'

Kit was suddenly tired. 'I do. And that's why I want to make sure Kilcanon can remain sustainable.'

'Sustainable…' His father gesticulated and as he did so he let go of his glass. It fell in horrifying slow motion, whisky flying from it in a sweet-smelling amber shower, until the one-hundred-year-old crystal bounced off the sharp edge of the marble hearth, shattering into hundreds of tiny, razor-like shards. Everyone shouted out, the women jumping to their feet, Kit and his father taking an instinctive step back and both dogs bounding up from their fireside bed in a panicked tangle of howls and whines.

'Iain!'

'Damn fool, look what you made me do.'

'I'll get a cloth and a dustpan…' Bridge, of course, sidling out of the room as fast as she could; unusually for a Buchanan, she hated confrontation.

'Dad, have you cut yourself?'

'Oh, Iain, really. The car will be here in twenty minutes. Come with me. I'll fix you up. I told you to control your temper. No wonder Kit never comes home and I'm sure Maddison will never want to come here again. What must she be thinking?' His mother's voice faded away as she steered his father out of the room and up the stairs.

Kit turned to Maddison, an apology ready on his lips, but it remained unuttered. She wasn't looking at him; all her attention was on one of the dogs, still whimpering by the fire. He touched her arm to reassure her but it wasn't fear he saw on her face, it was concern.

'The dog...' she half whispered. 'I think it's hurt.'

Sure enough, although Heather had retreated to the doorway, her tail and ears down but otherwise unhurt, Thistle had barely moved from the old red rug that had been the dogs' library bed for as long as Kit could remember.

'Thistle?' Heedless of the glass still scattered everywhere, Kit dropped to his knees beside the dog, still sitting whining by the fire, one paw held at a drooping angle. Thistle's ears trembled and his tail gave a pathetic thump, his huge dark eyes staring pleadingly at Kit. 'Are you hurt, old boy?' He extended a gentle hand towards the paw but Thistle moved it back, his ears flattening as he let out a low growl. 'Come on,' Kit said coaxingly but the next growl was a little louder.

Heather, still at the door, began to pace, her tail still drooping. Kit glanced up at Maddison. This must be her worst nightmare. She was wary enough of the huge dogs as it was—one doing a lion impression and the other growling like a bear was unlikely to reassure her. 'Now I understand the point of corgis. A little easier to wrestle into submission! I don't want to hurt him further but I do need to see that paw.'

She was pale, her lips almost colourless, and there was

a faint tremor in her fingers, but she made an attempt at a smile and crouched beside him. 'I think one of us needs to reassure him while the other examines his paw.'

'So which end do you fancy, claws or teeth?' Kit wasn't being serious, he was intending to send her to get some water and some help, but to his amazement she laid a gentle hand on Thistle's head, slowly rubbing the sweet spot behind his ears and crooning to him in a low voice.

'Who's a brave bear? I know. I know it hurts but you need to let us look at it.' Her voice and the slow caress of her hand were almost hypnotic and Thistle gave a deep sigh, slumping down, his massive head on her knee. Maddison continued to talk to him, gentle words of comfort and love, one hand still rubbing his ear, the other sliding along the dog's shoulder until she was supporting the dog's paw. Thistle gave a quick jerk in pain and then lay still again.

With a quick glance at Maddison to make sure she was all right, Kit slowly and carefully turned the great paw over. The three dark pads, usually velvety soft, were damp, the fur between matted with blood. 'I think he's got glass in there,' Kit said as quietly as he could. 'Are you okay down there while I get some tweezers, water and some antibacterial cream?'

He rose to his feet as she nodded, and backed towards the door, one hand reassuring Heather, who had stopped pacing to sit staring anxiously at her litter mate still half lying in Maddison's lap.

And Maddison… Kit's breath caught in his throat. The fire lit her up, turning the strawberry-blonde hair gold, casting a warm glow over her pale skin. She was unmoving, her face set, partly through concentration, partly to hide the fear he knew she felt. With the blood from Thistle's paw on her hands and soaking into the white hem of her dress, she looked like Artemis straight from the hunt. Fiery, blood-stained warrior queen.

His heart gave a painful lurch, as if the ice encasing it were cracking. But that was okay. It was thick enough to handle a few cracks. He was in no danger of melting anytime soon.

'I can't wear this.' Maddison plucked at the long skirt and stared at Kit's mother anxiously. 'Really my, I mean, Lady Buchanan.' She hated that she'd stumbled over the words but what the fricking heck? She'd never thought she'd need to know the right way to address a viscountess before.

If Kit's mother *was* a viscountess. Was that even a thing?

'Don't be silly,' Lady Buchanan said briskly. 'Your own dress is covered in blood.' Her mouth twisted in an unexpectedly vulnerable movement. 'Attending my son's widow's marriage is hard enough. We'll be the victims of more than enough vulgar gossip without bringing the bride of Dracula with us.'

'That's a good point. I promise I'll try not to spill on this.' Maddison eyed her reflection nervously. There was an awful amount of fabric to keep clean and away from candles, especially in the floating skirt and the long, see-through chiffon sleeves. Apart from the neckline. There wasn't nearly enough material there; she swore she could see her navel if she looked hard enough.

'It's just so nice to see it being worn again.' Lady Buchanan's eyes were wistful as she rearranged the beading that encircled the low, low neckline and looped higher up Maddison's chest like a necklace. 'Bridget won't touch any of my clothes and dear Eleanor, well, it wasn't really her style. I wore this the first time I met Iain, at Hog-

manay right here in this house. I wore a cape over it so
my father didn't make me get changed. It was a little risqué back in the seventies.'

It was still risqué as far as Maddison was concerned.
But the mint green suited her colouring and besides…
'It's vintage Halston,' she breathed reverentially. 'A design classic. It's an honour to wear it.' Even if it wasn't
standard wedding attire, Maddison suspected she'd have
got less attention in the blood-stained dress.

'It's the least I can do. You were so quick-thinking and
brave, helping poor Thistle like that. Kit thinks he has
all the glass out but Morag is going to stay late and wait
in for the vet just in case. I'd have stayed myself but it's
important we attend this wedding with our heads high.
Never let it be said that the Buchanans retreat from a challenge although…' Her voice broke off, her eyes so sad
that Maddison wished she could give her a hug.

But could she hug a viscountess without permission or
was that some kind of treason? And besides, she wasn't
confident that she could lean forward in this dress *and*
stay in it.

'It was nothing. Thistle was very brave.'

'It's not just Thistle you're helping though. Kit seems
different, less brittle. Happier. To see my boy smile I'd
hand over one hundred dresses.'

Maddison tried not to squirm as the sincere words
washed over her. It couldn't be denied that she was making Kit happy, but not in the way Lady Buchanan meant.
Kit's mother was talking about his heart, not his body.
One she was happily familiar with, the other she suspected had been locked away several years ago.

And she was pretty sure he had no intention of handing over the key. Even if he did, was she the right person
to unlock it? What did she know of families and castles

and long-standing traditions? She didn't belong in a place like this; she never would. Coming here was a reality check she badly needed. She could enjoy Kit's company, share his bed—but she would never be the right person to share his life. Cinderella might have made the move from the fireside to the castle, but the trailer was a step too far down. And pretend as she might, she would never shed her past completely.

CHAPTER ELEVEN

'HAVE I TOLD you that you look…?'

'Inappropriately dressed?' Maddison supplied, resisting the temptation to hoick the sides of her dress together back across her chest. She'd give anything for a pin right now.

'I was going to say hot. Definitely hotter than the bride.'

'That's always my goal at weddings.' Maddison stepped even further into the shadows at the back of the hall. 'At least it's so gloomy in here I'm hoping no one knows this is actual skin on show and assumes there's some kind of nude-coloured top going on.'

'When Eleanor decided on candlelight I don't think she took into consideration just how much light these old banqueting halls need. It feels more like Halloween than a wedding.'

'She looked beautiful though. Eleanor.' Maddison hadn't expected the surge of jealousy when the bride, a mere thirty-five minutes late, had glided ethereally down the aisle. She hadn't known what to expect from Kit's first and only love but it hadn't been the dark-eyed, dark-haired, diminutive beauty who had floated along in a confection of lace. No wonder both brothers had fallen for her, chosen her over their sibling bond.

Even her voice was beautiful, chiming out her vows in

clear bell-like tones. Maddison, hidden in a back corner, shrank into herself, uneasily aware of just how gaudy her own brilliant colouring could look, how brash her own decisive tones.

'She always looks beautiful.' But Kit didn't sound admiring or wistful. Just dismissive. 'It's all she has, really. She's good at turning those big eyes on you and making you think she matters, but when I look back at our year together I can't remember much that she said of any substance. Still, Angus wants someone to look good when he's hosting parties and to pop out an heir or two so they'll both be happy.'

Maddison winced as his words sliced into her. That was her plan, wasn't it? Find someone who wanted a compatible partner to keep the home fires burning, be a corporate wife and raise the kids. That was her goal. Planned for, prepared for, ready for... Maddison looked from Kit, slightly dishevelled yet absurdly sexy in his tux, to Angus, sweaty, balding, one arm proprietorially round his bride, and swallowed, a lump in her throat. It didn't seem such a laudable goal any more.

Kit followed her gaze and huffed out a short laugh. 'Good Lord, Angus is already half-cut. Some wedding night this is going to be.' As he spoke Eleanor looked round and caught sight of Kit. Was that regret in those huge eyes? Regret for turning him down the first time? Or regret for not hooking him in the second?

'I don't think I can stand much more of this. We've definitely done our duty,' Kit whispered into her ear, his breath heating the sensitive skin, sending tingling, hopeful messages straight to the pit of her stomach, to her knees, so she wanted to melt into his voice, his strength, his touch. 'Fancy finding a real party?'

Normally Maddison would be in her element in a gathering like this. Kit had pointed out several titles, a brace of millionaires and a group of heirs and a wedding was the ideal place to start up a conversation with any eligible man. Even though she wasn't looking for a UK-based guy, a picture of Maddison and the heir to an oil fortune posted somewhere Bart would see should be very satisfying. But somehow in the last couple of weeks she had lost any interest in impressing Bart.

Kit was right. Maybe he had been interested in her the way she was originally and her attempt to be his perfect woman had bored him. And if he hadn't been, then would she really want to build a whole life on a pretence? 'Sure. Only…' Maddison gestured at her dress. 'Where on earth can I go dressed like this? Studio 54?'

'You'll be fine where we're going. No one will raise an eyebrow.' He stopped to consider, his gaze travelling slowly down the deep vee in her neckline. Neckline? Navel line. 'Okay. They might raise *an* eyebrow, both eyebrows. But if we're lucky you might score us free drinks all night and they'll crown you harbour queen.'

'Harbour queen? Is that a thing?'

'It definitely should be. What do you say?'

Maddison cast a quick look around the high-ceilinged, grey stone room. It had been decorated to within an inch of its five-hundred-year-old life, the walls draped in a deep red fabric, the floor covered in matching carpeting, huge vases of red and white flowers dotted in every alcove, on every table. A violin quartet were playing traditional music high up in the minstrels' gallery and food and drink circulated freely. But even with the opulent decor, with the candles glittering from the candelabra on the wall and the gigantic chandelier, the gloom penetrated and, she shivered, the temperature remained chilly.

'It seems kind of rude to just go.'

'You're right. Besides, the ceilidh will start soon and in that dress you're going to be every man here's partner of choice. Think your neckline will stay intact after a round of Gay Gordons?'

Maddison had no idea what a Gay Gordon or a ceilidh was but the suggestive glint in Kit's eye warned she might be better off not finding out. 'As I was saying, it seems kind of rude to just leave but there's so many people here I guess no one will miss us.'

His smile was pure wickedness. 'I think you've made the right choice.'

It took a while before they actually left. Kit wanted to make sure he had fulfilled his role as Master of Kilcanon and switched on the professional facade so familiar from the office as he circulated the room, shaking hands, kissing cheeks and making easy small talk as if he had been born to it.

Which of course he had.

The whirlwind charm offensive finished at the bridal party with kisses for the bride, her mother and bridesmaids and a hearty, back-slapping conversation with the bemused-looking groom before they finally slipped out of the room.

'No one will be able to accuse me of not giving the wedding my full blessing,' Kit said as they collected their coats, heading out of a small side door into the cool, dark evening rather than making their way back along the long formal hallway to the gigantic front door.

'I think you scared the groom. He looked like he thought you were going to kiss him at one point.' Eleanor had kept that same cool half-smile on her lips, Maddison had noticed, but there had been a hint of hurt in her eyes. What had she been expecting? Pistols at dawn?

They made their way around the rectangular building, their way lit by small hidden lights on the path, the sounds of merriment floating out of the opened windows into the evening air. Angus's house wasn't as old as Castle Kilcanon or as elegant as the big house but it made up in size and ostentation what it lacked in authenticity. Surely it didn't need quite so many towers?

Looking up, Maddison saw the darkest sky she'd laid eyes on since she had first moved to New York four years ago, a deep, velvety blackness studded with stunningly bright flickers of light. Normally this level of darkness would panic her but Kit had tight hold of her hand, as if he knew that she might react.

Maddison's pulse began to throb. Nobody had anticipated her needs, her moods in such a long time. She squeezed his hand thankfully and breathed in deep. The air was so pure, so fresh it almost hurt her city lungs, better than any perfume or room spray.

The path brought them out onto the long, sweeping driveway and their taxi waited at the end, beyond the imposing wrought-iron gates, the modern equivalent of a drawbridge. Maddison gave a heartfelt sigh of relief when she saw the headlights; her shoes were pinching, her toes were cold and her bones so chilled she wasn't sure she'd ever feel warm again.

It was the same driver who had taken them to the wedding. Maddison suspected he was probably the only taxi driver in Kilcanon, which gave her little comfort as he set off at a white-knuckled fast pace down the dark and twisting road. Kit settled back in his seat, silent as the car flashed through the night, covering the three miles in what surely must be record time but, as the car raced to the top of the hill and the first lights in the village could be seen in the dip below, Kit reached out and took her hand again, lacing his fingers through hers with a strong, steady pressure.

There was an intimacy about holding hands in the dark that went beyond the kisses, the caresses, the passion they had shared yesterday. Maddison swallowed, a lump burning in her throat. She shouldn't get used to this. He didn't do love, remember? Neither did she.

Only she wasn't quite as sure about that any more. She wasn't sure she would swap this taxi for the fanciest of limos, the man next to her for a Kennedy, last night for a lifetime of security. Maddison stared out the window at the darkness. In that case what did she want—and was she in danger of trading all she'd ever dreamed of for heartbreak?

Maddison had expected that they would head either to a private house or to the whitewashed grand hotel that dominated the corner where the main road hit the harbour, but the taxi drove straight on, bypassing the hotel, bypassing the grand Victorian villas looking out to sea, bypassing the small and friendly pub she'd noticed earlier. The moon was high and full, laying out a silvery path along the dark sea, and Maddison had an urge to follow it and see what strange land it took her to.

Finally, once they had swept right around the harbour road and reached a small row of cottages, the taxi pulled up. Maddison opened her door, gratefully gulping in some air, her stomach unsettled by the fast and twisting journey. She looked around, confused. In front of her a door stood open but the inner door was closed and the windows tightly shuttered, although she could hear music coming from within.

'Where are we?'

Kit had walked around to join her. He extended a hand

to help her out of the car and gestured towards the door. 'This is where the locals come to play. Ready?'

Maddison cast a long, covetous look back along the harbour wall towards the hotel, shining beacon-like, a promise of hospitality, warmth and civilization. 'Sure.'

'Good.' And Kit opened the shut inner door and ushered her inside.

The first thing that hit her was the noise. Or the lack of it. Just like any good western, the room came to an abrupt silence as she was propelled through the door to stand gaping on the threshold. The second thing to strike her was the simplicity: whitewashed walls, wooden tables and stools, a dartboard and pool table visible in the adjoining room. The third thing she noticed was the heat, the glorious, roaring heat that came from a generous log fire.

The fourth and final thing Maddison realized was that, if she had been inappropriately dressed for a wedding, here, in a room full of jeans, plaid shirts and sweaters, she looked like a bordello girl amidst the cowboys. Only more underdressed.

'Kit!' The man behind the bar broke the stunned silence and slowly, like dominoes falling into each other, the room came back to life. Conversations restarted, darts were thrown and through the alcove Maddison could hear the unmistakable clink of pool balls being lined up. She hadn't played for years. Nice girls didn't hang around pool tables. Another thing she missed.

'All right, Paul.'

Maddison was barely listening as the two men launched into a series of 'how are you?'s and 'what have you been up to?'s. The accents in the little bar were stronger than any she had come across before and it was easier to let the voices wash over her than try and make sense of the conversation, which, from what she could glean, revolved around fishing anyway. A pint of something amber was handed to her and she took it. Beer. She didn't drink beer, not any more, not since high school, an illicit keg on the beach wearing her boyfriend's varsity jacket even though she wasn't cold. Because it marked her. Marked her as an insider.

She sniffed the beer cautiously, breathing in the nostalgia of the tangy, slightly metallic aroma, then took a sip. It was delicious. She took another.

'There's a seat by the fire.' Kit had finished his conversation and turned to her. 'Fancy it?'

'For now.' She smiled slowly, licking the slight froth from her lip as she did so, and watched Kit's eyes darken to navy blue. 'But later I want to play pool.'

Was this what a relationship was? Discovering new parts of someone, being surprised by them, delighted by them, in new ways every day. Eleanor had always been the same—cool, collected, affectionate but in a way that made it clear she was in control. He saw it now for what it was: a way to keep him in line, wanting more. And he'd never allowed anyone else close enough to find out what one facet of their personality was like, let alone several.

But here he was. And here Maddison was. The hardworking assistant, smooth and reliable. The clue solver, her quick brain jumping ahead, unabashedly delighted when she was first with an answer. The opera lover, enthralled by the music, lost in a world he couldn't touch. The warrior, conquering her fear to help a creature in pain. The lover, tender, demanding, exciting, yielding.

And now—the pool shark. It wasn't just the dress distracting him; she had borrowed a T-shirt from Paul, the barman, to even up the odds somewhat—there wasn't a man in here who could have played her in that dress and survived. It wasn't the adorable way she bit her lip as she focused on the cue ball or the way she caressed the tip of the cue while sizing up her shot, although both of those gave her a definite advantage. No, the truth was she was very, very good. Or lucky. He hadn't decided which.

She was also more than a little drunk, having moved on to whisky. She had unwittingly committed sacrilege and asked for a blended whiskey but Kit had jumped in to change her order to the local single malt, although he had allowed it to be poured on ice. Her face at the first sip had had the entire bar in stitches but she had persevered a little too well—was that her second glass or her third?

'Another round?'

Was she talking about whisky or the pool? Kit wasn't sure he could take either. 'I wouldn't mind some air first,' he suggested.

Maddison narrowed her eyes at him, reminding Kit irresistibly of a cat in her unwavering focus. 'Scared?'

'Terrified. My reputation may never recover.' Truth was some of his shots had gone awry because she was so damn adorable when she was competitive, but he wasn't going to admit that. It would just make her win all the more complete.

'Okay. Air and then I whip your ass again. Deal?'

'Deal.'

He steered her out of the door, realizing as he hit the street that she wasn't the only one feeling the effects of the whisky. Kit was mellower, calmer than he had felt in a long time. The cool night air was a welcome relief from the heat of the bar, the sound of the waves soothing after the laughter, loud talk and music pumping through the two small rooms. Kit reached for Maddison's hand, breathing in a sigh of relief as the peace hit him.

Only for the peace to retreat as the past roared in to engulf him once again. A past he would never be free of, not here, no matter whose hand he held, how much whisky he sank. No matter how much he tried.

'Hey, are you okay?'

Kit loosened his grip on Maddison's hand with a muttered apology. 'I thought this time was different, this time I could handle it.'

He crossed the road and leaned on the railings, the only barrier between land and sea, staring out at the moon path.

She joined him at the railing. 'They all seem to like you in there.'

'I haven't been back there in years. Not since…' He didn't finish the sentence.

'They treated you like a regular.'

'I was once. Place like that, once you're a regular you're always a regular.'

'Sounds nice.' There was a longing in her voice.

'It was. The hotel and the pub belong to the tourists, to the incomers, to people like my parents. Even though I lived at the big house I never ran with the set. The bar belongs to the villagers. When I was home I was in the lifeboat crew. I helped build the jetty.' He nodded over at the wooden structure bobbing about in the gentle waves. 'Euan was with me but there was a difference—no matter how much he rolled up his sleeves and pitched in, he was still the Master, the future Laird. Half those folk in there live in tied cottages. They'd be paying rent to him one day. Now I guess they'll be paying their rent to me.' The prospect was bleak. He didn't want the inevitable separation his title would bring.

'Your father wants you home.' It wasn't a question.

Kit nodded. 'He does and he doesn't. He thinks I

should be here learning about the estate but he worries that I'll want to change things. He wants the finance I can bring if I sell my house and bring my investments to the estate but not the power that will give me. He wants a Master of Kilcanon but not me.'

'What happened, Kit? How did Euan die?'

The question was inevitable; they had been approaching this conversation all day. He took a deep, shuddering breath, allowing himself to really confront the past, confront his role in it, for the first time in three long years. 'We were ridiculously competitive. Mum says we would fight over anything and everything. I had to prove I was as good as him despite being younger—despite not being the future Laird. He had to prove his asthma didn't stop him.' Kit gazed out at the bay. He could still see them: two boys night fishing from a dinghy, kayaking over to the nearest island, still visible in the dusky night.

'Anything I could do he had to do better and vice versa, but we were really close even so.' His lips compressed into a hard line. 'We sailed, fished, camped, built dens. It was ridiculously idyllic, looking back. Just look at it, Maddison. Some people hate growing up in a place like this but we thrived. Like some *Boy's Own* adventure. Only it was real life.'

'Sounds amazing.'

'I knew I had no future here and I resented that, I guess. The estate wouldn't support me as well—second sons are useful spares but they can get in the way. So I headed to Cambridge at eighteen, started to build a life away from Kilcanon although I always yearned to come home. We would pick up right where we left off in the holidays, trying to get the better of each other. I just didn't realize that nothing was off limits.'

'Some things should have been.'

Maybe. It was odd now, looking back. Remembering how hurt he had been. The sense of betrayal when Euan had just continued the game that had started before Kit could walk, carried it on to the ultimate conclusion. 'I refused to show Euan how much he had hurt me. I had my pride, after all. I wished he and Eleanor well and I walked away as if I didn't give a damn. I agreed to be best man at their wedding. But it wasn't enough. He wanted my blessing, for me to tell him it was all okay. We were okay.'

'So what did you do?' Maddison placed her soft hand on his; the gleam of victory mixed with whisky gone from her eyes, her pointed chin no longer lifted in triumph, rather her whole body leaned into him in wordless sympathy.

'Do? I refused to give him the satisfaction. I stayed in London, built up my publishing business, dated, came home for holidays and did everything I could to prove that I was better. I was insufferable. Had to coppice the most trees, catch the most fish, build the longest bit of fence, bring home a different girl each time, be the most popular brother with the locals. I was the life and soul of every party. He couldn't compete but it didn't stop him from trying.'

It was easy to look back now and see how angry he had been. Maybe they should have had a good fight and got it out of their systems with some well-aimed punches rather than letting the anger fester for four long years.

'One Christmas we got into a pointless row. We'd often raced across the harbour—row boats, sailing boats, motor boats and, being the insufferable brats we were, kept a running tally. I thought I was ahead, he thought he was and I wouldn't back down. In the end he told me, in the most condescending high-handed way, that if I needed it that much then, okay, we would say it was me.' Kit took another long look at the sea: boyhood playground, beautiful, endless, merciless. 'Of course, I wasn't having that. I insisted we sort the matter out immediately. One last race, winner takes all. He told me not to be stupid and I pushed and pushed until…by then we were both determined to win no matter what the cost. I didn't know how high the cost could be.'

He swallowed, memories washing over him, the spray of salt water on his face, the burning in his arms and legs, the sweet, sweet moment of victory turning sour as he realized something was very wrong.

'His asthma?'

Kit nodded. 'An attack right out there and of course the silly sod had forgotten his inhaler. I went back for him, God, I don't think I've ever rowed as fast in my life, but I wasn't fast enough. I got him to shore, called an ambulance but…I was too late. Too late to save him, too late to forgive him.'

He paused for a long moment. 'This was always the place I longed to be. I was so jealous of Euan, that this was his while I lived in exile.'

'So why haven't you moved back now your parents want you here?'

'How can I? I killed my brother as surely as if I had pushed him off the cliff. I knew his chest was bad that Christmas but I couldn't see beyond my own hurt pride. I forced him to race me and he died. How can I live here? How can I ever be happy when he's in the ground, knowing I put him there?'

'Oh, Kit.' Her arms were around him, holding him tight, her lips on his cheek, on his jaw, his neck. Her fingers tangled in his hair, her voice enfolding him with whispered comfort. 'You do belong here, Kit, but it's not Euan you have to forgive, it's you. Let it go, Kit.

Forgive yourself. Isn't that what Euan would want? Let it go. Live.'

Kit stared out to sea, Maddison's heat, her fire slowly warming him, bringing him painfully back to life. *Isn't that what Euan would want?* Was it? He had no idea.

He put his hands on her shoulders, standing back so he was at arm's length, so that he could see her face, her eyes, her truth. 'Why would you think that?'

'Think what? Think that three years of self-imposed exile, three years of guilt, of estrangement is enough? Because it is, Kit. You didn't kill your brother. He knew the rules, he was an active player, sometimes the instigator, always the main competitor. What happened to him is beyond sadness, beyond grief, but it isn't your fault.'

Kit desperately wished he believed that, but his mind flashed back to that bleak December day. To the pain and anger in his father's eyes, the anguish enfolding his mother, Bridget's sobs and Eleanor's stony-faced grief. The identical looks on their faces when he'd walked wearily into the hospital waiting room. The looks that had told him quite clearly that they knew exactly where the blame lay.

And he had agreed. Had willingly shouldered the toxic burden and let it infect his whole life. He deserved it.

Maddison cupped his cheek, her hand branding him with its gentleness. 'What did Euan want that whole time he was married to Eleanor? For *you* to forgive *him*. He wanted his brother back. What would he say now, if he was here?'

To get over myself. But it wasn't that easy. 'It's not just you that you're hurting.' Her voice was gentle but her words inexorable, beating away at his carefully erected shields. 'Your parents, your sister. They miss you. The way things are they've lost two brothers, two sons. You can't bring Euan back, Kit, but you can give them back you. You can become part of the family again. And sure, it'll hurt. You'll miss him every time you have to make a decision he should have made, perform a task that was his, visit a place he loved, but that way you'll preserve his memory too. Because right now? You're denying him that.'

Kit stared down at her. Was she right? Was his decision to stay away, to keep apart from his family, to carry the burden of Euan's death alone selfish? An excuse to wallow in his grief? Coming home, being part of the family again, moving on would hurt, not with the dull, constant ache he'd carried for the last three years but with sharp, painful clarity, but maybe, just maybe, it was the right thing to do. The right way to honour and remember his brother.

CHAPTER TWELVE

HE HADN'T SLEPT a wink. Kit stared at the window, the first rosy tints of dawn peeking through the flimsy curtains—sunrise came early this time of year. As boys he and Euan would often be up and out, determined to wring every second of adventure out of the long summer days.

Maddison was soft, warm, curled into him like a satisfied kitten, and he shifted, careful not to wake her. She murmured and turned, the sheet slipping to expose the creamy point of her shoulder, red-gold hair tumbling over it like spun sugar. He could nudge her awake, kiss her awake…

Kit slid out of bed and grabbed his clothes. If he woke her then he would make love to her and that, that would be amazing on many levels, especially as it would stop him thinking, stop his brain turning her words over and over and over. But it was time he faced his situation head-on—and he wouldn't be able to do it with a naked Maddison so temptingly within reach.

Everything she had said made sense. He thought that he was truly, fittingly punishing himself by staying away, but all he was doing was running from his troubles. He needed to come home, part of the time at least. He needed to shoulder the responsibilities that were his to bear now that he was Master of Kilcanon. He needed to do more

than suggest business ideas to his father; he needed to
provide the capital, the manpower and the know-how
he could so easily manage. He needed to celebrate his
brother's legacy by being part of it, not tarnish it by hiding from it.

Maddison shifted again and the sheet slid a little lower.
Kit stopped and stared, his mouth dry as he drank her in.
Funny to think he had known her just a few weeks, and
that for the beginning of that time he had barely noticed
her at all. She looked so different asleep: softer, sweeter,
more vulnerable.

But she *was* vulnerable, wasn't she? The realization
hit him like a freezing spring wave. That efficient exterior was nothing but a carefully honed act; at heart Maddison Carter was a lost little girl searching for a happily
ever after. What had she said she wanted? *Hayrides and
clambakes and a huge family Thanksgiving?* He wasn't
entirely sure what a clambake was—but he was pretty
sure that he wasn't planning to find out.

Kit grimaced, reality stabbing through him along with
the dawn sun's rays. *What was he doing?* She worked
with him, worked *for* him and he was no Prince Charming. He could offer her a few weeks of fun but he couldn't
give her the porch swing, the four children, the clambakes
and fireworks. He had his own life to sort out—he didn't
know where he would be living, what he would be doing
in three *months* let alone three years, thirty years. He
didn't think he could promise three months. He didn't
know how to.

And Maddison needed security like most people
needed air.

Maybe she didn't want security from him. Maybe she
was happy with things the way they were but he couldn't
risk it. Couldn't risk her getting hurt. Or, a little voice

whispered, himself; he couldn't get too used to having her around. She would be heading away, back to the future she needed, she craved. This thing, whatever it was, had got too deep, too intense far, far too quickly. He curled his hands into fists. There were many difficult decisions he needed to face today but this one was easy. He needed time and space away from Maddison Carter—it was the best thing he could do for her.

Maddison came to with a jolt, aching all over, a sweet, luxurious ache that almost begged her to push harder, again and again. She rolled over, unsure for one moment where she was, why she felt this way: sore, sated, satisfied. The windows were barely covered, the sun shining through the thin filmy curtains. She slumped back onto the soft pillows, the memories running through her mind like a shot-by-shot replay. Sex had never been like that before. Never been so intense, so all-encompassing. She had never been so lost in someone else, so lost to pleasure.

She sat up, her heart thumping.

What had she been thinking? To be so dependent on another person with no guarantees at all that the words, the touches, the intimacy meant anything, would lead anywhere. She had taken her entire rule book and just ripped it up. Maddison curled her hands into tight fists as reality set in, the cold and harsh light of day displacing her sleepy, sated dreams.

Okay, reality check. Last night had been about emotion-driven sex—that was all. That was why it had been so very intense. So all consuming. So very, very good… She was still riding high on adrenaline after her own bout of confessional honesty. It hurt, that opening up, allowing someone in. It hurt to face her own flaws. Sex was some kind of all-purpose plaster, helping make everything feel better, mind, body and soul. And then Kit had trumped her, tearing open his own secrets, facing his own demons.

No wonder their lovemaking had been so hot, both of them trying to lose themselves, forget themselves, seek absolution in the other's touch. But that was all it was. All it could be.

Maddison stretched out an arm and brushed the other side of the bed. It was cold; Kit must have left her some time ago. She pulled her phone off the nightstand. It was still early, not yet seven. He must have left her before dawn. She looked around. No note, no sign of him at all.

A chill brushed her chest and the ache in her limbs intensified, a little less sweet, a little less luxurious. Now the ache just made her wince, a physical reminder of her own vulnerability.

What if he regretted it all? Not just the sex but the emotional honesty? What if he decided their closeness had all been a mistake? There was no way she was going to hand all the power over to him; no way was she going to allow herself to be made vulnerable. She needed to re-erect her barriers and fast.

Maddison showered and dressed quickly, mechanically, building up her armour layer by layer with each brush of her hair, each sweep of the mascara wand, each blotting of her lipstick. Armour was preventative, protective. It kept you strong, kept you alive to fight another day. And the very fact that she felt that she might need it told her everything: she had let Kit in too deeply, too quickly, too intensely. And she didn't trust him not to hurt her.

She didn't trust herself not to let him.

She sank into the easy chair by the bedroom window and stared out at the stunning view, all blues and silvers and greens. It was a living picture, one she could never get tired of as the sky shifted and the sea moved restlessly. In the distance a gannet dropped, a reckless, speedy plunge into the water below, and her stomach dropped with it. She had been that reckless. She had plunged into intimacy with no thought of tomorrow. Would she, like the gannet, resurface with nothing to show for her dive?

She knew better. How many times had her mother told her that *this is the one*? The man who was going to rescue them. The man who was going to give them a home, make them into a real family. Every time Tanya Carter fell all the way in straight away, offering herself up like a sacrifice only to wonder why every time she was left with her heart ripped out, alone and defenceless. Maddison had learned early that you kept your heart locked away, you didn't let anyone into your soul—and you made sure you came out on top, always.

Only where had that knowledge got her? She hadn't allowed Bart into her heart and he had still left her—only for her to crash headlong into an ill-thought-out flirtation. She'd known Kit was dangerous early on but hubristically had thought she was invincible, that she could handle him. And what had happened? She had allowed Kit perilously close. But not all the way in. She wasn't that stupid. Thank goodness.

The ache in her chest intensified. She was so tired of being lonely, that was all. She was ready for her safe, secure happy ever after. No more deviations.

But was she really ready? Maddison sighed, staring blindly out at the sea. These last few weeks had thrown her badly off balance, all her plans, her dreams now up in the air. Did she want to try and get Bart back? She tried to picture the future she had dreamed of but the vision was blurry. No, she wanted more than a loveless marriage of convenience. Did she want to put all her efforts into her career? At least that was going right—but what if she missed out on meeting the right guy? Ended up fifty, alone and childfree?

She wanted it all. Kit's face floated into her mind, that amused smile on his mouth, laughter in the blue eyes. Maddison's mouth twisted. Had she learned nothing? He wasn't even here. Her heart began to beat painfully, each thud reminding her that she was alone once again.

Maybe she needed to look backwards before she looked forwards. Maybe it was time she faced just who she was, who she had been. Maybe that way she would find the answers she needed.

She checked the time again. Seven-thirty. She could do with coffee, juice, something to push away the ache in her head and her chest. What was the etiquette with breakfasting in castles anyway? She doubted that a maid would come in with a breakfast tray. She should find her way to the kitchen and sort out a coffee and a plan. A plan always made everything better.

Resolutely Maddison got to her feet but before she moved a step the door swung open to reveal Kit, fully dressed, shadows emphasizing his eyes, his stubble darker than usual. He looked as if he hadn't slept a wink. Maddison's heart began to beat faster, adrenaline mixing with anticipation and dread. His mouth was set in a grim line, his eyes unsmiling.

'I brought you a coffee.' He held out a huge mug and she took it gratefully, cradling it between her hands, drawing courage from the warmth.

'Thanks, I was about to venture out in search of the kitchen but I didn't have a ball of string long enough to guide me back.' She kept her voice deliberately light and carefree and saw some of the tension leave him. 'It's a beautiful day. Which is a shame because I'd really like to explore the area, I've hardly had a chance to do more than glimpse it, but I really need to be getting back.'

He must know that was a lie. He knew she knew hardly anyone else in London, knew that all her time was spent either working for him, testing out routes with him or on her own with a takeaway. But he didn't challenge her. She hadn't been expecting him to but disappointment stabbed through her anyway. 'I was thinking of staying here a few more days.'

I, not *we*. Not unexpected. 'That's a good idea.'

'I went fishing with my father this morning. There's a lot we need to discuss. About the future of this place. My role in it.'

'Kit,' she said as gently as she could. 'You don't need to explain, not to me.'

He carried on as if she hadn't spoken. 'I feel bad that you have to make your own way back, though. There's a taxi booked to take you all the way to Glasgow and I've bought you a first-class ticket back to London. As a thank you for coming with me.'

'You didn't have to do that.'

'I did.' His mouth tilted. 'You gave up your weekend again. It was very kind of you.'

'Well, thank you.' She took a sip of the scaldingly hot coffee, the pain almost welcome in this falsely polite exchange. 'I meant what I said yesterday, Kit. I'm not Camilla. We didn't make any promises and I'm not the kind of girl who reads wedding bells into every kiss.'

'Not unless you planned it that way.' There was a hint of warmth in his eyes and she wanted to hold on to it, blow it into life, but she held back, wrapping her dignity around her like a protective cloak.

'You know me, always with the plan.' And that, Maddison realized, was the part that was so hard to say goodbye to. He did know her. Almost better than she knew herself. More than anyone else in the whole wide world. And that wasn't enough for him. She wasn't enough.

She'd done good work here. She'd helped him break down some of his guilt, helped ease some of his burden, shown him that he was a man worth knowing. Maybe she'd paved the way for someone with more confidence, someone who didn't care about rejection, someone who knew what they were worth to come in and finish the job. And obviously that thought hurt because she was a little raw right now, but that was a good thing, right? She cared about him; he was her friend and he deserved happiness.

And he had done the same for her. The last couple of weeks she had been *happy*. He'd given her the tools to set her free; she just needed to use them. She was a work in progress, not set in stone after all. The future was hers if she had the courage to embrace it.

'What time is the taxi coming?'

'Soon. It's a couple of hours to Glasgow and a long train ride. I thought you would want to salvage some of your weekend.'

'I'd better pack, then.' She glanced over at the Halston dress hanging forlornly on the wardrobe door. Last night it had been fantastically, recklessly glamorous. Today it looked limp and a little worse for wear. Like its wearer. 'Don't feel that you have to keep me company, Kit. I have a few things to do and I'd like to make sure I say a proper thank you to your mother before I go. Honestly. I'm fine.'

He paused then nodded, dropping one light kiss onto the top of her head before turning away. It wasn't until Maddison watched Kilcanon disappear behind her that she realized that he hadn't even said goodbye.

* * *

Kit swivelled his office chair round and stared unseeingly out across the London skyline. A view that denoted success, status. Just as his expensive chair, his vintage desk, his penthouse office did.

It was cold comfort. In fact there was precious little comfort anywhere. Not here, in this gleaming, glass-clad, supersized office. Not at night in a house far too big for one person, especially a person who barely spent any time there. He'd never noticed before just how bland his house was, like a luxurious and tasteful hotel, not a home. Had he chosen a single one of the varying shades of cream, olive, steel or grey, positioned any one of the statement pieces in the large empty rooms? No, it looked almost exactly the same as it had when the expensive interior decorator had walked away. Like a show home: all facade and no heart.

A bit like his life.

Kit's mouth pressed into a hard line. He knew better than most how hard Maddison's life had been, how she was searching for a place of her own, for security. And what had he done? Made her feel so unwanted that her only option was to leave. Leave a job she loved, a fantastic opportunity she had been headhunted for, in order to avoid him. The irony was that his own notice was in and he would be moving on himself in a couple of months. She should have stayed; he could have moved her to another department if she really wanted to avoid him.

He'd been relieved, that morning in Scotland, at her apparent lack of emotion. Alarm bells should have been screeching. He should have looked deeper but he'd seen what he'd wanted to see. What it was easier for him to see. Again.

He'd told himself that he was doing the right thing,

that giving her some space was exactly what they had both needed. But when he'd got back to London she had gone. Family emergency, apparently. Which was interesting because he knew full well that she didn't have any family, not that she was in touch with anyway.

So, it wasn't hard to deduce that she had disappeared in order to avoid seeing him. He should be glad. It made a difficult situation a lot more tenable. No tears and constant phone calls from Maddison; she had more class than that. His mouth thinned. He couldn't just let her vanish into thin air; he should make sure she was okay, that she had somewhere to go. He owed her that. Otherwise he was no better than that idiot on the porch swing.

After all, Bart had obviously had no idea of Maddison's worth, but Kit didn't have that excuse. He knew exactly what she was, *who* she was; he knew just how brightly she shone. Had pushed her away, afraid of being burnt by her flame. The whole time he had been in Scotland he had wished that she were there, had wanted to discuss the compromise he'd made with his father with her. Wanted to hear her thoughts on his plan—a plan that involved spending half the year in Scotland and branching out as a freelancer again. Using his entrepreneurial skills to help shore up and revitalize the Kilcanon economy.

He'd told himself that pushing her away was for her own good, that she deserved someone better than him but, he realized with scalding shame, he'd been lying to himself all along. He who prided himself on his unflinching honesty. He'd pushed her away because he was scared, because she made him *feel*. She'd made him feel hope. And how had he repaid her? He needed to make sure she was okay. He needed to say sorry. He needed to tell her exactly how brightly she shone.

A call to New York established that Maddison hadn't returned there and that Hope hadn't heard from her. Kit racked his brains. She had never said where she was from. All he knew was that it was a coastal town in New England. That narrowed it down to thousands of miles of coastline, then.

Kit turned back to his desk and, with a few quick taps, brought Maddison's personnel file up on his screen. He stared at the small yellow envelope. As her line manager he had every right to look in there, more than a right; he had a duty to record appraisals, chart her performance. But, no matter what he told himself, he knew he wasn't looking as a line manager.

He wasn't even looking as a concerned friend.

He missed her. He was pretty damn sure he needed her. Terrifyingly sure that actually he was desperately and irrevocably in love with her.

Love. Was that what this was? This emptiness? This need? This willingness to fall on his sword a thousand times?

He clicked on the icon.

There they were—her application documents, anonymous forms, filled in, filed and forgotten. Until now. He opened her résumé and began reading. She had graduated summa cum laude from Martha George, a small liberal arts college in New York State, and, while there, had spent her summers working as an intern for various PR agencies before joining a new agency soon after graduating. Two years later she was applying for a job at DL Media.

He scanned further down. Graduated class valedictorian from Bayside High on Cape Cod...Bayside High... *got her*.

But he needed more. He couldn't just turn up in a

strange town armed with a photo of her and track her
down, could he? He closed the document, opening up
her employee details instead. Name, address, Social Security number...there it was. Next of Kin. Only it was
blank. She had cut her mother completely out of her life.

What must that be like? His own parents were still
hurting, still recovering from Euan's death, from Kit's
own emotional and physical distance, but they were there,
always there. What must it be like having nobody at all
to rely on?

Kit opened another couple of documents at random:
appraisals, the move from PR to editorial, her references.
It was all in order and yet it told him nothing. Finally he
clicked on the last document, her college reference. It
was a breakdown of her entire time there, classes taken,
grades achieved—and her scholarship recommendation.

He read through the recommendation, words jumping out.

> *Despite her difficult background...*
> *Three jobs...*
> *Tenacious and hardworking...*
> *Ambitious...*
> *Legal emancipation...*
> *Needs a chance...*
> *No parental support, emotionally or financially...*

Seeing her past written there so baldly hit him in a
way her confession hadn't. No wonder she pushed everyone away. No wonder she always had to be in control,
couldn't show that she needed anyone.

She had never been able to rely on anyone.

Well, hard luck. He was going to be there for her
whether she wanted him to be or not. And when he knew

she was okay, then he would walk away. If that was what she truly wanted. Only if that was what she truly wanted.

He'd thought that keeping the rest of the world at bay was what he'd deserved, that he owed Euan a lifetime of remorse and loneliness. Wouldn't it be better to honour his brother's legacy by living? By feeling? The good *and* the bad.

Kit walked back to his desk and read the reference again, noting down the address.

He was going to find out exactly what made Maddison Carter tick, and when he had done so he was going to fix her. He was going to make everything better for someone else for once in his life, no matter what it cost him.

CHAPTER THIRTEEN

MADDISON'S HANDS GREW clammy and she gripped the steering wheel so tight the plastic bit into her palms. Ahead of her the road segued smoothly onto the bridge that separated Cape Cod from the mainland.

The bridge that would take her home.

It was eight years since she had bid it farewell in her rear-view mirror. Waved and sworn never to return. Up until today she had kept that vow.

But it was time to face her demons, confront her past—then maybe she could move forward. Maybe she too would finally deserve some kind of happiness. Her stomach twisted and she gulped in air against the rising panic. Would she be able to find happiness without Kit?

No. This wasn't about Kit. This was about her, Maddison, finally taking stock of who she was and where she had come from. This was about moving on. This was about learning to be happy. If she could…

The bridge soared over the narrow strip of water separating the Cape from the mainland. Mouth set, eyes straight ahead, Maddison maintained a steady speed over the bridge and onto the highway, which ran the full length of the Cape all the way up to Provincetown on the very tip. She wound down her window and the smell hit instantly: salt and gorse. Despite everything she breathed in deeply, letting the familiar air fill her lungs. Despite everything it whispered to her that she was home.

Her turn-off was thirty miles up the Cape, at the spot where the land narrowed and twisted, like an arm raised in victory. She turned instinctively, driving on autopilot, until she found herself entering the small town of Bayside.

Bayside always looked at its best in early summer, when everything was spruced up ready for the seasonal influx that quadrupled the town's population. The freshly painted shopfronts gleamed in the morning sun, the town had an air of suppressed anticipation just as it did every May, a stark contrast to the weary fade of September.

But some things had changed; several cycle-hire stores had sprung up offering helmets, kiddie trailers and tandems as well as a bewildering assortment of road and trail bikes. Maddison's mouth twisted as she remembered how she had been teased for riding her rusty bike around the town, not driving like her classmates. She guessed she had just been ahead of the curve. The cycle shops weren't the only new stores; driving slowly, Maddison noticed an assortment of new delis, coffee shops, organic cafes and bakeries, many of which wouldn't have been out of place in the Upper East Side or on Stoke Newington Church Street. It was a long way away from the ice-cream parlours and burger joints of her youth.

Bayside had always been a town divided, not once, but two or three times. Locals versus visitors. Summer-home owners versus two-week vacationers. Vacationers versus day trippers. And at the bottom of the heap, divided from everyone, were the town's poor, dotted here and there in trailers or falling-down cottages, on scrubland worth millions less than the prime real estate on the ocean edge. That had been Maddison's world.

Her stomach tightened as she drove out of town, past the small, dusty road that led to Bill's Bar, a small, shabby establishment frequented only by locals—her mother's second home. If she took that road and pulled in would she see the all-too-familiar sight of her mother, propping up the bar, another drink in front of her? She accelerated past, heading for the Bayside Inn where she had reserved a room. Once she'd asked them for a job and been turned away. Now her money was as good as anyone's.

Two hours later, showered and refuelled by some excellent coffee, Maddison was back in the car, continuing on the road out of town following the shore. The town was situated by a huge natural bay and the beaches were sheltered, the water warm and safe; in low tide it was possible to walk out for what seemed like miles and still only be waist deep. The beautiful sand-dune beaches on the other side of town plunged swimmers straight into the icy swell of the ocean, where seals frolicked within swimming distance—and where the seals swam the great whites weren't far behind. Property overlooking the ocean on both sides was at a premium and Maddison drove past tall electronic gates prohibiting access to the vast, sprawling houses within, their views worth more than their opulent interiors.

Maddison pulled into the ungated driveway of one of the oldest and more modest houses: a two-storey white-shingled house. True, anywhere else the five-bedroomed dwelling with its beautiful wraparound porch, outside pool and beach views from every room would be pretty impressive, but it lacked the helipad and pool houses of some of its more vulgar neighbours. On one side stood a separate double garage, and Maddison looked up at the apartment overhead, that sense of coming home inten-

JESSICA GILMORE   163

sifying. This was the first place where she had ever had the luxury of security.

She rang the bell and waited, wiping her hands on her skirt, trying not to jiggle impatiently. No answer. Maddison looked around, hope draining away. Why hadn't she called ahead? The house might have changed hands, or the owners be away. This whole impetuous road trip was probably a waste of time, a self-indulgent wallow in memory lane. She took a step back, poised to turn away, but the movement was arrested by the sound of a key turning. Maddison turned, hope hammering in her chest, the relief almost too much when the door opened to reveal a familiar face. Mrs Stanmeyer. A little older, but her blonde hair was still swept back in an elegant coil, she was still as regally straight-backed, exquisitely dressed in linen trousers and a white silk shirt.

'Hello, can I help...?' The voice trailed off. 'Maddison? Maddison Carter? Oh, my dear girl.'

As Mrs Stanmeyer's face relaxed into a welcoming smile and she stepped forward, arms outstretched to pull Maddison into a hug, the pain in Maddison's chest, the load she had carried since she was eighteen, the load that had seemed unbearable since she left Scotland, lessened just a little. Enough to make it manageable.

'Maddison, oh, my dear, come on in. I am so very glad to see you.'

Maddison found herself ushered into the wide, spacious hallway. Little had changed, she was relieved to see, the house still a tasteful blend of creams and blues, beautiful but practical in a home where children ran straight in from the beach and most of the day was spent outside. Mrs Stanmeyer led her through the living/dining/family room that made up most of the first floor and out onto the deck where a trio of cosy wooden love seats were pulled up invitingly.

'It's so lovely to see you,' Mrs Stanmeyer said as they settled themselves onto the seats, iced water flavoured with fresh lemons on the table before them. 'I have often wondered how you were.'

For the first time in eight years guilt hit Maddison. How could she have cut everyone off so completely when some people had done nothing but offer her help and support?

'This is the first time I've come back,' she admitted, her eyes fixed on the sand dunes and the gleam of blue sea beyond. 'I'm sorry. Sorry I didn't call or email you, sorry I didn't try. I just wanted to wipe it all out. Start again.'

'And how has that gone for you?'

'I thought it was going perfectly. I thought I had re-invented myself, that I was untouchable.' She grimaced. 'But I guess I never stopped judging myself. In the end I was the one still looking down on me, never believing I was worthy of anything, deserved anything. Maybe that's why I spent the last few years chasing after all the wrong things.' She swallowed hard, the lump in her throat making words almost impossible. 'And now it's too late. I'm worried that it's too late.' Her mouth quivered and she covered it with one hand.

'Oh, Maddison. It's never too late. The girl I knew, the girl with three jobs when she was just fourteen? The girl who supported herself at sixteen and still graduated as class valedictorian, she knew that.'

Maddison looked up at that. Was that how Mrs Stanmeyer saw her? Not as a monumental mess but as a survivor? 'Supported myself and graduated thanks to you. If you hadn't given me a job when no one else would, offered me the maid's room, sorted out the scholarship to Martha George, I don't know where I would have ended up.'

The older woman reached out and laid a hand on Maddison's arm. 'I didn't do anything, Maddison. If anything I felt guilty for not doing more—a child of your age here all winter on her own, cleaning for me! But you were so determined and so proud, I knew you wouldn't take charity. As for the scholarship, all I did was recommend you. You did the rest yourself.'

For the first time in maybe forever a glow of achievement warmed her. She *had* worked hard, saved hard, studied hard. Hadn't allowed her beginnings to define her end. But she knew that without the home, the money, the trust Mrs Stanmeyer had shown her it would have been a far harder journey.

'I wondered...' Maddison twisted her hands together, trying to find the right words. 'I wondered why you helped me, if maybe it was...if I was...' She glanced through the open glass doors to the large sideboard, at the collection of family portraits gathered there. She had dusted each of them time and time again, searching for some kind of resemblance between herself and the two blonde, elegant daughters and the boyish, handsome son. There were more photos now, babies and small, round children playing in the sand. 'Did you help me because your son... Is he my father?'

The smile faded from Mrs Stanmeyer's face, replaced by a weary sadness. 'Oh, Maddison. If you were my granddaughter I hope I'd have done better than employing you as my maid and housing you in a room over the garage. I don't think Frank even knew your mother. He was away interning the summer you were conceived.'

Warring emotions hit her, intense disappointment that she could never be part of this family mingled with relief that she wasn't the guilty secret hidden away in the maid's room after all. 'Do you know who it was? Who my father is?'

Mrs Stanmeyer shook her head. 'No, but I knew your mother. You look very much like her, you know, the same hair, the same eyes—and the same ambition. I'd known your grandmother a very long time but I really got to know Tanya the summer before you were born. She was hoping for a scholarship to Martha George too, and I was already on the admissions board.'

Maddison stared. Her mother had applied to the elite liberal arts college? She didn't remember her even opening a book, let alone studying. At least she certainly hadn't after Grandma died.

'My mom?' Her voice squeaked despite herself and she stopped, silent. She wasn't supposed to care.

Mrs Stanmeyer nodded. 'It was a scandal when she fell pregnant with you. Everyone said it was such a waste of potential. I think some thought it a judgement—she was just so alive, so free, so sure she could do it all. She told me she didn't care what they said, that she was excited about the future, that she would raise you and study at night. Like you she was very independent. She moved out of your grandmother's house into the trailer when you were still a baby, determined not to ask for help. I think they clashed a lot.'

'They did, but they loved each other too,' Maddison admitted. 'She was devastated when Grandma died.' She took a sip of the ice-cold water, trying to reconcile this picture of a vibrant, ambitious teen mom with the bitter reality. 'What happened? Because the woman I knew? She had no ambition beyond the next drink, the next boyfriend.'

Mrs Stanmeyer shook her head. 'I wish I knew. I saw a

little of her when you were a baby and a toddler and everything seemed fine. I was a friend of your grandmother's, you see, since we were girls ourselves, and I always took an interest in your mother. I knew she found it hard, making enough money, keeping up her studies and raising you, but she was very optimistic. Your grandmother's illness hit her hard but at that time my own girls were growing up, had their own teen worries and troubles and I didn't see your mother—or you—for several years. I heard gossip, of course, but I discounted it as mutterings of scandal-loving old cats. Maybe I shouldn't have been so quick to judge them. When I next saw her it was as if something had broken inside her. She seemed to have given up. I tried to help but she pushed me away, many times.'

Maddison's eyes burned and the pressure in her chest swelled to almost unbearable degrees. It had been so long since she had thought of her mother without scorn and anger but she could all too vividly imagine the struggling young woman, breaking down under the burden of poverty and hardship. And sitting here contemplating a bleak future of her own making, a future without Kit, she understood, a little, the intoxicating appeal of just checking out of life.

Maybe her bleakness showed on her face because Mrs Stanmeyer's voice was very gentle, very kind. 'What's brought you home, Maddison, after all this time?'

She blinked, trying in vain to hold back the tears that had been building but not allowed to fall since the moment she had driven away from Kilcanon, each one scalding her as it escaped. 'I thought I had it all planned out but I'm lost. And I have no idea how to find my way.'

'Do you have any plans for today, dear?' Mrs Stanmeyer—Lydia, as she had instructed Maddison to call her—put a plate of pancakes, bacon and maple syrup in front of Maddison as she spoke. 'Eat up. You are far too thin.'

In some ways the last twenty-four hours had been like stepping into a much-loved and cherished daydream. Mrs Stanmeyer had insisted she cancel her room at the inn and stay with her, putting Maddison in the whitewashed corner room with views out over the ocean on two sides. When Maddison had been the live-in maid she had always pretended that the room was hers. It wasn't the largest or the fanciest, but the views were superb and the sloping ceiling gave it a quaint, old-fashioned air.

'Thank you.' Maddison picked up her fork, not needing much more encouragement to get stuck in. Maybe it was the sea air, maybe the best night's sleep she had had in years, but she had woken with a hearty appetite. 'This looks amazing but you really shouldn't have gone to so much trouble.' Maybe not, but seeing as she *had*... Maddison speared a piece of bacon and pancake, dousing them liberally in the amber syrup, before allowing herself to savour the taste. 'I need to get in touch with the office and take some leave officially. I just kind of left...'

Did she even have a job anymore? After all, she was technically absent without leave; she doubted she could claim compassionate leave for an imaginary family crisis. How could she, organized, always-planning-ahead Maddison, have just walked out on her job—would there even be a place for her in New York? Maddison shivered, cold despite the sun on her shoulders. She had thrown everything away in her impetuous flight.

The doorbell rang and Maddison pushed her chair back, automatically readying herself to answer it. 'Don't be silly, dear. You eat.' Lydia gave her a gentle push back into her seat as she walked past her and into the hallway.

Maddison scooped some more food onto her fork but didn't move it off her plate, her mind whirring. She would do what she had to here and then what? Sort out her job situation. Contact Kit.

Should she have left Kit without telling him how she felt?

How could she have told him when she'd barely admitted it to herself?

'Maddison.' She looked up as Lydia called her. There was a curious tone in her voice, curiosity mixed with satisfaction. 'It's for you.'

For her? Who on earth could be visiting her? Maybe someone at the inn had mentioned seeing her, maybe an old school friend had heard that she was back—but no, she hadn't been much of one for friends. Her high-school boyfriend had married in his early twenties, but even if he hadn't she couldn't imagine he'd cared enough about her to hotfoot it over the second she sailed back into town.

Her stomach shifted and she clasped one hand to it. Surely not her mother...

Maddison got to her feet, reaching out to the table for support, and moved slowly into the hallway and blinked, trying to focus on the tall, dishevelled man standing there. 'Kit?' She wasn't sure if she thought it, breathed it or shouted his name aloud. 'What are you doing here? You look tired,' she added as he came into focus. His skin was almost grey, his eyes bloodshot and his chin darker than usual with extra stubble.

'Isn't that the point of a red eye? I left London yesterday afternoon, spent several hours in Toronto and landed in Boston...' he checked his watch, swaying a little as he did so '...about three hours ago.'

He sounded so matter-of-fact. As if his turning up here were completely normal. She blinked. 'But why?'

'If I were you, Maddison, I would take poor Mr Buchanan into the kitchen and feed him coffee and pancakes before you interrogate him any further. I am heading out for the day so please both make yourselves at home. There are spare bathing suits and towels in the drying room if you want to go to the beach. Help yourself to anything you need.'

Before Maddison could say anything Lydia had whisked out of the door, leaving them quite alone. She stood still, staring at Kit. She wanted to touch him, check she wasn't imagining things, but she didn't quite dare.

'Was that coffee I heard mentioned?' Kit asked hopefully. 'I drank at least a gallon in Boston before collecting the hire car but I think it wore off somewhere around Plymouth.'

'Coffee? Yes, come on in.' It *must* be a dream, Maddison decided as she led him through into the kitchen. In which case she was going with it; she hadn't had a dream this comforting in, well, in forever.

There was still a stack of pancakes in the warmer and some bacon in the pan and she ladled a substantial helping of both onto a plate, handing them and a large mug of coffee to Kit.

He received them rapturously, almost inhaling the first cup of coffee and half the plate of food before leaning back with a satisfied stretch. 'These are good. I couldn't get a first-class flight or a direct flight so I have suffered more hours than I care to admit of limited leg room and plastic food. But for these pancakes I would fly all the way to Australia.'

'But you didn't fly all this way for pancakes.' Maddison pushed her plate away; even Kit's hearty enjoyment of his breakfast hadn't rekindled her appetite.

'No.'

'How did you find me?'

'It's a good thing I like treasure hunts. You've covered your tracks pretty well. Actually,' he confessed, pouring a second large cup of coffee, 'I didn't. Expect to find you here, that is. This address was my first—and only—clue.'

Maddison cast around for the words that would somehow make it all right. The words that would make her worthy of a man who had flown across the world to find her with nothing but an old address to spark the hunt. She didn't have them.

'Why?'

'I wanted to make sure you're all right.'

She stared at him incredulously. 'You wanted to make sure I was all right? So you flew to Toronto and then to Boston and then drove here just to check up on me?'

'That about sums it up,' he agreed. 'I was worried about you. I didn't handle Scotland very well.' His eyes gleamed with warmth and something deeper, something she hadn't seen in them before and yet recognized instantly.

Maddison was suddenly, unaccountably shy. She didn't know if she could handle whatever he'd come here to say, not yet. Not until she'd done what she'd come here to do. 'How tired are you?'

'I don't know. Part of me is so wired on caffeine and sunshine I could run a marathon, the other part exhausted enough to sleep for the proverbial hundred years. Why?'

'I wondered if you wanted to go on a treasure hunt. With me.'

Kit smiled then, a slow, sweet smile that wiped the weariness off his face, and Maddison's heart leapt as she watched his eyes spark back to life. 'A treasure hunt? What's the prize?'

She wanted to answer *me* but how could she presume

he wanted her, would think her any kind of prize? Sure, he had flown here but he hadn't told her why, had made no move towards her, uttered no words of love. It might have been pique or anger that had set him off to hunt her down.

'I'm not sure,' she said instead. 'But we'll know it when we find it.'

CHAPTER FOURTEEN

SHE LOOKED VULNERABLE: too thin, too pale, all the vitality leached out of her, and all Kit wanted to do was hold her close and tell her that it didn't matter, none of it mattered. But he couldn't, not yet. Because to her it did. And that meant it mattered to him too. Whatever Maddison had returned home to do, he would support her with, help her with.

Maddison drove, pointing out that he hadn't slept in goodness knew how many hours and was liable to find himself on the wrong side of the road even if he didn't doze off, and Kit didn't argue, happy to sit relaxed in the passenger seat, enjoying the view. Maddison's home town was picture-perfect, all blue skies, beaches and quirky, local shops all located in painted, wood-shingled buildings. It was like a film set.

'So, what are we looking for?' he asked at last as she turned into a small housing development. Cheerful detached houses sat on hilly lots, each garden flowing into the next, trees all around them. He could imagine children biking up the driveways, playing ball by the hoops fastened in many of the garage roofs.

She didn't answer for a long moment, pulling up outside a corner house. It was a pretty blue wooden house, a covered porch on one side. Maddison stared at it, her heart in her eyes. 'Me,' she said finally. 'We're looking for me. I want to see where it all went wrong, where I went wrong.'

He wanted to contradict her, tell her that she didn't have a wrong bone in her body, but he sensed this wasn't what she needed, not today, and instead just nodded. He'd guessed as much. 'Okay. Is this where we start?'

'This was my grandma's house.' She killed the engine and shifted to face him, her eyes very green in her pale face. 'My mom was very young when she had me and I didn't know my dad. When I was little she worked a lot so I came here. My grandma told me that she wished I could live there forever and I wished it too, that I could spend every night in my little yellow bedroom with the rocking horse. But my mom wanted to prove she could do it on her own and so most evenings she'd pick me up and take me home. Then, when I was seven, I got my wish. We moved in. Only my grandma was really sick.' Her mouth quivered.

Kit wanted to pull her in tight and tell her everything was okay. But it wasn't, not yet. Not until she had told him, whatever she needed to. 'Then what happened?'

Maddison stared at the house, her eyes unfocused as if she could see her younger self playing in the wooded yard. 'Then she died. My mom was supposed to inherit the house, only there were medical bills and she had to sell it. I think that's when it all got too much for her.'

'How about you? How did it affect you?'

She didn't answer for a long moment, her hands twisting in her lap, then turned back to the wheel and restarted the engine. It wasn't until she was backing out of the driveway that she answered, her voice hoarse with repressed tears. 'Like I'd lost my world. I guess I had.'

It took nearly a quarter of an hour to reach her next

destination. Maddison headed out of town before taking an abrupt turn down an untreated road, the woods encroaching on both sides of the rough track. At various intervals the trees were hacked back and small cottages or trailers built in the scrubby wastelands. Kit held on as the car bumped over stones and potholes. 'I hope you got a good insurance deal,' he said through gritted teeth.

Maddison didn't answer, her focus on the road ahead. Finally, just when Kit was sure his insides had been turned into a cocktail definitely shaken not stirred, she pulled into a rough clearing. At the back, on breeze blocks, stood a trailer, the windows boarded up and the door swinging off its hinges. Surely not...

Kit stared at the trailer, unable to disguise his revulsion. 'Please tell me this is where you lost your virginity or went all Blair Witch,' he said. 'Please don't tell me you lived here.' But she was afraid of the dark. She'd mentioned being hungry and cold. He'd known it was bad. He just had hoped it wasn't this bad.

'It was only meant to be temporary. Till Mom got some money and a proper job.' Her voice cracked. 'We had a fund, the Maddison and Mom fund, and we were going to use it to travel, to get a proper house, to go to Disneyland. But it was hard to save even before Grandma died and afterwards...I'd get ill or needed new shoes or there were bills and so the fund kept getting depleted even though Mom worked all the time.'

'Who looked after you while she worked?' But he already knew the answer. 'You were a child. Alone, out here?'

'She said I was never to tell. That if they knew they'd take me away.'

Kit thought back to his own wild childhood. Roaming free, swimming, sailing, hiking, utterly secure in his parents' love. He'd never realized just how lucky he had been. How lucky he still was in many ways. How much he had taken for granted, how much he had pushed away.

Maddison carried on, her voice expressionless, as if she were reading from a script. 'She got more and more tired and then she was just angry all the time. One night she picked up the phone to call for pizza and the phone had been cut off. She was so mad, swearing and screaming and kicking things—and then she left. Picked up her car keys and walked away. I thought she'd gone for pizza but she didn't come back and when I woke in the morning she was passed out on the sofa. She'd never really drunk before that but I think she just needed to stop thinking— and the drink helped her forget for a time at least.'

It didn't take too much detective work to guess the rest. 'And she carried on drinking?'

Maddison nodded. 'Soon I became that child, you know, the one no one wants to sit next to in case they catch something. It's hard to keep clean when the hot water is cut off and you don't have a washing machine. It's hard to look smart when all your clothes are second- hand.' Her voice dripped with bitterness and Kit's heart ached to hear it. Ached for the lonely, neglected child.

'And no one did anything? Your teachers? Social workers?'

'A few tried to talk to me but I said I was fine. I didn't want to be taken away. This might not look like much but it was all I knew. Mom made just enough of an ef- fort when she had to come in to school, at least she did back then. I'm glad she's not still here,' she said, her voice shaking. 'I'm glad she got out.'

The trailer looked like no one had lived there for a very long time and Kit was relieved when Maddison re- versed and pulled away. He wasn't sure he could have looked inside the trailer and not cracked. 'Do you know where she is?'

'Mrs Stanmeyer said she got clean the year I left. Apparently she finally got her degree and got a job as a teacher, can you believe it? Married three years ago and moved to Chatham. She has a little girl, she's about two. My sister.'

'Are you going to go and see her?'

Maddison's mouth trembled. 'I haven't decided.'

'I'll come with you, if you want me to.'

'Thank you. Not today. I'm not ready. But maybe tomorrow.'

She was talking about tomorrow. With him. Kit waited for panic to hit him but it was gone as if it had never been. Tomorrow was just a word.

'Okay, in that case, where next?'

'Next?' Her mouth curved into an unexpected smile. 'Clue Three. The reinvention of Maddison Carter.'

She took them back into town, driving straight through the centre and turning into a large car park situated beside playing fields and an official-looking building that proclaimed itself 'Bayside High, Home of the Sea Hawks.'

'Sea Hawks, huh?' Kit tried to lighten the mood. 'Were you a cheerleader? I bet you looked amazing in one of those skirts.'

'No, girls like me didn't get to be cheerleaders. Although you're right, I would have looked pretty darn good in that skirt.'

'So which were you? The jock, the princess. The geek? Ally Sheedy?'

He was relieved to hear her choke out a laugh. 'Which do you think? I was Ally Sheedy both before and after the makeover. Only mine was better. A real reinvention.'

'I'm glad to hear it.'

'In junior high I began working. I was too young for a proper job so I hustled for work: babysitting, car washing, grocery shopping, anything I could do to get money so I could dress better, get a bike, try and fit in. By the time I reached high school I knew I needed more. I needed to take control of my life so I took on as much work as I could get, studied like mad and started to plan my exit route. I moved out the day I turned sixteen and became a live-in maid at Mrs Stanmeyer's.'

'At sixteen? Was that even legal?'

Maddison nodded. 'She hated that I insisted on working. She would have let me have a room for free, helped me out with money for much less work, but I refused any sign of charity—I'd been the town's trash for long enough. I wanted to earn every cent, make sure everyone knew I wasn't like my mother. I loved living there. I had the room over the garage. It was the first time I'd felt safe in a really long time.' There was a wealth of untold detail in that last statement and Kit curled his hands into fists, hating how it was too late to make any of it all right.

'I just wanted to fit in,' she almost whispered. 'I wanted to be one of the cool kids, the ones who were so secure they knew exactly who they were and what they deserved.'

'That's understandable.'

'It was no use trying with the girls, my social status was too low. So I targeted the boys. Targeted one boy. It was almost too easy. I could afford to dress better, get my hair cut and I knew boys liked to look at me. The next step was finding out what else he liked and making sure I liked it too, that we met at the same movies, in the same comic-book store, that we always had something to talk about. No one could believe it, Jim Squires, captain of the football team, and Maddison Carter. But when he held my hand in the hallway or I wore his varsity jacket I knew I belonged. At last. I was safe.

'That's when I knew what I wanted. I wanted to leave this Maddison behind and become someone else, the kind of girl who expected to walk down a hallway holding the hottest boy in school's hand, the kind of girl that took dates and friends and proms and an allowance for granted. The kind of girl who had never worked one job, let alone three, who had never set foot inside a trailer. And so when I left here I made it up, invented the life I wished I had. I think at times I even believed my own lies, I've been living them so long. I'm pathetic.'

'Pathetic?' Kit stared at her, incredulous. Was that really what she thought? What she believed? 'You had nothing and you didn't let it stop you. You worked your socks off to achieve your dream. I admire you, Maddison. You're the strongest, bravest person I know. You are absolutely incredible.'

The words reverberated round and round her head, his eyes shining with sincerity and truth. Maddison wanted to believe him but she couldn't, not yet. She pulled away, driving away from the school, away from her memories, away from his words.

Maddison didn't stop until she reached the car park by her favourite beach. She parked haphazardly and jumped out, the sun's warmth a shock after the air-conditioned car. Kit stepped warily out of the car but she didn't acknowledge him, instead turning and walking across the car park, along the boardwalk and past the clam shack until she reached the beach. The smell of fried clams hit her, mingled with the salt in the sea air. The scent of a dozen beach parties.

Despite the heat of the day it was quiet, just a few preschool families about—the schools not due to break up for another couple of weeks. Maddison pulled her shoes off and walked, barefoot, through the foot of the dunes, wincing as her feet struck the heated sand. Kit matched her step for step, not saying a word, allowing her to set the pace.

'I had this fantasy that my dad was one of the summer-home owners. That his parents hadn't let him acknowledge me but that one day he would stride into school and scoop me up and take me away to live that gilded life. They'd come to town, the summer kids, with their platinum credit cards and their boats and their country-club memberships, and I wanted to be one of them so much it actually hurt, right here.' She tapped her chest.

'Once I got to high school I knew that my daddy wasn't coming for me, that he probably didn't even know I existed. But I still wanted that life. When I moved to New York it was with one goal: to find the right man who could give me the right kind of life and marry him.'

Kit nodded. 'All you wanted was a family. You told me that almost straight away. Four children who would have the most perfect childhood ever. I don't think that's such a terrible crime, Maddison. If you wanted to marry for status or jewels or a platinum credit card of your own, then that would be understandable, considering what you've been through, but you didn't. You wanted a family. A family you could keep safe.'

'And then I started to spend time with you.' She stopped and swallowed, trying to find the right words. 'It had all gone wrong. I thought I knew exactly what I was doing, had found the right guy, but Bart derailed all my plans and knocked my confidence. I arrived in the UK knowing I had to start all over again. When you suggested I spend my weekends doing the treasure trails with you I agreed mainly because I thought it might make Bart jealous, but soon it was more. A lot more. I liked your company. I liked you. And I thought, why not? I was only in the UK for a short while, why not have some fun? Deviate from the grand plan just for a while. I didn't expect to fall in love with you.'

Her words hung there as she kept walking, afraid that if she stopped or turned back then he would walk away. Would leave her. 'But I did. I did fall in love with you. Me, Maddison Carter with my plans and my dreams and my whole *love is for losers* mindset. Guess I wasn't as good at the game as I thought, huh? The ironic thing was that if you had been anyone else it would have been fine, but how could I tell you the truth when you were so adamant that love wasn't for you? How could I open up when you have the kind of background I've been searching for? What could I say? "Please, Kit, I used to want to marry someone rich and important but that's not why I've fallen for you." I wish you weren't. I wish you didn't have any of it. I don't want you to think I played you. Because when I was with you I wasn't playing at all.'

She hadn't planned on telling him any of this, but once the words had spilled out she realized that she was free. Free of her past, her secrets, her schemes, her plans. She had no idea what happened next but that was okay. And if Kit turned, left and she never saw him again, then that was okay as well because she had given it her best shot. A real shot, not a fake, perfectly thought-out, planned response.

She'd given him her heart.

Maddison turned, drinking him in. The faint sea breeze ruffled his hair as he stood at the foot of the sand dunes, his eyes fixed on the endless ocean. 'Why did you come here, Kit?'

'To find you,' he said simply. 'I left Scotland full of plans and the one person I wanted to share them with wasn't there, had just disappeared. I didn't think you were a quitter, Maddison, in fact I knew you weren't, so for you to just up and disappear? Whatever was going on it seemed to me you needed my help. I wanted to help.'

He passed a hand through his hair, rumpling it into an even more disordered state. 'I was a mess that morning in Scotland. Everything had changed in twenty-four hours. Thanks to you I could confront my feelings about Euan, admit it wasn't just guilt I felt but anger—anger at him for dying, for competing, for not fighting hard enough that night. Anger at myself for pushing him. For holding on to my bitterness when I had long since fallen out of love with Eleanor. Thanks to you I really spoke to my dad, about that night, about the future.'

'Sounds intense.'

'Oh, it was quite the fishing session. And then there was you. In my bed. Making me feel things I still wasn't ready to face—that I had been in no way the kind of man that deserved a girl like you. It seemed easier to just let you go but as soon as you were gone I realized I wanted to fix everything, fix me, make myself worthy of you.'

He stepped close and took her hand. 'I missed you, Maddison. I missed you planning every little detail, I missed you searching out every clue, I missed you finishing my crossword, I even missed that damn list. I missed the way you challenge me.' His eyes dropped to her mouth. 'You only spent two nights in my bed but I haven't slept right since. My dreams are full of you, Maddison Carter.'

'I had to come back here,' Maddison said, needing him to understand. 'I needed to face who I was, who I am now. But all I see is that if you're not with me then my life is empty, even with all the security in the world. You flew across the world for me.' Her mouth wobbled. 'I don't deserve that.'

Kit raised one of her hands to his lips and her heart leapt at the old-fashioned gesture. 'You do. You deserve it all. All the security your heart desires.' He smiled down at her. 'Four children, the house, anything you need.'

'Your family needs you, Kit. Your father needs you even if he won't say so.'

'I know and I have obligations in Kilcanon that I've ignored for long enough. I hope you would be happy to spend some of the year there, but we wouldn't have to live in Scotland all the time. We could have a place in London or a house here on the Cape, whatever you wanted.' His mouth twisted into a smile. 'Fourth of July, clambakes, hayrides, Thanksgiving—I'm willing to give it all a try.'

The last clamp finally loosened from her heart. 'I think as long as we're together I have everything I need.'

'So you're saying yes?'

'To what?' But she knew; it was in the blazing blue of his eyes, the curve of his mouth, the heat in his hands.

'To me, to us, to forever.'

Maddison finally allowed herself to reach up, to pull his head down to hers, to press her mouth to his. It was like coming home at long, long last. 'Yes,' she breathed against the warmth of his lips. 'I'm saying yes. To forever.'

EPILOGUE

One year later

KIT SHIFTED FROM foot to foot, anxiously scanning the
rows of chairs, looking beyond the seated people to the
sun-filled horizon beyond. *Where is she?* He took a deep
breath. He should be calmer; after all, they *were* actually already married. Maddison had been very keen to
marry him in his kilt but had reluctantly conceded that
the Cape Cod beach in summer wasn't the most appropriate place for thickly woven wool and a formal tux—
and Kit hadn't wanted to wait a full year before claiming
his bride. The answer was a happy compromise—two
weddings. A small, private spring service in Kilcanon
church and now, two months later, a blessing and party
on the Cape.

He scanned the rows of people, all decked out in their
summer best: his parents and Bridget were in the front
row, looking relaxed and happy after a couple of weeks
of sun and playing tourist. His father seemed years
younger—handing some of the business responsibilities over to Kit had obviously relieved him of a great
burden. They still clashed—they wouldn't be Buchanans
if they didn't—but his father grudgingly admitted that
some of Kit's ideas weren't too crazy and had thrown

himself into setting up the new distillery with enthusiasm. Bridget had finished university this month and had asked Kit if there was a place for her on the family estate, an offer he had accepted straight away. Bridget's presence would make it easier for Maddison and him to spend the summers and long vacations here on the Cape, just as he had promised her they would.

Next to the Buchanans sat a beaming Mrs Stanmeyer clutching a hanky just in case—she had cried throughout the first wedding and had declared her intention to do exactly the same this time round. Further back Kit noticed Hope, his old assistant, clutching the hand of a handsome dark-haired man, a soft smile on her face.

In the back row a beautiful woman in her early forties sat tensely on the aisle seat, her hands locked, her face set. Maddison still didn't have an easy relationship with her mother, their interactions were very formal and stilted, but they were both trying. But he knew that Maddison adored being a big sister, having blood kin of her own. And, stilted or not, Maddison had hosted Thanksgiving in the house they had bought on the Cape with her family, old and new, around her.

And at that moment the aria she loved so much began to swell out all around them, the guests got to their feet and Kit turned, met a pair of sparkling green eyes and was lost once again.

Maddison hadn't wanted to be given away—after all, she didn't have anyone to ask—so instead of leaning on someone else's arm she was clasping a small hand. It might not be customary for the bride and her flower girl to walk down the aisle hand in hand but Savannah wasn't just a flower girl, she was her little sister. She was hope. Testament that people could change, that the future was unwritten.

The small hand tugged at hers and Maddison bent down.

'Kit looks really handsome,' her small sister whispered and Maddison dropped a kiss on the fair curls, careful not to disturb the carefully arranged flowers. 'I know,' she whispered back.

He didn't look as formally handsome as he had in Kilcanon, clad in the black and green family tartan, but she liked the soft grey linen suit almost as much, just as she loved this flowing, simple lace dress she was wearing as much as the corseted, fuller wedding gown she had worn in Scotland. No veil this time, just fresh flowers in her hair, her feet bare as she walked through the sand towards the sea, towards her groom, towards her future.

She couldn't believe that it was all real. That this was her life now. The sand squished beneath her bare toes, the sea rippled just a few metres away and the sun beat steadily down, but it all felt like a dream. A perfect dream. It wasn't the future she'd thought she'd wanted but it was a million times better.

Maddison had kept her job at DL Media for the first few months of their engagement while Kit juggled freelance editing with revitalizing the Buchanan estate, but he had asked her advice so often she had ended up taking a formal role in Scotland, overseeing all the marketing of the estate and its various subsidiaries. It meant spending the bulk of the year in Scotland but Kit had promised they would always return to the beachside cottage here in Bayside for the summers, for Thanksgiving and any other time she wanted to see her sister, and Maddison loved the dramatic Scottish coastline. It felt like home.

The music died down as she reached the end of the

aisle and she let go of Savannah's hand, offering hers to Kit instead. How could she feel so shy? Almost unable to look him in the eye. They were already married, after all! But here she was, standing here, in front of the community she had hidden from, run from and returned to, promising once again to worship Kit body and soul and listening to his steady voice promise her the same.

The official closed her book and smiled. 'I now pronounce you husband and wife. You may now kiss the bride.'

Kit's eyes darkened with intent and Maddison's pulse began to race. Their friends and family were all on their feet, clapping, but the sound died away as the blood pounded in her ears and the world narrowed until all she could see was Kit. 'My favourite part,' he murmured as he stepped closer. Maddison quivered as his hands lightly caressed her bare shoulders and he leaned in to brush her mouth with his. She closed her eyes and fell into the deepening kiss, pulling him closer, not wanting the moment to end.

She'd never thought that girls like her would get a happily ever after but today, in this moment, she was more than happy for Kit to prove her wrong—and to keep proving her wrong. Forever.

* * * * *

"It's not funny, Kit. If anything happened to you…"

He raised himself up on one elbow and looked searchingly at her. He reached for her arm, gripping it gently. "If anything happened to me, then what?"

She could hardly think with him touching her. "I don't want to think about it."

"What don't you want to think about?" he pressed. "What are you afraid of?"

"I—I wouldn't want you to get hurt protecting me." Her stammer was a dead giveaway that her emotions were in turmoil.

"I wouldn't want anything to happen to either of us. For you to get hurt on my watch is unthinkable to me. Come here. Let's talk about it." He pulled her forward until she fell against him on the floor. He gathered her closer and entangled their legs.

"Kit—" She half gasped his name.

"On second thought, I don't feel much like talking." He lowered his mouth to hers. Natalie had been wanting this for so long she was past considering the wisdom of it. Kit started kissing her with a hunger as great as her own. In an explosion of need she began kissing him back, forgetting everything as she poured out her feelings for him.

THE TEXAS RANGER'S FAMILY

BY
REBECCA WINTERS

First Published in Great Britain 2016
By Mills & Boon, an imprint of HarperCollins*Publishers*
1 London Bridge Street, London, SE1 9GF

© 2016 Rebecca Winters

ISBN: 978-0-263-91984-4

23-0516

Our policy is to use papers that are natural, renewable and recyclable products and made from wood grown in sustainable forests. The logging and manufacturing processes conform to the legal environmental regulations of the country of origin.

Printed and bound in Spain
by CPI, Barcelona

Rebecca Winters, whose family of four children has now swelled to include five beautiful grandchildren, lives in Salt Lake City, Utah, in the land of the Rocky Mountains. With canyons and high alpine meadows full of wildflowers, she never runs out of places to explore. They, plus her favourite holiday spots in Europe, often end up as backgrounds for her romance novels, because writing is her passion, along with her family and church.

Rebecca loves to hear from readers. If you wish to email her, please visit her website, www.cleanromances.com.

I'm a lucky author to have a great editor like Kathleen Scheibling, who lets me write about the kinds of heroes I love. She's the best!

Chapter One

Texas Ranger Kit Saunders took cover behind a fat pine tree and watched with his binoculars from a distance. Seven people accompanied the honey-blonde widow standing at the grave site at the Evergreen Cemetery on this hot July afternoon in Austin.

The woman was Natalie Harris, and her husband, Rodney Parker Harris, age thirty-three, was being laid to rest. As far as any of the mourners, including his widow, knew, the deceased had been an accountant with LifeSpan Pharmaceutical, a huge private corporation in Austin. A week ago he'd been found at the low-end Sleepy Hollow Hotel, dead of a gunshot wound to the temple.

Kit's captain, T. J. Horton, had assigned him to the case only yesterday.

The police had run the victim's DNA through the database and, according to their report, the name Rodney Harris was the latest in a string of aliases. The name on the deceased's original birth certificate was that of escaped felon Harold Park from Colorado, who'd disappeared eight years ago.

Park was on the FBI's Most Wanted list. After serving only two years of a sixty-year sentence for murder, embezzlement, armed robbery and grand larceny, he and another prisoner, convicted killer Alonzo Morales, had escaped during a transfer from the ADX Federal Penitentiary in Florence, Colorado, to Canaan Federal Prison in Pennsylvania. Since that time both fugitives had gone by many false names that prevented the Feds from recapturing them.

The preliminary report from the detective here in Travis County suggested the gunshot wound was self-inflicted, but nothing would be official until all the forensic evidence had been reviewed. Something didn't add up in Kit's mind. It didn't make sense that the felon would kill himself. A clever killer could have set it up to look like suicide.

A search of Harold-alias-Rod's bank records revealed that $400,000 had been deposited into his checking account one day and withdrawn the next. The day after that, he'd been found dead in his hotel room. The size and date of the large deposit were inconsistent with his earnings from the pharmaceutical company, and the abrupt withdrawal was just plain suspicious. Normally that kind of money would have been put in a money market or the stock market at least.

Since Harold-alias-Rod had crossed state lines and had been an armed, dangerous killer, the police had asked for the Texas Rangers to take over. These were early days in the case. The police report also stated that Mrs. Harris had hired an attorney who'd attempted to serve him with divorce papers on the day he was shot.

Since they weren't yet divorced and he'd absconded with money she had half rights to under property laws, it appeared she could have a motive to see him dead.

But if Harris had still been living a life of crime and the money was stolen, then there may have been accomplices involved—maybe even other ex-felons from his past life—who might be potential culprits. If the widow was innocent of any wrongdoing, then she herself might be a target for interested parties still looking for the missing money.

Kit hadn't met Natalie Harris. The only information he had on her so far was that she was a twenty-eight-year-old pharmacist and had a sixteen-month-old daughter named Amy. There was no sign of the toddler at the graveside.

He was going to have to build this case from scratch. Knowing of the service today, he'd decided to study the people who showed up and take pictures with a long-range lens. Oftentimes a murderer appeared at the funeral to gloat. Of the seven people present, two were females, but he didn't sense they were family. He had the rap sheet on Alonzo Morales with a mug shot and would know if he saw that face again.

Before long the people assembled at the burial turned to leave and go their separate ways. Kit's first frontal view of Mrs. Harris being helped by the mortuary staff came as a shock to his senses. She was a true beauty; maybe five foot six. He took a picture of her. The classy, tailored black suit couldn't disguise the mold of her shapely body and legs. Everything about her appealed to him, which came as a shock. It had been a long time since he had reacted this way to a total stranger.

Kit didn't know what he'd expected. Maybe to find a widow in tears? But from a distance he got the impression she hadn't given in to whatever emotion she was feeling. Her lovely classic bone structure was undermined by features that showed no animation. Shock could do that to a person in mourning.

But since she'd filed for divorce, maybe she'd passed through her period of grief long before the papers had been served. Whether elated he was dead at her hands, relieved he was gone by another person's doing, or sad or even haunted by the way he'd died, the frozen mask he saw in front of him revealed no secrets.

Was he staring at a killer? If he was close enough to look into her eyes, he might be able to get a feel for what was going on in her psyche.

His gaze followed her to a silver Toyota parked on the roadside. The clergyman helped her in before walking to the car ahead of hers. Little by little everyone drove away from the cemetery, leaving the workers to finish their jobs.

Kit would give her a half hour before he phoned to set up a time to meet, preferably before the day was out. He needed to know her background. Was she a home-grown Texan? How long had she known the man she'd married? What about her parents or siblings? The police report didn't have many details about her background and a dozen questions filled his mind.

Tonight he planned to drive to Marble Falls to watch his younger brother, Brandon, compete in the steer wrestling event at the Charley Taylor Rodeo Arena. Brandon was headed for a world championship competition in Las Vegas this coming December and Kit was excited for him. Until he'd made the decision to go into law enforcement, Kit had competed big-time in the same sport. But when he'd made up his mind to follow in his father's footsteps, he'd given up the rodeo and ended up losing his girlfriend Janie at the same time. She knew that the Saunders brothers had suffered over the loss of their Texas Ranger father in a shootout when they were fifteen and seventeen. Fearing the same thing would happen to Kit, she'd broken it off with him, not wanting any part of a career that could end his life right in the middle of it, leaving a grieving wife and children.

Five years ago Janie had fallen in love with Brandon's hazer, Scott Turner, and they'd married. As of today they had one child. He was happy for her. Any residual pain from their breakup had disappeared a long time ago. When all was said and done, he was content enough with his bachelor existence. His mother and brother needed support and he could be there for them.

Kit would be thirty-one next month. He liked being single and free of emotional baggage. Out of his three best friends in the Rangers, two of them, Cy and Vic, were now married and incredibly happy. That left him and Luckey, who'd been married for a short time before his wife had decided she hated what he did for a living. Their divorce had pretty well scarred him.

Kit was thankful he'd avoided that problem before vows had been said. Janie had done both of them a huge favor. From time to time since then he'd gone out with various women, but no one female after Janie had made a lasting impression.

He made his way back to his truck and started up the engine, driving out of the cemetery to the main road and heading for his town house at Chimney Corners in Northwest Austin. Oddly enough Mrs. Harris lived in the same part of the city; no great distance from his condo. That would cut down his driving time. He'd grab a bite to eat and then make the call. If he could interview her soon, he'd leave for Marble Falls and pick up his mom en route to the arena. It would be good to spend some time with family.

NATALIE PULLED HER Toyota Corolla into the driveway and pressed the remote. She was still getting used to entering the garage devoid of Rod's white Sentra. The police had impounded it when they'd investigated the crime scene at the hotel a week ago.

But the second the garage door lifted, she realized someone had been there since she'd left for the graveside service. The lawn mower and equipment for the yard had been moved around. Items from the shelf, including a Christmas tree stand, had been thrown on the cement floor, preventing her from driving in. What on earth?

Frightened that a burglar had broken into her house, she backed out to the street and parked along the curb a few houses away to call Detective Carr. He'd been the one who'd come to see her following Rod's shooting in the hotel where he'd been living temporarily. The detective had told her to call him if she needed anything.

Her hand shook as she waited for him to answer.

"Mrs. Harris?"

"Yes. I'm so glad you're there. I just got home from the service to find my garage in disarray. I think someone has broken into my house. He could still be inside."

"Where are you?"

"In my car, parked down the street."

"What make and color?"

"A silver Corolla."

"Stay right there. Officers will be at your home within minutes."

"Thank y-you," she stammered and hung up. There'd been too many shocks already and now this...

She sat there trembling as she stared at her house, watching to see if someone would come out. Before long, two police cars arrived. Three officers got out and started casing the place, and the fourth walked toward her car. She rolled down the window.

"Mrs. Harris?"

"Yes. Thank you for coming."

"If I could have a key to your home, we'll check inside."

She pulled her keys out of the ignition and gave him the one that would unlock the front door. "There's a crawlspace under the house. You have to get to it through the laundry room. Someone could be hiding in there."

"We'll check. Stay right where you are."

Natalie nodded and waited. There were several cars

parked on each side of the street. Any one of them could be the intruder's. After several minutes the same officer came back outside.

"Whoever ransacked your house is gone." He handed back her key. "Please pull into your driveway, but stay in the car until you hear from Detective Carr. He'll follow up and give you instructions."

"Okay. Thanks for coming so quickly."

NO SOONER DID she watch the police drive away than her phone rang. She clicked it on. "Detective Carr?"

"Mrs. Harris?"

The deep, attractive male voice didn't sound like anyone she knew. "Yes?"

"This is Miles Saunders with the Texas Rangers." Natalie's heart skipped a beat. Why was a Texas Ranger phoning her? She thought they only worked on big federal cases. "Detective Carr contacted me. I hear you've been burglarized while you were attending your husband's graveside service."

"Yes."

"I'm about six minutes away. Leave your car in the driveway and go into the house through your garage. I'll park on the next street over and walk through a few neighbors' yards to knock on your back door. Use a hand towel to open it. Don't touch anything. A forensics team will arrive right away to go through everything. They'll come to your front door."

"A-all right."

She heard the click as he disconnected, still unable to believe what was happening. She knew there were unscrupulous people who read through the obituaries and chose to break into people's homes on the day of a funeral.

Taking a deep breath, she started her car and pulled into her driveway. She got out and entered the house through the garage as instructed, passing through the small laundry room into the kitchen. Cupboards were open and foodstuffs were on the floor.

Natalie had only been gone two hours, but it looked as though a wrecking ball had been at work. As she walked through her two-bedroom rambler, she saw that drawers and closets had been ransacked. Her bedding had been thrown on the floor and her mattress lay halfway off the box spring. Numerous items lay strewed on the floor of both bathrooms. She checked the nursery and found it in shambles. Some intruder had gone through every room, causing total upheaval.

She was wild with anger. Last evening after returning from her work at the pharmacy, she'd thoroughly cleaned the rambler in case someone dropped by after the graveside service. The house would be neat, clean and filled with flowers.

She'd inherited this house from her deceased mother, and she and Rod had made it into their home. But their marriage had started to fall apart soon after Amy was born, and now he was dead and her family home was a disaster.

Half a dozen floral arrangements had arrived during the week, but several of them had been knocked over. Water had spilled on the carpet. The fireplace screen had been knocked over. Cushions were piled on the floor in the living room and den. The drawers of her computer desk had been pulled out, the contents dumped on the floor. Several framed prints had been taken off the walls and the backings torn. Whoever had gone through her house had been desperately looking for something.

While she waited for the Ranger, she reached again for her cell and placed a call to Jillian.

Her good friend lived just across the street and had been looking after Amy since Natalie had gone back to work. The little girl was good company for Jillian's eighteen-month-old daughter, Susie, and the arrangement allowed Jillian to earn a little extra money while her husband, Bart, served another tour of duty overseas with the marines.

"Jillian? You're not going to believe this," Natalie said when her friend answered. "I just got home from the service and found that my house has been broken into"

"You're kidding!"

"I wish I were. Life has been a nightmare since I got that call from the police about Rod. Can you keep Amy a little longer? I have to wait for some Ranger to come over."

"What? Why?"

"I have no idea. And a forensics team. As soon as they're gone, I'll be over to get her."

"Don't you worry about anything. There's no hurry."

"Yes, there is. You've gone beyond the call of duty to watch her on a Saturday afternoon. That wasn't our arrangement. I plan to pay you double."

"Natalie—don't be ridiculous. You've been through a horrible experience. What are friends for?"

"You're the best, Jillian. I'll be over as soon as I can."

The second she hung up, Natalie's landline rang, startling her. She moved to the kitchen to answer it but checked the caller ID first. It was blank. Would it be one of those hang-up calls she'd gotten twice this week already?

Natalie hated to answer without knowing who was on the other end, especially after this break-in, although it could be one of many important calls she was expecting—the police, the bank, the attorney, the mortuary, her boss at work, her coworkers, church friends, her insurance agent. But right now she was in no state to talk to anyone and let it ring until the person on the other end gave up or left a message.

She looked around but couldn't tell if anything was missing. She'd developed a bad headache and needed a pain pill.

One look in the bathroom mirror made her realize she needed to freshen up before the Ranger arrived and she washed her face, remembering too late that she wasn't supposed to touch anything. The burial plot in the newer section of the cemetery hadn't been planted with shade trees yet. The heat had caused her to break out in perspiration, but she didn't have time to change out of her lightweight linen suit.

After drying her face, Natalie refreshed her lipstick and gave her tousled, collarbone-length hair a good brushing. When she heard the knock on the back door, her brush fell to the floor. Her nerves were that bad.

She walked down the hall, past the nursery and into the kitchen. She used a dish towel to open the door leading to the backyard. Whatever picture of the Ranger she'd had in her mind didn't come close to the sight of the tall, thirtyish, hard-muscled male in a Western shirt, jeans and cowboy boots.

Her gaze flitted over his dark brown hair only to collide with his beautiful hazel eyes appraising her through a dark fringe of lashes.

"Mrs. Harris? Miles Saunders." She felt the stranger's probing look pierce her before he displayed his credentials. That's when she noticed the star on his shirt pocket.

This man is the real thing. The stuff that made the Texas Rangers legendary. She had the strange feeling that she'd seen him somewhere before, but shrugged it off. This was definitely the first time she'd ever met a Ranger.

"Come in." Her voice faltered, mystified by this unexpected visit. She was pretty sure the Rangers didn't investigate a home break-in.

"Thank you." He took a few steps on those long, powerful legs. His presence dominated the kitchen. She invited him to follow her into the living room.

"Please sit down." She indicated the upholstered chair on the other side of the coffee table while she took the matching chair. There was no place else to sit until the room was put back together.

He did as she asked. "I understand you have a daughter. Is she here?"

The man already knew quite a bit about her, she realized. "No. I left her with my sitter who lives across the street."

He studied one of the framed photos that hadn't been knocked off the end table, even though a drawer had been pulled out. "She looks a lot like you, especially the eyes. She's a little beauty."

Natalie looked quickly at the floor, stunned by the personal comment. He'd sounded sincere. So far everything about him surprised her so much she couldn't think clearly.

He turned to focus his attention on Natalie. "You're very composed for someone who's been through so much. Your husband's funeral was just this afternoon, wasn't it?"

"I'm trying to hold it together. If you'd taken any longer to get here, you might have found a screaming lunatic on your hands." She was nervous and talking too fast, but she couldn't help it. "Why would the Texas Rangers want to talk to me? I already answered the detective's questions after they found my husband's body at the hotel. It's hard for me to believe he took his own life, but even more difficult to believe anyone would have wanted to kill him."

"Why do you think it wasn't a suicide?"

Averting her eyes she said, "In my opinion he was too selfish to do it. That's what I told the police. Now I've probably shocked you."

"Not at all. Tell me something. Was your husband right- or left-handed?"

"Left."

"The report said the gun was found in his left hand, but the angle of the bullet raises some questions. Your answer convinces me the gunshot wasn't self-inflicted."

She sat back in the chair. "So someone killed him? Am I a suspect?"

"If this weren't crucial, I wouldn't have insisted on talking to you today. I'll explain, but we're going to need some time, unless you want me to come back this evening."

"No, no." Might as well get this over with. "I'll call my sitter and prepare her for a longer wait. Excuse me." Natalie got up from the chair and hurried into the kitchen to call her friend on her cell phone.

"Don't hate me for this, Jillian, but the Ranger is here now and it sounds like this is going to take a while longer."

"You poor thing."

"It's all a little scary. Would you mind keeping Amy? I hate to do this to you, but he's made it sound like it's really important."

"The girls are playing in the toy room and having a great time. Don't worry about us. I'll give them both dinner. You take your time."

"Bless you, Jillian."

She hung up and rushed back to the living room.

The Ranger eyed her directly. "I know you're full of questions, so I'll get to the point. Your husband's death was a homicide. But that's not the whole of it."

She knit her hands together. "What do you mean?"

"The police stumbled onto some information that has resulted in the case being handled by the Texas Rangers. My captain has assigned it to me. That's why the detective informed me of your phone call instead of following through himself."

"I still don't understand." Something told her she wasn't going to like what he told her.

His expression sobered. "Your husband wasn't the man he claimed to be."

Her adrenaline surged. "What do you mean exactly?"

"I wish there was a way to soften the blow for you. The man you knew as Rodney Parker Harris was actually born Harold Bartlett Park. He was born and raised in Denver, Colorado."

She felt as if her lungs froze while the revelation sank in. "Surely you're mistaken!"

"DNA doesn't lie. His grandparents raised him after his parents were killed in a car crash when he was seven, but they couldn't control him. In his teens he ran away and got into serious trouble. In time he used various aliases and committed crimes that put him in prison for a sixty-year sentence."

"Sixty?" Her cry resounded in the room.

"That's right. He'd only served two of them when he escaped eight years ago during a prisoner transfer to another facility. He eventually ended up here in Austin. There's been an arrest warrant out on him for years."

A gasp escaped her lips. She sprang to her feet. "You're telling me that I was married to a *felon*?"

His eyes looked at her with compassion. "I'm afraid so. You're welcome to see the DNA test results. They prove he's the same man who'd been on his way to another prison when he made his escape with a fellow inmate. That killer is still at large."

Fear raced through her as her thoughts leaped ahead. "Do you think he's the one who broke in here?"

"In time I'll find out who did this."

She shivered as he pulled a paper from his back pocket and handed it to her. "This is what we call a rap sheet."

Her fingers trembled as she opened it. Another cry resounded in the room as she saw the mug shot of the man she'd been married to. It was Rod, but a younger Rod with long black hair and a beard. The good-looking man she'd fallen in love with had short-cropped, dark blond hair and was clean-shaved.

Natalie looked down the list of his crimes that had earned him a sixty-year prison sentence. *"Murder?"* The knowledge that she'd been living with a hard-core criminal caused her to break out in a cold sweat. This was her precious Amy's father?

Her hands went clammy.

Horrified, she dropped the paper and ran to the bathroom where she threw up. When there was nothing left, she rinsed out her mouth and brushed her teeth. To her shock she saw the Ranger waiting for her in the hall while she clung to the sink to recover.

"I wish there'd been an easier way to break this to you," he murmured. "If you want to lie down, I understand."

His kindness got to her. She let go of the sink. "I'd like to pretend none of this is real, but I know it is or you wouldn't be here. No wonder the Texas Rangers are involved. Since I was in the process of divorcing him, I'm sure the police have already decided I killed him."

She left the bathroom and walked to the living room on shaky legs.

"They have to look at a death from every angle." His brows lifted. "Do you own a firearm?"

"No."

"Did your husband?"

She took a steadying breath. "Not that I ever knew about."

He eyed her speculatively through veiled eyes. "Why do *you* think the police would automatically assume you wanted him dead?"

"Because he'd been unfaithful to me. Now that I know the truth about him, it wouldn't surprise me if he'd been with different women throughout our marriage. This is unbelievable." She couldn't disguise the tremor in her voice. "When I had proof of his infidelity, I told him I was filing for divorce and asked him to leave the house."

"How did he handle that?"

"He didn't take me seriously until I warned him I'd call the police to put a restraining order on him. To my surprise he actually packed up and left. It almost seemed too easy, but it makes sense if he knew the FBI was hunting for him."

The Ranger shifted his weight. "Mrs. Harris, the detective's opinion of what happened was only speculation while he investigated your husband's case. It was turned over to me too quickly for any conclusions to be drawn. I haven't seen all the forensic evidence yet. Now that I'm in charge, I prefer to investigate the facts without bringing any bias from other sources. That's why it was so important I spoke with you today. For the time being we're going to keep any more information from being leaked to the press."

"Thank you for that."

"You've received a shock—you're still pale. Sit down and I'll fix you a cup of coffee."

She pressed her lips together. "I imagine you could use some, too. Come into the kitchen. I'll answer your questions while I make it. I need to stay busy." Her suggestion coincided with the doorbell ringing.

"That'll be the team. I'll let them in."

"They'll need to check the garage, too."

"I'll tell them. I also want them to take your fingerprints. I hope that's all right."

He left her long enough to go to the door. Three people, two men and a woman, came in carrying equipment. They put on latex gloves and got to work. After meeting Natalie, one of the men took impressions of her fingers at the kitchen table while the other two checked the room for other prints.

When that was done they went about their business through the rest of the house, dusting surfaces and looking for evidence. The moment was surreal.

The Ranger stepped over several items on the floor to sit at the table. The high chair stood in the cor-

ner. She felt his gaze while she fixed coffee for them.
"Where do you want to start?"

"Before we begin, you need to know I'll be recording our conversation."

Natalie nodded. "Do you take cream or sugar?"

"Both."

So did she. She prepared two mugs and brought
them to the table, sitting opposite him. After being
sick to her stomach, the coffee tasted good, the sugar
reviving her. He appeared to enjoy his, too, draining
most of his mug before sitting back.

"Tell me about yourself first. I saw two women at
the graveside service."

"You were there?" she asked in disbelief.

"Watching from a distance. Were either of them
your relatives?"

"No. I am an only child and my mother died several
years ago. My parents divorced when I was twelve.
My father had an affair and married the woman. They
moved to his hometown in Canada. I never saw or
heard from him again."

"You've been through a lot of heartache in your
life," he observed with empathy. "Now, I'd like you
to tell me about how you met your husband, and I'll
also need you to identify the people in these photos
for me." He handed her the camera and she blinked
when she saw the display, astonished that he'd taken
pictures at the cemetery. She swiped her finger across
the screen, scrolling through the images before giving
him back the camera.

She stared into space. "My husband and I met just

over two and a half years ago. It was November. A controlled-substance delivery from LifeSpan Pharmaceutical didn't check with the head pharmacist's order. The shipment usually comes in a brown box with tamper-proof tape. When I saw that the wrong order had been delivered, I called the plant. Several conversations took place before a man in accounting came on the line. It was Rod.

"He said the problem would be taken care of. The next thing I knew he came to the pharmacy with the correct shipment."

"Where do you work?"

"In the pharmacy at the Grand Central store on Spruce Street, about a mile from here."

"How long have you been a pharmacist?"

"I received my degree seven years ago and I've been working there ever since. The head pharmacist, John Willard, and his wife, Marva, were two of the people at the service today."

"Tell me about the other woman who was there. The older one."

"Ellen Butterworth is a woman from the church who was good friends with my mother."

"I see. All right, back to your story about Rod."

"I thought it was unusual that someone from the accounting department would make the delivery instead of a courier, but Rod reminded me that we'd spoken on the phone once before about a separate issue. He told me he liked the sound of my voice and wondered what I was like, so he'd taken it upon himself to bring the package in person."

"You'd never met him in person before?"

"No. But now that I know he was a criminal, it wouldn't surprise me if he'd seen me somewhere and found out about me ahead of time."

"It wouldn't surprise me, either. Go on."

"Rod came by several times after that and talked me into going out to lunch with him. I was flattered. He was very kind when I told him about my mother's battle with MS. She'd only just died before he came into my life. I found him attractive and we started dating. I learned that he'd been in the military but had been released from service when he was wounded in the lower leg."

"Did you see any proof of his military service?"

"No. I had no reason to question it. He said that during his time in the military, his folks were killed in a car crash in Houston, where he'd been born and raised. The military had helped him find a job from their outreach program and he was interviewed by LifeSpan to work in their accounting department. In time he'd moved his way up and eventually became the director of Finance. One thing led to another and he asked me to marry him."

Her gaze flicked to his. "After looking at that rap sheet, I can see that everything he told me was a spectacular work of fiction." She shook her head. "His healed gunshot wound had to have come from another source that had nothing to do with fighting a war."

"Not the war he described to you. He was injured fleeing arrest after he escaped."

She groaned. "Here I've been living with a killer,

thinking all along how horrible combat must have been for him. He fed me lie after lie and I believed him."

"Harold Park was a consummate sociopath who fooled everyone, including his employers."

The Texas Ranger was trying to make her feel better, but the fact that Harold had lied to more people than just her gave Natalie no comfort.

Chapter Two

"What is it they say? Truth is stranger than fiction?" Natalie's voice quivered. *"The lies..."* She couldn't believe it.

The Ranger nodded and she saw the concern in his eyes. "A good con artist can charm his way into just about anything he wants. He must have wanted you badly. The man worked his way into LifeSpan using fraudulent documents created by a master forger. Harold was the best at what he did."

A shudder swept through her body. "And my mother had just passed away. I was at my most vulnerable." Bitterness welled up inside her. "I fell into his lap like the proverbial apple dropping from the tree. He knew a good thing when he saw it…a woman all alone with her own house paid for and a good job. Exactly the right kind of person for a fugitive to marry to hide his past life of crime."

"Don't go there, Mrs. Harris. He was too clever to give himself away to anyone—he'd eluded the police for years. His mistake was getting caught with another woman. When did you realize it?"

She moistened her lips. "Amy had just turned a year old and I'd planned a little evening party for her with the idea that Rod could be there when he got home from work. But he didn't make it. He called me and said he'd been detained in a meeting but he'd make it up to us. I'd been putting up with those kinds of excuses from the time she was born, but that was the moment it occurred to me my husband was slipping away from me.

"About a month later I called him at work and found out he wasn't there and hadn't been in all day. I knew something was going on he didn't want me to know about."

A grimace marred the Ranger's rugged features. "Did you finally confront him?"

"Yes. About two and a half months ago I was having lunch with my best friend from college. She and her husband live in Arizona, but they'd flown in to attend a friend's wedding and we got together. She happened to mention that she'd bumped into Rod at the short-term airport parking. He'd told her he was dropping off my cousin for a flight."

Natalie shot Saunders a glance. "I don't have a cousin. He'd told my friend a blatant lie. At that point I knew in my heart he'd been having an affair, maybe even several."

After a silence he said, "What's your friend's name and phone number? I'd like to speak to her."

"Colette Barnes. She's in Phoenix." Natalie opened the contacts folder in her cell phone and found him the number.

"Did your husband admit to the affair when you confronted him?"

She bit her lip. "Yes. He was amazingly forthright about it. He accused me of having lost interest in him after Amy was born. It was a lie. He accused me of going back to work to avoid him. That *wasn't* a lie. I needed to get back to the job I knew because intuition told me our marriage wasn't going to make it." She took a deep breath. "It was my mother's story all over again. An unfaithful husband who didn't want to deal with his child."

"Except that your story wasn't your mother's, not by a long shot. A dangerous killer used you. The circumstances aren't comparable. When did you go back to work?"

"Two months ago."

"When you first mentioned divorce, what did he say?"

"He looked all penitent and said he didn't want one. Rod claimed the woman meant nothing to him. He promised never to see her again, but by then I was done. He was so cold and hadn't shown real remorse for any of his behavior, including missing his daughter's first birthday. I couldn't understand it and felt like I'd never known him. Now I know why," she reflected with a heavy heart.

"I've seen his type before. He's the kind that never formed emotional attachments early in life."

She nodded. "He's exactly like that. Later on that night I asked him to pack up and leave the house. I told him I was going to hire an attorney and he'd need one, too. Though the house is in my name, he threatened that he was eligible for half the property and would sue me for it.

"That's when I knew I'd married a stranger. If he wanted to fight over the house he'd never paid for without any concern for his daughter's future, there was no hope for us. I told him we'd have to work out everything in court. But he died before that day came." She paused for a moment. "I never wished him dead, but he's been dead to me for a long time."

Before the Ranger could say anything, the head of the forensics team came into the kitchen to say they were through. Saunders walked them to the front door, where they talked for a few minutes. After they filed out, he turned his attention back to Natalie.

"It turns out that whoever invaded your home must have had a key. There's no sign of a break-in."

"Maybe it was that other inmate you were talking about."

"Maybe, maybe not. But either way I'd say that's enough questions for now. I'll help you clean up your house before I leave."

"Oh, no. That won't be necessary, but thank you."

He zeroed in on her with his gaze. "I insist. Until the surveillance team arrives, I'm not letting you out of my sight."

A chill ran down her spine. "Surveillance?"

"Absolutely. I'm having you and your house guarded around the clock."

Her heart thudded with anxiety. "So you think I'm in danger, then?"

"Rod was a career felon. He could have enemies who wouldn't hesitate to hurt you or your daughter."

"But why?"

"Come on, let's get your place cleaned up while we talk. If you'll give me a towel, I'll get the water out of the carpet."

"You don't need to do that."

"I want to."

She couldn't budge him. In the end she found him a towel that had been thrown on the floor next to the linen closet. "Here you go. I'll clean up the nursery then I'll go for Amy. Jillian needs to be relieved—she's been such a help. I think I'll take her one of these floral arrangements, maybe that large one with the daisies and roses."

"They're beautiful. Who sent them?"

"My boss. The one from the photo. John Willard. He and his wife have proved to be terrific friends."

The Ranger got down on one knee to perform his task and Natalie's eyes lingered on the striking picture of virility he made. She decided he must be a man in a million to pitch in when he didn't have to. She tore herself away and hurried to Amy's room to put everything back in place. When she returned to the living room, she found it and the den restored and in perfect order, with nearly all traces of water gone.

She discovered her guest in the kitchen, washing his hands. When he looked over his shoulder at her, she smiled. "If I didn't know better, I'd think you'd been sent from Hire-a-Husband, that company you see around town. Are you married, Ranger Saunders?"

He chuckled. "No. I haven't had that experience yet."

"After interviewing me, you must be thankful."

"Not every marriage ends in pain—I'm sorry. That sounds incredibly insensitive."

"Not at all."

She watched him dry his hands as he turned to her. "Before any more time passes, I want you to save my cell number in your contacts. If an emergency arises, you can call me any hour of the day or night."

"Thank you," she answered. She retrieved her phone and entered the number he gave her. "Now, will you tell me why you're having me watched?"

His hands went to his hips. "Did you know that LifeSpan fired your husband a month ago?"

"No," she whispered then sank down on the nearest chair. "That would have been after we separated. He never told me." She buried her face in her hands. "What happened?"

"LifeSpan has been losing money. One of the other accountants under your husband started checking back and discovered payments made to a company he could find no record for. They were payments your husband authorized. A full investigation has been started. They're still tracing back to see how long it had been going on. So far they've found over nine-million dollars missing since the beginning of his employment with them."

Natalie gasped. "Rod did that?" She simply couldn't believe it.

"Yes, but the only portion of that money to show up in his personal records was four-hundred thousand."

Her head lifted. "He always wanted to keep our bank accounts separate. It's all making sense now. Four-hundred thousand?"

"Your husband withdrew it from his checking account the day before he was killed, and I'm guessing that whoever trashed your house wanted to get their hands on it."

She shook her head. "We've never had that kind of money, not even with our combined salaries." Her body trembled. "I've been living with a monster."

"It's evident he's been a disturbed man most of his life. I'll learn more when I speak to his grandmother. Though her husband died recently, I understand she's still alive and was able to give the police a few facts about Park. I need to question her."

Natalie's incredulous gaze met his. "That means Amy has a great-grandmother! I can't fathom it. They have to have been in pain for years wondering what had happened to their grandson after he escaped."

"I'm sure that's true. One day soon we'll get all the answers. Will you be available to talk some more tomorrow? Since it'll be Sunday, morning or afternoon will be fine for me."

He was coming by again? Her pulse picked up speed for no reason. "Do you want to come over at eleven or so? Amy will be ready to go down for her nap around then."

"Eleven it is." He walked through to the living room and looked out the front window. "The surveillance team is parked out front in a carpet-cleaning truck. They'll keep an eye on you around the clock to make certain you're safe. I'll see myself out the back door."

She watched his tall, rock-hard physique slip out through the kitchen and disappear from view once he reached the neighbor's yard. Natalie clung to the open door. He'd convinced her that she and Amy could be in danger, but as shocking as all the revelations had been, he'd had a calming effect and she felt confident she wasn't alone in this horror story.

KIT PHONED THE surveillance team from his truck to give them instructions. Once he let them know he was leaving the premises, he drove to the freeway and headed for Marble Falls. He'd have to drive fast to be on time for his mother.

Needing to talk, he used voice commands to dial Cy, a fellow Ranger who was working on another case. He was gratified when he heard his friend's voice over the speakers.

"Hey, Kit. I saw you in TJ's office earlier. What's going on?"

"I've been given a case the captain doesn't want anyone else to know about yet, but I'd like your advice."

"You don't need anyone's advice."

Kit made a strange sound in his throat. "I think I do."

"Where are you?"

"Headed for the rodeo in Marble Falls. Brandon's competing tonight."

"He's racking up great times so far."

"Let's hope he can keep it up. He wants to win that championship in the worst way."

"My bet is on him. Kellie and I are planning to join you for the Las Vegas trip in December. So, what's going on? What did you want to ask me?"

"How did the boss take it when you told him you were going to go undercover as Kellie's husband?"

A long silence followed. "Don't tell me you're planning to do the same thing with this new case?"

Kit exhaled a sigh. "You've just answered my question."

"No—forget what I said. Tell me about the case."

"The wife of the guy who was found dead in his hotel room a week ago could be in serious trouble—someone broke into her house today. But having a surveillance crew watching her could scare off the bad guys. I want to catch them in the act. I'm thinking about posing as her cousin who is taking his retreat from the parish he serves to be with her for the next week."

"A *priest*?"

"Yeah. I'll wear a collar."

Cy made a funny choking sound. "Have you told the widow what you've planned?"

"Nope. I wanted to run it by you first. If you think my plan holds water, then I'll tell the captain. If he gives his approval, then I'll talk to her."

"What haven't you told me yet?"

"Get ready for an earful."

In the next few minutes Kit had revealed everything to his friend, including the fact that the widow had a sixteen-month-old daughter. When he'd finished, a loud whistle came from the other end of the line.

"Harold Park has been on the FBI's Most Wanted list for years! You mean to tell me his wife didn't have a clue?"

"As far as I can tell, not one."

"Maybe she's as big a con artist as he was."

"No. When she saw the rap sheet, she went white as a ghost. I followed her to the bathroom and watched while she lost her lunch. That kind of reaction couldn't have been faked.

"Seriously, Cy, I would have treated this like a normal case until Detective Carr called me about the burglary.

"If you could have seen her house, you'd know that whoever is after the money isn't going to stop. My hunch is that the money he embezzled over the years has been laundered, but he kept four-hundred thousand for quick cash. Someone knew he had it and came to the house hoping to find it stashed there. But they only had that short window of time. I'm afraid they'll be back for a more thorough search. That puts Mrs. Harris and her daughter at risk and changes the way I planned to go about solving the case."

"I hear you. Knowing what I know now, your priest idea sounds inspired. It makes sense that a family member would stay for a while to help her in her time of grief. The collar will stop any gossip, especially if she's attractive."

Kit didn't comment.

"Is she?"

"Is she what?"

"Attractive."

"Yes."

Cy waited for his friend to continue. "Just yes?"

"Yes. Just *yes*!"

"Whoa! For you to clam up like this means she must really be a knockout. Right?"

"That's not what's important here."

"The hell it isn't! I've been there, remember?"

"I do remember. Vividly. That's why I called you." Cy had ended up marrying the woman he'd been protecting.

"You shouldn't have any trouble with the captain. No matter how you do it, he knows Kit Saunders always gets his man. But he'll give you the same advice he gave me. Be careful you don't cross the line."

Kit knew exactly what his friend meant. A strong attraction could complicate a case while you were trying to remain professional. "That won't happen to me. This woman's in shock."

"So was Kellie. But it wore off. When it wears off for Mrs. Harris, that's the time to worry."

"Thanks for the warning, Cy," he muttered. "Give my best to Kellie. Talk to you later."

He ended the call and dialed TJ. Might as well run it by him. Depending on the captain's answer, Kit would have some preparations to make before eleven in the morning when he saw *her* again. He'd have to keep his head down and try to concentrate on his work instead of those eyes, green as lush spring grass.

NATALIE HAD ALREADY used up a week of her ten-day paid leave for family bereavement. She was thankful for a few more days to play with her golden-haired daughter before going back to work.

She was just the sweetest little thing, Natalie thought, as Amy ambled around the house on fairly steady legs, pushing her little grocery cart. Natalie adored her and sang her favorite songs over and over again while she got her dressed and fed her breakfast.

One day Amy would have to know about her father, but that time wouldn't come for years yet. Since he hadn't been around at all since moving to the hotel, she rarely said "dada." Her vocabulary consisted of about twenty words. She loved her farm animals and had *cow* and *pig* down pat. Amy particularly loved the "Eensy Weensy Spider" song and always said the word *spout* very loudly when the time came.

At quarter to eleven Natalie let Amy drink her milk from a sippy cup then put her down for a nap and sang nursery rhymes until the toddler's eyelids fluttered closed. After tiptoeing from the bedroom, Natalie walked back to the kitchen to clean off the high chair and straighten up. The Ranger would be arriving in a few minutes.

She hurried into the bathroom to give her hair a brush-through and put on some lipstick. Today she'd dressed in a blue-and-white print blouse with jeans and sandals. When her cell rang, she went to her bedroom where she'd left it on the bedside table.

She knew when she saw that there was no name on the Caller ID that it had to be him. Miles. The two hang-up calls had come in on her landline. She clicked Answer. Maybe he wouldn't be coming, after all. "Hello?"

"Mrs. Harris? Ranger Saunders here. How are you this morning?"

The vibrancy of his deep voice curled through her. "I'm fine, thank you."

"If I didn't know better, I'd believe you. I'll be by in a minute. I'll be driving a dark red Altima and I'll come to the front door this time. You mentioned putting your little girl down for a nap—I'll knock so I don't disturb her."

"That's very considerate of you. I'll listen for your knock."

"All right, then." He clicked off.

Natalie left her bedroom and paused at the nursery door. She'd played hard with Amy and figured she'd stay asleep for an hour, but probably no longer. By that time, presumably, the Ranger would have finished whatever it was he needed to do and gone.

The news had been shocking enough when she'd learned that Rod had been found shot. But whatever news the Ranger still had to share couldn't possibly be as ghastly as what she'd learned about her husband yesterday. *He'd committed murder.*

Rod hadn't even been his name... She shuddered to think that she'd been married to him all that time. *They'd had a baby together.* Natalie felt violated. She hadn't slept well.

She was still deep in torturous thought when she reached the living room and heard a soft knock. As she opened the door, another shock awaited her. The Ranger who'd left her home yesterday had been so transformed she almost didn't recognize him except for those fabulous hazel eyes and dark brown hair.

Standing in front of her was a tall, well-honed priest carrying a suitcase. He wore a traditional, short-sleeved, tab-collared clergy shirt in a vivid blue color and a pair of black pants. His white collar stood in contrast with the tan of his complexion, and even more brilliant was his smile. It took her breath.

"If you'll invite me in, I'll explain."

Natalie had been staring at him. His remark caused the blood to rush to her face. She opened the door wider so he could pass.

He put the suitcase down on the floor in the small entry hall before following her into the living room. "Your daughter is asleep?"

She nodded. "Please sit down. Can I offer you coffee or a soda?"

"Nothing for me, thanks." This time he opted for the couch while she chose the same chair as before.

"Once in a while we get a case that requires full-time watch to protect an endangered party. After talking to my captain, I see two ways to go about handling your case. We can continue to guard you with a surveillance crew outside your house 24/7 or you can have someone living with you on the inside."

Her pulse started to race. "When you say someone, do you mean *you*?"

"That's right. How would you feel if your fictitious cousin Todd Segal from Wyoming spent his retreat from his parish here, to help you through your bereavement for the next week or so? The choice is yours, of course, but I'd prefer to protect you myself."

The gorgeous Ranger was resourceful, too. She was awed. "I have to admit you look the part." Inwardly she was shaken by the idea of his living in her home.

"Good." His lips twitched. "Being a priest who happens to be your only living relative, aside from your absentee father, won't raise any eyebrows. Those who know your situation will be happy you have someone from the clergy who is family and looking after you since losing your husband. I'll be able to protect you while I carry out the investigation."

Natalie couldn't sit still and got up from the chair. "You think that inmate who escaped with Rod is after the money, don't you?"

He studied her features. "I only mentioned him in passing. After eight years, anything's possible. We have no idea what new contacts Rod's made in that time. I've barely scratched the surface of this investigation. How soon do you plan to go back to work, by the way?"

"On Wednesday."

"That'll have to change, I'm afraid. Until the culprit is caught, it's not safe for your little girl to be left with your friend. This person might resort to kidnapping to get the money."

The color drained from Natalie's face but the Ranger quickly continued.

"Since we don't want any harm to come to you or your daughter, it makes the most sense for you to stay home and take care of her until we know it's safe for you to go back to work. This is an emergency situation. My boss will make the arrangements with Mr. Willard at the pharmacy so your position isn't jeopardized while you take more time off."

Natalie could hardly keep up. She was reeling. "Thank you for that."

"The sooner we can get this case solved, the sooner you can get back to the life you've made for yourself. While you're home, we can work more quickly."

We? "What can I do to help?"

"I need to know your husband's habits, his friends. I'll be going through your personal accounts and phone records. Did he have a laptop?"

"Yes, but he took it with him."

"It wasn't found at the hotel, but the police impounded his car. Maybe it will have turned up there, along with his cell phone. I'll find out when I get the forensics report. Have you gotten rid of any clothes and belongings he may have left here?"

"He only left a few things behind. I don't want anything he owned. I don't even want to see it. Whatever was found at the hotel can be donated or thrown out."

"I'll let them know. As for his things here, we can go through them together. You might recognize clues that wouldn't make sense to anyone else. I guess the crucial question is…would you be uncomfortable with me staying here for a while? Will it make your daughter unhappy? If the answer is yes to either of those questions, then I'll have you watched and proceed on my own."

Everything was happening so fast she could barely

process it. Natalie put her hands in the back pockets of her jeans. "I can tell you'd prefer working from here."

"I would. I came dressed for the part, just in case." He sensed her hesitation. "But please don't let that sway you. We'll get the job done either way."

He seemed decent up front. She didn't know why, especially given the way Rod had deceived her, but she trusted him even though they hardly knew each other. "I want this menace gone from my life as soon as possible. I have confidence in you."

"Thank you for that. My gut tells me the person who ransacked your house isn't finished, and if I'm here 'round the clock I may be able to speed up the process of catching him. But you have to be absolutely comfortable with the decision."

She'd been pacing the floor but came to a standstill. With her own personal Texas Ranger guarding her and Amy day and night, what was there to be worried about? "I *am* comfortable with it," she stated quietly, "but I don't have an extra bedroom."

"That's not a problem. I have a bedroll out in the car. I can put it down anywhere. Hopefully, I won't prove too much of an inconvenience."

"If there's any inconvenience, it will be my daughter waking you up in the middle of the night when she starts crying. It doesn't happen very often, but I'm warning you now her lungs are in perfect working order."

His half smile melted her insides.

"While she's asleep I'll go out to the car and bring in my bedroll and groceries."

"Groceries?

"I told you I came prepared. I stopped at the store on the way here. I'll put my things in the den, out of sight."

He'd thought of everything, she marveled. "Let me give you the second remote for the garage so you can pull your car in. I've got an extra house key for you, too. I asked Rod to give them back to me when he left for good."

"Thank you." He followed her into the kitchen where she started searching through a drawer.

"How soon do you think the police will release his car?"

"I'll find out tomorrow."

"I only ask because the baby quilt I made for Amy is missing. I can't think why it would be in his car, but it's the only place I haven't looked. We only ever went places as a family in my car. He said his was for business only."

"Everything they found when it was impounded will be returned to you."

She nodded and handed him the key chain with the remote.

"Be right back."

So far, so good.

Kit walked outside, aware the surveillance team was still parked a little ways down the street. He phoned them and told them they could leave, but he wanted them back at six-thirty in the morning.

After activating the remote, he drove into the straightened-up garage and then pulled Natalie's car inside, next to the laundry room door. He got out and made a first trip into the house with the groceries.

While she put the items away, he went back for his tool bag and suitcase. He took his things to the den with its floor-to-ceiling bookcase on one wall. The entertainment center took up the other wall. He noticed more framed pictures on the end tables; pictures of Natalie with a woman he guessed must be her mother.

He could see where Natalie Harris got her beauty. And the barefoot little girl in a ruffled, lemon-colored top and shorts who now came into the den with one of her push toys had the look of both of them. She stopped short of bumping into Kit's shoe and looked up at him with her grayish-green eyes.

Was she about to cry at seeing a stranger? It didn't even matter—Kit decided she was the cutest little girl he'd ever seen.

Natalie had come into the den and leaned down to address her daughter. "Amy? This is Ranger Saunders. He's going to stay with us for a while."

"Ranger Saunders is too hard to say. You can call me Kit."

Surprised, Natalie stood. "Kit? I thought you said your name was Miles."

"It is, but most people call me Kit. It's my nickname." He hunkered down next to Amy. "Hi, honey. What's your name?"

"Tell him you're called Amy," her mother urged. "You can say it. Ay-mee."

"Me," her daughter mimicked, leaving out the *A*.

He smiled and pointed to his chest. "I'm Kit. Kit."

"You can tell her mind is working on it," Natalie murmured.

"Kit," the little girl finally pronounced.

"Yes." He nodded, pleased she'd picked it up so quickly. "I'm Kit, and you're Amy. Now what's that toy you're pushing?"

She immediately started moving it around, showing him she understood.

"That makes a fun noise," he said, encouraging her.

Pretty soon she'd circled the room. When she looked to see his reaction and smiled, it tugged on his emotions.

"Cow," she said and ran out of the den on her sturdy legs.

Natalie eyed him in amusement. "She's gone for her favorite animal in her toy box."

While they exchanged a silent glance, Amy came back clutching the brown-and-white-spotted plush cow in her hand. She toddled over to Kit, almost stumbling, and held it up. "Cow."

"That's right. It's a cow." Kit took it. "Moo."

"Moo-oo," she repeated with all the earnestness in her then hurried out of the den.

"Oh, Kit. I'm sorry. Now that she's got a captive audience in you she's going to bring you all her farm animals."

"I'm not complaining." He sat on the couch and put the cow on the coffee table. Before long the golden-haired cherub returned and handed him a purple pig. "What's this?" he asked her.

"Pig!"

Her enthusiasm caused him to burst into laughter. "That's a colorful pig. What sound does it make?"

Amy tried to imitate the oink. He couldn't believe she was so adorable.

"Oink, oink," he grunted. Her giggle delighted him. "You're without a doubt the cutest, smartest little girl on the planet. That's because you've got a terrific mother." Though her father had been a criminal, he'd done one thing right in his life to have helped create this angel.

"Come on, sweetie." Natalie swept her up in her arms. "Let's go out to the kitchen and give you a little snack."

Kit followed them, enjoying the interplay between mother and daughter. After Amy had been put in her high chair, Natalie fastened a bib around her neck. Then she sliced half a banana into small pieces and put them on the tray. He took a seat at the table to watch while the little girl took her time eating each mouthful of the fruit.

He glanced at Natalie. "Since you weren't expecting a guest to stay with you, I thought I'd fix us some lunch with the groceries I bought. How does that sound?"

"I was just going to ask if you'd like a sandwich."

"Sounds good, but I'll do it."

She smiled, but he didn't know what else was on her mind because her cell phone rang, reminding him of the reason he was here.

"Go ahead and answer it, but put it on speaker."

Her smile faded before she reached for the phone and checked the Caller ID. "It's Jillian."

"Good. Let her know a cousin is visiting you and you won't be going to work for a while, so you won't be needing her services. The less she knows, the better."

"I agree." Her voice trembled. She clicked on. "Jillian—"

"Hi. I just want to know if you're okay."

"I'm much better today."

"That's good. You sound better. I saw a car in your driveway earlier. If you have company, call me when you have time to talk."

"It's all right, I have time now. I was going to call you today, anyway. My cousin Todd is here from Wyoming for a few days, so I'm taking more time off of work and won't be needing you to look after Amy next week."

"Oh. Okay... I'm glad you have family with you."

"Me, too. Thank you for everything you've done for me, Jillian. I'm hoping life can get back to normal soon."

"I hope so, too. Take care, Natalie."

"You, too. I'll call you soon."

"Okay. 'Bye."

She'd done well. The plan was in place.

Chapter Three

Natalie disconnected and turned to Kit, who was making sandwiches. "Jillian knows there's a lot I haven't told her."

"But you told her enough so she won't be planning on babysitting for you next week. This way she and her daughter will be safe."

"Thank heaven for that. If anything were to happen to her because of Rod…"

"It won't. That's why I've taken precautions."

While he assembled cold cuts and cheese, she reached for a paper towel and got busy cleaning up the pieces of banana Amy had thrown on the floor. Natalie darted the Ranger a look of frustration. "A week in my house and you'll find that half her food doesn't make it to her mouth. If you have any little nieces or nephews, you know what I mean."

"Not yet. My brother, Brandon, is a professional steer wrestler—he's headed for the championship competition in Las Vegas in December, as a matter of fact. One day he'll settle down and have a family."

"How old is he?"

"Twenty-eight. Two years younger than I am. This will be his last year on the circuit."

"How exciting! Are you a rodeo fan, too?"

"I used to be a steer wrestler myself. We took turns being wrestler and hazer for a long time. But I quit when I went into law enforcement."

"From steer wrestler to Ranger. Both put your life at risk."

He studied her features. "Have you ever been to a rodeo?"

"Many times while I was in college. Remember my friend in Phoenix? She used to be a barrel racer. We rode horses on her parents' property and it was fantastic to watch her speed around the barrels. I tried it, but I was a complete failure. She taught me about the various events. Steer wrestling is incredibly dangerous."

"But you liked it?"

"I loved it all!"

Kit was enjoying their conversation so much he almost forgot he should be working on her case. Talk about crossing the line. Already he was getting too close to it.

Within ten minutes they sat eating lunch while Natalie fed Amy some Cheerios. Kit chuckled to watch her tease her daughter. She'd move her hand around and Amy's little mouth would follow, open in anticipation.

"Tell me something, Natalie. Has Amy ever ridden on a jet?"

Her eyes widened. "No."

"What would you think if we took her for her first ride tomorrow morning to Denver? I need to talk to

Rod's grandmother in person. The detective said she's been told her grandson passed away. Seeing Amy would do her a world of good and could jog her memory. I'm hoping she'll be able to give me some background information about his teenage years that might help me fit some of the pieces of the puzzle together."

Natalie's face lit up. "If she was a loving grandmother, then I know she'd be thrilled to see her great-grandchild. I could take some pictures of them together for Amy's baby book."

Kit was pleased with her reaction. "I'll make the arrangements. It's less than a two-hour flight. We won't have to be there long."

"I thought about her last night…Rod's grandmother. What's her name?"

"Gladys Thomas Park."

"He never said a word about a living relative. The poor thing lost a married son and a grandson. How cruel life can be…" Her voice trailed off.

"All the more reason for us to go there and surprise her. In the meantime, where will you be the most comfortable to answer some more questions?"

"The living room. Amy will bring her trove of treasures from the nursery and stay busy going back and forth for another few hours."

He got up and cleared the table while she wiped Amy's hands and face and got her down from her high chair. When she told him she'd finish up, Kit went to the den for his suitcase. He took it to the bathroom and swapped his clerical shirt for a casual sport shirt.

Any time he needed to answer the door, he'd quickly put it back on.

When he returned to the living room, Natalie and Amy looked up from the floor where they were working on a puzzle. They made a beautiful sight. Both pairs of eyes wandered over him. "So my cousin is on vacation from the priesthood this afternoon?"

"Yup. It's Ranger Saunders reporting for duty. If you're ready to get started, I'll turn on the digital recorder." She nodded and he proceeded. "First question. Your income taxes. Where do you keep a copy?"

"Rod prepared them at work and kept everything there."

"Then I'll have to speak to the people at LifeSpan. Did he have the Sentra when he met you?"

"Yes. He said he'd bought it three years earlier."

"From a dealership here in Austin?"

"I don't know."

"Did he continue making monthly payments on it?" Amy toddled over to give him a horse from her farm collection. "Thank you, honey." She smiled and got busy again.

"No. Rod said he'd paid it off."

"Do you know where he kept the title?"

"At the office with everything else. You've probably never met a wife so in the dark about her husband's dealings. It never occurred to me not to trust him. I've been so naive, I'm embarrassed and ashamed."

He grimaced. Harold Park had put her on a short leash. He sat forward in the chair and handed Amy a dog she'd dropped. He made a barking sound she tried to imitate before handing him a goat. "There's no shame in trusting someone."

Natalie looked up at him. "My mother never trusted my father and always questioned him about everything. They had a lot of fights. At twelve I was old enough to understand their marriage wasn't happy. I swore that if I ever got married, I would never do that to my husband. If she were still alive, I'd ask her to forgive me.

"After what's happened to me, I'm thinking my father must have done something to ruin their marriage from the beginning, but Mom tried to shield me from the worst of it. She didn't believe in divorce. Thank heaven, she didn't live long enough to find out I married a true, hardened criminal. Mother and daughter both lucked out, didn't we?"

Kit took a deep breath. "Bad marriages happen to wonderful people. Tell me about the early days before Amy came along. What did you do? Did you take trips, go out a lot? Did you make friends with other couples? Did he have a favorite sport or hobby? I'm trying to get a picture of the pattern of your lives."

The answers to those questions and many others— How much time did he spend away from home? Did he take the occasional business trip? Was he an early riser? Did he get home from work late? If so, how often? Did she go to his work once in a while? Which people at work did he associate with?—took up the rest of the day. Natalie's observations led Kit to realize Harold Park had been the worst kind of controlling husband.

By nightfall Natalie had fed Amy dinner and now

whisked her off for her bath. Kit took advantage of the time alone to prepare for the trip and make half a dozen phone calls to get his investigation started.

Their flight to Denver was booked for eight fifteen. It meant they'd have to be at the airport by six thirty. Kit hadn't been on a trip since April when he'd flown to Billings, Montana, to watch his brother compete at the Wrangler Rodeo Competition.

Natalie peeked into the den to say good-night. Kit looked up from the desk. "We'll need to leave the house at six."

"We'll be ready."

"I've already taken the liberty of putting Amy's car seat in the back of my car. When we reach the airport, it will go on the plane with us. Technically, Amy qualifies as a lap baby, but I want her secured no matter what. In Denver we'll install it in the rental car."

"Thank you for taking care of that. I've been wondering how it was all going to work. Don't stay up too long. Good night, Kit."

"Good night, Mrs. Harris."

"Please call me Natalie."

He nodded.

Once she'd vanished, he walked through the house to make sure windows and doors were locked. When he finally stretched out on the floor of the den in his sleeping bag, Kit rolled onto his side. He'd put his .357-caliber SIG Sauer halfway under his pillow, very much hoping he wouldn't have to use it while he stayed here. Natalie was living through a horror story with her daughter and didn't need anything else to add to her pain.

He was determined to solve this case as soon as possible because already he could tell he was emotionally involved to a greater degree than he should be.

"Be careful not to cross the line," Cy had warned him.

Unfortunately that advice had come too late. In truth Kit found himself looking forward to tomorrow with more excitement than the occasion warranted.

AT 11:00 A.M. they entered the Cottonwood Nursing Home in downtown Denver. Amy had sat on Natalie's lap for most of the flight, but she seemed happy enough to be held by the Ranger as they spoke to the people at the front desk. Everywhere they went, whether it was the tourists on the plane or the staff here, people stared at the fabulous-looking, dark-haired priest holding Natalie's little golden girl.

"Father Segal? If you'll go down the hall and around the corner on the left, you'll find Gladys Park in room 120. She's had bouts of pneumonia that have weakened her. This is the best time of day to visit. Once she's had lunch, she usually sleeps and it's difficult to wake her."

As they walked along, Natalie got a good feeling about the clean, nicely decorated facility. If Gladys's care was as good, that was the most important thing. When they reached her door, they found it open. The ninety-two-year-old woman was in bed with the head raised. She was listening to the radio.

Kit nodded to Natalie. "Go ahead and talk to her while I hold Amy."

Her heart pounded extra hard as she walked over to the side of the bed. She'd already made up her mind to keep certain facts to herself to be kind. The woman's eyes were closed. "Gladys?"

"Yes," she responded without opening them.

"My name is Natalie. I've come to visit you."

"That's nice."

"I used to know your grandson Harold."

A long silence ensued before the woman turned her head toward Natalie. "You knew Harold?"

"Yes. I was married to him. We live in Austin, Texas."

That revelation caused her eyes to open. "Come closer. My eyes aren't what they used to be."

Natalie leaned toward her. "Can you see me better?"

"A little. What's your name?"

"Natalie."

"You married Harold? When?"

"Two and a half years ago."

"I haven't seen him since he was sixteen. He went to prison. He must be thirty-three now."

"He passed away last week," she said gently. "Of complications from an infection. But we have a daughter, sixteen months old. Her name is Amy. Would you like to see her?"

Gladys tried to lift her head off the pillow but she was too frail and feeble. "You brought my great-granddaughter to see me?"

Tears filled Natalie's eyes. "I did. My cousin, Father

Segal, came with us." She looked over her shoulder at Kit who moved toward her. She reached for Amy.

"Can you see her?"

"Bring her closer."

Natalie leaned in close with her little girl. "Amy, this is your great-grandmother Gladys."

The older woman lifted her hand to touch Amy's. "Oh…my precious girl. I wish I could see better, but I have glaucoma." In the background Kit was taking pictures of the three of them with his phone.

"She's golden blond and has gray-green eyes."

"Harold had gray eyes like his mother. His parents were killed in a car crash you know."

"Yes. Harold told me."

"We did what we could for him, but he was inconsolable. I think something happened inside his head. When he got older, he got mean and kept running away. We didn't know what to do to help him. I didn't know he'd been released from prison. I'm glad he met someone like you after all those terrible years. You sound so kind."

"Natalie is a very kind woman, Mrs. Park," Kit interjected. Natalie moved far enough away so Kit could lean toward Gladys.

"Who are you?"

"I'm Natalie's cousin. She wanted you to meet your great-granddaughter before any more time passed. We flew here from Austin with Amy."

Tears trickled out of the corners of the older woman's eyes. "My prayers have been answered."

"What prayers were those?" His question was so tender, the sound of his tone pierced Natalie's heart.

"That I would hear some news of our grandson. Now that you've brought my great-granddaughter to see me and let me know Harold has gone to heaven, I can die knowing he met a wonderful woman and had a baby."

While the older woman wept, Natalie buried her wet face in Amy's hair.

"Is there anything I can do for you, Gladys?" Kit asked.

"Did you know Harold?"

"No," he answered. "Tell me about him."

"He was a beautiful-looking boy and a good child."

"Did he have good friends?"

"Not after he changed. There was one boy he ran around with. They got into trouble all the time."

"Do you remember his name?"

"Salter. Jimmy Salter. I'll never forget him. His parents couldn't do anything with him, either. My husband and I felt like such failures…you can't imagine."

"What did your husband do for a living?" Natalie interjected.

"He was an architect for a firm here in Denver. We had hopes our son might be an architect one day." Her voice faded.

"In his last years of freedom Harold became an accountant."

"Harold? An accountant? Oh, my. He hated school."

"Which high school did he attend?" Kit asked.

"Tabor High."

"Did you work when you were a young, married

woman?" Natalie discovered she wanted to know everything this woman could tell her.

"Oh." She gave a half laugh. "I taught girls' physical education at Tabor High for thirty-eight years. I used to run marathons. Now I can't make this body work anymore."

"Amy runs constantly. I think she might have inherited that trait from you."

Natalie's gaze swerved to Kit's. Streams of unspoken thoughts ran between them. "Do you have friends who visit?"

"Oh, yes. People from our church. I've been well looked after. My husband saw to that. But we couldn't do anything for our Harold." She wept again.

"Yes, you did," Natalie contradicted her. "You gave him a wonderful home after his parents died. No one could have done more, but I'm sure you're tired now. I'll come to visit you again soon and bring Amy. I want her to get to know you."

There was no more talk. They'd worn her out. Natalie held Amy until her little girl started to squirm to get down. Kit must have seen the signs and plucked her out of Natalie's arms. Gladys had gone to sleep.

With tacit agreement they left the room and walked down the hall to the reception area. Kit approached the desk. "We had a nice visit with Gladys and can see she's well taken care of. We'll come again soon."

"She'll love that."

Natalie left her name and phone number in case they needed to call her. Then she joined Kit and they left the nursing home for the rental car.

Kit got behind the wheel. "What do you say we stop at a drive-through for lunch and go to a park for a little while before we have to head to the airport? It'll give Amy a chance to run around."

"That's a wonderful idea."

Before long they located a nearby park. They found a nice spot for their picnic and Natalie laid Amy down on a quilt to change her diaper. With that accomplished, she disposed of it in the diaper bag then sanitized her hands.

Kit opened the sacks. Natalie fed Amy some yogurt with fruit. She ate part of Natalie's grilled-cheese sandwich while Kit tucked into a ham-and-cheese melt. They drank soda and laughed at Amy's antics as she walked around on unsteady legs in the grass, carrying her cow. It went everywhere with her.

"I don't think I fooled Gladys. She had to have known he'd escaped from prison and was a fugitive. I'm just thankful she didn't press me."

Kit eyed her thoughtfully. "In my opinion she was so thrilled you gave her news about Harold and let her see her great-granddaughter, she was willing to go with what you told her."

"She's a lovely, bright woman. So was her husband. It means—"

"It means Harold's parents were great people, too," he interrupted her. "Something *did* go wrong inside his brain. It's tragic, but it happens. Are you glad we came?"

"Oh, yes, Kit. Thank you for making it happen. I've learned so much…the kinds of things I'll be happy to tell Amy about when she's older. But what about you? Do you think the name of that former friend of his could give you a lead?"

"I'm counting on it, but I'll look into it tomorrow. Tonight I'd like you to call your friend in Phoenix and ask her when would be a good time for a visit. We'll fly out there. The sooner the better. Wednesday if we could."

Natalie felt a fluttering in her chest. "I'll call her after nine when she's off work."

"Good. I need to talk to her in person. Her answers could prove crucial to this case."

Natalie waited until Amy drank the fresh milk she'd poured into her sippy cup. "All right, young lady, it's time to get you back to the car."

Time to bring an end to this amazing day with Kit Saunders, Texas Ranger *extraordinaire* in every sense of the word. In three days Natalie's life had undergone a drastic change. She could tell she wasn't the same person who'd walked into her house on Saturday to find it violated the way Rod had violated her. The life she'd had with him seemed light-years away.

TUESDAY MORNING KIT was up and out of the house early. He left a note for Natalie that he needed to get to headquarters and that a surveillance team in a television-repair van was parked near the house to keep watch over her until he got back.

He'd dressed in his clerical shirt and headed for the office. Before he did anything else, he needed to talk to his boss. Everyone who saw him walking down the hallway did a double-take before he reached the captain's inner sanctum and knocked on his partially open door.

"Come in."

Kit did as he was told. "TJ?"

The gray-haired man looked up and gave Kit the once-over. "I thought I'd seen it all. Don't get any ideas about changing careers, *Father* Saunders. We need you around here."

"Thanks." Relieved to find his boss in a good mood, Kit sat.

"Give me an update."

After five minutes TJ had been brought up to speed. "What's your next move?"

"I'll be in my office for a while. I've got to check out the information on Jimmy Salter. After that I'll touch base with Forensics. Tomorrow I plan to fly to Phoenix. Mrs. Harris's friend may hold the key to the person who killed Harold Park."

TJ regarded him shrewdly. "I take it you've cleared Mrs. Harris as a suspect?"

"I'm one-hundred-percent certain she's innocent of everything except falling in love with an expert con man."

"Are you taking her with you again?"

"Yes. I believe her friend will be more comfortable with Mrs. Harris there."

"What about the toddler?"

Just thinking about the little girl put a smile on Kit's face. "Amy will be coming, too. I don't want her separated from her mother."

"So it's Amy now." TJ looked amused.

Kit could see where this conversation was headed and got to his feet. "I won't take up any more of your time."

"Watch your back. Let me know if you need more help."

"Thanks, TJ."

Once he'd settled at his desk, Kit made two calls to Denver. The first was to the school board to request information on Jimmy Salter and his family from their records. His second call was to the police in Denver to have them search their files for a rap sheet on a Jimmy Salter. Thanks to Mrs. Park he had approximate dates to go on.

With that accomplished he called Forensics. Stan, the lead forensics expert, invited him to come downstairs to discuss what he knew at this point in the case.

Before he could leave, his cell rang. He saw Natalie's name and his pulse sped up. Maybe she'd reached her friend. "Hi."

"Hi. You told me to phone if I got one of those hang-up calls. It just happened."

Kit checked his watch. It was ten to ten. "I'll get someone on it immediately. That's three so far, right?"

"Yes. The two last week and now this one."

"Okay. Did you reach your friend?"

"My call went to Colette's voice mail. I asked her to call me back ASAP."

"Then I'm sure she will. I'll be here awhile if anything else comes up. How's Amy?"

"Running around as usual with toys in both hands."

He chuckled. "See you later."

On the way down the hall Kit almost collided with his friend Luckey, who grinned. "Well, well. Do I call you *Monsignor*?"

"It's Father Segal."

"On you it actually looks believable. Cy told me you've gone undercover on the Harris case and she's really hot."

"I didn't say a word about her."

"That's why Cy figured it out. Where's the fire?"

"I'll tell you later."

"I want to know chapter and verse. If you need backup, I'm available."

"Thanks. I just might need you."

Kit hurried past him and took the stairs two at a time to reach the bottom floor where the forensics department was located. Once through the doors he stopped at the office of another colleague. Rafe.

The man smiled. "The collar looks good on you, Kit."

"Thanks."

"What can I do for you?"

"Check on the call that went to the Rodney Harris home maybe five, six minutes ago." He wrote down the number of Natalie's landline. "I need to know who made it, anything you can."

"Will do."

"I'll be in with Stan when you've got any information for me."

He moved on and found Stan comparing pictures

on a screen. "Stan? Have you got prints from the Harris home yet?"

"We're still working on them, but we have the prints off Harris's cell and laptop. There were several different sets on and inside the car. They found a couple of long black hairs on the front passenger seat. We're running the prints that aren't Harris's or his wife's through the AFIS database. I'll email you a copy of the results." He eyed Kit but didn't remark on the collar.

"Great."

"Les has finished going over the car. It was totally clean. By that I mean there wasn't anything in the glove compartment, no litter. Nothing."

"When he checked the spare tire, did he see anything that could give us a clue where the car was serviced or purchased?"

"No. He found the laptop and cell phone in the trunk. They found a thumb print on the lid and we're looking at it now. The two items were wrapped in a baby quilt, of all things."

"Obviously it was wrapped to hide it from view."

"You'll notice two hundred and eighty thousand miles on the car."

Interesting. Why would an accountant have done so much driving? "Later in the day someone from the staff will drive it over to Mrs. Harris's house with the deceased's personal effects."

"Thanks, Stan."

Kit would look through everything with her later. He hoped Natalie could remember how many miles were on the car when she'd first met her husband. If he had a travel allowance, Kit knew the mileage on the car would be way over the limit.

"Kit?" He turned to see Rafe coming toward him.

"What did you find?"

"That call originated from a throw-away phone."

"I thought so. Appreciate it."

Whoever had broken into Natalie's house was anxious to get back in. Maybe the culprit thought the money had been stashed in the attic, unless he'd checked it out the first time. Kit phoned Stan.

"Kit?"

"One more question. Did the forensics team take prints on the trap door leading to the attic at the Harris residence?"

"Let me check." He came back on the phone quickly. "No."

"Okay. Thanks."

Forensics should have checked that. Kit would do it after he went back to Natalie's house. Now that he was through here, he'd head over to LifeSpan Pharmaceutical and get the status on the investigation of the accounts fraud.

When he reached the car in the underground parking, he removed his clerical shirt and put on the brown Western shirt he'd brought, the badge attached to the front pocket. Then he phoned Natalie.

"Hi. I just found out Rod's car will be delivered to your house later today. They'll phone you first. I just wanted you to know what to expect. You'll be happy to learn that the baby quilt you made was found in the trunk."

"Oh—I'm so glad. I hated losing it. Thanks for letting me know."

"Of course. While I have you on the phone, do you have any idea of the mileage on Rod's car when you first started going out with him?"

After a silence she said, "No. Like I said, I simply wasn't that curious. Sorry."

"Not a problem. See you later."

But before he could put his key in the ignition, his cell rang. After a glance at the Caller ID he answered.

"Brandon? What are you doing calling me at this time of day? I thought you'd be out practicing with Scott!" He always liked talking with his brother.

"You're not going to believe what happened. Scott was in an accident this morning and went to the hospital with a broken leg."

"You can't be serious." Kit's eyes closed tightly. His brother had just lost his hazer for at least three months. The timing couldn't be worse considering his schedule on the rodeo circuit. "How did it happen?"

"A semi's brakes failed and it T-boned Scott's Silverado before it ended up in a field. It was a miracle no one was killed, but Janie's a wreck." Brandon sounded shaken.

"I'm sure she is." He ran a hand through his hair. "What hospital is he in?"

"Seton."

Kit would have to give Scott a call.

"I don't know what to do, bro. We have a competition coming up this Saturday night in San Antonio. I've got to find another hazer, but that takes time."

"Ask Whitey. He's worked with you before."

"I'm afraid he's off his game these days."

That meant Whitey was drinking again. "Try Pete."

"He's not up to speed anymore."

"Then spread the word you need a hazer fast!"

"I'm sure I'll find one, but not in time for Saturday night."

Kit had too much on his mind to give his brother's problem a lot of thought. "Can you afford to give this rodeo a miss while you search for someone else?"

"I guess I might have to."

Kit heard the disappointment in his voice.

"Kit?"

He could hear it coming. "Yes?"

"Are you working on a big case these days?"

"Yup. In fact I'm in the middle of it right now and I have to go. I'll call you later when I get a chance." He rang off and headed across town. It didn't surprise him that his phone rang again as he pulled into the guest parking lot at the LifeSpan Pharmaceuticals.

He clicked on. "Hi, Mom. I heard the news."

"It's a darn shame, Kit."

"I agree."

"But Brandon was counting on winning in San Antonio. Is there any way you could haze for him on Saturday night? You know better than anyone how important it is, and there's no one better on a horse than you."

That's right, Mom. Butter me up to make me feel guilty.

"I'm working undercover on a big murder case. It's

possible I might have to be in Arizona this weekend."
Natalie and Amy would be with him. He found he
didn't want anything to get in the way of his plans. "If
I can see a way to do it, I'll call him, but don't count
on it."

Though his mother didn't say a word and never
would, he could hear her thoughts.

*Your father never put his Ranger duties ahead of
his family when it counted.*

And that hurt.

Chapter Four

Natalie was in the middle of making tacos for dinner when she heard her cell ring. There was no Caller ID, but Kit had given her a heads-up earlier in the day. "Hello?"

"Mrs. Harris? I've brought your husband's car home. It's in the driveway with the key in the ignition. I've left it unlocked."

"Thank you so much."

"You're welcome."

After she hung up, she turned to Amy who was in her playpen chewing on one of her doughnut toys. "I'll be right back, sweetie."

She left the kitchen and hurried through the house to the front door. When she opened it, she found it strange to see Rod's Sentra again, knowing he was out of their lives permanently. Her feelings were so dead where he was concerned, she felt as if she'd turned into an entirely different person.

She opened the trunk and reached inside for the quilt. The cell phone and laptop were in there, too. She gathered everything in her arms and shut the trunk before rushing back into the house.

Natalie put the things down on the couch but carried the quilt to the kitchen. "Look what I've got, honey!"

Amy pointed at it, but kept playing with her red doughnut. While she was still content, Natalie took the quilt to the laundry room to be run through a wash and dry cycle. Before doing anything else, she walked to her bedroom and gathered the rest of Rod's things from her closet. Kit had mentioned wanting to look through them, so she carried them to couch.

Once he'd checked everything, she would throw out the last vestiges of Harold Park. A shudder ran through her body. She couldn't wait to be rid of anything that reminded her of him. That included his car. She'd take it to a used-car dealer to sell or, better yet, donate it.

While she finished cutting up some tomatoes and avocado, her cell rang. She saw that it was Colette and took the call.

"Oh, Colette. Thanks so much for calling me back."

"Of course. I feel terrible that I couldn't fly to Austin for the graveside service, but Chad had his appendix removed that morning and I had to stay home with him."

"I understand totally. To be honest I'm glad you didn't come." Natalie's voice shook.

"What's wrong?"

"Do you have a few minutes?"

"Sure I do."

Natalie gave her friend a brief account of what had happened.

"My gosh, Natalie. I don't believe it. Rod was a felon?"

"Afraid so. There's so much to tell you, but not right now. The reason I'm calling is because the Texas Ranger who's working on the case wants to fly to Phoenix to talk to you about the day you saw Rod with that other woman."

"You mean the woman who wasn't your cousin?"

"That's the one. When would it be okay to come? He says the sooner the better. Amy and I will fly there with him."

"Come tomorrow. Chad is feeling better every day. I'll meet you at the airport to save you time."

"That would be wonderful! I'll tell him and get back to you on the exact time."

"Good. I'll wait for your call. Stay safe."

"With a Texas Ranger guarding us, I'm not worried. Talk to you later."

No sooner had she hung up than the phone rang again. She picked up and said hello.

"Hi, Natalie." Kit's deep voice resonated through her. "I'm almost to the house. I don't want you to be alarmed when I let myself in."

"Thank you." He was so considerate, she was amazed. "Just so you know, Rod's car is out in the driveway. The key is still in the ignition."

"In that case I'll park his car in front so I can drive into the garage."

"I'd like to get rid of it, maybe through a donation if I can." The words rushed out of her, revealing her state of mind.

"Forensics is done with it, so you're free to do whatever you want."

"I still haven't found the title."

"Don't worry about it. You can donate without one."

Relief swept through her. "That's good. I have news for you. Colette called and said we can fly to Phoenix any time tomorrow. She's offered to meet us at the airport."

"That's terrific news. I'll see you in a minute."

Natalie lifted Amy and put her in the high chair with one of her toys. Then she folded up the playpen and put it back in the nursery. Before long she heard the garage door lift. To know he would be there in a minute made her excited, and it had nothing to do with the fact that his job as a Ranger was to keep her safe while he solved this case.

In a very short time she'd gotten use to this temporary arrangement and had made dinner with him in mind. *Remember it's only temporary, Natalie.* But try telling her heart that when he appeared in the kitchen wearing the clerical shirt. There was no way to shut out his arresting masculine appeal.

"Something smells good."

"Are you hungry?"

"Famished."

"I've made tacos."

"Give me a minute and I'll join the two of you. Here's the key to Rod's car."

When he disappeared, she got out a jar of junior sweet potatoes and lamb for Amy. Kit walked in a few minutes later wearing a claret-colored polo shirt and jeans. It was getting harder and harder to keep her eyes off him.

"Help yourself to anything you want, Kit."

His smile made her pulse race. "Since you're busy feeding the cherub, can I fix you a plate, too?"

"I'd love it."

She'd fried half a dozen tortillas. One taco was enough for her. But when she saw that he'd eaten four filled shells along with a large helping of tossed salad, she wondered whether she'd made enough.

He finally sat back in the chair and centered his hazel gaze on her. "That was delicious."

"I can make more."

"If I take another bite, I won't have room for the chocolate-marshmallow ice cream I bought."

Natalie grinned. "So that's your favorite dessert?"

"One of them. I'll get it. Would you like some, too?"

"Sounds good."

"Do you think Amy would like a taste?"

"Of course, but she's not getting the chance yet. Once she discovers chocolate, all my hopes of feeding her healthy foods will go right out the window."

Laughter rumbled out of him, grabbing the little girl's attention.

"Kit—" Amy spoke his name with a happy smile.

"That's my name, sweetheart." The tender look he gave her daughter touched Natalie deeply.

Kit dished out two bowls of the ice cream and handed one to Natalie.

She took a mouthful. "This is yummy. I haven't had this flavor in years."

His dessert disappeared in a hurry. "I've loved it since I was a little kid."

"What else did you love as a boy?"

"Oh…the usual. Snakes, fireworks, anything scary or that went boom."

A chuckle escaped her lips. "Your poor mom."

"Yup. With two sons to raise, she had her hands full while Dad was out on a case."

Her head lifted. "A case? What kind? What did he do?"

He eyed her through narrowed lids. "He was a Texas Ranger."

"Was?"

"Dad was killed in a shootout when I was seventeen."

"Oh, no—I'm so sorry." She bit her lip. "How hard to have lost him that early in life. I'm surprised it didn't put you off becoming a Ranger."

He shook his head. "Just the opposite. In 1842 Sam Houston got a law passed that provided for a company of mounted men to act as Rangers under Captain John Coffee 'Jack' Hays. My ancestor was one of them."

"You're serious?"

"Yup. Three of the other Rangers who are my close friends are also descendants from the original company. The guys at headquarters have nicknamed us the Sons of the 40."

"Wait a minute. I saw the four of you on TV. You brought down that huge drug ring!"

He nodded.

"I thought I'd seen you before." She studied his rugged features. "I guess it isn't all that surprising that you wanted to be like your father. The Texas Rangers are legendary and honorable. The kind of men any child would look up to."

"That described Dad."

Natalie thought of her own father. Those adjectives didn't apply to him.

"Captain Hays and his company of forty defeated the Comanche raid at Bandera Pass, protecting the southern and western portions of the Texas frontier. Their story was passed down through my father's side of the family. I knew that one day I wanted to be a Ranger, too."

"I guess with a heritage like that, you couldn't help but want to follow in your father's footsteps."

"Something like that. Throughout high school and college I did steer wrestling, but it couldn't last. So I quit to go to the police academy. Eventually I was taken on as a Ranger."

"Amy and I are very thankful you did," Natalie said in a quiet voice and got up to clear the table. Much longer and she'd be begging to hear the rest of his life story.

He'd told her he was single. Much as she wanted to know, she didn't dare come out and ask if he was romantically involved with someone. It was none of her business.

"I left Rod's things on the couch with his laptop and cell phone. If you want to go through them, I'll do the dishes and give Amy her bath before putting her down."

"Thank you for dinner. I didn't stop for lunch. You

have no idea how happy I was to smell your food cooking."

She laughed. "As long as I'm staying home, plan on eating any or all of your meals here. It's nice to have someone to cook for." Natalie could have bitten her tongue off for saying that, but it was too late.

An hour later she walked into the living room having put Amy to bed for the night. She found Kit searching through the files on Rod's computer.

"Have you discovered anything that could help you?"

"No. He was too savvy to leave clues behind. I've been through his clothes, but they're several years old and nothing stands out. If you'll notice, he removed the labels so it would be difficult to trace where they'd been purchased." Kit stood. "Do you mind if I bring in the step ladder from the garage? I want to look for prints on the attic lid and climb inside to take a look around."

The attic? "Go right ahead." She'd almost forgotten the house had one.

"I'll be as quiet as I can."

Natalie didn't doubt it. So far he seemed to be an expert at everything he did. While he put on plastic gloves and got busy, she went to the kitchen for a garbage bag to put Rod's old clothes in to take to Goodwill.

To her shock Kit came down the ladder carrying a medium-size suitcase. His gaze flicked to hers. "Have you ever been up in the attic?"

"Never."

"Have you ever seen this suitcase?"

She shook her head.

"Let's see what's inside." Natalie followed him into the kitchen and he put the case on the table. "It's locked, but I have tools." He went to the guest bathroom for his bag. She marveled that within seconds he'd opened the lock.

When he lifted the lid, she gasped.

"Well, well. Two firearms. Both .45-caliber Colt automatics," he muttered and picked them up one at a time. "They're loaded, ready to go."

Natalie's hand covered her mouth. The police had been to her house but they hadn't been in the attic.

"Now we know at least one item the intruder was looking for. It's clear your husband knew this person and gave him a key to get into the house. Since Rod was killed before this person could find out where the guns were hidden, it makes me think there was a third party involved in all this."

"Anyone that desperate should have realized the attic was the perfect place to hide them," Natalie commented. Certainly she hadn't thought of it. But Kit wasn't like other people. He had the instincts only a few men were blessed with. That's why he was a Texas Ranger.

"Maybe he was afraid you'd get back from the funeral before he could search the attic and be found in the act." He shot her a piercing glance. "Thank God, you didn't go in the house when you saw the state of the garage. If that person had still been in there, he could have taken you hostage."

Or worse.

Natalie weaved in place and grabbed the back of a chair for support.

Kit closed the suitcase. "I'll take this to Forensics in the morning. Excuse me while I put the ladder away."

When he came back into the kitchen, he removed the gloves and tossed them in the trash. "Let's go sit in the living room." He motioned for her to lead the way and she settled into an armchair. He went to the den for his laptop before sitting on the couch.

"I spent most of the afternoon at LifeSpan and discovered how your husband was cheating the company. Right around the time he started working for them seven years ago, he set up a dummy corporation that looked like any of the dozens of companies LifeSpan pays for their services. But, of course, it didn't perform a service.

"The money went straight to a bank where it was deposited into a falsified account. He made constant withdrawals and pocketed the money under another of his assumed names."

Natalie was scandalized. "What did he do with it?"

"It's my guess he invested it in various ventures—real estate, maybe—under yet another alias to hide what he was doing. The point is, the auditor who worked under your husband couldn't understand why the offsite, independent auditor hadn't caught the problem years ago."

"That's horrible."

"Agreed. He stole millions from the company. It seems likely to me your husband bribed an independent auditor to go into business with him and paid him a percentage for looking the other way. Or that person was a criminal like Rod. Your husband was fired a month ago when the independent auditor couldn't be found to substantiate Rod's claims that he'd done nothing wrong. The FBI is staging a full investigation."

She stirred restlessly. "I hope that money can be recovered and given back to LifeSpan."

"I could wish for the same thing, but my main concern right now is to keep you safe until we know who invaded your home and the culprit is arrested. Let's hope your friend in Phoenix has some information that can help. Give me a minute to make the reservation."

Kit pulled out his cell phone and got to work and it didn't take him long before he was tucking it back in his pocket. "I have to take the guns to the lab, so we'll drop them off on the way to the airport. Our US Air flight will leave at eight-thirty and put us in Phoenix by ten-ten. That means we'll have to leave here by 6:15 a.m. Does that work for you?"

She nodded. "Amy's already asleep. I'll get everything packed and be ready."

"Good. Do you mind if I do some wash right now? The clerical shirt is drip dry, so there's no problem."

"Of course, I don't mind, but I can do it for you."

"Thanks, but no. I've fended for myself for years. To be surprised with a dinner you fixed was a treat I didn't expect."

"In that case I'll phone Colette right now."

While he gathered his things to take to the laundry room, she called her friend and gave her the time and terminal. "One more thing, Colette. The Ranger will be dressed in a blue shirt with a collar, like a priest."

"You're kidding—"

"It's a long story. I'll tell you the details after we get there. If anyone should ask, he's my cousin, Father Todd Segal."

"Natalie—"

"I know it sounds bizarre, but he's saving my life, literally."

"I believe you. See you tomorrow morning. Do I dare tell you I can't wait to meet him? A real Texas Ranger?"

"Yeah. I'm still having trouble taking it all in."

"What's he like?"

Natalie wasn't going there. "He's the personification of the perfect Ranger."

"I get it. Code for gorgeous, right?"

Right. Something had to be wrong with her to be talking like a high school girl to Colette when she was in the middle of a grave situation that could cost more lives.

"I'll see you tomorrow, Colette."

She hung up, afraid to say anything else because Kit had come back into the living room. Natalie looked up at him. "I'm going to go pack a suitcase for Amy and me, and then get to bed so I can wake up in time for our flight."

He nodded. "Get a good sleep. While we're gone tomorrow, another surveillance team will watch the house."

"Kit?" she said in a tremulous voice, getting to her feet.

"What is it?"

"Thank you for everything you're doing. I'm so grateful I don't know how I'll ever be able to repay you."

"This is my job, Natalie."

"I know, but you've helped me get through one of the darkest periods of my life. You've restored my faith in the idea that there are good men out there, although probably not many as exceptional as you. Good night."

NATALIE'S WORDS CAUSED Kit's throat to swell. For the first time since working as a Ranger, Kit had become personally involved in a case. He had no business caring about her or her daughter except on a professional basis, but it had happened, anyway. If he were honest with himself, he could admit to a strong physical attraction to her at the cemetery before they'd even met. It was the kind of chemistry that couldn't be explained.

The only thing to do from here on out was to focus on the case and cut out all ideas of spending unnecessary time with her, such as watching a movie together before they went to bed. *Concentrate, Saunders, or you're in big trouble.*

He turned out lights, secured the doors and got ready for bed. He still wasn't ready to sleep so he checked for new messages on his laptop. The response from the police in Denver sparked his interest first and he opened it to find the rap sheet on Jeremy Roos Salter. So he *was* in the criminal database!

Jeremy Roos Salter, 33. Born: Denver, Colorado. Home address: Lima Street. Aliases: Jessie James, Walter James, Sal Jameson. Currently serving a life sentence at Atwater Federal Penitentiary, Northern California, for arson, aggravated assault and the murder of two police officers. Incarcerated seven years ago.

That meant Harold and Jeremy could have been committing crimes all through their teens before the law caught had up with them. The visit to Gladys Park had produced a big lead for Kit. He intended to fly to California to have a talk with Salter.

While he was still up he called Information to find out if there were any Salters living in Denver. There were quite a few, but none on Lima. Tomorrow he'd phone every listing. Maybe he'd stumble across someone related to Jeremy or who could tell him something about the family that once lived on that street.

Stan had sent him a message saying the thumbprint found on the lid of the laptop had been sent to the criminal database because it hadn't matched Mrs. Harris's prints or her husband's. He'd requested that the results be sent to Kit ASAP, and Kit was anxious to see them.

One last item of business before he quit for the night. He reached for his cell and texted his brother.

No time to call hospital. Give Scott my condolences. Won't be in Texas this weekend. Hope you find a hazer fast. Kit.

He put down his phone and closed his laptop, refusing to feel guilty. For years he'd watched out for Brandon, but this was one time his duty to work came first. But a nagging little voice reminded him it wasn't all duty, not where Natalie was concerned. Not by a long shot.

"THERE'S COLETTE. SHE'S wearing the yellow blouse and cowboy boots," Natalie said as they walked off the plane into Terminal Four on Wednesday morning.

Her friend's long, chestnut-brown hair rippled as she hurried toward them and hugged both Natalie and the baby. "It's so good to see you."

"I feel the same. Colette, meet my cousin, Father Segal."

Colette smiled at Kit and shook his hand. "I'm so glad to meet you, Father. I'm thrilled you're helping Natalie through this difficult time."

"It's my pleasure."

"Since I know you're in a hurry, I thought we'd go up to the third level and have a meal in the restaurant. They have high chairs. Maybe Amy will let me hold her after we're seated."

"I'm sure she will."

"Let's go."

Kit followed the women, carrying the diaper bag and car seat. The restaurant Colette had chosen was the perfect place for an interview.

Once they'd ordered lunch Natalie excused herself and took Amy to the restroom where she could change her diaper. Kit handed her the bag.

His eyes lingered on her retreating figure, dressed in a peach-colored top and jeans that outlined the soft curve of her hips. With those long legs and that honey-blond hair, he was sure every male in the place must be watching her progress.

The reason he was there at all suddenly dawned on him and he switched his gaze to Natalie's friend. "I appreciate your being able to meet us here, especially since I hear your husband is still recovering from an operation."

"I'd do anything for Natalie and my husband is much better—he plans to go to work tomorrow. I just hope I can help you."

"Whatever you can tell me about the woman you saw with Rod Harris will be useful. I'll be recording our conversation." She nodded. "Could you describe her physically for me?"

"She couldn't have been more than five-two, five-three. She had a small frame, maybe a hundred and ten pounds."

"What about her hairstyle?"

"Dramatic. Her hair was long and black. She had it swept around back and coiled near the top of her head with a clip. She had dark brown eyes."

"Race?"

"Her coloring made think she was Hispanic."

"Did she speak with an accent?"

"No, not that I noticed."

The waitress arrived with their food and, after she excused herself, Kit resumed his questioning. "How was she dressed?"

"Very stylish. A designer-type dress and high heels. She went a little heavy on the makeup. You're probably surprised I noticed so much, but it was because she was so striking, almost like a fashion model. Rod said she was Natalie's cousin, but I found that surprising because I'd never heard about her."

"I wish all the witnesses I interrogated had your memory. Did he introduce her by name?"

"He said something like Myra or Mara, but he was in a hurry and I didn't quite catch it."

"That's fine."

"I wish I'd been more observant," Colette murmured. "Now that I know the truth, I guess he just wanted to get her out of there as fast as he could."

"I'm sure of it. Did she have a suitcase with her? Maybe a tag that would identify where she'd come from or where she was going?"

"Not that I recall. I was in a hurry myself."

Kit nodded. "How did he treat her? Like a friend or a lover?"

"I didn't pick up on anything more than that they knew each other."

"Do you remember the car he was driving?"

Colette frowned. "I think he was standing next to a white car, but I can't be positive."

"Good," he said as Natalie returned and put Amy in the high chair. The little girl pointed to him. "Kit."

"Hi, sweetheart." He put a cracker on the tray for her.

Natalie's friend broke into a smile. "She knows you."

"She catches on fast." He smiled back.

"Amy has her mother's smarts. One day I hope to have a baby as adorable as this one."

"I'm sure you will." Natalie's spring green eyes darted to Kit. "Sorry I was gone so long. The place was crowded. Forgive me if I'm interrupting you."

His gaze played over her. "There's nothing to forgive. I've already asked all my questions pertaining to the case. Colette here has a keen eye—she remembered details I wouldn't have expected. It helps immensely."

The three adults started to eat their lunches and Amy munched happily on her crackers. Kit addressed Natalie's old friend.

"Tell me about your barrel riding days, Colette. Do you still compete at the rodeo?"

"Not anymore. Sounds like Natalie has been telling tales out of school."

"That's because you were an excellent barrel racer," Natalie countered. "And guess what? Kit—I mean, *Father Segal*'s brother is a steer wrestler. In fact he's competing at Nationals in Las Vegas in December."

Colette's eyes lit up. "What's his name?"

"Brandon Saunders from the Lazy S Ranch in Marble Falls, Texas."

"Father Segal used to compete in the same event," Natalie interjected.

"Really. How come you're not still riding?"

"My career forced me to give it up."

"That happened to me, too. Those were the good old days. I'll have to keep an eye on your brother's numbers. When is his next event?"

"Saturday night in San Antonio, but I don't know how he'll do because he lost his hazer this week."

Natalie's smile faded. "What happened?"

"His hazer, Scott, was in a car accident and has a broken leg. Brandon's got to find a replacement, fast."

Colette finished the last of her sandwich. "Good ones are hard to come by. That's bad luck. I feel sorry for both of them. Hazers are almost invisible unless they make a mistake, but a bull dogger couldn't get a low score without an outstanding one to keep that steer close."

Her comment made Kit feel even guiltier.

She looked at Natalie. "How soon is your return flight?"

"In an hour. We'll go downstairs in a few minutes. Amy has almost finished."

Natalie had been feeding her a jar of chicken and stars. Kit couldn't get over what a great little traveler she was.

"In that case I'm going to leave you two in time to get some grocery shopping done before I drive home." She rose and hugged the baby and Natalie. Then she turned to Kit. "It's been a pleasure meeting you, Father Segal."

He got to his feet. "Thank you for getting together on such short notice. Your testimony is more helpful than you know. If you think of anything else, don't hesitate to call me on my cell. Here's my card." He handed it to her.

"I promise." She started to dig through her purse but Kit shook his head. "This lunch is on me. Drive safely."

"I will." Her glance rested on Natalie. "We'll talk soon."

"I'll call you. Thank you again."

Colette made her exit and Natalie wiped Amy's face and hands, then turned to Kit. "We're ready to go downstairs. Amy's been awake since first thing this morning, so I think she'll probably nap most of the way home."

"She's been a model child—honors go to her mother."

"I can't take the credit. She came this way."

Kit decided not to argue. But he'd watched how Natalie handled her daughter and could tell she was a terrific parent.

He left money for the bill on the table, picked up the bag and car seat, and ushered the girls out of the restaurant, anxious to get back to Austin. It pleased him that he and Natalie would be going home together. He found himself enjoying her company more than he should.

His thoughts returned to the case. Stan should be getting back to him with the rest of the information on the fingerprints. He was also eager for the FBI agent to send him the background on the missing independent auditor for LifeSpan. As for the black hairs found in Rod's car, they might be a match for the hair on the woman Colette had seen with Park. She could be an unsuspecting girlfriend or she might be an accomplice, corrupt to the crown of her head.

There was a lot Kit needed to go through and analyze. But he decided that while he was waiting for more answers, he would fly to California in the morning and speak to Salter. Hopefully he could get it all in and be home by tomorrow night. He couldn't get this case solved fast enough.

Chapter Five

After a homemade spaghetti dinner, Natalie gave Amy her bath and put her down for the night. She'd grown restless on the airplane and hadn't napped the way Natalie had hoped. Kit had taken over and held her for a while, playing with her toes. Amy had loved it when Kit pointed to each toe; laughed each time he touched one. The stimulation had kept her awake, but happy. Now what she needed was a good night's sleep.

Natalie found Kit in the den, laptop open while he talked business on the phone. He saw her and motioned for her to come in. She sat in one of the comfortable armchairs, pleasantly tired. It had been great to see Colette again, but their visit had been too brief.

"How's the cherub?" Kit asked when he finished his call.

"Out like a light."

"I'm not surprised. Your little girl has done enough flying for a while."

"She's never had a more exciting week in her life. A new man in the house, jet-plane rides—"

His eyes studied her for a moment. "It makes me happy that she doesn't mind having me around."

"Mind? She's crazy about you. It astonished Colette when Amy said your name in the restaurant."

He flashed her a smile that turned her heart over. "That made my day. Thanks for flying to Arizona with me. I wanted your friend to feel comfortable."

"I enjoyed seeing her again, even if it was only for an hour. Was she really able to help you, or were you just saying that to be polite?"

"Anything but. It was well worth the trip. Now I need to find a pattern using the evidence I've gathered, but that means I have to fly out again tomorrow morning. I'll be going alone this time."

"Are you able to tell me where?"

"California. I'm going to interrogate Jimmy Salter at the federal prison."

"You mean Rod's—childhood friend went to prison, too?"

"Afraid so. He killed two police officers."

"I can't believe it." Natalie looked at Kit. "How long will you be gone?"

"I could be home by tomorrow night, but probably the next day. Since Salter is a lifer, you never know about getting him to talk. He might cooperate and tell me something important about Harold.

"Then again, he could refuse to speak. But when I tell him your husband was murdered, it may jar him into revealing a critical piece of information I could use. But don't be concerned. You'll be watched at all times while I'm away. They'll follow you if you want to drive to the store or whatever."

"I know that." She averted her eyes. "I just don't see how you can stand to face a cold-blooded killer."

"It's part of my job."

"I know, but it's so awful."

"The satisfaction of capturing a dangerous criminal makes it all worth it."

Natalie lifted her head. "You're an amazing man."

"Like I told you before, my childhood was filled with snakes and things that go bump in the night." Kit's half smile didn't dispel her concern for him.

"Do you ever have nightmares?" she asked.

"I've had my share, but not because of my career. The one that returns on occasion has to do with letting my father down."

Natalie swallowed hard. "Was he a demanding man?"

"Not at all. He was kind and straight as an arrow. I thought he was next to perfect."

"Well if I had a chance to meet him, I'd tell him the size of your footsteps match his." The second she'd spoken, heat swarmed her cheeks.

Kit's gaze held hers. "When I have that nightmare again, I'll remember your words."

Natalie stood from her chair. "If you've got to make an early morning flight, I'll say good-night."

"Once I've installed a camera over the front door, I'll call it a night, too."

The man was doing everything possible to keep her

safe. "Is there anything I can get you before I go to bed? There's still some iced tea left over from dinner."

"No, thanks. It was delicious, but if I want any more, I'll get it."

You heard him, Natalie.

She turned and retreated through the house to her bedroom. But after she got into bed, she couldn't fall asleep. She shouldn't be upset because he had to leave for a day or two to carry out his job. And it wasn't because she was afraid for him. That wasn't the problem.

Something else had happened to her; something she could never have imagined. Natalie's attraction to Kit had grown roots. How was that possible in so short a time?

To get him off her mind, she reached for the remote and turned on the TV on the dresser.

The next thing she knew, she was waking up to a Thursday morning news show. She shut it off and got out of bed.

After throwing on a robe Natalie walked down the hall to the nursery. Amy was still sleeping. When she reached the den, she saw Kit's sleeping bag rolled up and propped in the corner. Her watch said eight-fifteen. He'd gone.

She moved to the living room and looked out the window. A van marked Kitchen Remodels was parked a few houses down. To be watched over made her feel secure, but she felt an emptiness because—

Oh, stop it, Natalie.

Upset with her herself, she took a shower, washed her hair and got ready for the day in shorts and a sleeveless blouse. Amy was up and playing in her bed when Natalie entered the nursery.

"Good morning, my little love."

Her daughter answered her with a smile and some baby chatter. Once she'd had a diaper change and Natalie had found her a cute little sunsuit to wear, they ate breakfast. While Natalie was feeding her, Amy said Kit's name.

"Kit's not here, honey." So her daughter was missing him, too. Things just weren't the same today.

Before it got too hot, she grabbed her cell and took Amy out back, setting her in her playpen on the patio with some toys. Natalie started the mower and cut the small back lawn, then moved the little kiddie pool off the patio and onto the grass.

It was filled with plastic ducks and geese. Amy loved to throw the beach ball into it, then climb in and throw it back out, along with the ducks. Later Natalie would put a little water in so Amy could splash.

While the little girl toddled around the yard, Natalie lay on the lounger to watch. The emptiness she'd felt earlier hadn't gone away. Resigned to be in this condition until Kit came back, she returned a series of calls to people who'd left messages.

Once that was done, she phoned Information and got a number for car donations for veterans and was pleased to discover that a towing company could collect the Sentra before the end of the day and would leave her a receipt. Relieved to have taken care of that so easily, she turned on the hose and put some water in the pool.

Amy loved it and they played until it was time for

lunch. At nap time, Natalie brought in the mail then cut the grass out front. With Austin on water restriction, the sprinklers went on at four in the morning at her address on Wednesdays only. The lawn didn't look that great, but it couldn't be helped.

The last thing on her list was to put the key to Rod's car back in the ignition. Just as she finished and came back into the house, her cell rang. She looked at the Caller ID and clicked on.

"Colette?"

"I hope it's all right to talk for a few minutes."

"Of course."

"Is the Ranger still there?"

Natalie gripped the phone tighter. "No. He's away. Probably until tomorrow."

"I'm alone, too. Chad has gone to work for a few hours and I've taken today off in case he doesn't feel well and comes home early. To be honest, he was going crazy around here and driving me crazy too. I've decided that husbands make horrible patients. Anyway, I just had to call you and—"

"I know what you're going to say," Natalie interrupted. "Yes I find him terribly attractive and wonderful, but he'll wrap up this case soon and that will be the end of it."

"Want to make a bet? I saw the way he looked at you when you took Amy to the restroom." Natalie's heart pounded. "I hope he's not married."

"He's not."

"That's good, because no priest or married man should watch a woman the way he watched you."

"Don't be ridiculous." Natalie was afraid to believe it.

"I'd say it's a good thing Father Segal isn't really a priest because from where I was sitting, he was already in big trouble."

"Colette—"

"It's true, and you had the same expression in your eyes when you looked at him. What's great is that Amy likes him, too."

"She does. This morning she noticed he wasn't here and called out his name."

"See?"

"See what?" Natalie asked with impatience.

"If you're honest with yourself, you'll admit that you fell out of love early in your marriage. It's about time you met someone else. And, Natalie, I have to tell you that Ranger Saunders is fantastic with a capital *F*."

Colette never minced words. She attacked head-on. That was one of the reasons Natalie loved her friend so much. "I agree with you," she said in a shaky voice. "But I don't dare read anything into what's going on. He's never given me even a hint that he might be interested."

"It's there in his eyes and in his body language."

"I think you're imagining things because you want me to be happy."

"I do want you to be happy, but only with the right man."

"Thank you for being the greatest friend in the world."

"Ditto. Keep me posted about what's going on. Call me anytime if you need to."

"I will. You're the best, Colette. 'Bye for now."

Amy slept on, so Natalie looked around for something else to do. She threw out two of the flower arrangements that had died, wishing they could have lasted longer. People had been so kind to her she decided to write thank-you notes. It would keep her from thinking about Kit, out interrogating a killer.

Her day wore on and by the time she and Amy were eating their dinner, the tow truck driver had come to the door to give her the receipt for the car. She watched through the screen as Rod's car was hauled away. She was relieved to know the surveillance team was keeping watch. Tomorrow she'd take the bag of his clothes to Goodwill and that would be the end of any physical reminders. *Except* for photographs.

Those were in a scrapbook Natalie had put away on a shelf. One day Amy would want to see pictures of her father. Natalie hoped that by the time Amy started asking questions about her daddy, enough years would have gone by that she'd be able to deal with them.

After Amy's bath, she put her to bed and was just coming out of the nursery when her phone rang. She hurried to the kitchen, hoping it might be Kit, but when she checked the screen, it listed an area code and number for Denver. With a frown, she answered.

"Hello?"

"Is this Mrs. Harris?"

"Yes."

"This is Mrs. Issac, the director at the Cottonwood Nursing Home. You asked that we contact you about Gladys Park. I'm sorry to have to tell you that she died in her sleep this evening." Natalie gasped. "She was comfortable to the end. There'll be a little memorial service here for her on Monday at noon. Her close friend and her pastor are arranging it, but I knew you'd want to be notified."

"Thank you so much for letting me know. It means the world to me. I don't think I can make it to the service, but I'll have flowers sent."

"That would be lovely."

Natalie disconnected and buried her face in her hands. Another death. Emotion overwhelmed her and she broke down sobbing.

BEFORE KIT PULLED into the driveway, he waved off the surveillance team. With his business concluded early, he'd taken the next flight out of San Francisco.

He drove into the garage and went into the house, where he found Natalie in the kitchen, crying her heart out.

"Natalie?"

She lifted her tear-streaked face. "You're back—" she cried in surprise. "Oh, Kit, I'm so glad you're here."

Without thinking, he pulled her into his arms and held her while she wept. "What's happened?" he asked. His lips brushed her silky blond hair.

"G-Gladys died this evening. I got the call a few minutes ago."

He gathered her tighter.

"What if you hadn't arranged for us to fly to Denver when you did? I would never have known her. Thank heaven you took pictures while we were there. Amy will cherish those when she gets older." Natalie lifted her head so their mouths were only inches apart. "If it weren't for you, I don't know how I would have gotten through everything. I owe you so much."

Kit kissed the tears on her cheek but eased her away from him, even though it was the last thing he wanted to do. "I'm glad we went, too. Come on. Let's go in the living room and talk. I take it Amy is down for the night."

She nodded and led the way.

He waited until she sank onto a chair before settling in at one end of the couch. "When is her service?"

"Monday. At the nursing home. I told the director I couldn't be there, but I'd send flowers." She wiped her eyes with the backs of her hands. "How did your prison visit go?"

"Salter was uncooperative, but I spoke to several other inmates. One of them told me he knew the forger who'd made fake IDs for Salter and some of the other prisoners. The name was Barni Esger. It could turn out to be a promising lead if I can find a connection between this person and Rod's forged documents."

"Where is this forger?"

"He's serving time in federal prison at Leavenworth in Kansas."

She groaned. "All those men in prison… That means you'll be taking another trip."

"Yes."

She lowered her head. "Did you tell Salter that Rod had been killed?"

"I did. He showed no emotion, which isn't surprising." He eyed her for a moment. "I saw that the Sentra is gone."

"I took care of it today and donated it to the veterans."

"That would have been my choice, too. How's Amy?"

"She said your name at breakfast. She was looking for you."

He'd missed both of them. Kit wasn't supposed to develop attachments, but there were a lot of things that weren't supposed to have happened since he'd met her. Such as putting his arms around her to comfort her. It had felt so right.

"If you're hungry, there's plenty of food in the fridge."

"I ate on the plane, thanks. Any more hang-up calls?"

"No. It's been quiet. I'm glad you're back safely. I know you have work to do, so I'll say good-night."

Keep your mind on the case, Saunders. "See you in the morning."

After she disappeared, he went to the den and opened his laptop. Another response from the criminal database. Neither of the two guns had been fired recently, and any prints had been wiped clean. The thumbprint on Park's laptop had turned up a mug shot of a female. She'd been arrested for possession of drugs and petit larceny eight years ago in Denver, Colorado.

The same time as Harold Park.

The woman had been charged with a misdemeanor and was jailed for eighteen months.

He scrolled down.

Juanita Morales, alias Myra King, Mara Fletcher, Myrna Foyle. Female, 24, 120 pounds, 5'3". Blond hair, blue eyes.

Kit's head reared in reaction. He'd hit the jackpot! Juanita had to be the sister or wife of Alonzo Morales, the convict who'd escaped with Harold. Assuming she'd dyed her hair and worn colored lenses eight years ago, this could very well be the woman Colette had seen at the airport with Natalie's husband.

He scanned a copy of the rap sheet and emailed it to Colette. He'd like to hear what she had to say about the mug shot. He also wanted to know the precise location where she'd seen them in the airport parking area. Tomorrow he'd get one of the guys at headquarters to go through the airport security tapes for footage of Harold and his companion.

After he'd sent the message to Colette, he read through his other emails. The rest of the prints from the house and car matched those of Harold Park and Natalie Harris. Nothing surprising there.

He'd suspected all along there was a third party involved in this case. Linking Juanita to Alonzo made the most sense. Juanita was probably the one who'd provided the transportation to drive the two fugitives out of state during their escape. Everything had been planned. Which one of them had ransacked Natalie's home?

Together they'd picked LifeSpan to defraud, but they would have needed all kinds of fake ID and forged documents to make it happen.

With his mind racing ahead, he suddenly realized his cell was ringing. He reached for it and recognized the Arizona number. "Is this Colette?"

"Yes! I saw the image you sent me and didn't want to keep you waiting. *She's* the woman I met! The coloring is different, obviously, and she's lost a little weight since that photo, but I saw her up close and those are her exact features."

"That's all I needed to hear. Your information is going to help me solve this case."

"I hope that's true. You asked where I ran into them. It was in the short-term east parking with access to the Jeppesen Terminal on level four, kind of in the middle."

"That will help us locate the right security cameras. Thank you for calling me back."

"Of course. I can tell Natalie is in the best of hands. Good luck, Ranger Saunders."

After he'd hung up he emailed headquarters and asked that a team pull the tapes. He'd take a look at the footage after his return from Kansas.

With that sent, he checked the front door camera, pleased to see that no one had come to the door but the man from the towing service.

Content that all was well for the moment, he locked up the house and got ready for bed. It was a long shot to fly to Leavenworth tomorrow, but he intended to build this case with as much evidence as possible. He'd been supplied with a rap sheet on Barni Esger, and while he might not have any reason to cooperate, Kit had to try.

Before his arrest, the Dane who'd immigrated to Colorado with his father when he was a teen, had been a professional photographer celebrated for his scenes of the Colorado mountains. For years he'd used his studio in Fort Collins, Colorado, to cover up his real work of producing fake credentials for dozens of hardened criminals throughout the country.

Despite what Kit's instincts told him, he had no proof that Esger had been involved. But any information he could get out of the man would be valuable. For Harold to obtain an accounting job with LifeSpan in the first place, he'd have had to reinvent his whole life. He'd fooled so many people for so many years. The Morales duo, too. Had Esger set them up with fake documents, as well?

One of them had killed Harold. Kit was sure of it. Had they discovered he'd double-crossed them? Had they turned on him because that had been their plan in the first place? Who knew the ins and outs of their ménage à trois? He'd like to lock them both up for good.

Kit was looking forward to the day when Natalie was safe and could put all this behind her.

When he climbed into his sleeping bag, he imagined being curled up with her. She always smelled delicious. What a loving heart she had, crying over Rod's grandmother. He admired her immensely for the way she was handling the horror of having been married to a criminal.

Another woman might have fallen apart, but not Natalie. Her strength of character was awesome to witness as she carried on with her life for the sake of her daughter.

Amy was a little angel. He'd never felt an attachment to a child before. How ironic that it would be Harold Park's daughter who pulled at Kit's heart strings with such force. Maybe it was because of Park's criminal background that Kit wanted the very best for that golden-haired little girl and her beautiful mother.

When Kit's father had been killed, he'd thought he'd experienced the very worst thing that could happen to a person. Though his father's killer had been killed, too, Kit hadn't been able to get over the pain. It took years of maturing to teach him that sometimes horrible things happened to the most innocent people. Other people suffered heartache, too. Ridding the world of the people who'd terrorized Natalie with frightening phone calls and break-ins had now become his first priority.

ON FRIDAY AT noon Kit walked into the interrogation room at the Leavenworth prison carrying an envelope. A prison guard stood by the door.

Esger was sitting behind a table with his ankles shackled. The balding man was sixty but looked older. His dark blue eyes studied Kit's star-shaped badge.

"You're excellent at what you do, Esger, I have to admit. Your forgeries fooled the very best for years. The inmates at Atwater sing your praises."

"Of course, but a Texas Ranger didn't come here to compliment me."

Kit took his time. "You're aging in here, Barni. I'm prepared to slice two years off your twelve-year sentence if you'll help me out on a particular case."

The prisoner stared at Kit for a long time. "What do you want to know?"

"Eight years ago Jimmy Salter and Harold Park made contact with you. I've got it on record that they came armed with a small fortune for you to transform their lives. " *Unfortunately those testimonials came from the inmates who knew Salter and were nothing more than hearsay.* "Now I'm here to find out if you made documents for their friends Juanita and Alonzo Morales, the husband and wife team working with them."

"They were brother and sister," Esger muttered before looking away. Kit was elated by that vital slip of information.

"That's it, Barni. That's all I want to know."

The forger cocked his head to the side. "So all I have to do is tell you that information and my sentence will be reduced by two years?"

"That's the deal. Your confession will be signed and notarized by the warden."

"How do you know I won't lie to you?"

"I don't. But if I find out later that you *did* lie—and I *will* find out—then I'll have your sentence extended for ten more years on the grounds of perjury before a federal officer of the United States.

"You've already served three years of your sentence. Doesn't it sound good to know two more years can be lopped off simply by telling the truth? You'd only have to serve seven more and be out of here by the time you're sixty-seven. There'd still be a lot of life to live, pictures to take of the Colorado mountains. Interested?"

Kit pulled a document out of the envelope and set

it in front of the prisoner along with a pen. "Go ahead and read it. Nothing will happen to you if you don't sign it. I'll walk out of here and you'll go on serving your original sentence."

Esger picked up the piece of paper and began to read. "This says I supplied documents to all four of them."

"That's right. If it's not true, then I'm wasting your time and mine."

His eyes narrowed on Kit. "Before I do anything, I want to talk to my attorney."

Kit nodded to the guard who opened the door. Esger's attorney entered the room, accompanied by a second guard. Kit stepped out to chat with the warden. After a few minutes Kit and the warden were allowed back inside.

"Well, Esger?" the warden asked.

The forger looked skeptical. "If I sign this, is it true I'll be out of here in seven years?"

"It is. But if you lie, that paper also states that ten years will be added to your original sentence. To make it legal and binding, I'll sign my name below yours. Your attorney will sign it and the guards will witness it. Won't it feel good to do something helpful for a change?"

Esger hesitated a moment longer and then signed the document. His attorney, the warden and the two witnesses followed suit.

Barni Esger's signature helped tie the loose ends together, making a solid case against three killers wanted by the FBI, one of whom was already dead. Kit had yet to learn what crimes Juanita had committed since her release from jail. But for now he couldn't have been happier.

He went to the warden's office and had a copy made of the signed confession before he left the prison with it and headed to the airport twenty-five miles away in Kansas City. He would have to hurry; his US Airways flight would be leaving at 4:00 p.m. That would put him in Austin around seven-thirty.

It was close to eight when he phoned TJ from his car in the airport parking lot to tell him the outcome of his visit to Leavenworth. "They're all involved in the LifeSpan embezzlement scheme. I'm waiting for a few more bits of information and then we can begin a manhunt for the Morales duo."

"That's fine work despite your unorthodox methods. Using the prison warden—that's a new one. I see you've logged a lot of flying miles in less than a week. Take a day off before you burn out. That's an order."

"In that case, I have a rodeo event I'd like to attend this Saturday and I'll need an officer to stay at the Harris home while I'm gone."

"I'll arrange it. Don't get stomped on."

"No, sir." With a laugh Kit hung up and started changing into his clerical shirt when his phone rang. He looked at the screen and took the call.

"Hey, Brandon—"

"Boy, am I glad you answered. I need your help in the worst way, bro."

"You mean you haven't found a hazer yet?"

"Yeah, I have. Corky Tibbs."

"I remember Corky. He's a great choice."

"I know. He said he'd haze for me until Scott is back, but he can't start for two weeks. I still haven't found anyone to ride for me in San Antonio tomorrow night."

Kit sucked in his breath. He'd thought he'd try to get there to watch his brother tomorrow night, but not to be part of the show. He'd turned him down once. Maybe he could help him out tomorrow night. But it all depended on Natalie, because he wasn't going to leave her unattended with Alonzo and Juanita still on the loose.

"Tell you what. Give me an hour and I'll phone you back if I can do it. That's the best I can offer."

"I knew I could count on you."

"Brandon—I only said if, so don't—"

His brother clicked off before Kit could finish the sentence.

After he hung up he finished putting on the shirt and took off for Natalie's house. En route he phoned Luckey. Kit had no idea if his friend would be available. He could be deep into a case or he might already have plans. But it was worth a try to find out.

"Well, if it isn't Father Segal," Luckey teased when the call connected.

Kit chuckled. "Tonight it's just plain Kit, even if I'm wearing a collar. I'm glad I could reach a live voice."

"Don't tell me you don't have anything to do on a Friday night because none of the guys would believe you. What's up?"

"My brother needs me to haze for him tomorrow night in San Antonio. Are you working a case or could you guard Natalie for me?"

"You mean at her house?"

"No. She says she likes the rodeo so I thought I'd take her and Amy with me so she can watch. I'd need your services during the event. Here's why."

He spent the next few minutes filling his friend in on the case. "One or both of the Moraleses is after the money and the guns. None of those items are in the house, and I'm convinced they'll come after Natalie when they break in again and realize that fact. She's not safe until they're caught."

"Sure I'll help. It'll be fun to watch you in the saddle."

"You don't have to do this, Luckey."

"You've helped me out plenty of times and my weekend is wide open. The boss told me to expect a new case on Monday."

"I'll owe you big time. I'm on my way home now. If Natalie says she wants to go with me, I'll call you and we'll make plans."

"Home, huh?"

"Don't start, Luckey."

"Yup. You have it bad. I'll wait for your call."

NATALIE HAD JUST put Amy down for the night when her cell rang. Her pulse raced before she answered. "Hi, Kit. Are you still in Kansas?"

"Nope. I'm pulling into the driveway and I wanted to give you a heads-up."

She was so happy he was back she had to be careful not to show it. "It's perfect timing. Amy's just fallen asleep. If she'd seen you, she wouldn't have wanted to go to bed. She said your name several times today. She can't figure out where you are." His chuckle worked its way to her insides.

She could hear the garage door opening while they were still on the phone. "Maybe we can fix that problem this weekend," he said and then disconnected, leaving her hanging.

When he walked into the kitchen wearing his collared shirt, her heart was still thudding. He looked... sensational. "Welcome back, Father Saunders. Would you care for something cold to drink?"

His gaze held hers. "I'd like a cola if you have one."

"I have a six-pack."

"Give me a minute to freshen up."

While he disappeared, she pulled two out of the fridge and went into the living room to wait for him. He returned quickly, wearing a polo shirt, and reached for his soda before he sat on the couch. After taking a long swallow he said, "How was your day?"

"Uneventful, thank heaven. How was yours?"

"My trip to Leavenworth turned all of my hunches into truths."

She sat forward in her chair. "Tell me everything."

"I made a deal with Esger, who signed a confession in front of the prison warden. In exchange, two years have been taken off his twelve-year prison sentence. He provided false ID to your husband, to Salter, to the other prisoner who escaped with your husband, Alonzo Morales, and to his sister, Juanita Morales.

"She probably drove the vehicle that took them to Fort Collins where they would have paid a fortune to Esger to fix them up with false documents. When they'd planned out their con, they came to Texas. The woman Colette saw with your husband was Juanita. I sent Colette a rap sheet on the other woman and she made a positive identification of the mug shot."

Natalie jumped to her feet. "Then two killers are still at large."

"That's true, but we know who they are and what they look like. Thanks to Colette, I'll be able to close in on them much sooner. When I've pieced a little more information together, I'll organize a manhunt to bring them in."

She stood there looking at him in awe. "You only took on this case a week ago, and already you know everything. You must have come to this earth with special gifts."

He darted her a quick smile. "No. I was born naturally curious. I was always asking why. It drove my family crazy."

"Be serious for a minute. Do you ever take a break?"

"I'm taking one this weekend."

Natalie didn't know what that meant. "I'm glad to hear you have a personal life. You must be sick of sleeping on the floor with one eye open all the time."

"I don't mind. It's all part of the job." He finished his cola. "How would you and Amy like to drive to San Antonio with me tomorrow? She's a great little traveler. We'll stay at a motel close to the arena and order a crib for your room. There's an animal exhibit at Little Buckaroo Farms Amy will love. You can push her around in her stroller."

What?

"I'm going to haze for my brother at the rodeo tomorrow night. My friend Luckey will guard you during the steer wrestling event. But if you don't want to come, a surveillance team will watch you here all weekend. The decision is yours."

Don't want to come? Natalie had trouble catching her breath. "I'd love to go, but I don't want you to feel you have to take us along. Amy and I will be fine here."

"Wouldn't you like a break that doesn't include traveling on a jet?"

"Well, yes, but—"

"But what?" he broke in, sounding tense all of a sudden.

"But nothing," she said with a smile he reciprocated, thrilling her out of her mind. Natalie sensed he wanted her with him and she wanted to be there. She was overjoyed that he'd invited her. "What time do you want to leave tomorrow?"

"Whenever we feel like it. The drive to San Antonio only takes an hour and a half. I'll need to meet Brandon at the arena an hour before his event. Why don't we take off after breakfast and check in at the motel before we visit the animals?"

"That sounds perfect. Amy will be worn out after that and take a nap before we go to the arena to watch you compete."

"Then it's settled. Now, if you'll excuse me, I have half a dozen phone calls to make."

She could imagine. "While you do that, I'll do a

little packing and get ready for tomorrow. See you in the morning."

For once she didn't mind saying good-night because she knew she'd be with Kit all weekend. She couldn't wait to watch him in the arena. Any time spent with him was precious.

By the time Natalie slid under the covers she knew she was suffering from a full-blown case of hero worship.

Truth really was stranger than fiction because in one week she'd fallen hard for the gorgeous Ranger. With every passing minute she was getting in deeper and deeper. Last night when he'd put his arms around her to comfort her, she'd struggled not to return the kiss he'd given her on the cheek. If only he knew how badly she'd ached for the taste and feel of his mouth on hers.

Chapter Six

"Look, Amy! That's a cow! A *big* one."

Kit chuckled as Amy imitated him and said, "Big cow." He'd been pushing her around in the stroller with Natalie at his side. Despite the heat, the Little Buckaroo Farm turned out to be pure delight. Seeing it through Amy's eyes made the experience so much fun, Kit didn't want it to end.

Hundreds of other families exclaimed over the animals. The goat-milking entertained everyone. "Shall we go see the horses now?" He pushed on and stopped in front of the fence so Amy could have a clear view of the horses in the corral.

Natalie leaned down. "See the horses?"

"Hus!" Amy pronounced. Both Kit and Natalie broke into laughter.

"That's right, little cutie," Kit agreed. "You're looking at a *big* hus."

When they least expected it, the bay closest to them let out a loud, high-pitched neigh that startled a lot of people and frightened Amy. "Kit!" She cried his name and squirmed around, holding up her arms. He undid the strap that held her and pulled her into his arms. She clung to him, crying her heart out.

A lot of bystanders smiled to see her hugging the priest. Natalie eyed the two of them. "If you had any question of how much she likes you, it's just been answered. You've received my daughter's seal of approval. She didn't even think to turn to me."

To hold her warm little body against him with her arms around his neck brought a huge lump to his throat. "I'm a grown man who was raised around horses and it startled me, too. I'm glad she feels safe with me. But maybe coming to the farm wasn't a good idea."

"Don't be silly. She loved it. She'll get over the scare."

When he would have put Amy back in the stroller, she fought to stay in his arms.

Natalie shot him a glance. "I think it's time to go back to the motel." He agreed.

She started pushing the stroller toward the main gate. He followed, carrying the precious princess who continued to let out shuddering little half sobs. By the time they'd reached Kit's car she'd calmed down.

He put Amy in her car seat, but she didn't like it. "I'll sit next to her," Natalie told him. "A nap is exactly what she needs."

After Kit put the stroller in the trunk of the Altima, he started the car and drove them to the Bucking Horse Motel near the arena. They had rooms side by side. He opened the rear door to help Natalie out.

"I think I'd better take her into my room without you, Kit. Otherwise she might never settle down."

"You're probably right, but let me make sure it's safe." After he'd checked the room, he came back out. "I'll call you when I'm ready to leave."

Once she'd lifted Amy into her arms, he handed her the diaper bag and watched as they disappeared inside. He got Amy's stroller out of the trunk and put it outside Natalie's room for Luckey to put in his car. He could hear Amy's whimpers as he let himself into his room.

His friend would already be inside. They'd arranged for him to arrive at the motel ahead of time so no one would be aware. His presence would free Kit to leave for the arena to meet Brandon, who'd arrive in his own truck and trailer. He'd be bringing Kit's favorite horse and his gear.

When he walked in, he saw his dark-blond friend stretched out on the bed in his Western clothes, watching TV.

"Thanks for coming. I appreciate you doing this big favor for me."

"Hey. This is the kind of work I like. Where's Mrs. Harris?"

"Next door. Room 14." He told Luckey what had happened at the farm. "Let's hope Amy has forgotten when she wakes up. The stroller is outside her door. Amy will be easier to handle if Natalie can wheel her around at the arena. Brandon has reserved seats for you on the front row near the chute."

"I've already got that covered."

"What do you mean?"

"Vic's here, too."

"What have you done?"

"I told the guys you were going to be the hazer tonight. Cy wanted to come, but he's on a case and can't leave. Vic was free and wants to watch you ride. He also wants to get a look at Natalie Harris. So do I."

Kit shook his head then laughed. In truth he was relieved two of the best Rangers alive would be helping to guard Natalie. "I have something to show you."

Luckey sat up. Kit pulled out a file and handed him the rap sheets with the mug shots on the Morales siblings. "I have to assume they've been watching the house, so it's possible that one of them might have followed us here and the other is planning to get into Natalie's house. One of the surveillance team will be inside, ready to arrest him or her on sight."

"Let's hope it happens, and then you can zero in on the killer still at large."

"I have no idea which one will be tailing Natalie and me. If it's Juanita, she could be in her old disguise of blond hair and blue eyes. But my hunch is on Alonzo who might even try to kidnap Amy or Natalie or both. I'd imagine they must be desperate to find the money and the guns."

Luckey put the rap sheets on the dresser. "Get your mind off the case and concentrate on helping your brother bring in the best time tonight. Leave the worry to Vic and me."

"I will." Kit clapped his friend on the shoulder and phoned Natalie. She picked up on the first ring.

"Kit?"

"How's Amy?"

"Blissfully asleep."

"Good."

"Are you ready to go?"

"Yup. I'm walking out the door. Luckey's here and he'll phone you when it's time to leave for the arena."

"I'm excited to watch you and your brother compete."

"I haven't hazed for him in a while."

"Don't give me that bull. No pun intended." He laughed. "I happen to know a hazer has to foresee all possibilities of trouble and correct them in a split second. You couldn't turn in a bad performance if you tried."

"I'm flattered by your confidence in me. See you back here after the rodeo. Stay safe."

"You, too. Go get 'em, cowboy!"

Luckey stared at him as he hung up. "Yup," he murmured.

"Don't say it. Don't say anything."

"Oh, I won't!" A big grin broke out on his tanned face. "That conversation said it all."

"See you later. I'm out of here."

Kit left the room still wearing his clerical shirt and got into his car. He'd stowed his riding clothes and cowboy hat in the trunk. Brandon would be waiting for him in his trailer behind the livestock pens.

He checked his rearview mirror repeatedly on the way to see if anyone was following him, but he saw nothing suspicious.

Kit arrived to find his brother standing outside with one of his team members. The second he saw him, Brandon ran to the car, practically pulling Kit out of the driver's seat to give him a hug. "Thanks, bro. You're saving my life. I know you're on a case."

"It's all right. I've got it covered."

His brother did a double-take when he pulled away from him. "What are you doing in that outfit?"

"Part of my cover. Let's go inside the trailer so I can change."

"Where's your gear?"

"In the trunk."

"I'll get it." Brandon was so grateful, it was as if he couldn't do enough for his older brother. It didn't take long for Kit to put on his rodeo clothes.

"Terry's already walked our horses inside," Brandon informed him.

"How's Flash?"

"The vet checked both horses over this morning. Yours is in great condition. I've seen to that. Let's go."

The familiar smell of the animals took Kit back to the time when he'd competed on a regular basis. It seemed a lifetime ago. Since then so much in his life had changed, starting with his move to Austin and the beginning of his career as a Ranger. He'd gained three close friends who were like brothers.

He loved this life.

If he hadn't chosen this profession, he would never have met Natalie. The thought of any harm coming to her or Amy filled him with rage. But he needed to take Luckey's advice and stay centered on the job ahead of him for Brandon's sake.

If his brother could win the national championship in Las Vegas, the prize money would be enough to keep the family ranch running. Kit determined to do his best for him.

Flash, Kit's black-and-white gelding, nickered as Kit rubbed his forelock. "Good to see you, buddy. I've missed you, too." He slipped his horse some sugar cubes. "I'm going to eat my pre-competition Snickers, so you should be able to binge, too."

He saddled and bridled Flash. After putting on his riding gloves, he joined his brother in the corral to put his horse through some paces. With the right animal, everything felt right. Flash felt right beneath him.

Brandon rode alongside him. "It's like old times, bro."

Kit nodded. "Feels good to be riding with you again."

"You don't know what it means to me."

"Sure I do."

"Scott feels terrible."

"I can imagine, but accidents happen. Corky will do a great job for you."

Brandon checked his watch. "It's time for me to head back in for the parade."

"I'll be right beside you when it's time. I bet you'll do it under 3 seconds." To bring down the steer in 2.9 would be hard to do but it wasn't impossible.

"I've got to get in that range to keep my average."

"Hold that thought." They high-fived.

Kit watched with pride as his brother rode in. Flash was frisky so he rode him around for a while then headed to the arena to wait their turn. Natalie would be in the bleachers by now.

He patted his horse. "We've got to do our best tonight. Brandon needs a win and we don't want to disappoint Natalie with a poor performance."

In the background he could hear the "Star Spangled Banner" sung by a local country singer, then the roar of the crowd and the applause. Finally came the announcements to open the San Antonio Rodeo.

"This is it." He walked Flash inside to a place where the other hazers were lined up. Some of the riders were familiar and they nodded to him. Because of his standings, Brandon would be second out of the box. Kit found his spot in line. Before long it was time for him to back into the box on the timed-event side of the arena.

"Next up, Brandon Saunders, mounted on his champion horse Ringo, from Marble Falls, Texas. Tonight his substitute hazer is Miles Saunders. They were known in the past as the dynamic brother duo!"

Kit heard a roar from the crowd. He watched his brother on the other side of the chute. He looked fierce. Kit knew that rush of adrenaline every rider experienced while they waited. When Brandon nodded his head, they released the steer and Kit rocketed out of the box to bookend the steer and ride close enough to touch it. Brandon picked it off fast while Kit rode on to rein in his brother's horse.

"That's a time of 3.0! Brandon is definitely on his game tonight!"

A huge roar went up from the crowd again.

The relief Kit felt left him overjoyed for his brother. After losing Scott, he'd had to fight through the bitter disappointment, but tonight he'd pulled it off. When the last steer wrestler had performed, the announcer said Brandon's time was the best of the night. *Hallelujah.*

Since his brother had to wait around to pick up his gold buckle for the night, Kit left both horses with Brandon's team and walked back to the trailer to get his clothes and put them in his car. Then he headed to the bleachers. Now that his part was over, the only thing driving him was the need to be with Natalie.

Even from a distance he spotted her gleaming honey-blond hair. He had no idea where Luckey or Vic had positioned themselves, but it didn't matter because she looked happy. There was an empty seat next to her and Amy sat in her stroller in front of her, drinking water from a bottle.

As he walked toward her he heard a familiar voice. "Miles?"

It was his mother, but he'd been so intent on reaching Natalie, he was slow on the uptake. She sat on Natalie's right side and grasped his hand. "I'm so proud of you boys I could burst."

"Thanks, Mom."

He bent to kiss her cheek, but his gaze had centered on another pair of eyes that were focused on him, glowing a hot green. Kit moved past his mother.

"You were fantastic out there," Natalie said in a quiet voice. "Come and sit down."

As he stepped around the stroller and took his seat, Amy saw him and held up her hands, dropping the water bottle. "Kit!"

Not immune to that entreaty, he undid the strap and pulled Amy into his arms. "Did you see the horses?"

"Hus." She gave him a big smile and kissed his cheek several times. The gesture went straight to his heart, as did Natalie's smile. The bareback riding event had gotten under way, but Kit couldn't concentrate on anything while he held Natalie's daughter on his lap.

"You have a new little rodeo fan, Father Segal. And here you were, hoping you could still pull it off. If you want my opinion, they should give you hazers a gold buckle. Your mother agrees with me."

"How much does she know about us?" he whispered.

"Your brother told her I'm a friend," she whispered back. "I've enjoyed sitting next to her. She taught me a lot about steer wrestling while we watched."

Kit should have remembered his mother would be here to cheer them on. It hadn't occurred to him that the two would meet.

Luckey and Vic had to be around here somewhere. The rodeo would go on for another half hour, but for his friends' sake Kit didn't want to force them to be here any longer. Besides, Amy was restless. "Get ready to leave when the bareback riding ends. I'll carry the stroller while you bring Amy."

"Okay."

He moved Amy into her arms. The diaper bag sat behind the seat of the stroller. He picked up the water bottle and stowed it inside. As soon as the announcer called for the tie-roping to start, Kit stood and carried the stroller past several fans to the aisle on the other side of him. Natalie followed with Amy who hadn't liked being moved. He'd talk to his mother later.

When they reached the parking area he headed straight for his car and put the stroller in the trunk. Once he'd unlocked the car, Natalie fastened Amy in the car seat. He held the front door open for her and then went around to slide in behind the steering wheel.

Relief swept through him that his brother had the winning time. But more than that, he was thankful there'd been no incident to mar the night for them. He watched to see if they were being followed. En route to the motel his cell rang. He attached his Bluetooth earpiece and answered.

"Great job out there!"

"Thanks, Luckey. I take it you didn't spot Morales or his sister."

"Not tonight."

"I'm relieved to hear it. You're free to go and enjoy the rest of your evening."

"I'll tell Vic."

"Good. Just remember I'm here for you guys when you need my help."

"We know that. It was a real pleasure meeting Mrs. Harris. I told Vic I wish I'd met her first. She's a stunner, and even better, she's nice."

"Agreed." Nice went a long way in Kit's book, too. "Talk to you later." He ended the call.

Kit flashed Natalie a sideways glance, loving the sight of her profile. She was feminine to the core. "If there was no threat, we could have stayed through the whole program. Sorry to have to pull you away if you were enjoying it."

"It was the perfect time to leave. Amy kept squirming. I was pretty sure I'd have to take her out when she'd finished her water." She turned toward him. "Your mother is a lovely person. I can see where you get your coloring."

"Most people think I look like my dad."

"Then he must have been one tall and attractive Texas Ranger, too."

"Luckey's the one the females flock to," Kit said to hide his emotions. "He's still single—that's why we nicknamed him Luckey."

She chuckled. "What about Ranger Malone? Is Vic his real name?"

"He's part Lipan Apache. His Ranger ancestor was named Victorio and Vic was named for him. But he likes the short version."

"That's fascinating. And how did you get the name Kit?"

"When I first joined the Rangers, my boss said, 'Your reputation at the police academy precedes you. Like Kit Carson, "You're clean as a hound's tooth."' The nickname stuck."

"I can't imagine a greater compliment. It fits you to a tee. I can vouch for that myself. If your father were alive, he would have been proud of you and your brother tonight."

"I'm sure you're right."

"Your mom was ecstatic."

"You know mothers."

"Yes. I had a great one, too."

"It shows."

"Thank you," she whispered.

"Have you noticed Amy's fallen asleep?"

"She's had a big day."

"And a big scare from a big hus."

Natalie's quiet laughter stayed with him. Before long they arrived at the motel and he drove to the parking space in front of his room. Kit wanted to stay in the moment and not get out. The need to take her into his arms was so strong he turned to reach for her, but there was a knock on the window.

He jerked around in surprise, thinking it must be one of the guys.

Janie?

In the next breath he opened the door and got out of the car.

"Sorry, Kit. I didn't mean to startle you."

Kit couldn't concentrate because Natalie had gotten out of the car and had opened the back door to retrieve Amy.

"I promised Scott I'd come to watch Brandon's performance and take pictures. Your brother said you were staying at the Bucking Horse. Scott wanted me to thank you for pinch-hitting for him. It's because of you that Brandon wound up with a 3.0."

He looked back at Janie, barely registering her comments. "Tell Scott I'm sorry about his accident. We're all hoping he gets better soon so he can end the season in Las Vegas with Brandon." He closed the door and locked the car with the remote.

"I will. It's…it's wonderful to see you again, Kit."

"It's good to see you, too. Now, if you'll excuse me, I have to go in." He started to leave. She followed him.

"Brandon didn't tell me you're seeing someone. I was so surprised when I saw her sitting by your mom."

A lifetime ago he might have been glad that she minded, but not anymore. If anything, he was irritated that she hadn't called him on the phone to tell him all this. Or better yet, hadn't made contact at all. If he were Scott, he wouldn't be happy to know his wife was here alone talking to her old boyfriend. Her unexpected appearance had shattered the moment for Kit.

"Be safe driving home," was all he said before he headed for Natalie's door.

ONCE INSIDE THE motel room, Natalie had put a sleeping Amy in the crib then darted over to the window to look through the curtain. The attractive dark-blonde woman talking to Kit obviously knew him well. Natalie felt a stab of jealousy she couldn't help.

For the woman to come up to the car to get his attention spoke of long-time familiarity. Kit's jaw had hardened when he'd recognized her. Until she'd knocked on the window, Natalie had felt Kit might have been going to kiss her. But in an instant the mood had been broken.

She jumped when she heard the soft knock on the door. Natalie smoothed the hair off her hot cheeks and opened it. "Hi."

"Is Amy still asleep?"

"Yes."

"We need to talk." He spoke in a quiet tone and

walked in, locking the door behind him. "I shouldn't have let you come into the room alone before I could check it."

"I wasn't thinking."

"For once I wasn't concentrating. It was a slip that could have ended in disaster. Sit down while I call the front desk and ask them to bring in a cot. I'll be sleeping by you tonight. I'll tell them to put it outside the door so it won't wake Amy."

She was so happy he was going to stay with her, she could hardly contain it. He walked over to the bedside table and phoned housekeeping. Then he sat on the side of the bed while she sank into a chair.

"I take it that woman is a friend of yours."

His gaze traveled over her features. "She's Scott's wife. They have a little boy."

"Oh!" That was enough to stifle her fear that he was in an ongoing relationship with her.

"I knew her long before any of us knew Scott."

Her heart plummeted. "Us?"

"Brandon and me. Janie was my girlfriend during our steer wrestling days. I thought the day would come when we would get married."

"What happened?"

"I decided to go into law enforcement rather than be a rancher. She knew the pain our family had gone through when our father died. To know I'd chosen a career that had killed my father upset her to the point that she broke up with me."

Groan. "That must have been devastating."

"I suffered for a while. But time passed and I realized it was the best thing that could have happened. She met Scott—a good, steady rancher and horseman. I was free to do the work I enjoy, knowing I wasn't tearing my wife apart because she was afraid for me." He sat forward. "Luckey had a wife like that. After a year they divorced because she couldn't take it."

"I can understand that. Are you over Janie?"

"A long time ago," he said without hesitation.

That sounded definite. After a pause she added, "Do you think she's over you?"

"Yes. I'm convinced she tracked me down here because she was curious to see the woman who was sitting at the rodeo with my mother."

"I presume that was her coveted place for a long time. I get it. Did you tell her who I was?"

"I said nothing and told her I had to go in. I'm working on your case, but my brother got careless and told her where I was staying. He knows better, but he forgot. It's the reason I don't have much of a personal life while I'm on a case."

"It's all right, Kit."

"No, it isn't." He got to his feet and put his hands on his hips. His brows met in a frown. "I promised to protect you, but I let my brother's need take precedence over my duty to you. Never again."

"Your boss had it right. Like Kit Carson, you're as clean as a hound's tooth. Cut yourself some slack for getting interrupted by your old girlfriend. That wasn't your fault. Don't forget that two of your Ranger buddies guarded me at the rodeo. If anyone is to blame, it's me, for getting out of the car before you told me to. I'm the one who could have walked in on someone waiting in the room."

"Thank heaven it was empty," he muttered with emotion. "If Morales had been inside, he could have taken you and Amy hostage. If my boss knew what had happened, he'd probably throw me out of the Rangers and he would have every justification."

Natalie got up from the chair. "I see why you're so upset. This has taught me a lesson, too. I'll follow your directions to the letter. Will that be good enough for you?"

His rigid body relaxed and he let out a deep sigh. "It's going to have to be. Why don't you get ready for bed while I see if they've brought the cot?"

"Okay."

Natalie disappeared into the bathroom and got undressed. Her pajamas and robe were hanging on the hook on the back of the door. She put everything on and brushed her teeth. When she came out, she noticed the cot opened up in front of the TV. Kit had pushed a chair into the corner and was talking on his cell phone.

She took a peek at Amy then got into the double bed, turning on her side away from him.

A few minutes later the light went out. She heard the creaking of the cot. Kit had to be exhausted. "Kit?"

"Yes?"

"My heart was in my throat when your event was announced. The second the chute opened, it looked like two torpedoes shot forward. It was over so fast I didn't have time to blink. What both of you did out there today was incredible. You have to be thrilled. You know your brother is thankful. So enjoy the triumph of this night. Please."

Maybe five minutes passed before he spoke, but it wasn't the comment she'd expected. "That's hard to do. Vic got into trouble on a case because of a mistake he made. It almost cost him his badge."

"What happened?"

"Someone kidnapped his son from elementary school."

"Oh, no—"

"The guy was caught and arrested. When Vic interrogated him at the jail, the kidnapper refused to tell him where he'd taken his son. Vic went crazy and grabbed him. I saw him through the window and stepped in to stop him."

"He was only trying to find his son."

"True. But he forgot to be careful. That's what happened to me tonight. It won't happen again."

"Did he find his son?"

"Yes, thank God."

Kit wasn't about to let this go and she realized there was nothing she could say that would make him feel better. Naturally he'd been distracted by the woman he'd once planned to marry. But Natalie reasoned to herself that if he had loved her more than anything, he wouldn't have become a Ranger.

When she'd given up hope of any more talk he spoke again. "The only way I can savor this night is knowing you and Amy weren't harmed because of my distraction. You have to know your little girl is adorable. I'll never forget the look of fright on her face when that horse neighed. She hugged me so hard, I can still feel it."

"Her response was instinctive." Natalie had witnessed it. Anyone watching would have thought Kit was her father. Amy knew where to turn for safety and affection. Not in all the time Rod had lived at the house did he embrace Amy like that.

"Get a good sleep, Natalie."

"I could wish the same for you, but I know that as long as you're guarding me, you'll never get the kind of sleep you need."

"I manage."

Tears trickled out of her eyes onto the pillow. *Sweet, wonderful Kit...*

AFTER PHONING THE officer inside the house to let him know they were back, Kit drove the Altima into Natalie's garage at six Sunday evening. Much as he would have loved for them to stay and play in the swimming pool at the motel and not come home until dark, he refused to take any more unnecessary risks while Morales and his sister were still at large. Instead they stopped at several parks to allow Amy to run around while he stood guard, then drove home and ate their meals en route.

Kit helped Natalie inside with Amy. While she took care of her daughter, he went into the den with the officer and shut the door.

"Now we can talk. Tell me what's gone on."

"No one tried to break in, but several people came to the house. The first person rang the bell about one yesterday afternoon. The man left a lawn care brochure on the front door handle. I put it on the kitchen table. Today a couple of women knocked on the door around eleven. They were Jehovah Witnesses and left the *Watchtower* magazine."

"While you're still here, I'll pull the tape on the camera." Kit walked through the house to the front door and opened it. After he returned to the study they looked at the footage. "The lawn man doesn't resemble Morales, but could have been paid by him to case the place."

Kit kept looking until he saw the women. "They're the wrong ages and body shapes to impersonate Juanita. But they could be working for her."

"Maybe they've decided the money and guns aren't here and the people who came by the house were on the level."

"Maybe," Kit muttered. "Thanks for doing a great job. I'll take over from here."

He walked the officer to the back door. When he'd gone, Kit gathered the material left on the kitchen table and went to the den. First he called the Better Business Bureau and learned that Greenside Lawn Service was a legitimate business. Next he contacted the company to verify the employment of the man whose name had been stamped on the pamphlet. Everything checked out.

After phoning the Jehovah Witnesses Kingdom Hall number printed on the magazine, Kit asked if their people had been passing out magazines in northwest

Austin. No one could give him a definitive answer. Call back tomorrow.

He intended to do that after he went to the office in the morning. Kit had already set up a 9:00 a.m. meeting with the FBI agent working on the accounting investigation at LifeSpan. While he was checking some new emails on his laptop, his phone rang. He picked up when he saw who was calling.

"Cy? I thought you were on a case."

"I am, and something has turned up that might have a bearing on yours. Can you talk?"

"Yes."

"When I gave TJ an update on my investigation, he informed me about your case and suggested we share any new information."

"Does he see a link?"

"I think it's more of a hunch."

"If you're coming in to headquarters in the morning, let's talk then. I plan to be there by six-thirty."

"I'll be in around seven and find you."

"Sounds good."

"Luckey told me you nailed it at the rodeo. That's no surprise. Brandon could very well be the champion in December."

"We're hoping."

"So how are the widow and the priest? I've felt left out."

Kit's smile turned into a chuckle. "You guys never give up."

"As I recall you were relentless while I was protecting Kellie. Has the boss's advice been a help?"

He took a deep breath. "You *know* it hasn't."

"Yup. That's what I thought. See you in the morning." He was gone before Kit had a chance to say goodbye.

Kit would need surveillance on Natalie first thing in the morning. He made one more call, this time to headquarters to set it up. No sooner had he rung off than his phone sounded again. It was ten after ten. His mother. He'd been expecting this.

"Hi, Mom."

"I hope you have a minute to talk. We didn't get a chance at the arena. Thank you for hazing for Brandon. Thank you for being a wonderful son." Kit heard the tears in her voice.

"Luckily the captain gave me a day off that allowed me to do it."

"Brandon was so grateful. He told me Mrs. Harris is a friend of yours."

He'd been waiting for her to say something about Natalie. "She is."

"That little girl of hers is darling."

"Agreed. Mom? I'm still working on a case so I'll have to say good-night."

"All right."

"When this latest one is wrapped up, we'll all get together and take a little trip somewhere." He knew his mother worried about her bachelor sons, but that was an area where he couldn't help her out.

"I'd love that!"

"So would I, but I've got to go. Love you, Mom. Talk to you soon."

By the time he walked through the house to check the locks and turn off the lights, he discovered Natalie had gone to bed. Their talk last night had changed the atmosphere between them. She'd blamed herself for getting out of the car before he'd given her the signal.

All day she'd been careful to do everything right. Now she'd disappeared on him. He needed this case to be solved so they could behave naturally with each other.

Janie's unexpected appearance had made him realize he'd crossed the line in his mind. And in so doing, he'd left himself vulnerable. That meant he'd have to watch every step to ensure Natalie and Amy's safety, but it was getting harder and harder to do. Against his better judgment, his desire for Natalie had been growing, and now all he really wanted to do was to pull her into his arms and kiss her senseless.

Chapter Seven

Kit's watch alarm went off at six. He got up and out of the house before anyone else stirred. After leaving a note on the counter that he'd be at headquarters if Natalie needed to talk to him, he left in his car. A rug-cleaning service van was parked across the street. He nodded to the guys and drove downtown.

At work he stopped in the makeshift lunch room where he poured two cups of coffee and grabbed a couple of doughnuts. When he reached his office, the first thing he saw was a forensics report in his in-basket. He put the food on the desk and reached for the printout.

The DNA from the black hair found in Rodney Harris's car was a match for the DNA of felon Juanita Morales. Kit didn't need to read the rest. The case was coming together. Where in the hell were she and Alonzo hiding out? How soon could Natalie expect another visit?

"Kit?"

Cy had arrived. "Come on in and have breakfast with me."

"Don't mind if I do." They sat across from each

other. Cy bit into a doughnut. "The guys were right. Anyone would think you're a priest." He squinted at his friend. "Is the collar providing enough protection?"

"What do you think?" Kit muttered before taking a sip of the hot coffee.

"I can only speak from my own experience. A week into my undercover role as Kellie's husband and I wanted it to be real. I take it that's the place where you are about now."

"You're not a Ranger for nothing." Kit let out a frustrated sigh. "I swear I'm going to go crazy if I don't catch up with the Morales duo soon."

Cy leaned forward to reach for his cup. "That's why I'm here. After talking with TJ, I sent you an email. Open it and take a look."

Kit turned to the computer and found Cy's email.

Marcos Garcia, 63, of Sunset Valley, Austin, Texas, convicted of wire fraud affecting a financial institution, has been sentenced to 18 months in prison. He's been ordered to pay restitution totaling $400,000 by US District Court Judge Richard Salazar.

The Assistant US Attorney who handled the case stated that Garcia was an employee of the Empire Guaranty Mortgage Company based in Houston. He was responsible for preparing loan packages and forwarding the documents to financial institutions that provide financing and advisory services for assets management.

Kit looked up from his reading. "How do loan packages like these work?"

"In legal transactions, financial institutions purchase loans originated by mortgage companies, allowing the mortgage company to receive immediate payment and the financial institution to collect the interest."

"How exactly was Garcia implicated?"

"During this scheme, he signed a number of loan documents using various names. He forwarded these documents to multiple investor financial institutions, one of which was Austin Metroplex Bank. In effect, Garcia set it up so that there were numerous loans all connecting back to a single property, a fact that was not disclosed to the financial institutions."

"Ah."

"The proceeds of the fraudulent loans were subsequently wired into the account of a company associated with Empire Guaranty Mortgage Company. It's a bogus company. The name Julia Varoz comes up on the records, but there's no live body to prove she exists. As a result of Garcia's actions, Austin Metroplex Bank was one of nine financial institutions to suffer a loss. The total fraud scheme amounted to approximately twenty-five million dollars."

Kit let out a whistle. "Why does TJ feel this case touches on the one I'm investigating?"

Cy's brows lifted. "Julia Varoz is missing and so is four-hundred-thousand dollars. You're looking for Juanita and Alonzo Morales. One or both of them ransacked Natalie Harris's house looking for that exact sum of money."

"So TJ is thinking Julia could be Juanita, but the alias hasn't come up on the criminal index."

"Not yet. The connection I see is that Park withdrew four-hundred thousand from his account the day before he was murdered. Garcia owes that amount in restitution for his crime, but he's behind bars and Julia Varoz is missing."

"So maybe all four of them have been pulling off two cons at the same time," Kit mused aloud.

"It's possible."

Kit's thoughts shot ahead. "Juanita might be the girlfriend trying to find that money to help Garcia when he's released from prison. Maybe she turned on Harold."

"I don't know. But think about it... Garcia's only serving an eighteen-month sentence. Maybe Park double-crossed them and hid the money where they couldn't get at it."

"Esger made fraudulent documents for Juanita, but she might have found another forger to make her a new Varoz alias in order to run that dummy account for Garcia. But to find the right forger is a tough order."

"Yup." Cy finished off his coffee. "I've got to get going, but I wanted to give you something to chew on. Knowing you, you'll find the common denominator."

"Back at you. Your instincts are never wrong, Cy. Neither are TJ's. This could be huge."

He stood. "We'll just keep pecking away."

"Amen to that."

Deep in thought after Cy left, Kit went to the conference room to meet with the FBI agent working on the LifeSpan accounting fraud. He added his input. After they concluded their meeting, he left the building for the Kingdom Hall Center.

AS SOON AS Natalie put Amy down for her nap at two, she went into the kitchen and called the nursing home in Denver. Today a service had been held for Amy's great-grandmother. The older woman had been on Natalie's mind.

"Cottonwood Nursing Home."

"Hello. My name is Natalie Harris. I'm calling to speak to someone who handled the funeral service for Gladys Park earlier today."

"Oh. That would be Mrs. Issac. I'll connect you." In a moment another voice came on the line.

"Hello? Mrs. Harris?"

"Yes. Thank you for answering. I want to know how the service went for Gladys Park. I sent flowers and wondered if you'd received them."

"We certainly did. The carnations were just lovely."

"I'm glad. Can you tell me anything about the service?"

"Well, the pastor said a few words and then one of the patients here spoke. Several of her friends from the church came. Also the podiatrist who took care of her sore feet right before she died. Gladys was well loved."

"I'm so glad to hear it. By any chance was there a picture taken? I'd like to have one for my daughter's scrapbook."

"I did take some for the pastor with his camera. He wanted to post the photos at the church in Gladys's memory and asked me to be sure I caught one of the floral arrangement with her name on it in gold letters."

"I'd love to have copies. Could I have his phone number?"

"Of course. You left your information when you were here. I'll email his number to you right now."

"Thank you so much."

"You're very welcome."

Natalie got off the phone and opened her laptop. As soon as she received the information, she phoned the number of Pastor Sidney Clark. Her call went to his voice mail. She left a message with her phone number and hung up.

She had no idea when she'd hear from him. Time was weighing heavy on her hands. Kit hadn't called and he'd left early this morning. Amy had asked for him several times throughout the day, and every time the little girl said his name, it echoed in Natalie's heart.

It was no good waiting for the phone to ring. She picked it up and dialed Jillian, but her voice mail picked up, as well. Colette would be at work, so it would be better to talk to her tonight.

Natalie went to her bedroom and turned on her TV. She skimmed through the channels. As she was trying to get interested in a program on supernovas, her cell rang. The screen indicated a Colorado area code. She reached for it and said hello.

"Mrs. Harris? This is Pastor Clark returning your call."

"Thank you so much, Pastor. I spoke with Mrs. Issac from the nursing home and I understand you had pictures taken at the service for Gladys Park."

"Yes. For the posting board in the foyer of the church. I like our flock to know and remember our church members."

"That's a lovely thing to do. She's my daughter's great-grandmother. I've made a baby book for her and I'd love to have copies of the photos. Would it be possible for you to send them to me?"

"Of course. I'll ask my secretary to forward them to your email address." Natalie gave him her information; he promised to take care of it right away.

"You have no idea how much this means to me. Before we hang up, could you tell me how long you knew Gladys?"

"Oh, my, maybe twenty years. She and her husband Joseph were faithful members."

"I married her grandson late in her life and only met her last week. I took my daughter with me so she could see her."

"I visited her later that very day," he commented. "She told me how happy your visit made her. Bless you for coming to see her. She died holding on to that memory."

Natalie's eyes filled with tears. Without Kit, that trip to Denver would never have happened. "I'm thankful she had you to watch over her, Pastor. You don't know how much I appreciate your kindness. Do you know where she was interred?"

"Fairmount Cemetery next to her husband and their son and his wife."

"One day when my daughter is older, we'll go there. I'll look forward to receiving those photos. Thanks again."

"You're welcome, Mrs. Harris. God bless you."

Thrilled to have made contact, Natalie got off the phone and went to the kitchen to make some kind of a treat for Kit to thank him. She took her laptop with her and put it on the kitchen table.

What would he love? After some thought she decided to make brownies. Once they'd cooled she would ice them with peppermint frosting then pour melted chocolate chips over the top. The trick was to cut them into squares before the chocolate set. Her mom's recipe had always been a huge hit.

An hour later Amy awakened. Natalie brought her into the kitchen and set her up so she could play with the tins in the kitchen cupboard. She dangled the measuring spoons on a ring in front of her. Amy saw them. "Mama." She lifted her hands.

"Say 'spoons.'"

"Spoons."

"Yes." She kissed her cheeks. "Spoons."

Laughter bubbled out of Natalie. She found a wooden spoon so her daughter could pound on the bottoms of the saucepans. While she started cutting the brownies, she heard the text alert from her phone and glanced at the screen.

Driving into the garage.

Kit was home! Joy, joy, joy.

WHEN KIT WALKED into the house he was bombarded by the delicious smell of chocolate. He had to stop when he reached the kitchen because Amy sat surrounded by pots and pans and utensils, blocking his path.

"Kit!" She showed him the measuring spoons she held in one hand. "Spoons!" In the other she gripped a wooden spoon that she pounded on everything she could find. He burst into laughter and got down on his haunches. Picking up a potato masher, he tapped along on a couple of tins.

In the midst of all this he shot Natalie a glance. In her nautical-striped top and white shorts, those long legs made his breath catch. "I think your daughter might be turning into a drummer. Look at her go!"

Her radiant smile was unexpected after the tension between them last night. "I've been listening to her repertoire since she got up from her nap. Show her the ice cream scoop and ask her what it is."

He did as she suggested and held it in front of Amy. "What's this?"

"Scoop!"

Her answer amused him so much he picked up a heart-shaped cookie cutter. "What's this?"

"Cookie!"

That was close enough. He was having too much fun to quit. He found the spatula and lifted it.

"Spat!" She'd put her heart into it.

"Yes. *Spat*ula. You're even smarter than I realized." Kit leaned forward and kissed the top of her golden curls. She smelled sweet, like Natalie. Heavenly.

"You're home early," Natalie observed.

He looked up into those fabulous green eyes. "Yup. I could smell those brownies all the way to headquarters and decided to come home in time to sample them. Is that permitted?"

"I made them for you." She put half a dozen of the small squares on a plate and carried it to the table with some napkins.

"What's the occasion?"

He watched her open a jar of Vienna sausages and hand her daughter one. "It's a special thank-you. Would you like coffee or tea?"

"How about milk?"

"Coming right up." She poured him a glass and brought it to the table. Kit got up from the floor and joined her.

"What did I do to deserve all this?"

"I talked to the pastor who officiated at the service for Gladys today. He said our visit gave her peace before she died." Kit could tell she was fighting tears. "I'll never forget that you made that visit possible. You could have gone on your own to get information. But being the kind of person you are, you included Amy and me, even though it would have been easier for you to go alone."

"It was my pleasure, Natalie."

"You're such a good man. The pastor said that Gladys and Joseph Park were revered members of the congregation. That means everything to me. One day I'll take Amy to visit her grandparents and great-grandparents at the cemetery." She cleared her throat. "He had pictures taken at the service to post at his church. I asked him to email me copies for Amy's baby book."

"Have they come yet?"

"I'll look after I put Amy in the high chair. It's time for her dinner."

While she dealt with her daughter he started eating the brownies and couldn't stop until he'd eaten every one. "Are the rest of the brownies in the pan for me, too?"

She looked down at his empty plate with a faint smile. "What do *you* think?"

"I think you've won my allegiance for life. You could have a million-dollar career selling these."

"I'm glad you like them."

"I promise to save you one."

"Don't worry about it. I can always make another batch."

"Promise?"

Her eyes smiled at him before she fed her daughter some carrots and beef from the baby food jar. He got busy putting everything on the floor back in the drawers and cupboards. By now Amy was being treated to some Goldfish crackers. Her eyes lit up. "Fish!"

Kit grabbed one and put it in his mouth. "Fish. Yum!"

"Yum," she mimicked. He laughed.

Natalie grinned as she checked her emails. "Better watch what you say around her. She's a sponge."

Kit ate another fish and Amy promptly imitated him.

"Oh, good! The pictures have come. There are two

of them. One of the casket and the other a group photo."
She studied them for a minute. "The secretary took
the time to label each person. How nice. The flowers
on the casket are beautiful. Take a look." She slid the
laptop in front of Kit.

He knew these pictures meant a lot to Natalie, but
the people held no significance for him until he saw
the name Dr. Varoz.

She had blond hair, but it was *Juanita Morales*. He'd
bet his life on it.

By the merest chance he'd found the woman Cy
was searching for in relation to the mortgage fraud
case. There was no time to lose. He flicked his gaze
to Natalie.

"Excuse me for a second. I need to call the director
of the nursing home right away."

"Use my phone. I called Mrs. Issac not too long ago,
so her number should be right there in my call history."

"Thank you." He waited for his call to be answered
then asked to speak to the director.

"This is she."

"It's Father Segal calling from Austin."

"Oh, yes, Father. How can I help you?"

"Mrs. Reese just shared the photos from the service for Gladys Park. Can you tell me about the blond
woman, Dr. Varoz? She was in the group photo. Was
she a church member, too?"

"No. She filled in for the regular podiatrist who
went on vacation."

"Who was that?"

"Dr. Nyman."

"I see. How many times did Dr. Varoz come to see Gladys?"

"Just once, last Friday. Gladys was feeling poorly so she stayed awhile to keep her company."

"Do you know why she came to the service?"

"She'd been at the nursing home to see another patient. I guess she decided to attend the service since she'd spent time with Gladys on Friday."

It meant Gladys hadn't supplied her with the information she'd been looking for. Today she'd hung around; possibly hoping to find out where Gladys's possessions were located.

"Can you tell us who handled her financial arrangements? Mrs. Harris would like to get in touch with them."

"The attorney for Mrs. Park."

"Do you have a name?"

"Let me check. Yes, here it is. The firm of Farbes and Lowell." She gave him the phone number.

"Thank you for that information. Sorry to bother you."

"No problem at all."

He hung up and gave Natalie her phone. "I'll be right back."

On an adrenaline rush he hurried into the den and phoned Cy on his cell. "Come on, bud. Pick up."

The second he heard his friend's voice he pounced. "You'll never guess who was at the funeral service for Harold Park's grandmother today. Julia Varoz, alias Juanita Morales."

"What?"

"Yup. TJ's hunch paid off. I'm looking at a picture of her as we speak. She's wearing her blond disguise, posing as a podiatrist for Gladys Park. That puts her in Denver earlier today. When Natalie's house was ransacked and no money was found, she must have left for Denver. This is the break we've both been looking for."

"I'm calling TJ. We need to put out an APB on her immediately."

"I'll email you the picture from Natalie's laptop and meet you at headquarters."

He ended the call with Cy and phoned downtown to get the surveillance team back to guard Natalie. When he started for the kitchen he discovered she'd taken Amy into the living room to play with her toys.

She stared at him. "What did you see in those photos that sent you flying out of the room?"

"Juanita Morales."

Natalie gasped.

"She was the assumed podiatrist while the real doctor was on vacation. Juanita is a professional. After doing her homework she knew exactly how to get into the nursing home without creating suspicion."

Frown lines marred Natalie's pretty face. "She must have thought Rod had hidden the money with Gladys. What an evil mind."

There was a lot more he could tell her but not right now. "We're setting up a manhunt to find her. Hopefully it will lead us to her brother. I have to go to headquarters, but I won't leave until the surveillance team gets here. They should be out front any minute."

He picked up the beach ball and rolled it to Amy.

She was so excited she scrambled to her feet to push it toward him. Laughter rolled out of her as they played the game, and it hit him that he loved this little girl. And, heaven help him, he loved her mother, too.

LONG AFTER NATALIE had put Amy down for the night, she still was too wired to go to bed. She changed into pajamas and a robe and went into the den, preferring to watch television on the larger screen. The room was small and could only accommodate the desk and a couch not much bigger than a love seat.

She noticed Kit's bedroll propped in the corner. If he'd tried to sleep on the couch, his feet would have hung over the end. No way would he have gotten any rest. Ever since he'd moved in she'd been worried about him sleeping on the floor, but he never complained.

Tonight he'd gone off without dinner. Those brownies wouldn't hold him for long. She was as bad as a wife who worried about her husband. *But he's not your husband, Natalie.* She could remind herself over and over again, but the fact remained she'd fallen in love with him.

And she had to face another truth. Amy was used to seeing him around the house and had grown attached to him. The longer he stayed here undercover, the more impossible everything was becoming. This wasn't a natural situation.

She needed to discuss it with Kit and decided to wait up for him. A plan had been forming in her mind that seemed to make good sense. Upon her mother's death, Natalie had begun receiving a monthly payment from an annuity. The money automatically went into a Certificate of Deposit to be used for a rainy day. And although Austin was experiencing hot and sunny weather, Natalie's rainy day had come.

She had to do something to free herself and Amy from a situation that was growing more and more untenable. *You're going to be hurt if you don't take action.* Separation was the only answer.

Nothing held her interest on TV, so she reached for a book on Lincoln she'd barely started and made up her mind to get into it. Anything to take her to a different world for a little while.

Near midnight she heard the hum of the garage door lifting and closed her book. Instead of getting up to greet Kit, she stayed on the couch to give him time. In a minute she heard sounds from the kitchen and then she heard him in the hall headed for the guest bathroom. When he walked into the den, the soft light from the lamp made him look grim.

"Kit?"

He lifted his head. "You're still up?"

"I've been waiting for you. Bad night?"

Kit raked his hair, a sign of frustration. "Have you ever gotten up early, ready to get everything done, then realized the people you needed to deal with weren't available yet?"

She nodded. "I know the feeling well."

"That's what it's like for me tonight. All the business I need to do has to wait until tomorrow." He sat on the upholstered chair. "I assumed you'd be asleep by now. What's on your mind?"

"You've got some icing from the brownies on your chin."

He flashed her a quick smile before wiping it off and licking his finger. "Guilty as charged. I finished the last of them."

"Without any dinner?"

"They're better than dinner."

She loved this man with a vengeance. "I can see you're exhausted."

"Not too tired to talk to you. What are you worried about?"

"Our situation."

His eyes narrowed. "I thought it was working just fine."

"It is. You've kept Amy and me perfectly safe, but we don't know how long it's going to take to find those two criminals. You're shackled here in order to protect me. If Juanita Morales was in Denver today, it's not likely they're going to try to break in here again."

"Your point is?" he asked tersely.

She flinched. "You need to be free to conduct that manhunt."

"Explain 'free' to me."

"It's no longer necessary for you to remain here undercover. I realize I still need protection, but that can be done by a private agency that provides bodyguards. I have money in a CD to pay for it. The last thing I want is to deplete your department of officers who have to watch me day and night."

His jaw hardened. "Until this case is solved, the department has an obligation to protect you, so forget dipping into your resources. Is there anything else on your mind?"

"Yes. Amy may only be a toddler, but she's attached to you in a way she never was to Rod. If you're not living here, she'll get over expecting you to walk in the door."

He expelled his breath. "I'll make other arrangements for you tomorrow if you want me to. I'm sorry you're trapped here so she can't play with her little friend across the street. This shouldn't have to go on for too much longer. I also realize you miss your job. Your whole life has been put on hold."

"So has yours, Kit. You're not able to enjoy a private life while you're on a case like mine. But from now on you can go to your own home at night and sleep in your bed instead of on the floor. You must be sick of wearing that clerical shirt. If I were in your shoes, I'd be eager to get rid of it."

While she'd been talking, he'd gotten up to roll out his sleeping bag and pillow. To her surprise he stretched out on top of it still dressed. "You're right. I *am* sick of it. I'm also exhausted."

"I'll leave so you can get some sleep."

"Wait—don't go yet. What about going into a temporary witness protection program with Amy? Would you consider that? You wouldn't have to leave Texas. You'd be removed to a place where you could enjoy a little more freedom but still be kept safe until the threat was over."

Natalie blinked. "Wouldn't the cost of that be more prohibitive than surveillance?"

"Forget the money aspect. Does it appeal to you?"

"No. I'd much rather stay in my home in surroundings that are familiar for Amy. I'm fine here. We both are. You're the one I'm worried about. You've been multitasking, trying to keep us safe and still be a Ranger. You must have eyes in the back of your head."

He chuckled. "That would be a first for the books."

"It's not funny, Kit. If anything happened to you…"

He raised himself up on one elbow and looked searchingly at her. He reached for her arm, gripping it gently. "If anything happened to me…what?"

She could hardly think with him touching her. "I don't want to think about it."

"What don't you want to think about?" he prompted.

Heat enveloped her. "This is a ridiculous conversation."

"You started it," he countered. "What are you afraid of?"

"I—I wouldn't want you to get hurt protecting me." Her stammer was a dead giveaway that her emotions were in turmoil.

"I wouldn't want anything to happen to either of us. For you to get hurt on my watch is unthinkable to me. Come here. Let's talk about it." He pulled her forward until she fell against him on the floor. He gathered her close and entangled their legs.

"Kit—" She half gasped his name.

"On second thought, I don't feel much like talking." He lowered his mouth to hers. Natalie had been wanting this for so long she was past thinking about the wisdom of it. Kit started kissing her with a hunger as great as her own. In an explosion of need she began kissing him back, forgetting everything as she poured out her feelings for him.

One kiss turned into another until she was trembling with desire. His hands and his mouth fueled the fire that was licking through her body. She'd never known rapture like this.

"I'm sorry, Natalie. I've tried to keep my distance, but it isn't possible. I want you—you have no idea how much." He buried his face in her neck.

"I feel the same way, but I was afraid you might be too chivalrous to kiss me, even if you found yourself wanting to."

He groaned and brought his face back to hers, kissing her until she hardly knew herself. "I've been denying myself since the day we met," he confessed against her lips. "It's been hell."

She no longer had to wonder what it would be like to lie in this Texas Ranger's arms. When she felt able to take a breath she said, "That night in the car outside the motel, I wanted so badly to let you know how I felt about you, but I was afraid you might not feel the same way."

Whatever he would have said was silenced by the ringing of his cell phone. Afraid of what it meant, she eased away from him so he could answer it.

"Cy, what's going on?" The Ranger wouldn't be calling him at one in the morning without a good reason.

Natalie felt Kit's body tense and knew he'd just been given some important news. When he ended the call, he wasn't the same amorous man who'd been kissing the daylights out of her. In an instant he'd turned back into the Ranger.

"I have to go to headquarters," he stated. "A surveillance team will be here in a few minutes."

Natalie got to her feet, knowing better than to badger him with questions. While he got ready, she went into the kitchen and packed up a couple of sandwiches for him to take. They met at the door leading into the garage. He'd put on his tan shirt and badge. "The guys are out in front, so you're in good hands."

She nodded and handed him the sack. "You need food to keep you going."

"Thank you, but I hope you know I need this more." He put his hand behind her head and kissed her until she was swaying. "I'll be in touch with you tomorrow."

"Whatever is going on, good luck, Kit."

Natalie locked up behind him and hurried through the house to the front window to watch him drive away, taking her heart with him.

Chapter Eight

Kit had told Natalie he was going into headquarters, but he planned to meet Cy at the jail.

Thanks to some fine investigating by the Colorado police after Kit had told them about Julia Varoz, they'd gotten a tip from the secretary working for Dr. Nyman. She'd met Ms. Varoz when she'd come into the doctor's office on Friday morning wanting an appointment.

When told he was on vacation, she'd left the office and said she'd be back. The secretary had followed her out to get something from her own car and noticed the woman drive off in a new black Lexus.

When the APB went out, some Texas patrolmen had spotted her Lexus and stopped her on the highway inside the Texas border. They'd arrested her on multiple counts of impersonating a doctor, fleeing arrest on the mortgage fraud scheme, murdering Harold Park and possession of fake IDs.

Overjoyed there was only one killer left at large before Natalie's case could be closed, Kit drove to the jail munching one of the ham sandwiches she'd made for him. Cy was waiting for him in the parking lot. He got out of the car.

"You did it, bud. You found her."

They walked inside. "Not me. Natalie. She was inspired to ask if there were pictures taken at the service for Gladys. In fact she's been inspired all the way along."

"But you were the one who flew her to Denver in the first place and got that information on Salter."

"Either way, we still have to find Alonzo."

"Maybe if we interrogate Juanita together, she'll crack."

"It's worth a try. This is a big win."

"I bet the boss even smiled when he heard about her arrest."

They passed through the checkpoint and walked down a corridor to the interrogation room. The guard at the door nodded to them.

"We're here to question the prisoner." They showed their IDs.

"You're on the list." He opened the door. Another guard stood inside.

Juanita, in striped prison garb, sat on the far side of the table. Her hands and ankles were shackled. She was thirty-two years of age but looked older, harder, than the mug shot taken eight years ago. The blond wig was missing. Her black hair hung loose to her shoulders and Kit noticed she'd had a recent manicure. Purple nails.

She sat back in the chair with her chin held high. "Ooh—two Texas Rangers." Her dark eyes flashed and she said something vulgar.

Kit went first. "Your bad mouth won't get you anywhere, Juanita."

"I'm not talking!"

His brows lifted. "You might care *if* you cooperate. You and your brother, Alonzo, are wanted for the murder of Harold Park. If Alonzo pulled the trigger instead of you, it could shorten the length of your prison sentence."

She eyed him with defiance. "Sure it could."

"You're the one with the problem, not me. Are you waiting for Marcos to get out of prison? Is that why you wanted to steal the four-hundred thousand from Park, so you can pay off the bill Marcos owes? Is he your lover? We've got you on a security tape at the Austin airport parking with Park. Was he your lover before you turned on him?"

No response.

Cy started in. "That was quite a haul you made from the dummy mortgage company. Twenty-eight-million dollars—that must be how you paid for the Lexus you were driving. It's going to lead us to your brother, but if you want to give us some help, it could buy you less time in prison. Think about it."

Juanita remained cool and collected. They weren't going to get anything out of her. By tacit agreement Kit and Cy left the interrogation room and headed for the exit.

"Do you think she'll consider your offer?"

Kit shook his head. "I don't know. Let's see how another twelve hours in jail affects her."

When they reached Kit's car, Cy said, "How's it going with Natalie?"

"Funny you should ask."

"Uh, oh."

Kit threw his head back. "She told me it was time for me to go. As if I didn't already know."

"What was her reason?"

"She said Amy was growing too attached to me."

"That's no surprise. What are you going to do?"

"I've got the surveillance crew guarding her 24/7. Do you know she offered to use her own money to hire a private bodyguard service to spare the department's budget?"

"As Luckey said, she's nice, in all the ways that count. Beautiful, too."

"Yup."

"I'm going to go home and get some shut-eye. How about you?"

"The same. I haven't been to my condo in over a week. See you in the morning. We've got a lot of work to do."

"You can say that again."

They parted company and Kit headed for his condo, finishing his other sandwich on the way. When he arrived at his place, he was pleased to see that his cleaning lady had kept it dust free. Once he'd grabbed a quick shower he climbed into bed and set his watch alarm for 7:00 a.m., then turned onto his stomach. Lying on a mattress definitely beat sleeping on the floor, but it didn't feel right being alone.

The place felt empty. There weren't any warm bodies in the house with him. No chance of stepping on a beach ball or a cow. No out-of-this-world brownies sitting on the kitchen counter begging to be eaten. No sweet-smelling female waiting for him on the couch. No little angel calling out his name, holding up her hands to be hugged and kissed.

Natalie had been right to suggest a change in their arrangement. Tonight he'd wanted her so badly there would have been no stopping him if Cy hadn't phoned when he had. Letting go of her was the hardest thing he'd ever had to do.

What kind of a Ranger was he to take advantage of the woman he'd promised to keep safe? It didn't matter that she'd responded with the same hunger that drove him. He should have been the one in control. Until he closed the case, he didn't have the right to stay at her house overnight.

Tonight he'd taken off the clerical shirt and wouldn't be putting it on again. Father Segal was no more and already Kit felt as if he was in mourning.

WHEN KIT CAME to the next morning, he realized he'd slept through his alarm. It was eight-thirty. After a quick shave, he dressed in jeans and a shirt. Attaching his badge to the pocket, he left the condo. En route to headquarters he grabbed breakfast at a drive-through.

Cy was already at his desk as Kit walked by. "You're as late as I am. TJ has called a meeting for nine."

"That gives me five minutes." Kit went into his office to phone Natalie. She'd be up by now. He wouldn't be able to get through the day until he'd talked to her. She answered on the second ring.

"Kit?"

"Good morning. How did you sleep?"

"Fine. You must have loved being in your bed."

"I did. Listen, I'll be by later today to get all my things, but I'll phone you when I'm on my way. How's the cherub?"

"She's in her high chair making a big mess of her breakfast."

He chuckled. "Sounds like she's in top form." Natalie didn't mention whether she'd asked for him, and he resisted inquiring. "Thanks for those sandwiches. They saved my life last night. I discovered that no matter how delicious they are, man can't live on brownies alone."

She let out a little laugh. "Are you at work?"

"Yes. I'm about to go into a big meeting with the boss." He refrained from telling her to give Amy a hug from him. "Have a good day, Natalie. If you need me for any reason, just call."

"I'll remember. Stay safe, Ranger Saunders."

He hung up, not liking the formality. If what had happened between them last night was an aberration on her part, he didn't want to know about it. He'd left her house with an ache that had stayed with him, and she was the only person who could take it away.

Half a dozen Rangers were seated in TJ's office when he walked in. Cy had already arrived. Kit took a place next to Ranger Rodriguez.

"I've assembled you men to brief you on our manhunt for Alonzo Morales, responsible for the twenty-eight-million-dollar mortgage fraud that stole funds from nine banks. He's been on the Most Wanted list for eight years.

"Due to the brilliant work of Rangers Saunders and Vance, Morales's sister, Juanita, a known felon also on the Most Wanted list, was arrested last night driving to Austin from Denver. We're convinced that either she or Alonzo killed Harold Park, but she's not talking, having worked two cons—the Empire mortgage fraud case and the LifeSpan accounting fraud case.

"We believe Morales is in the Austin area searching for the four-hundred-thousand dollars, a percentage of the eight million embezzled by Park that's missing from the pharmaceutical corporation. We have to assume that he's armed and dangerous.

"You've all been given photos and rap sheets. His pictures are everywhere in Texas as well as the western states. Stay alert and report anything you hear to me, Saunders or Vance. That's all."

Everyone filed out except Kit.

"Captain? I wanted to inform you that I'm no longer staying at the Harris home undercover. Now that Juanita is jailed, one danger has been removed. So I'm having Mrs. Harris guarded outside the house by around-the-clock surveillance until we catch Morales."

"Smart move to free yourself up," TJ responded.

Kit averted his eyes. "Yes, sir."

Kit left the room to go back to his office. He needed to talk to the attorney in charge of Gladys Park's finances. If by any chance Harold had been in touch with his grandmother before his death, Kit would find out. He also wanted the attorney to know Gladys had a living relative, little Amy Harris.

When he reached the office of Farbes and Lowell and told the secretary he was calling on behalf of the Texas Rangers, Mr. Farbes came right on the line.

After Kit explained his business, the man sounded shocked. "You mean to tell me Harold Park married and had a child?"

"Yes."

"This is amazing. Joseph Park was a very successful architect and kept a considerable sum of money in trust, which he left to his wife. After his death she drew up her own will. Upon her death she asked that any money was to pass to their descendants or, in the absence of any living descendants, to their favorite charity.

"Since Harold was never found, my offices were preparing that charitable donation, but it hasn't yet taken place. I would need to fly to Austin and meet the mother of Harold's child. Depending on verification of birth records, that money could be put in trust for her."

Excitement for Natalie swept through Kit. "I'll email you all the pertinent information after we get off the phone. How soon can Mrs. Harris expect to hear from you?"

"I'll contact her within the week, Ranger Saunders."

"Thank you. She'll be waiting for your call."

Kit hung up, dazed by the turn of events. He couldn't wait to tell Natalie.

After he sent the necessary documentation to the attorney, he phoned Natalie and explained he was coming over to pick up his bedroll and toiletries.

On his way out the door he received a call from the circuit servant for the Kingdom Hall area. The two women who'd come to Natalie's door were indeed Jehovah Witnesses and had been passing out their literature in her neighborhood. Both the lawn service man and the missionaries had been legitimate. Kit could cross them off his list of persons of interest.

NATALIE WAS NERVOUS about seeing Kit again so soon. It was only eleven. She'd told him she'd slept fine, but that was a lie. She'd been awake most of the night and wished she hadn't suggested that he go back to his house. The need to be in his arms was causing her physical pain.

Amy had babbled about him all morning. If she saw him, she'd want to play. Natalie couldn't allow that to happen and put her down for a short nap. After a protest, she finally fell asleep.

Natalie showered and dressed in a skirt and blouse. After brushing her hair she put on a little more makeup than usual to conceal the fatigue lines. She didn't want him to think she expected a repeat of last night, in case he was regretting the lapse. But the truth was it downright frightened her, the possibility he might never kiss her again.

While she made fresh coffee, Natalie reasoned that she knew he wasn't a man who played women. But what kind of a message had she been sending him, waiting up for him as she had last night? No doubt he could sense how crazy she was about him—subconsciously she'd wanted it to happen. Any normal man would have made a pass, even a highly principled Texas Ranger. But she'd been so embarrassingly eager in her response...

The sound of the garage door lifting was music to her ears. Her cheeks felt hot just knowing he was here. When Kit walked in, she stayed busy emptying the dishwasher. "Hello, stranger," she teased without looking at him. "Long time no see."

"It seems like eons," he drawled in his deep voice, sending ripples of delight through her. "I've come with some amazing news."

She wheeled around and got caught in his all-encompassing gaze. "You've captured Alonzo Morales?"

"I wish that were the case. This is something else that directly affects you. Where's Amy?"

"Taking a nap."

"Then why don't we sit down."

Her heart thudded. "All right. Would you like coffee? I'm going to have some."

"That sounds good."

In her nervousness she spilled some of the hot liquid as she poured it into the mugs. After wiping up, she added cream and sugar and took them to the table. He held the chair out for her then sat across from her.

No more priest's collar. The formality was killing her.

"Thanks for the coffee. This is what I've needed all morning." He sipped the hot brew. "All right. Today I had a talk with Mr. Farbes, the attorney who handled the affairs of Gladys and Joseph Park. He was very interested to learn that the Parks have a living relative in Amy, and he will be contacting you and setting up a time to meet."

The mug almost slipped out of her hand. "Are you talking about an inheritance?"

"Yes. I have no idea of the amount, but he did say that Joseph Park was very successful in his profession. I'm sure he'll answer all your questions, but I wanted to tell you now so his phone call doesn't surprise you. Now, if you'll excuse me, I'll gather my things."

In a stupor-like state Natalie finished her coffee. It didn't take Kit long to appear with his arms loaded. He went out to his car and came back in empty-handed.

She looked up at him, feeling the wrench of loss. He'd only been here temporarily, but her soul was already grieving to know he wouldn't be staying with her anymore. "Again I find myself thanking you for everything. I never would have thought to inquire about Gladys's financial situation.

"I keep thinking back to the graveside service. I was in a state of shock, but not for long because one of the legendary Texas Rangers came to my rescue and restored my world in a brand-new way. Don't say you were just doing your job. I don't want to hear it."

His expression remained solemn as he responded. "I'll text you every day to keep you informed about your case. I have every reason to expect we'll catch Morales before the week is out. Then you can get back to work and Amy can go back to playing with her little friend across the street."

A text? He didn't even want to hear her voice? She supposed it was the perfect way for him to keep feelings and emotions out of the conversation. Perhaps he didn't regret last night, but he was backing away so she wouldn't get any ideas about it happening again.

"What about the camera at the front door?"

"We'll leave it for now. There's a chance it could still provide us with a clue. For the time being I'll keep the key and the remote."

But you won't use it, her heart cried.

"Thanks again for the coffee. Enjoy your day and don't worry. The arrests of Marcos and Juanita have been made public. The news is everywhere, so we can be pretty sure Alonzo will hear about it and make a mistake. When he does, we're ready for him."

Kit disappeared too quickly for her to say anything else. She had the crazy urge to run after him, but what good would it do to chase him? It would be too painful and humiliating. Apparently he'd quit her cold turkey and it was all her fault.

She went to her bedroom and changed into a pair of shorts and a T-shirt. Amy would be up soon and she would take her out to play in the backyard.

As she dressed Amy for play time, Natalie decided she would also take her laptop out to the patio table and pay bills. It would help fill her day.

When it was nearly time to go in for lunch, Natalie's phone rang. It was a Colorado area code.

"Hello?"

"Mrs. Harris? This is John Farbes from Farbes and Lowell in Denver. We represent the estate of Gladys Park."

"Oh, yes. Ranger Saunders told me you'd be calling."

"Would it be possible for me to come to your home at noon tomorrow to speak with you about your daughter?"

"That would be fine."

"He told you the reason?"

"He did, yes."

"Good. I'll see you soon, then." The attorney confirmed Natalie's address and suggested some of the documents she might want to have on hand for their meeting. "Thank you, Mrs. Harris."

"Thank *you*."

KEEP BUSY OR GO CRAZY.

Kit swung by the grocery store to do some shopping. Then he drove to his condo to put everything away. His sandwiches didn't taste like Natalie's. He drank half a quart of milk. Still not satisfied, he reached for the pack of chocolate-chip cookies. As he was opening it, his cell rang. The government number on the ID could mean several things.

"Ranger Saunders speaking."

"This is Officer Walton at the jail. Juanita Morales's arraignment before the judge is scheduled for three o'clock. She's asked to speak to you first. Alone."

Well, well, well. It sounded as if she was getting nervous. That was a good sign and worth his trouble to find out what she wanted before she headed to the courthouse.

A half hour later it was like déjà vu as he entered the interrogation room. He turned on his digital recorder.

Juanita didn't display the attitude of the day before. Overnight she'd lost her confidence and looked pitiful in her shackles.

"You're going to be taken before the judge within the hour. Say what you have to say."

This time her eyes didn't flash. They looked dull. "Did you mean what you said about cutting time off my sentence if I give you information?"

"That depends on how valuable it is."

"Harold's wife is in danger."

Her statement burned like acid. "What makes you say that?"

"Alonzo and I were the ones who ransacked her house."

"What were you looking for?"

"Four-hundred-thousand dollars and two guns. My brother was sure they were there, but we found nothing."

That money has to be somewhere. "Tell me where he put the millions he helped Marcos embezzle from nine banks."

"He lost most of it on bad investments and gambling."

"Were you involved with Marcos?"

"No. I hated him." That came as a surprise. "My brother should never have gotten mixed up with him."

"How did they meet?"

"My fault. I had a boyfriend in Denver who was an accountant. I learned a lot from him. When my brother said he had a plan to escape prison if I helped him, I couldn't turn him down. Our parents died early and he kept me alive. This was my way to pay him back. I drove him and Harold to Texas. When we got there, I needed a job.

"Marcos advertised for an accountant. I applied and he hired me. Before long I could see what he was doing and wanted to leave. He threatened to kill me if I didn't do what he wanted. By then he knew my brother was an escaped felon. They both used me."

"Tell me something I don't know."

"I didn't kill Harold. I've never killed anyone." The hard as nails woman teared up. Somehow Kit believed her. "My brother was furious because Harold had double-crossed him. Alonzo was the one who had the plan to escape eight years ago. He thought he could trust Harold. My brother put a gun to his head and gave him one last chance to tell him where the money was hidden before he blew his brains out.

"Harold swore it was in the house, hidden in a place no one would think to look for it.

"Alonzo called him a liar. My brother always did have a violent temper and he shot Harold just as he was about to tell him where to look. After we left the hotel he ordered me to go to Denver to find out if Harold had hidden the money with his grandmother. Alonzo needed that money to pay some gambling debts and he said if I didn't go, he'd kill me."

Kit checked his digital recorder to make certain everything was getting picked up. So far, so good. He looked at Juanita.

"Where did he hang out?"

"With friends in the back of Raul's Billiards in Round Rock. I'm sure he's not there now." No, but it could give Kit a lead. "It took time to come up with a plan, but it put space between me and the police who were looking for me after Marcos was arrested." She grimaced. "It was a wasted trip. Harold's grandmother told me her life story, but there was no mention of the money."

"Why did you go to her funeral service?"

"How do you know about that?"

"I have my ways." Thanks to Natalie.

"I thought maybe I'd hear the pastor say something in passing about her belongings and where they'd been stored, but no such luck. I called my brother and told him.

"That's when he said he was going back to Harold's house, and he said that if Harold's wife got in his way, he would kill her to get the money."

Kit's blood ran cold. He got to his feet while she was still speaking.

"That trip has put me in this hellhole. My brother won't come to my rescue because I know too much now. After he finds the money, he'll bribe someone to kill me in prison."

Kit exhaled sharply. "I'll see what I can do."

He left the jail at a dead run. The second he got in the car he phoned Cy at headquarters. "Hey, bud. Big break in the case. I'll explain after I've picked you up.

Wait for me at the entrance to the underground parking. I should be there in five minutes."

After ringing off, he phoned TJ and told him about Juanita's confession. "I'm headed for Natalie's to take her and Amy to my condo. I'm taking Cy with me to set a trap." He would hide Cy in the back of his car.

"I'll send a surveillance crew to your condo."

"Will you also call Judge Leemaster? Tell him I have the recording of Juanita's confession. She wasn't the killer. I want him to keep that in mind."

The proof on his digital recorder ought to persuade the judge to give Juanita some kind of break, no matter how small. When she'd talked about her brother, he'd seen real fear. The details of their childhood would probably be a horror story he wouldn't wish on anyone.

"Consider it done. And, Kit? Watch your back."

"I intend to."

Chapter Nine

Natalie had just started a wash when she heard noises from the nursery. Amy had awakened from her nap and wanted out of the crib. At the same time she received a text on her phone and her heart leaped. Driving into the garage.

Kit had come again when she'd least expected it. He entered the kitchen like a man on a mission, his piercing gaze zeroing in on her. "Quick! I need to get you and Amy out of the house *now*. I'll explain later. Cy is with me. He's putting the car seat in my car. While you get Amy ready, I'll load the playpen, the high chair and a few other things you might need."

Within five minutes the three of them had gathered the most important items and clothes and put them in the trunk of Kit's car. Amy called Kit's name and he paused long enough to kiss her before settling her into her car seat with some of her favorite stuffed animals.

While the two Rangers went back into the house, Natalie sat next to her daughter to comfort her. "Kit will be right back. We're going on an adventure," she said, trying to calm her own pounding heart. They had to be in grave danger for him to burst into the house the way he had.

When he came out to the car, he was alone. He pressed the remote, then backed out onto the street. She noticed that the surveillance van had gone.

Kit talked Ranger business on his phone as he drove. Wherever he was taking them she'd find out when they got there. Amy chattered the whole time, excited to be doing something different. Without Kit around, Natalie realized she and her daughter had been going stir crazy in the house.

"We're home," Kit announced. They'd come to the area called Chimney Corners, not far from where Natalie lived. He pulled into the driveway of a town-house condo complex and drove into the garage.

They entered one of the units through the kitchen where he deposited the high chair. As he helped her get her things inside, she looked around the living room, spying some framed pictures of Kit and his family on the end tables. He'd brought them to his home. She'd wondered where he lived, never expecting to see the inside of it.

He set up the playpen so she could deposit Amy with some toys. "For the time being she can sleep in the playpen while you sleep on the couch. It's amazingly comfortable, I promise. I'll get you sheets and quilts. I'm afraid I only have two bedrooms upstairs and I use one as my office. It's a small place, but perfect for me until I buy a home with horse property."

She darted him a glance. "You think we might have to be here for a while?"

"I can't predict." He disappeared up the stairs and brought down bedding and pillows. "You can use the bathroom near the foot of the stairs. The fridge is stocked, so feel free to help yourself to anything."

Natalie took Amy's snacks and jars of baby food into the kitchen. Before long everything had been organized.

She went back to the living room where she found Kit playing with Amy. He'd taken her out of the playpen and was stacking blocks with her. The little girl loved the attention of the tall, handsome Ranger.

So do I, Natalie thought.

"Can you tell me what's going on now, Kit?"

He looked over his shoulder before gravitating to one of the chairs. "I was called into the jail earlier. Juanita decided she wanted to make her confession in the hope the judge would go a little easier on her. She explained that her brother killed your husband because he'd double-crossed him."

"That was your theory all along."

"The confession substantiated it, but my blood chilled when she said Alonzo is convinced the money is still hidden in your house, and that he's willing to kill you in order to get to it. Because Juanita's arrest was publicized, she's certain he'll go back for it any time now."

Natalie felt a shiver run down her spine.

"While you're here, a surveillance crew will remain outside the condo for your safety. Cy will be at the house, waiting for Alonzo to break in, no matter how long it takes."

"I'm sure Juanita's brother isn't working alone."

"You let me worry about that."

She sucked in her breath. "Won't he see you letting yourself into my house?"

"That's not the plan. One of the guys will drive a car with a real estate logo and put up a For Sale sign in your front yard with a number to call. After he leaves, we're hoping Alonzo will think you've been frightened off. Believing that the house is vacant, he'll come for the money. The ruse might work, but it might not. In any case Cy will be inside waiting for him. I'll provide backup."

"Where will you be?"

"In the big tree growing in the backyard on your neighbor's property. On the first day I came to your house through the back, I noticed it would provide the perfect perch."

Oh, Kit...

She opened the Little People Farm that Kit had grabbed for her to bring. Amy loved it and started arranging all the animals.

"I need your cell to call Mr. Farbes. He'll have to put off his visit until Alonzo is captured."

Natalie had forgotten all about the attorney. She reached for her purse and handed him the phone. While they talked, she got up and went into the kitchen to put some milk in Amy's sippy cup in case she was thirsty. As she turned to go back to the living room with it, Kit was right there.

"Oh—sorry. I didn't see you." She would have run into him if he hadn't steadied her shoulders with his hands. The contact shot darts of awareness through her body. "How did Mr. Farbes take the news?" She could hear her voice shaking.

Kit's hands moved to her upper arms. He squeezed them before letting her go. Natalie wished he hadn't touched her. "He'll be happy to come when this nightmare is over."

"I'm so glad you remembered." She moved past him and returned to the living room. Amy saw her and raised her hands. "Mik."

Kit was right behind her. "Milk," he said back. "That was almost perfect, Amy."

"As you've noticed, *L*'s and *H*'s are hard for her." Natalie handed her the cup and sat on the floor next to her. Her pulse raced when Kit stretched out on the floor, too. His hard, lean body was too close.

With one hand propping up his head, he teased Amy by taking her animals away one at a time. When she grabbed one from him, he reached for another. They played back and forth until he had her giggling uncontrollably and she dropped the cup she'd been holding.

"I don't believe my daughter has ever had this much fun."

When he flicked his gaze to her, his eyes danced. "I haven't, either. I know we planned to distance ourselves, but circumstances have thrown us together again and I find this little cherub to be excellent company."

"If she could say the words, she'd tell you the same thing." Natalie was starting to feel emotional. "Kit—

thank you for getting us out of harm's way. Your whole life has been upended because of me."

He grasped the hand closest to him and kissed her palm. The action was so intimate she could hardly breathe. "I like being upended. These are the perks of being a Ranger. You never know what your next case will bring.

"When I went to the cemetery to take pictures, I didn't like the fact that I was attracted to you even before we'd met. I knew you were a person of interest to the police, but I found myself not wanting you to be guilty of a crime. Someone else should have worked this case instead of me, but the pull you had on me overruled my good sense. When I told the boss my plan, he had reservations about it, but he didn't try to stop me."

She averted her eyes. "I'm afraid my good sense failed me when you gave me the choice between having the surveillance team watching me or having you guard me yourself. I liked the idea of my cousin Todd visiting me for the week. But I was thinking selfishly and didn't consider that Amy could be affected."

"She may be little, but she exudes her own personality."

"She definitely does. You asked me if I thought she'd be disturbed to see a strange man in the house. I didn't have to think about it because…because I sensed the goodness in you. So did she."

He reached for Amy and held her in the air while he was on his back. "Do you want to swim?" He moved her like she was a fish.

"Swim!" she echoed, loving this new game.

"That's right, sweetheart. Swim, swim."

When he put her down, she protested.

"Do you want to swim again?"

"Swim gain."

"Did you hear that, Mommy? She said she wants to swim again. She's speaking in sentences. I knew you were a smart girl." He moved her around some more, dipping her near Natalie several times. The giggling continued.

By now Natalie was laughing along with Kit. She couldn't imagine heaven being more wonderful than this. *Make it last*, her heart cried. But of course it couldn't because he'd be leaving when it got dark to face a known killer.

Forcing herself to bring things to an end she said, "It's time for your dinner, Amy. I bet you're hungry after that workout. Let's get your diaper changed first." She got up from the floor and reached for her daughter. The bathroom counter would be a good place for that.

"'Bye, Amy," Kit said, still lying down.

"Bye-bye."

Natalie took her into the bathroom. She put a towel down then reached into the diaper bag for a Pamper. Soon her daughter was ready. She carried her to the kitchen and put her in the high chair. After washing her hands, she reached for a jar of noodles and turkey and selected peaches for dessert.

Kit came in a few minutes later. "Feel like breakfast for dinner?"

"Always," she answered.

"I make a Texas omelet almost as good as your brownies. Even my mom says they're better than hers."

"That's because you learned from her."

"Yup. It's about the only thing I cooked that I didn't ruin."

"I had a few disasters myself growing up."

They bantered throughout the delicious meal, exchanging life stories. While they ate, Amy found her little shopping cart in the living room and pushed it into the kitchen, purposely running into Kit's chair. He'd spoiled her so much she was wearing herself out with excitement. Natalie figured her little girl would fall into a deep sleep once she put her down. It was growing late.

Kit insisted on doing the dishes, so Natalie went into the living room to empty the playpen and lay out a quilt for Amy. After putting her in her footed pajamas, she lowered her into the playpen and handed her the cow she treasured.

"Nite, nite." She kissed the top of her head.

Amy didn't like being put down. She stood at the railing. "Kit—" she called out in a loud voice. It sounded so urgent, Natalie burst into laughter. He came running.

"I think she wants you to say good-night."

He hunkered down in front of the playpen. "It's time to go to sleep, sweetheart. Nite, nite."

All of a sudden the tears came. Amy stood there not knowing what to do with herself. "Mama—Kit—"

"I'd better go back to the kitchen," he whispered.

One more kiss to the top of her head and he left the

living room, already bathed in darkness. Amy whimpered for a few minutes then sank down. Natalie sang a couple of songs she loved. Pretty soon silence reigned. The little girl had finally fallen asleep.

Natalie made up the couch for bed. Kit had brought down sheets designed with Texas Longhorn steers. She loved them. His mother had probably put sheets like these on his bed when he was a boy.

Natalie had liked Kit's mother very much during the short time they'd had to talk at the rodeo. The pride over her sons had shone in her eyes. Who wouldn't be proud? Kit was in a class of his own.

With everything done except to put on her pajamas, she walked into the spotless kitchen and found Kit on the phone. He spoke in low tones so she couldn't make out the words. He was probably talking to Cy.

How they handled what they did for a living was beyond Natalie's ability to comprehend. But she was incredibly thankful for men like him, and she couldn't imagine him doing anything else.

Being a Ranger was part of who he was. Natalie was fiercely glad of it. She loved him with her whole being. No matter how risky life was for him every day, she wouldn't want him any other way.

She could tell the moment he ended his call that he was preparing himself to leave. She grasped the back of one of the kitchen chairs. "Is it time?"

"Afraid so." He got up from his chair and turned to her. His features looked chiseled in the semi darkness.

"Go get him, cowboy."

"I intend to." The fierce tone in his voice had a

heart-stopping effect on her. "How about a kiss for luck?"

She struggled for breath. "You don't need any but I might, so I'll kiss you anyway."

She moved toward him and put her hands on his well-defined chest. He was letting her do all the work. That didn't matter. She wanted to let him know how she felt and slid her arms up around his neck. Natalie had to rise on her toes to give him the kind of kiss she was dying for.

The world spun away as he crushed her in his arms and gave her a devouring kiss she would never forget. It said so many things they hadn't yet spoken to each other, but she didn't need a translator to tell her what she'd prayed would happen. As Colette had told her a week ago, it was there in his eyes and in his body language.

Her heartbeat merged with his. Their bodies molded together in one singing line of desire. Words weren't necessary; not when they were communing in the age-old way that brought bodies and souls to life. This magnificent Ranger made her feel immortal.

They'd only known each other a short time, but something so incredible had happened to her she knew his hold over her would last forever. There'd been such darkness in her marriage. Yet Kit had brought the light back into her life, the glory of being loved and cherished. Those were elements she'd never known before from any man and never would again. If she couldn't have Kit, she didn't want anyone else.

Aching with love, she cupped his face in her hands.

"Come home soon, Ranger Saunders. You're needed by an awful lot of people."

Natalie made a swift exit from Kit's arms and hurried into the living room.

THAT KISS HAD fanned the flame burning inside him. On fire with near-white heat, he'd left his condo and headed for her house.

Come on, Morales. Bring it on.

He parked his car one street over as he'd done that first night. He put his night-vision goggles around his neck. No one was in sight. He locked the car and darted through several yards. There were a number of fences to scale before he reached the tree in question. He'd done a lot of tree climbing in his youth. This one was easy.

When he reached midway and was well hidden by leaves, he phoned Cy.

"Where are you?"

"In the tree looking at the back of the house. Have the guys put up the sign?"

"About an hour ago."

"Good. I take it there's been no other movement."

"Not yet."

"In that case, I'm going to join you. Leave the back door open. I'll be there in two minutes." He disconnected and started down the tree. One more fence to climb and he'd be there.

When he crept in through the back door, it felt like home.

Cy was waiting for him in the kitchen.

Kit smiled. "Good to see you, bud."

"Likewise. Guess who else is here?"

Kit couldn't imagine.

"Vic."

"You're kidding—"

"Nope. After you gave me the tip from Juanita about Alonzo hiding out at the billiards place, I went over there to investigate. One of the girls who works at the front as cashier is terrified of him and hopes we get him. She said he always has two thugs with him and carries an AR-15. They operate like a gang and drive around in an old hearse.

"When Vic heard that, he volunteered to help us on this stakeout. There's a bulletproof vest for you on the chair there. Needless to say the boss wants this killer caught."

Good old TJ.

Kit put on the vest, then walked through the house feeling a ton heavier. He found Vic in Natalie's bedroom watching the windows through his night-vision goggles. They talked shop for a few minutes before Kit returned to the kitchen.

Cy eyed him. "What's your gut telling you, Kit?"

"The way Juanita explained it, I figure it's going to go down gangster style. She says Alonzo's a raging bull and he's got nothing to lose at this point. I have no doubt he'll blast his way in.

"The only problem is, I don't know how long we're going to have to wait. Juanita felt it would happen right away because he's desperate to settle his gambling debts. I hate tying up Vic when this isn't even his case."

"He insisted, and the boss knows we work well together. He'll send other guys to relieve us tomorrow if it looks like we'll have to be here longer."

Kit nodded and pulled out his weapon. "Which door do you want to guard?"

"Doesn't matter."

"I'll take the front and you cover the back. We'll trade off." Kit had a hunch they'd charge the front of the house and shoot the door off its hinges. Of course, anything was possible. He placed himself to the side of the glass so he could see the whole front yard.

His father had gotten into a situation like this. But the shootout had taken his life. Kit wasn't ready for that to happen yet. Tonight he'd found a new reason for wanting to live life to its fullest. Natalie may not have said all the words he wanted to hear, but he knew how she felt about him.

Go get him, cowboy.

Those were magic words. They'd freed him from the fear that she couldn't handle what he did for a living. During all the years since he and Janie had broken up, he'd been afraid to fall in love. He couldn't go through that again, only to be told that his career was getting in the way of total fulfillment.

Kit had seen how hard it had been on Luckey. The poor guy had suffered when his wife had said goodbye. To be told that you had to find a different way to make a living after a year of marriage would have been devastating. Luckey was doing better, but he was as gun shy about falling in love again as Kit had been.

Tonight Kit had been given a gift he hadn't expected. He didn't have to worry about that issue with Natalie. Even though she knew his father had been killed in the line of duty, she'd sent him off with her heart in her eyes, willing him to come back to her. That's what he intended to do. He could see a future opening up. A fantastic future with the cherub and, God willing, maybe even a few more.

While he kept watch, he checked in with the guys on his phone. Maybe tonight wouldn't be the night. Only a few cars had gone by. They talked strategies. The hours dragged on. He ate a couple of Snickers.

Around three-thirty in the morning when Kit had just about decided it wasn't going to happen, he saw a dark vehicle turn onto the street and park a few houses away on the opposite side.

He alerted the guys to get ready.

Three figures had gotten out and were creeping toward the house. No sooner had Kit warned his buddies than the front window shattered from the impact of a semi-automatic weapon, just as Kit had imagined. Shards of glass flew in all directions. With his adrenaline gushing, he waited against the wall until they started to climb inside.

Kit aimed his gun and shot the first two thugs. He would never forget the look of shock on Alonzo's face as he spun around in the moonlight before falling to the floor. Cy shot at the third intruder, but he turned and started running.

"Oh, no, you don't." Kit climbed up on the window sill and jumped to the grass. The thug shot at him, then took off toward the car. Kit raced after him and tackled him before he could open the door. It was like throwing a steer; the guy fell hard against the pavement and lost consciousness. With a grunt of satisfaction, Kit reached into his pocket to pull out his cuffs when a fourth man pointed a gun at him through the open rear window of the car. Kit hadn't counted on him.

"Get down!" Cy yelled. Kit had already obeyed the instinct and heard two shots fired. The last thing he remembered was a stinging sensation in his upper right arm.

NATALIE WOKE at seven and looked over at Amy. She was still asleep, her knees pulled up beneath her and her cute little bottom in the air. Her quilt was wrapped around her middle. It was a hilarious site. She quickly grabbed her phone and took a picture. Kit would laugh his head off.

Her body quickened when she thought of him. She had no idea how long it would be before she spoke to him again, let alone saw him. But it didn't matter because however long it took, she knew he'd eventually come home and she'd be here waiting for him.

While Amy was still out cold, Natalie got dressed in a pair of jeans and a blouse. After freshening up in the bathroom she went into the kitchen to make coffee. Just as she found the jar of decaf in the cupboard, she heard the phone ring. Her heart pounded. Maybe it was Kit.

She answered.

"Mrs. Harris? This is Milo, one of the surveillance crew out front. You're going to have a visitor in a minute. It's Ranger Saunders's mother. I didn't want you to be startled."

Kit's mother? "Thank you for letting me know."

"You're welcome."

She hung up, curious to know why the older woman had come. Kit's mother was probably here for an unannounced visit and would no doubt be surprised to find Natalie in residence. She was glad she'd gotten up and dressed.

She walked to the front door and opened it in time to see Kit's mother walking toward her. She was dressed in jeans and a top much like Natalie was wearing, but the older woman looked paler than Natalie remembered and for some reason she started to get nervous. "Mrs. Saunders?"

The woman's hazel eyes looked at Natalie for an overly long moment. "There's no way to make this easy for you, Natalie." Natalie's heart plummeted. "Kit was injured last night. His captain asked me to come over here because he knew Kit had brought you here and that you'd need to be told."

She gasped. "But he's still alive. Right?"

"Yes. By some miracle he is."

Natalie felt weakness overtake her as if she might faint, but she'd never fainted in her life. "Come in and tell me what happened."

"Oh. Your little girl is still asleep," Mrs. Saunders said quietly as they entered the living room.

"It's fine. Please. Sit down."

"I've just come from the hospital. I don't know all the facts yet, but he got shot in his upper arm."

"Oh, no—" Natalie exclaimed, causing Amy to stir.

"We simply won't know the prognosis for a while. The doctor explained that they have to look at the X-rays to find the extent of the damage. If it hit the bone, surgery might be required. He says there was little loss of blood, which is a very good sign. They've hooked him up with IV antibiotics and fluids. Whatever is decided, he'll need wound treatment and dressings. The ironic part is that he was wearing his bulletproof vest, but it doesn't cover the arms."

Natalie shuddered. "Mrs. Saunders?"

"Call me June."

"June, then. If it hampers his ability to use his arm, will that mean he can't be a Ranger anymore? Because I know that would just about kill him."

"That's my worry, too. We'll simply have to wait and see. On the bright side, you won't have to worry about your safety anymore. Kit took down the man who killed your husband."

Talk about the bitter with the sweet—

"He also killed one of the man's accomplices and wounded another, who has been arrested. Ranger Vance killed the fourth man, the one who was hiding in the getaway car and injured Kit."

It took a minute for Natalie to take it all in. She stared at Kit's mother. "You've been through this before."

"Yes. But this time we can be thankful Kit's life has been spared."

"I—I'm so thankful, I don't know how to react. How terrifying for you to have to hear news like this about your son." Natalie put her arms around the older woman, and the two of them simply held on to each other for a little while before June pulled back, wiping her eyes.

"I've been told your living room window was shattered during the gunfire. It might be best for you to stay here until the Rangers have finished their job and the people from Forensics are through. Then they'll have the mess cleaned up and new glass installed. I imagine that by tomorrow you'll be able to go home."

Natalie felt numb. Home without Kit was unthinkable. "How soon can he have visitors?"

"The surgeon told me not until tomorrow and maybe not even then depending on his condition. He's been through a lot of trauma physically and psychologically."

"But he's tough."

June nodded. "He's just like his father."

"Has your other son been told?"

"Yes. I called Brandon the second I had word from his captain. He'll arrive at the hospital before long to talk to the doctor."

"Why don't you stay here until you hear from him? I was just about to make coffee. Have you had any breakfast?"

"Not yet."

"Then let me get us some. I'm so thankful he's alive, I need to work off my excess energy and stay busy. I'm glad you're here with me. Amy and I would love the company. It's been very quiet with just the two of us."

"It must have been intolerable to be cooped up in your house."

"Not really." *Not at all. I've had Kit all to myself. Now there's no excuse for us to be together under the same roof.* "What I've missed is taking this little girl out to the park."

Amy awakened and stood in the playpen. "Mama." She held out her arms. "Kit!"

"Oh—" June laughed. "She knows his name. She's adorable."

"He's been playing with her." She walked over to the playpen. "Amy, this is June. Can you say June?"

She pointed her finger at Kit's mother. "June."

"Yes, sweetheart. June!" Natalie looked at Kit's mother. "Your son has won her heart. I'll just change her diaper and get her dressed. Then she can eat breakfast with us."

She picked Amy up and carried her into the bathroom. When she returned to the living room she saw that June had gone into the kitchen. She'd made the coffee for them and was toasting Eggo waffles.

"Waffles sound good." Natalie put the baby in the high chair.

"Kit has always loved them."

She got out the syrup and the butter. While June brought the plates of waffles to the table, Natalie found a jar of applesauce she'd brought with her. She broke a waffle into pieces for Amy and June poured the coffee.

They began eating their breakfast, but after a few mouthfuls of fruit, Amy wanted to get down. "My daughter is restless. Excuse me for a minute. I'll put on her sandals and take her outside for a little walk. In the rush to get here yesterday, I forgot to pack the stroller."

"I'll walk outside with you. Right now I'm afraid I can't sit still."

"Neither can I." Their eyes met in silent understanding.

Natalie was hurting for Kit, but she experienced a feeling of liberation to walk outside and know there was no danger lurking. The surveillance van had gone. Amy stopped and started many times, exploring this new world. It caused both women to laugh. Several times she stumbled. Natalie let her pick herself up.

Already too hot to stay out for long, they headed back to the condo. Their return coincided with June's cell phone ringing. She pulled it out of her pocket. "It's Brandon."

"Go ahead and talk while we get ourselves some water." Amy followed Natalie into the kitchen, where Natalie got down a glass and filled it for her. The little girl drank from it very well. Before long she wouldn't need her sippy cup.

June joined them. "I'm going to drive over to the hospital to talk to Brandon, but I'll be back."

"You go and be with your sons. You all need each other."

"Thank you for being so understanding. You're a sweet person, Natalie. I promise I won't be long and I'll bring any news." She gave Natalie another hug and leaned over and kissed Amy's cheek.

"Bye-bye, Amy."

"'Bye, June."

Incredible.

Kit's mother laughed. So did Natalie, who felt as

though ten years had just been added to her daughter's life. They walked June to the door and watched as she drove off. Natalie would give anything to go to the hospital with her, but that wasn't her place. Not until Kit either phoned or got word to her that he wanted her to come.

She closed the door. Only now was it starting to sink in that everything was over and the murder case involving her mentally ill husband had been solved. Life could get back on track. Everything was going to change. No more Kit in the house. She was free to go to work again.

But Natalie realized she didn't want things to change. She wanted to go on living in a world where Kit stayed with her and Amy forever. Her thoughts flew to him. This shooting could have had a life-changing effect on him.

What if the damage to his arm was bad enough that he couldn't be a fully active Texas Ranger anymore? He had to have a full recovery. *He had to.*

Chapter Ten

The doctor walked into Kit's hospital room and approached the side of his bed. "How are you feeling?"

Kit had awakened again and was surprised to discover it was four in the afternoon. "No pain."

"That's good. I'm here to tell you that the bullet perforated your upper arm in the best place it could have. It missed the bone and artery, so there's no need for surgery. We'll be able to treat this as a flesh wound."

"That's the news I've been waiting for. I've got to get back to work." *I've got to get back to Natalie.*

"Not so fast, Ranger Saunders. I won't be releasing you from the hospital until the day after tomorrow. You need bed rest while we tend to your wound and pump you full of more antibiotics. Infection is your biggest enemy. We don't want to give it a chance."

"I can do that at home."

"No you can't. We're keeping you on the IV and the dressings and wound care need to be handled here. I want your blood pressure to go down."

Kit could see this doctor meant business. "Can I have visitors now?"

"Only your immediate family. The whole department of the Texas Rangers has kept our phone ringing off the hook, but none of them except your closest friends are allowed to visit before tomorrow. After I've done my rounds and can see that you're improving, I'll lift the ban. Have I made myself clear?"

He sounded like TJ. "Understood."

"Before you're released, a therapist will be in to discuss your recovery and rehabilitation."

"How long will I have to do therapy?"

"That depends. Several months. I'd say no active field work for at least four, and only on my say-so."

Four? "Be honest with me. When all is said and done, do you think I'll be able to pass the Ranger physical?"

The doctor's brows lifted. "I honestly don't know."

"What's your best guess?"

"We can hope for maybe ninety-five percent."

Kit frowned. "That won't be good enough."

"You just got shot, Ranger Saunders. These things take time."

"Don't I know it," he grumbled. "Can I have my cell phone back?"

"Not before tomorrow. We've turned the landline off in this room, too. After what you've been through, it's vital you get your rest. Take some naps. Watch some TV."

"That's like watching paint dry."

"Exactly. Best therapy in the world." He started for the door.

"Doc?"

The man turned. "What is it?"

Kit knew he'd been rude. "Thank you."

"Just doing my job."

Kit had used that phrase on Natalie several times. He'd never been on the receiving end of it. "Thanks, anyway."

The doctor smiled. "You're welcome."

Left alone for the moment, the only thing that helped Kit handle this enforced bed rest was knowing Morales and his gang were dead or in jail. He was longing to debrief with Cy and Vic, but that would have to wait until tomorrow.

"Kit?" June peeked her head around the door. "Do you mind if we come in?"

"I've been waiting for you."

She came into the room, followed by Brandon. They both walked over to the side of the bed that was free of IV drips and monitors. Kit's brother grinned. "You're looking good for somebody who took down Austin's finest gang of felons. They all had rap sheets a mile long. The news said they came at you with guns blazing, including an AR-15. You've been labeled the new Elliott Ness. Dad's probably upstairs grinning from ear to ear."

"You think?"

His mother leaned over and kissed his cheek. "Thank God you're alive."

"I've been thanking Him."

Brandon said, "I've been thanking Him this didn't happen before my event in San Antonio. You're the best damn hazer I ever worked with."

"That's a compliment I'll remember, but I'm not dead yet. Mom, would you do me a favor and go over to my condo? Natalie's staying there. She needs to know I'm all right and that the worry is over."

"Your captain called me early this morning and I went right over to tell her what I knew. We had breakfast and took a walk with Amy. Natalie taught her my name. You've never seen anything so cute in your life."

Kit could imagine it and felt his eyelids sting with emotion. He had to clear his throat. "How is Natalie?"

"Handling it all like a trooper. She reminded me how strong you are. I needed that. I love both you boys."

Brandon eyed Kit and they exchanged a silent message. They knew this incident had brought their father's death back to their mother. "We love you, too, Mom. Come on. I'll take you out for a steak dinner, then we'll come back to say good-night."

"I'll see you later," Kit murmured, pleased that his mother had spoken to Natalie, but surprised the talking had made him so tired.

NATALIE WAS FEEDING Amy dinner when her cell rang. She clicked on. Maybe it was June. She'd said she'd be coming back. "Hello?"

"Mrs. Harris? This is Cy Vance. I've been at the hospital talking to Mrs. Saunders. She said the doctor won't let anyone talk to Kit on the phone or visit him until tomorrow. When she said she was going back to his condo to give you the latest news, I told her I would do it."

What?

"Your living room has a new window and all the mess has been cleaned up. If you'd like, I'll come by for you in the van and we'll move you back to your house. You and Amy will be able to sleep in your own beds tonight."

She groaned inwardly. The news that she could go home should have brought her relief. But she'd wanted to go to the hospital to tell Kit she'd stay at his place so she could help him when he came home.

"That's very kind of you. Are you coming now?"

"Yes."

"Then I'll gather up our things and be ready for you."

By eight-thirty, Cy had carried the last of the bags into her house. Everything looked as before, as though nothing had ever happened here. She thanked the Ranger profusely for helping her.

"It's the least I can do. Kit's going to be fine—he wouldn't want you to worry. If you need anything, call me."

"Of course. You've been wonderful." She watched him drive away before she closed the front door.

Amy had been playing right by her leg. She picked her up and took her to the nursery. Before long her sweet girl cuddled up in her crib with her cow and fell asleep after only two songs.

Finally alone to think, she phoned Jillian. They had a long talk. Jillian offered to look after Amy so Natalie could visit Kit in the hospital. What a great friend she'd been! She thanked her and rang off. There was one more call to make. Colette needed to know that Kit had solved the case and that a large part of it had been due to her.

Natalie put off calling her boss at the pharmacy. She wanted to see Kit before she committed to going back to work. Kit might need help for a while and she wanted to be the one to provide it. That was, if Kit wanted her to. She'd felt so confident about his feelings when they'd kissed goodbye, she had no idea what sorts of things had been on his mind since he'd been shot. If anything had changed, she wouldn't be able to bear it.

Being in her own bed felt good, but she would rather be at Kit's condo. She loved him so desperately. To think she could have lost him—emotion got the better of her and she started sobbing. And once they'd started, the tears continued to come, drenching her pillow.

THE NEXT DAY Natalie called the hospital, wanting to know when Kit was allowed to have visitors.

She was pleased to learn that she could go in between four and five, and she arranged with Jillian to drop Amy off at three-thirty so she could be at the hospital in good time.

She went through her normal routine with Amy, turning on the TV to have some background noise. There was a soap opera on one of the channels dealing with a case of stolen diamonds that had been hidden on the inside of the fireplace. She didn't think much about it until later when she stood in the shower washing her hair.

What a crazy place to hide something. Natalie was

positive the police hadn't looked inside her fireplace. Who would? But she couldn't let the idea go. After she'd toweled off and dried her hair, she slipped on an old T-shirt and went into the living room. She glanced out the window, feeling a little silly, and removed the fireplace screen, reaching inside the way she'd seen the woman on the show do it.

To her shock she felt a packet pasted against the bricks. She got her fingers around it and pulled hard. Out came two large and very dirty envelopes. Were there more? She reached in again on the other side and pulled out two more. Maybe there were others but she couldn't reach up that far. Good grief.

She took them into the kitchen and opened them on the table. Each packet contained a thick stack of hundred dollar bills, more cash than Natalie had ever seen in her life. Her eyes widened in disbelief. *The $400,000!* They never used the fireplace. Ever. Rod must have stashed the envelopes there, knowing they'd be safe.

Wait till she showed all this to Kit.

Excited about the find, she dug out a small, old suit-case. Kit would want Forensics to match serial numbers and dust the envelopes for prints, so she put all four packets inside and snapped it shut.

She washed her hands and arms up to the elbows then finished dressing. She chose to wear a filmy white blouse and khaki-colored wraparound skirt Kit had never seen. Before she left for the hospital, she walked Amy over to Jillian's. At first Amy acted shy, but then she saw her little friend and wiggled to get out of Natalie's arms.

Natalie hugged her friend and slipped out the front door while her daughter was occupied. She went back to the house and carried the suitcase out to her car. The hospital wasn't far away, but it took time to park.

She rode the east elevator to the fourth floor nursing station. One of the nurses told her that Kit already had visitors, but that Natalie could go in as soon as they left. The doctor didn't want him overly excited.

She had to wait fifteen minutes before being told it was her turn. Timed visits meant the doctor was still worried about him. Natalie's heart pounded as she entered his room, hoping his eyes would reflect his true feelings.

His head was raised, but his eyes were closed when she came in. He must be exhausted. She took in the IV tube and the bandage on his right arm. She walked quietly to his bedside and set down the suitcase.

She loved just looking at him. He was beautiful in a rugged, manly way. He opened his eyes, catching her in the act of feasting her eyes on him, but his gaze reflected concern. Why?

Natalie said the first thing that came into her mind. "You got 'em, cowboy."

He sighed deeply. "Not without help. Cy saved my hide when he told me to duck. If I hadn't…"

"Let's concentrate on the fact that you put away four felons. In honor of that spectacular feat, I have a surprise for you."

"Tell me it's your mint brownies."

"You can't eat those yet, but I've brought something I can guarantee will make you really happy."

"Is it edible?"

"I don't think you'd want to eat it, no. I'll give you a clue. I discovered it while I was watching a soap opera this afternoon. Maybe you saw it, too."

"I slept through reruns of *Bonanza*."

"Well, luckily I didn't sleep through *my* show." She brought the tray table forward, taking care not to disturb the IV. "Are you ready?"

Natalie put the small suitcase on top of the table and opened it.

Kit's eyes flickered then blazed. That's the look she'd wanted to see.

"Four-hundred thousand! It's all there. It was dirty business, but I counted it."

He stared at her. "Where in the hell did you find it?"

"Well, on this program today the culprit hid some diamonds in a packet inside the fireplace. I thought it was hilarious, but then again it was the only place in my house I could think of that hadn't been searched. Just for fun I stuck my hand up the chimney and *voila*!

"Those four dirty envelopes had been fastened to the inside with tape. You can tell your captain you've found the stolen money, at least what's left of those millions. It'll make you a bigger hero than you already are. I'll never say a word. But that's enough excitement for now."

She closed the lid and put the case back on the floor, then moved the table away.

When she returned to his side, he reached for her

hand and clasped it hard. "When the captain finds out, he'll make you a Ranger."

"Oh, no, there's only one Texas Ranger in our family." She'd been so happy, she'd gotten carried away, said something she hadn't meant to say out loud.

"I heard that," he said softly. "You *can't* take it back."

Natalie's mouth went so dry she could hardly swallow. "I don't want to. I love you, Kit. I've been in love with you from the start. I would never have agreed for Father Segal to live with me if I hadn't sensed I'd met the love of my life.

"I was afraid you'd think badly of me for having been married to a killer. The thought is so distasteful to me, I can't imagine what kind of thoughts you must have had at the beginning."

"If you'll lean over and kiss me, I'll give you an idea of what my thoughts were when you invited me into your house for the first time."

Natalie was already there. "I adore you," she whispered. "I'm glad you're a Ranger. I'll never complain about you going out on a case, as long as you always come home to me."

"I promise I will always come home to you, Natalie. Marry me. Right away—I mean it. We'll work out all the details later, but I want everyone to know you're going to be my wife."

"People are going to think we're rushing things."

"I don't care what anyone else thinks. I've been waiting for you for years."

"Oh, Kit—" Tears rolled down her cheeks. "I hated

to leave your condo yesterday. I wanted to be there when you got out of the hospital, but Cy showed up to help me move my things back home."

"I asked him to do it."

She kissed his mouth again. "Why?"

"Because I want to spend my convalescence at your house where Amy is happy. We'll have my couch brought over and I'll sleep on it. That town house is no good to us, anyway. I've been thinking about buying some property with acreage for horses. We're going to need a much bigger house."

Natalie smiled. "How big?"

"With enough bedrooms for more children. I'd like to hire an architect to design a Western-style home with lots of windows and timber."

"That'll be a project to keep you busy until you're back on the force."

"I'm afraid that's still iffy."

"No, it's not. You'll be back in no time."

He caressed the side of her face. "What did I ever do to deserve you?"

"You've got that the other way around." They couldn't stop kissing each other.

"My mother's already crazy about Amy."

"It was so funny yesterday. Oh, Kit—we can't wait for you to come home."

"One more night, then we'll never be apart again."

That sounded like heaven.

Epilogue

Tonight was their three-month wedding anniversary.

Natalie had prepared a special picnic and had driven to the new house they were building in Barton Creek. Kit had gone in for his physical and planned to meet her there afterward. She was nervous waiting to hear the verdict.

This morning his mother had come to Natalie's house and told her she wanted to look after Amy overnight. Whatever news Kit received, June knew how important this night was to the two of them. She wanted to give them time alone. Natalie had learned to love his mother and Amy was crazy about her nana. There'd be no more calling her "June."

The framework of the two-story ranch house had been erected. The drywall would go in next. Natalie walked inside. The front door hadn't been hung yet. She went up the staircase to the master bedroom where the adjoining veranda looked out over their ten-acre estate. Kit would only be seven miles from work, yet it felt as if they were far away from civilization.

As soon as the barn was built, Kit would bring

his horse from Marble Falls and buy one for Natalie. Vic had purchased a miniature horse for his son. Kit couldn't wait to get one for Amy, but she needed to be a little older first. He planned to take the daughter he was adopting on rides around the property. With the sixty-thousand-dollar trust fund she'd inherited, Amy could one day study to be anything she wanted—maybe an architect, like her great-grandfather. But secretly Natalie knew that Kit wanted to turn his little cherub into a cowgirl. Natalie loved the idea.

In a few minutes she glimpsed Kit's car through the trees, coming up the winding drive. Her heart picked up speed. *Please let him bring the news he wanted.* They'd both stayed busy getting this house designed and built, but she knew he couldn't wait to be back with the Sons of the Forty.

His Ranger friends dropped in whenever they could, but when they were on a new case, Kit might not see them for weeks at a time. He'd been going to his therapy sessions faithfully and doing everything possible to hasten the healing process.

But sometimes he would get discouraged. He didn't know if he could handle a desk job for the Rangers. That rush he got when he went out on a case would always be missing. About a month ago he was having a bad night and she'd asked him if he'd be interested in forming a private investigator agency. He would own it and run in a way only he knew how to make it successful. To her surprise, he didn't dismiss her suggestion. Just to know he was considering the idea gave her hope.

She watched him pull up and get out of the car. His

body language gave her the first indication that he wasn't happy. Her stomach clenched. She would have to be strong for him.

"Natalie?" Excitement was missing from his voice.

"I'm up in our bedroom, babe." She'd brought blankets and their sleeping bags so they could spend the night. With her heart pounding, she waited in the bedroom for him. He walked in and his gaze darted to the picnic she'd laid out. He took in the sleeping bags.

"Tell me what the doctor said."

His wooden expression said it all. "I'm not there yet."

"You'll get there. When does he want to see you again?"

"In a month."

"That's not a long time. Another month of therapy will make you stronger. By then our house will be finished and you'll be able to get back to work."

He nodded before his hands went to his hips. He was so gorgeous and she loved him desperately, but she couldn't help him.

"Come on. The sun is setting. Let's eat while we can still see our food." She'd made his favorite fried chicken and brownies, but there was no tempting him.

"I'm afraid I'm not hungry."

"That's okay. Shall we go to a roadhouse and do some line dancing? Your mom is keeping Amy overnight. We're free to do whatever we want."

"Natalie?" His eyes were like lasers. "I'm afraid you've married a failure."

She smiled and crossed the distance to press a kiss

to his mouth. "What's that awful cliché? It's always darkest before the dawn. Your day is coming."

He suddenly clasped her to him and buried his face in her hair. "What am I doing? You're so wonderful. How can you stand me while I'm feeling so sorry for myself? Forgive me, sweetheart."

"There's nothing to forgive."

"I love you." His fierce declaration was followed by a kiss to die for. They sank onto the double sleeping bag and clothes flew in all directions. Natalie lost awareness of time and place as Kit made sweet, savage love to her. Then it was her turn to worship him. The joy they brought each other went until late into the night.

She rested against his chest. "Are you hungry?"

"I think I am."

"Stay there." She reached for the cooler and pulled it close. "What would you like? How about a drumstick?" His appetite had come alive. He quickly ate everything she put in front of him, including all the brownies. But she didn't want any food.

"My, my. You really *were* hungry. I think you're ready to handle my news."

She could almost hear his brain turning her comment over. "You've decided to go back to work part-time?"

"No. I don't think I'll be going anywhere for a long time."

"I hate to admit it, but that makes me happy. What caused you to make that decision?"

"The truth is, Kit, this night is special in more ways than one. We're going to have a baby."

He jackknifed into a sitting position. "Natalie—"

"I haven't been to the doctor yet, but I know the signs. It's just like it was with Amy. Please tell me you're happy about it."

"*Happy?* Sweetheart, I'm overjoyed!"

She lay still as he ran his hand over her stomach. "Our little baby is inside there. I've dreamed about having another cherub."

"You're not just saying that?"

"How can you even ask that question?"

"Because I know you're upset that your career is still up in the air."

He kissed her neck. "Hearing that we're going to have a baby puts everything else into perspective. Another month and I'll know if I have to think about other work. Until then I'm going to do what I can to get better. Amy's going to have a little brother or sister. I can't wait!"

"I can't wait until the morning sickness passes. You're so lucky you're a man."

Deep laughter rumbled out of him; the kind she hadn't heard for a long time. She was thrilled.

"RANGER SAUNDERS? WELCOME back to active duty." The boss had assembled some of the Rangers in the conference room at the last minute.

"You've only been gone four months, but you've been busy in that time—you've gotten married, built a new house. Is there any other news we need to know about?"

Kit sat back with a smile. "We're expecting a baby in about six months."

The guys hooted and cheered. TJ smiled. "Kit and Cy both went undercover on different assignments and look what happened—they married the women they were protecting. Here's an APB for the rest of you single Rangers—watch out if you decide to go undercover to protect a woman in jeopardy. Okay. Get out of here."

Kit smiled at Cy as they left the room. Before they went their separate ways Cy said, "I'm glad you crossed the line, bud. Always go with your instincts."

"Back at you."

Only seven miles and he'd be home. Natalie didn't yet know he'd gotten the call from TJ saying he'd passed the physical. Kit couldn't wait to tell his wonderful wife, who'd never given up or let him lose hope. She was a gift.

He turned onto the road leading to the house. When he passed through the trees he saw Natalie up on the veranda. It was her favorite place to be. They kept a high chair up there and he could see Amy enjoying her dinner.

"Natalie!" He called to her and raced inside the house. Taking the stairs two at a time he ran through the hall and into their bedroom. She was there to meet him.

"You're back on the force!"

"How did you know? It was supposed to be a surprise."

She kissed him passionately. "A wife just senses these things."

"Dada!" Amy called out.

He turned to kiss his daughter. Life didn't get better than this.

* * * * *

MILLS & BOON®

Cherish™

EXPERIENCE THE ULTIMATE RUSH OF FALLING IN LOVE

A sneak peek at next month's titles...

In stores from 5th May 2016:

In stores from 19th May 2016:

Available at WHSmith, Tesco, Asda, Eason, Amazon and Apple

Just can't wait?
Buy our books online a month before they hit the shops!
visit www.millsandboon.co.uk

These books are also available in eBook format!

MILLS & BOON®

Mills & Boon have been at the heart of romance since 1908... and while the fashions may have changed, one thing remains the same: from pulse-pounding passion to the gentlest caress, we're always known how to bring romance alive.

Now, we're delighted to present you with these irresistible illustrations, inspired by the vintage glamour of our covers. So indulge your wildest dreams and unleash your imagination as we present the most iconic Mills & Boon moments of the last century.

Visit **www.millsandboon.co.uk/ArtofRomance** to order yours!

MILLS & BOON®

Why shop at millsandboon.co.uk?

Each year, thousands of romance readers find their perfect read at millsandboon.co.uk. That's because we're passionate about bringing you the very best romantic fiction. Here are some of the advantages of shopping at www.millsandboon.co.uk:

* **Get new books first**—you'll be able to buy your favourite books one month before they hit the shops

* **Get exclusive discounts**—you'll also be able to buy our specially created monthly collections, with up to 50% off the RRP

* **Find your favourite authors**—latest news, interviews and new releases for all your favourite authors and series on our website, plus ideas for what to try next

* **Join in**—once you've bought your favourite books, don't forget to register with us to rate, review and join in the discussions

Visit **www.millsandboon.co.uk**
for all this and more today!